THE ARRANGEMENT

THE RUSSIAN GUNS, BOOK 1

BETHANY-KRIS

Published by Bethany-Kris

www.bethanykris.com

ISBN: 978-1-989658-27-7

Cover Design © London Miller
Editor: Elle Leigh

For Bug. For your strength and your perseverance. For your little soul because you don't know the effect you really have. You inspired words, love, and friendship.

CONTENTS

PROLOGUE 1
CHAPTER ONE 4
CHAPTER TWO..16
CHAPTER FOUR 36
CHAPTER FIVE..51
CHAPTER SIX..62
CHAPTER SEVEN 81
CHAPTER EIGHT 93
CHAPTER NINE..107
CHAPTER TEN 127
CHAPTER ELEVEN 141
CHAPTER TWELVE 153
CHAPTER TWELVE 166
CHAPTER THIRTEEN 178
CHAPTER FOURTEEN 192
CHAPTER FIFTEEN 205
CHAPTER SIXTEEN 220
CHAPTER SEVENTEEN...233
CHAPTER EIGHTEEN 246
CHAPTER NINETEEN 261
CHAPTER TWENTY 275
CHAPTER TWENTY-ONE 288
CHAPTER TWENTY-TWO..302

Prologue

Anton sat behind an oak desk, fingers drumming an anxious beat on the wood.

Ivan caught his eye with a sympathetic frown. Their conversation had stalled into nothing at all. Neither knew what to say anymore. All the words they could dream up to yell at one another had been used in both English and Russian. They never argued, and if they did, it was rare. Closer than brothers, and they didn't even share blood. Very seldom did Anton find an urge to yell at his Sovietnik the way he had tonight.

"Soon," Ivan spoke up, tilting his head to the side. "You can give the order soon."

"Soon could be too fucking late."

"You have to take that chance."

"Fifty thousand dollars to his cousin said she wouldn't last the month," Anton argued, words practically spitting through clenched teeth. "The price he's going to offer out on her head isn't worth the blood in her body. She's a mafia princess, the daughter of a *boss*."

"Not to Sonny, because in all honesty, he knows the truth."

Anton ignored Ivan and continued on like the other man hadn't even spoken. "Still a boss's child, no matter which boss it is. You don't pay five grand to off a woman like Viviana."

"I know."

"Goddamn it, you don't *know* what that'd do to me."

"Her dead, or the price?"

"Fuck you."

Viviana dead would absolutely destroy Anton. All those years he spent waiting and watching, keeping that safe distance but planning to make his move would be wasted. He'd been so careful and meticulous about his words and

1

feelings for her when it came to his men and the rest of the Bratva organization, but there were some things he simply couldn't hide.

Love for one.

He loved her so fucking hard it hurt and had for almost a decade.

"You've paid less," Ivan pointed out.

Anton felt anger blaze through his veins like an inferno. "Are you comparing me to Sonny Carducci?"

"No, I'm just saying—"

"I've paid less for those who are worth less. You know I wouldn't give an order to off a woman unless it was absolutely necessary. And *never* would I hurt Viviana. My whole life has been nothing but for *her*. Nicoli made sure of that."

Before he could second guess his choice, Anton hit the speaker button on the conference phone on the desk, dialing in the number and allowing it to ring. A familiar voice picked up on the second ring.

"Boss."

"Boris," Anton greeted. "How are my things coming along?"

"As they have been. Another busy night."

"Anton, I'm telling you that this isn't the right time," Ivan whispered warningly.

The younger man held up a middle finger as his silent fuck you. He didn't take orders, he gave them.

"I want Viviana delivered to the safe house by tomorrow morning. Is that doable?"

Really, the question wasn't meant to be posed as a request. If Anton suggested something to one of his men, it was a clear demand that meant they needed to get it done and correctly, or there would be hell to pay. Sometimes he seemed a little quieter than most other men of his status, but beyond his confident, calm exterior lay the cutthroat attitude and behaviour of any crime boss. He didn't get where he was now by playing nice. No, he did what he had to.

After all, he had the very best teacher in his step-grandfather."

"Uh…"

Anton straightened in his chair. "Uh, *what?*"

"Tomorrow night might be a better option, Boss. That's all."

"The bull stays outside of the building after checking the floors does he not? He's yet to notice Viktor or you, so I fail to see—"

"Not tonight, Boss," the Brigadier interrupted with a remorseful tone.

"Excuse me?"

"They showed up at the dorm together, you know…"

"Not really," Anton snapped.

"Shit. *Together*, Boss. They were all over each other. He went in with her and hasn't come out. Okay?"

Anton almost choked on his tongue. *Oh, Viviana, no…*

"Listen, we can go in now, but—"

A strangled growl stopped the man's words up short. The Bratva prince didn't want to hear it; he didn't care. What was his was his, regardless of what came before the arrangement could be fulfilled. God knew he'd taken enough women to his bed for a random distraction over the last nine long years.

"In the morning. Do it then. Not a hair on her head is to be harmed or your blood will spill. Leave nothing behind."

"And the bull, Boss?"

Anton felt no guilt when he repeated, "Leave nothing."

Chapter One

A screech from Viviana's left side caused the pounding in her temple to increase.

"Vine, shut that damned thing off, would you?" Sam's husky voice reminded her of just who was in her bed and why she had yet to wake up. "You've hit the snooze half a dozen times. Don't you have a lecture?"

Grumbling, she rubbed at her eyes. Finally, she blinked enough to feel awake and smacked at the alarm until it stopped beeping. Tossing blankets off the bed, her feet hit the cold floor. She barely recognized the time flashing on the alarm, but what her bleary eyes could see was enough to tell she was running late.

Really, really late.

"Why didn't you wake me up?" Viviana asked, scowling.

A tanned hand waved indifferently. Sam couldn't even be bothered to open his eyes and look at her. Some bodyguard he was.

"Like today is any different from yesterday?"

"This lecture is important!"

Clothes that had been carelessly scattered the night before were plucked up in her hands. Too much vodka and an attractive man made Viviana a messy girl. Eventually, she located the dark black skinny jeans and ribbed tank she'd worn the night before. Sniffing the clothes, they smelled decent enough, so she pulled them on and kicked around more stuff to find sneakers.

The sound of a glock's chamber being manually discharged stopped her heart for a split second. It brought back memories she'd buried deep in the depths of her mind. It was a sound she never wanted to hear again. The black jacket in her hands fell to the floor as she chanced a look over at the door, then to the window.

Instinct, that's what her father would have called it, because it was in her blood and bones. It didn't matter that she was a girl, and girls couldn't ever join the Cosa Nostra, she knew a fucking gun. Viviana could hold one, shoot like any made man, but that was only because her father said she had to learn.

The Don's child had to know how to shoot.

Dropping to all fours, she heard Sam laugh deeply.

"Chill, girl. I'm just checking the clip; my piece needs to be cleaned."

"I hate guns." Her voice was strained, anxiety eating away at her lungs that couldn't seem to inhale. "Put it away."

"Can't. I gotta check the floor before you go," he replied quietly. When Viviana's scowl made another appearance, he added, "Sorry. Those are the rules. You wanted freedom, so they gave it. I'm just one of the conditions that came along for the ride, babe."

A nauseous feeling settled in her like a heavy weight. "I've been here a year and there hasn't been an issue. Why can't you just leave?"

Sam swung his legs over the side of the bed, the movement drawing her eyes in to the bands of muscle that stretched and flexed all over his tanned form. The light dusting of hair that covered his chest and created a thin line to the spot between his legs had her memory on overload with images from the night before. He was all-American with a touch of Italian on the tip of his magic tongue. Kind of handsome. Cussed like a sailor, had a perfectly deadly sort of aim with a gun, and always stayed far enough away to never draw attention but close enough that she was still aware of his presence.

"You want me to leave after last night?"

Viviana refused to dignify that with a response. His cock stood at attention: hard, glorious, and probably still smelling like her pussy. Oh God, smelling like her. Panic saturated her from the inside out.

"Last night ... tell me we used—"

5

"A condom," he interrupted. "Yeah. I don't fuck without one."

Sweet relief never felt so good. Sure, she was on the shot, but that didn't mean Sam wasn't out there fucking God knew who when he wasn't working.

Sam didn't pay Viviana's relieved sigh a moment of attention as he reached for his jeans. "I'll check the floors and you can go."

"What are we going to do?" she asked, shifting into a sitting position on the floor as he pulled on a pair of jeans. "Just ... not tell anyone?"

Sam cringed. "That's probably best."

Probably, she thought sarcastically.

Being the daughter of a former mafia boss, Viviana should have known better. You didn't sleep with your bodyguard, and if they were worth anything, your bodyguard didn't make a move to bridge the personal gaps between you. Sam had been good, too. For the last year he'd done just what he needed, followed orders to the letter, and kept her as safe as he possibly could.

And then last night happened ...

"Vine, you're freaking out over there when it's only me here. No one is gonna know we knocked boots if you don't say anything about it. I like my life right where it is, and I don't plan on swimming with the fish any time soon, so I sure as hell won't be saying a thing. If you want, I can request another man—"

"You're not made, right?"

Sam looked confused. "I'm not ... *yet.*"

She waved a hand between them. "Is this job your guarantee into it?"

The indignant sound he released was enough of an answer.

"It takes a little more than that, and you're not worth very much now."

"Well, great."

"No one likes to off a woman, Vine, especially if that

woman is Roman's daughter. Doesn't matter if he's six feet under or not now, they already got your momma and brother. I suppose killing you just seemed cruel and unnecessary in the grand scheme of things. Be grateful they're letting you live."

"Grateful? They're just waiting for me to screw up and then ..." Trailing off, Viviana made the shape of a gun with her thumb and forefinger and pulled the trigger at her temple. "*Boom.* I'll be the one swimming with the fish."

His unaffected, blank stare chilled.

"Your father might not be the boss now, but he was for a long time, and his daddy before him, too. Roman made a bad choice, so his men turned and did what they had to. Regardless, they'd show you more respect than an execution and a watery grave. You know that."

"A bad choice," Viviana repeated dully. That bad choice was her and a dozen other things that happened over two decades ago that she didn't want to think about. It was better if she didn't. There was less pain that way. "What the hell do you know about my father's *choices*? Just because those men spit what they call gospel doesn't mean they're not choking back on lies, Sam."

"Those *men* are *la famiglia*." Sam's warning rang loud and clear, causing Viviana to bite the inside of her cheek and look away. "As of today, they still consider you a part of that family. Gratitude and respect, Vine. Learn it."

"So says the man who fucked the *Don* of New York's daughter."

Sam grinned wickedly, pulling a V-neck T-shirt over his head. "Not the Don anymore. I was at the funeral, too. Besides, we can't do this again, right? I mean, you're a great lay, obviously, but I want my button and you're just a steppingstone to it."

"You can go to—"

"I'll make the call, Vine; get you another watcher. I'd rather be closer to New York, anyway. Sitting around in this place really isn't my thing. I know you're grieving, or whatever you want to call it, but it's been three years since your family was buried. Time to move on. It's not like some former mafia boss's daughter with no real connections can get her revenge, huh?"

Emotions betrayed Viviana by way of tears that welled up and threatened to fall.

"Fuck you, Sam."

"Already did, babe."

Standing to turn without another word, she slipped on the sneakers she managed to find under the corner chair before checking her face in the mirror. Red splotches had appeared on Viviana's cheeks from forcing back tears, lips still swollen from Sam's teeth biting and kissing the night before, and a small spot of red lipstick had smeared across the side of her mouth. Rubbing the stain with a makeup remover wipe from her dresser, she ran fingers through tangled waves of raven black hair as she tried to avoid the man's gaze behind her in the mirror.

"You know you're kind of beautiful, right?" Sam murmured behind her. His voice, thick with an Italian accent he could lay on heavy in a moment if he wanted, was rough and husky again. "They all say you look like your father, but you're a prettier version of your momma."

Brown eyes caught her own reflection in the mirror. What he said had some merit. With soft features, full lips, and wide eyes, Viviana certainly didn't go unnoticed by men. Regardless, she could pick out a dozen other parts of herself that she wasn't happy with. She hated the fact that her eyelashes weren't as long as her mother's once were, and that she mostly seemed to take after her in height, only standing a too-short five foot five inches.

Truthfully, Viviana didn't think she looked like her mother at all.

"We're not getting back into bed again, so you can stop it with your comments," she replied bitterly. Tilting her head to the side, the red mark he'd left on the spot between her shoulder and neck was on clear display. "I don't want your compliments."

Sam shrugged and dug through the mess on the floor to find his boots. "Just thought you should know, considering I didn't spend much time telling you last night. You're gonna make a man happy someday. The perfect little mob wife."

Leaning against the wall, he nodded at the calendar set up beside a small desk. "Your twenty-fifth birthday is coming up in three months, so when do you plan on settling down? God knows your uncle Sonny would love to see you married with a couple kids underfoot."

Shuddering at his words was the only indication she gave that she'd heard his statement. The uncle he spoke about was the same man who reportedly put a gun to her father's head and pulled the trigger. *Reportedly* because she knew it was truer than anyone else knew. He was also the man who took the throne of the Cosa Nostra within their family when her father was dead and gone. She had wondered later if Roman had seen Sonny coming, what with her uncle knowing of the deal her father had made with the Russians when she was only a toddler.

A snake, that's what her uncle was. A turncoat, untrue, traitor to her father and the family. His own brother marked the bullet and stained his hands a bloody red.

Blood didn't matter, though. Not in the family … or so Viviana had been told. Being a girl, it wasn't like she had been given the advantage of understanding the Cosa Nostra, its rules and values. In fact, just saying the word *mafia* or *mob* under her father's roof would get you one of his infamous looks, and then you knew you were in hot water.

The mafia doesn't exist.

Yeah, right.

Viviana's father had his own Wikipedia page, and her name was listed as his only surviving child right underneath.

"Don't talk about—"

The words were cut off by a loud bang. Once more, Viviana found herself on the floor, pushed there by Sam's hand.

Sam didn't join her on the floor; instead, she watched

him reach for the glock twenty-two he'd tossed to the bedspread. That same gun he scared her with earlier, but forgot about in their argument. He never should have dropped his piece. The gun was his third hand, but she had made him forget about that important rule for a split second.

A split second too long.

The near silent pop, pop, pops—one right after the other— made her squeeze-shut her eyes and cover her ears. That only served to muffle the shouts from the attackers and her scream. Raw, achingly loud, and terrified, that's how her fear sounded. Something warm soaked into the side of Viviana's shirt. The heavy scent of gunpowder stung inside her lungs and she screamed again.

"Shut her up!"

The voice was bottomless, scratchy with age, and thick with an accent that made a cold shiver of dread roll through Viviana's body. She hadn't heard a Russian drawl in years. It was the last thing she expected to encounter again, given they hadn't come for her after her family's murder.

"No!"

Viviana kicked out, turning to the side and stumbling over a mess on the floor. Reaching for the cell phone right beside the bed, she felt hands grabbing at her legs, pulling roughly and dragging her away from potential salvation.

If she could have reached the phone ... maybe ... maybe she ... Viviana was alone.

No one's daughter anymore.

The mafia princess without a crown.

"Don't touch me! *Sam!*"

The first man inside the doorway spoke, his words switching from English to Russian. Whatever he said, the man still pulling Viviana towards him as she kicked out and punched at him only grunted back in response. When her small fist landed a solid smack to his nose, his blue eyes narrowed before he shouted something she couldn't understand. He raised his large hand and hit her sharply on the cheek. It bloomed with instant pain. Air sucked into her frozen lungs; she was shocked and speechless that a man had hit her.

The man shouted again, and even in Russian, his warning was clear. Viviana watched stunned as the butt of a gun snapped down with a loud smack to his comrade's head.

"Fool, you're not to hurt her! He will have your life for that. Move, Viktor."

"Don't touch me," she hissed. Deciding fighting wasn't going to help her when he bared his teeth and spit more words she couldn't understand, Viviana exposed her own teeth in a last ditch effort to rebel. "Keep your filthy fucking hands off of me, scum."

"I said move. We need to leave." In a flash, the man named Viktor was pushed off Viviana, and someone else clouded her blurring vision. Hot tears fell as Viviana stared up with her lips trembling, hair stuck to a damp face, and the taste of blood saturating her mouth. "I am Boris, girl. Up with you, before some other drunk college student wakes and calls the police."

Both men wore flat black from head to toe, their hair slicked back making them look odd and startling. She guessed their ages to be late thirties to early forties, and by the job they had been sent to do, it wouldn't have surprised Viviana if they were only bulls for the Russian mafia. Bulls being a term the Bratva used to describe their bodyguards, as the men were often large, frightening, and known for their violent tendencies.

"S-Sam ... he—"

"Dead," Boris replied in a cold and distant tone, eyes flickering up to look behind Viviana's prone body. It wasn't a second later before he was bending down and grabbing at her wrists to pull her up to unsteady feet. "Do not act so shocked, Miss Carducci. You've witnessed death in one form or another. He is but a snail in comparison to the rest of the world you live in."

"I don't live in that world anymore."

Viviana glanced pointedly around her messy dorm

room. There were scattered papers on the desk and mismatched photos and mementos attached to the wall to hide the cracking paint. The room was as messy as a pigsty. Did she look like she was living her spoiled lifestyle as a mafia child? Wasn't it obvious she'd already cut her ties, or tried to?

"I'm a student, not a Don's daughter."

The words seemed to go unheard, as Boris pushed her at Viktor, who openly glared. Blood dripped down his nose to cover his scowling lips. A strange sense of satisfaction filled Viviana at the sight.

"Why are you here?"

Boris sighed as he opened the drawers to the dresser and pulled out a hoodie and other articles of clothing. The items were tossed into a pile on the floor.

"Your purse, where is it?"

"Why are you here?" Viviana repeated.

Viktor's hand stuck out again, fingers painfully gripping her jaw as he shook her face and snarled, "I've had just about enough of your nonsense, you little bitch. Now, answer his question!"

Her heart thudded louder, pushing out an achingly hard and fast beat. "On the hook behind the door." Suddenly, Viviana didn't feel so courageous. She attempted to hold back tears. "I don't have money; Uncle Sonny doesn't give—"

"I want to insure you have a passport," Boris interrupted, turning to half close the door they'd kicked open to find her purse. The contents scattered across the cheap, worn carpet. "Canada was not a safe place for you, and now we're taking you back. You have a deal to uphold. That is why we are here."

"My father is dead; that deal is void."

Viktor's narrowed eyes turned on Viviana in anger and she instantly flinched away. The last thing she wanted was him hitting her again. Viktor smiled, the sight causing her stomach to roll; blood covered his teeth, turning them garish and disgusting.

"Deals with the dead are still upheld in the Bratva, girl.

Their family upholds it personally. We make sure of that."

"By twenty-five, it was agreed," Boris said. "You were to be married, like it or not." With a jerk of his head, Viktor released her face. Exhaling shakily, she forced herself not to rub her aching jaw. "You're three months off from that date, so my Pakhan is requesting your presence."

"*Pah ... kan.*" Given the answering frown from Boris, Viviana knew her attempt at the Russian word was poor at best. "What is that?"

"Who," he corrected with a small smile. "The boss. You call them the Don or Boss, but we Russians call them Pakhan. Or Boss, depending on his mood. Nicoli—"

"Is dead, just like my father. So their deals should be, too."

"Stop arguing, it's done!" Boris snapped.

What she knew of the Russian mafia was very little, and the information she had gained over the years were from discussions she hadn't been meant to hear. Any interest Viviana outwardly showed for the Bratva—a family so similar to her own—after her father's death was brushed off with a warning about loyalty and blood. She just wanted to understand why they'd done what they did by arranging the marriage between her and the grandson of a Bratva boss.

"Who requested me?"

The question came out strained, sounding almost foreign. Weak and scared, that's what they made her. She was a boss's daughter—a mafia child. Never should she be feeble and pathetic. Still, Viviana was confused. Knowing they had several upper bosses, and given the structure in their business, well, it wasn't something she considered organized, so she had to know for sure who was requesting her.

"Who wants me, now?"

"You know who."

"No, I don't."

Boris checked his watch. "We don't have time for this. The border is a—"

"Who?" Viviana forced out.

"Anton."

Her shoulders slumped, confusion and fear rising in a mere breath of air. Anton Avdonin was the other half of the deal made between men who no longer lived. Anton, a man two years and two months older than she was, a full-blooded Russian who she only met twice in her life. He was also the grandson of a formally notorious mob boss in the Russian mafia, also known as the Bratva. Situated largely in Brighton Beach, New York, the Bratva was known to meddle in guns and narcotics trafficking, as well as money laundering and prostitution.

Viviana had a lot in common with Anton in some aspects. She was, after all, the daughter of one of the world's most dangerous Cosa Nostra Dons. Italian in bloodline, the Cosa Nostra started as a Sicilian-based mafia who considered their unit a family structure. They, too, handled running guns and drugs, as well as partaking in other illegal operations to make money.

Why, she wondered. Why now, when he could move on, forget about it, and take whoever else he wanted for a wife? Surely after nine years, whatever connection she thought they had was all but gone, right?

"But, he *can't*."

Boris eyed her like Viviana had grown a second head. Despite the situation, her nerves were making an appearance by way of the inappropriate laughter that bubbled its way out from her chest into dead air.

"He can. Anton is preserving the wishes of his dead grandfather and your father. It was important to him."

"But I'm useless!" she cried, feeling tears well and fall again. "Nothing to him—not Russian, not connected, and just ... a *fucking liability*."

With a sharp whisper in Russian, Boris grabbed her roughly and forced Viviana to move. The long barrel of a silencer pressed to her side. "Now, shut those lips of yours, Miss Carducci. We wouldn't want to wake up the rest of this dorm and cause more issues than necessary. A car is waiting for us at the entrance. Viktor will meet us five miles past the border after he cleans up."

Only then did she notice the plastic gas cans sitting outside in the hallway. Even though it was late afternoon and the hallways were seemingly quiet, there were still students and faculty in the building. "You can't burn—"

"I will tape your mouth shut, girl, if you can't keep quiet. I promise."

As he dragged Viviana from the room, she made the mistake of looking back.

Sam's still form was sprawled half on, half off the bed. Struck helpless, he was far too pale to be alive. Blood and matter had splattered across the wall behind him. Open, dead eyes stared blankly as blood ran red with spidery lines over the muscles on his arm, slipping in slow dribbles from his fingers to soak into the floor.

The vomit she had been holding back finally made its way out.

Chapter Two

Seated in a black SUV with heavily tinted windows, Viviana trembled in the passenger seat. The side of her shirt was soaked with blood—Sam's—and spatters of her own vomit. Bile rose in her throat again as she found herself staring at the large spot of morbid crimson.

"If you vomit in my car, I will knock you out and put you in the back. Are we clear?" Boris asked gruffly, sitting beside her, never once taking his eyes from the road. "It's bad enough you vomited on my shoes. These were not cheap, my dear, at nearly six hundred dollars a pair, and detailing this car will cost far more when it's blood and vomit they're cleaning out."

Wanting to keep that very thing from happening, she decided to engage him in conversation. "I didn't realize bulls were paid that much in the Russian mafia."

His dark laughter filled the vehicle. "A bull would not have treated you so well when you fought back, not to mention if you had made one bleed like you did to my friend. Besides, their job is to protect members and high family of the Bratva, not collect payments."

"I'm a person, not a payment," Viviana bit out, her teeth clenching.

"The Cosa Nostra will not be too bothered by your loss, girl. You are their liability."

Curling back her lips in disgust, Viviana hated that he wasn't wrong. "And what, now I'm Anton's?"

"I'm sure that uncle of yours will attempt some show at getting you back, hoping you'll be killed in the process. Worth the risk to Anton," Boris replied quietly. "Though, I cannot begin to fathom why. You're a pretty enough thing, that's for sure. Lord knows he's got enough women—taken enough women," he corrected with a shrug as he turned onto the exit for the TransCanada Highway.

"*Cooz* chaser," she muttered sarcastically. "Just what my mother always wanted for my husband."

"*Cooz?*" Boris sounded confused. "Italian slang isn't my speciality, but Russian on the other hand…"

"Pussy." She smirked as he coughed under his breath to hide the surprise that flitted across his features. "He likes to *chase* it. How many whores does he have on the side?"

Boris considered his passenger for a quick moment. "You will have to ask him those questions. He does not lack female attention, if that's what you're wondering."

Great.

"Do you think—"

"I am not paid to think about what Anton does behind closed doors," he interjected sharply. "I am a *brigadier*—your equivalent to a capo. You, girl, are my boss's … betrothed. That is all."

"I am not marrying him!"

"Discuss that with Anton."

She swallowed back her anger, wanting to keep him talking. "He's a little young to have reached his ranking, no?"

"His grandfather prepared him well. He was a made man—a *vor* in our terms—at eighteen, never finishing his studies formally but still well versed and intelligent. He's quick, cunning, and knew what he was doing because growing up, he had watched more than he spoke. The little Russian prince, his grandfather called him. They all called him that. It's in his blood, girl, what he was meant for. Most of us respected that, and when it came time, Anton was the best choice to take over, given his own father was too sick by that point."

"You don't think taking me after my father was killed for striking that deal with Nicoli Avdonin is bad leadership?" Viviana snorted, crossing her arms and turning to look out the window. "He's practically declaring war between the Bratva and the Cosa Nostra."

"Perhaps that is what he wants; have you considered that?" Boris asked. "His decisions have to be approved by the other Pakhans who may have issues because of his desires. There were reasons his grandfather and your father thought you two would be a good match. Besides the obvious reasons why they wanted the families to join in certain aspects, you have to know it was about more than just money."

He shrugged and added, "You shouted about not being Russian back at your dorm because the Cosa Nostra demands full-blooded Italians when joining. We do not, and any boys you birthed for Anton would still be eligible to join the Bratva, should they be what we're looking for when they become of age."

"My children would—"

"Not your choice to make," he interrupted swiftly with a raised brow. "You know this, girl. You were raised in this life. You avert your eyes and ears. Walls do not speak, and windows do not see. And if your husband wishes for you to know things, only then will he tell what he considers safe for you to know."

Viviana felt her jaw clench at his words. "It doesn't matter. I'm not marrying him."

Boris chuckled. "You've forgotten then, little Vine, what it was like nine years ago when you were a young sixteen and he only eighteen. You didn't know he was already a dangerous man, but you knew he would be. It did not bother you, and you were both willing to fulfill the arrangement, happily."

He'd shocked her speechless. Again, Viviana's memories were filled with years long past. Of a time when she was young, dumb, and head over heels for someone she didn't even know, not really. For years, her father had repeated words, conditioned and prepared her for a marriage that was simply understood—*accepted*—because he said it was so. While arranged marriages were rare in the modern mafia, it sometimes happened to gain more power or wealth, but it was never spoken of publically. Roman had made the mistake of celebrating Viviana's openly after she turned twenty, and it resulted in his death. Not that it would have made a difference when it came time for the actual marriage to take place.

The Italian daughter of a mafia Don had no business marrying the Bratva prince, they said. She should have been picking from the many sons of the Cosa Nostra batch. They would have been better suitors.

Sure ...

"I was only sixteen; I couldn't have known any better! And, anyway, how did you know that?"

"You don't remember me, but I was always there as a bull of sorts for Anton. While he worked under his father and grandfather, I was there with him, insuring he did what was correct and what we expected of him."

"You were *there*."

Viviana's breathing halted for a split second, taking in what he said. That meant he probably knew what it had been like during the only two meetings between Anton and her, how happy the families had been that they took so well to one another as young children, and then when they were older, how they had fallen in ...

"I didn't ... didn't love ..." She couldn't finish the sentence as shame pulsed through her core and ached from the inside out. The words would be a lie because she had. And if she were an honest woman, Viviana would have to say those feelings never really went away. How could they when in her life there was only one person who was supposed to be just hers? "I *didn't*."

"You did," Boris replied quietly, his hand reaching out to open the glove compartment. There, yet another small handgun sat atop a package of tissues. "Wipe your face, but do not touch my gun." He sighed heavily and shook his head. "It was a good match—still is—if you want it to be, Vine. Anton is taking major risks here. You were right in that assumption, but he is doing it for more than just the Bratva, too."

"I don't want to be his wife!" Not bothering to reach for the tissues, she slammed the glove compartment closed with a kick. "And I've been doing just fine since my parents died, without Anton or the Russians. Eventually, my uncle would have let this whole thing go."

Boris didn't bother to hide his displeasure. "*Eventually*, he would have killed you." Clicking his tongue chidingly, he muttered, "Probably would have made it look like a suicide. Do not act so stupid, girl. He cares nothing for the blood you share."

The truth in his words were a harsh reality that only added to her fear. Viviana wished she had grabbed for the gun in the glove compartment and turned the damned thing on him, but she knew it likely wouldn't have made the situation any better. Not wanting to cry again, she steeled her emotions, sitting up ramrod straight in the passenger seat and staring ahead at the miles of highway they still had to travel.

"Where are we going?"

"A safe place. More specifically, a place in Brooklyn. It's where Anton has always lived, and where we work out of, as you already know. Settle in, it's a long drive from Toronto."

Panic raged under her calm exterior. Viviana's uncle worked out of Long Island, mostly. "It'll be a war inside the city."

Boris still looked unaffected. "It's happened before."

"Not between the Bratva and Cosa Nostra. Would it be bigger than just New York?"

With a disgruntled grunt, he suddenly leaned over and opened the console between their seats. Viviana didn't get the chance to see what he grabbed before the flip door to the console was shut once more.

"Anton doesn't want you worried and bothered when you arrive. I need you quiet at the border. It's not so easy bribing officials, you know." With those words, his hand shot out, and a sting radiated deep in her bare arm. Striking out at him with a startled yelp, the car swerved. She glanced at where the pain originated only to see him push the plunger down in the needle he stabbed her with. "Mostly just a mild sedative that will keep you quiet for a half a day or so. It'll do the trip at least."

"What … what di-did … ju …" The words trailed off and Viviana slumped down in the seat almost instantly. *Mild sedative, my ass,* she thought drowsily. "I'm telling … Anton … you … tell Anton … drugged me."

Boris laughed. "You do that, my dear. Sleep for now."

Just as her body began drifting off into a forced slumber, a ringing sounded through the car's speakers. Boris answered in Russian, and she tried to keep her eyes open long enough to see his facial reactions to what he was hearing. The voice on the other end sounded vaguely familiar, but the wearier Viviana got, the less she was able to focus.

That was, until her name was spoken in the caller's mother tongue: *Viviana.* She hadn't been addressed by that name since her parent's death, and publically everyone knew her as Vine. It was a nickname given to her years ago by her older brother Tony when he was unable to speak her given name properly. She was always introduced as Vine. Never once did she use Viviana unless it was necessary.

But nine long years before, Anton had been the odd man out. He was the one person who called her by her given name; she had only ever been just Viviana to him.

In her chemical-induced slumber, she dreamt of an earlier time …

"Come on, they don't all call you Vine, right?" Anton asked in the dark.

"Yep, everyone."

His hand traced a light path across her naked legs wrapped in his under the blanket. She'd snuck into his room, since it was both their last night before they left from vacation to return to New York. It'd be a long while before they would see each other again. Really, Viviana just wanted to be close to him; one week was all it took for her to feel that way.

"Mom calls me Ant. I hate that."

She laughed. "Ant, really? Oh, God, that's horrible."

"Shut up, or you'll wake the house."

"Don't think your bull doesn't already know someone is in here with you."

Anton shrugged and rolled to his back with a sigh. *"He won't tell, and they wouldn't care. Well, maybe Roman would. You shouldn't be in a boy's room in the middle of the night, Vine."*

"I thought you liked Viviana better," she whispered, biting her lip and grinning.

"So, Viviana, why did you sneak out of your warm, safe bed to climb into mine?"

Before her sixteen-year-old self could think better of her actions, she leaned up and kissed him. His large hands tightened on her trim waist, gripping hard as the air turned thick. He muttered harshly under his breath.

"I wanted to say goodbye before morning," Viviana said as his thumbs brushed against her sides. Shivering at the new sensations driving through a body still too young to understand, he drove her a little closer, wrapping both tighter in the blanket. *"I'm not cold."*

"Me, either." Hands moved under the flimsy short and tank set she wore, hesitating only long enough to ask, *"Can I?"*

"Say it again," Viviana demanded.

Anton's brow furrowed, blue eyes lighting up in his confusion. *"Say what?"*

"My name."

Russian fell from his lips so smooth and deep, but there was one word above the rest that she understood well enough: Viviana. It ached so badly, the pads of his thumbs brushing away salty tears that escaped from the corners of her eyes. He was so careful, though, and oh so gentle.

"Giving this to me makes you mine, Vine. I don't care about who comes after, or the in-betweens. Not when we both know I'm going to be your last."

Viviana didn't have a reason to doubt him, but she sure as hell hadn't wanted to, either.

Chapter Three

Viviana couldn't shake the feeling of a heavy pressure holding her down. Blinking rapidly, she breathed and attempted to see, move, or just *do* anything.

Nothing happened.

An ache had settled in the creases of her arms and legs. Bending them only served to settle the throbbing pressure deeper into her muscles. Pain radiated from the right side of her jaw as she opened her mouth to call out. With dry lips, a soreness that wouldn't seem to disappear, and grogginess saturating her senses, she couldn't focus long enough to remember where she was. Never mind what had happened that got her ... *here.*

Where in the hell was she?

Breathing in, she could taste something familiar in the dark air. Like city air, gunpowder, cigars, and a woodsy cologne that reminded Viviana of home. Her fingers tightened in the blankets.

Hadn't she been at the university dorms with Sam last night? Hadn't she been drunk, and hadn't Sam taken her home? Didn't she go to that lecture in the morning?

"Sam?" Her voice was hoarse, words mumbled and barely intelligible. Her throat felt sore like she'd been screaming her lungs out for hours. "Sam, wake up."

It wasn't a second later that she heard shouts from somewhere outside her dark confines. A voice that resonated deep in her confused mind yelled angrily in a language Viviana couldn't understand. A woman dressed in a grey-and-white uniform, her hair tied back, looked about as frightened as Viviana felt as she scurried past the opened doorway.

The shouts continued before something shattered, the sounds of tinkling glass spreading over the floors echoing down the hallway. The familiar voice grew scarily quiet as he spit his words out with sheer venom.

Viviana didn't have to understand the words to know

the man was livid; just barely hanging on the ledge of control. More than once growing up, she had heard that kind of anger while she stayed hidden in the safety of her bedroom. Her father's voice carried through the house as he handled misbehaving men in the basement, or office, whichever served his purpose, depending on the soldier who'd done him wrong.

Forcing herself from the confines of the blankets, Viviana managed to get caught up in all the fabric and tumbled off the bed. Landing on the hard floor with a loud thump, she was surprised no one outside the room heard the noise. Crawling until standing was possible, she swayed on the spot, her legs feeling like a mixture of brittle sticks inside a bag of jelly. Nausea rolled through her insides like a tidal wave of sickness ready to drown and destroy.

Hangovers didn't feel like that. Nothing felt like that. Unless death did. She wasn't sure.

"Sam," Viviana called out again, heading toward the lighted hallway.

Had he checked the hallway before leaving?

Just as she reached the door, something on a small stand caught her eye. The light from the hallway illuminated the framed photograph enough that she could discern the people being pictured. Finally, she remembered.

The face of Nicoli—a former boss of the Bratva, and an ally to her father—stared back at Viviana. Her shaky hand reached out to touch the photograph, snapping back almost at the exact instant she realized what she was doing.

There would be no photo of Nicoli in her dorm, nor would there be a picture of him in any house she visited. It was only then Viviana remembered the sounds of a silenced gun firing off three deadly shots. Sam hanging limp and dead off the edge of a bed. A man hitting her face and spitting words in Russian.

Pop.

Viviana shuddered.

Pop.

Blood bled red in her memories, but the too big T-shirt she now wore hung loose around her bare legs, unstained and pristine white.

Pop.

She was in a car with a Russian … *Boris* … terrified and trying not to cry.

"Anton."

The name was thick on her tongue and heavy in her thrashing, thundering heart. Stumbling, she moved from the room and braced her hands on the wall, needing that solid ground to steady her swaying as she moved closer to the shouting.

"*Anton!*"

Looking at her hands, Viviana noticed the blood that once stained her skin was now clean. Fingernails had been buffed, chips filed down, and the natural white crescents at the tips shined brightly under the light. Confused, she reached up to run fingers through her black hair. Instead of the tangled waves from this morning—or was it yesterday now?—she was met with no resistance. The locks felt clean and soft, brushed all the way through and hanging loose down her back.

Someone had washed her. They took meticulous care in cleaning any evidence from her hands and body, changing the clothes she wore and leaving her somewhere they thought was safe for Viviana to wake up in.

Was it him, she wondered. *Was it Anton who did that for me?*

Beyond the fear and nerves, something that scared Viviana even worse resided in the pit of her stomach: *want.* She wanted that. Wanted to know he had touched her. Cared for her. Worried over her. But she shouldn't have wanted that at all.

Finally releasing her hold on the wall, she felt stable enough to walk on her own. Moving at a speed that was too fast for her still upset insides, Viviana made it to the partially opened French doors at the end of the hallway. With dark blinds covering the glass, no one on the inside noticed her approach, and the woman who had previously passed the doorway had long disappeared. The men's voices became louder again, fury hissing with a burn between every word she couldn't comprehend. Looking through a crack in the door, the sight staring back was shocking.

At least five men were inside the room, and while four stood upright, the one who had hit Viviana in her dorm—Viktor—was lying prone on the floor. With his head bent at an awkward angle, the barrel of a gun pressing to his right temple, Viktor gritted his teeth and continued to say the same phrase over and over in Russian.

"Boss, let it go," one man said quietly. "He's apologized, he's never skimmed off his boys or done you wrong in the past. Your grandfather would have done the same."

It wasn't his face Viviana's eyes were drawn to, or even the man that spoke in a language she could finally understand. Instead it was the hand holding the gun with a painful force. That hand didn't shake; there was no hesitation in the action. She had the distinct feeling if those fingers that had once touched her skin so softly pulled the trigger, they wouldn't find regret in that choice.

"*Eta ruka?*"

Anton's voice sounded darker than she had ever heard it. Hardened and cold, like shards of ice to her soul. Wearing only dark wash jeans that sat low around his hips, the waistband of his boxer-briefs were visible. The black hair, now kept a little longer than when she had last seen him, was wet and hanging over blue eyes. She couldn't help but wonder if those eyes blazed a dark blue in his rage like they did when he fucked and loved.

Every muscle tensed and shuddered as anger rolled over his broad shoulders, the six-pack of abs clenching like the white teeth he bared when he growled out once more, "*Eta ruka?*"

Viktor nodded, raising the hand his boss had tapped

with a boot. The chiseled line of Anton's jaw grew impossibly harder as he breathed heavily through his nose. Something unknown washed through Viviana's insides, sending her desire ramped up while fear prickled elsewhere.

"Do you think it is appropriate I let this go, Viktor?" he asked, warningly. The slight Russian accent in his dialect wasn't nearly as thick as some of the men around him, but the more irritated his voice became, the more prominent it sounded. "Do you agree with your brothers that your actions should simply be overlooked because of your lack of past transgressions? Would that be to your liking?"

"I—"

"It is a yes or no question!" The barrel of the gun pressed harder against the older man's temple. Viviana's heart stuttered. "I don't wish to hear your excuses, or apologies. I want a fucking answer!"

Viviana's fingers tightened around the doorknob as Viktor's voice turned quieter and he said, "Yes, I was wrong."

Anton gripped the gun, and he tapped the piece three short times to the man's head. "This hand," he stated, his foot tapping against Viktor's clenched fingers once more. "You hit her with this one, so open it up against the floor. *Now*."

"Boss!"

"Would you like to be next, Boris? I should take a pound from you, too, considering you didn't step in until after he'd smacked her around a little. I was very clear with my instructions. Neither of you idiots managed to follow them properly."

Anton stood straight, turning to face Boris, and giving Viviana a view of the wide plains of his back and shoulders. Stretched with bands of muscles, his shoulders were strong, wide, and shuddering with barely contained fury. Black ink crisscrossed his skin in a tribal design and a black star resided on both of his shoulders between the inky licks of color.

"The orders were clear, and you allowed him to break my protocol. At the very least, you could have used that sedative before you took her from the dorm, and he did not have to end that bull inside the complex. Those are issues I have to fix now. Too sloppy for a brigadier of your age and knowledge. Both of you are losing the thirty percent share from your boy's tributes this month, and maybe next, too. I haven't decided, yet."

"Yes, Boss," Boris replied quietly.

Anton turned back to Viktor, the gun in his grip aimed and ready. Viviana choked knowing what he was about to do, but still unable to turn away from the sight. "Hand out," he ordered again. With a shaky exhale, Viktor unclenched his fingers and laid his palm flat to the floor.

Closing his eyes, he apologized once more in his mother tongue. Anton kneeled down to thrust the gun against the back of the man's hand. "You will apologize to her. You are not to speak to her directly, or indirectly, without my immediate presence and permission. I do not want to see your face before I request it, and I suggest you stay away from my clubs and homes until this has blown over. Are we clear?"

"Yes."

"Yes, *what?*" Anton barked.

"Yes, Boss."

Without a second of indecision, Anton pulled back the hammer on his gun. Viktor flinched, and she felt suffocated by the realization that a man was about to be shot for hitting her. Bile rose in Viviana's throat as she pushed open the door and stumbled through. With it came the attention of every man in the room, and the appearance of their guns pointed directly at her.

*

Goddamn she looked good standing there—like she didn't care about them or their weapons. Anton's throat thickened at the sight of Viviana in only his shirt, her brown eyes drawn to his. The hardest thing he had to do was check his emotions out of the equation, reminding himself of just who was there besides her, and what they would see.

Guarding his expression, he felt his jaw tick.

"Please, don't," Viviana whispered, pressing her hand into her midsection. Her frame swayed and that only served to piss him off more. The medication hadn't worn off and Boris used too much. Someone's fingers needed breaking for that. "It's unnecessary, Anton. Don't do that, not for me."

When she swayed on her feet again, his expression softened, his heart rate picking up and shoulders temporarily relaxing. "Get her a chair." When no one moved, his hand jerked to the side, pulling the trigger of his gun. It went off with an echoing bang into the floorboards. Everyone jumped. "Why am I needing to repeat myself tonight?"

The man closest to Viviana—Ivan—shoved his weapon into the waistband of his dress pants before directing her to sit on the chair beside him. Her unease with five pairs of eyes watching her was obvious. With her shapely legs pressed tightly together and her hands tugging at the hem of his T-shirt to hide her thighs, she was practically naked in front of strangers.

Her cheeks were pink with embarrassment. Possessiveness flooded Anton's veins.

"Your coat, Ivan," Anton demanded with a nod at his lawyer. "Cover her."

When Ivan's suit jacket was spread across her legs, Anton watched silently as she fisted the fabric and thanked him softly. "It's no problem, Vine, but perhaps next time you could just knock instead of making a grand entrance like that, huh? Nearly got yourself shot," Ivan joked with a wink.

"Enough," Anton muttered. Did she know just by looking at him that he'd missed her so much? Immediately, her eyes dropped from his to find a spot on the floor. The rising rejection was hard to hide. "Viviana, you've met Boris …" She looked back up at the sound of his voice, "… and Viktor," he added, nudging the prone man on the floor with the toe of his laced up boots.

Viviana chanced a look away from Anton, seeking out Ivan who smiled. "And you," she added quietly.

"Yes." Anton nodded at Ivan who was pulling out a pack of cigarettes from the pocket of the jacket lying across her legs. "He is my *Sovietnik*." At her befuddled expression, he clarified with, "My Councilor, Viviana."

It was clear she still didn't understand. "I'm a lawyer. *His*, to be specific," Ivan said before lighting up a cigarette.

"Like a *Consigliere*."

Anton felt his anger flare slightly. "Similar, but we are not Cosa Nostra."

"I'm aware," she mumbled dryly.

"There are rules that need to be followed in this house for your safety. My office is off limits unless Ivan, or Erik …" he waved at the much older gentleman behind him sitting on a leather couch, "… or I accompany you inside. Whatever doors are locked are meant to remain that way. The attic and basement are barricaded with alarms and passcodes. They are not for you to enter, ever. If doors are closed, you knock and wait to be permitted inside."

"The doors weren't closed completely," she muttered, refusing to meet his stare.

Anton sighed. "Don't play word games or bother with the semantics. These rules are not vastly different from the ones you had growing up."

"I'm not a child, Anton."

"Then you know to knock before entering an office where my associates and I are residing."

"You were going to shoot him!" Viviana shouted.

His jaw gritted. "Another rule—you're not to step in when I am handing an issue."

"I want to leave."

"Then go back to my bedroom, and I will have the maid bring you whatever you need," Anton dismissed her and turned back to Viktor.

"No," she snapped. "Here. I want to leave *here*."

His unaffected, hard stare turned back on her. Those words hurt, but Anton wouldn't let her see how damned much. "Viktor," he said, nudging the man on the floor with his foot once more. "Up with you. I believe you have something to say to Viviana."

"I want—"

"Be quiet!" he snarled.

Shrinking back into the chair, she swallowed, her shaking hands clasped in her lap. "He doesn't need to apologize."

Anton was disgusted. "He absolutely does. Up, Viktor."

Viktor rose from the floor, brushed down his pant legs, and then regarded Viviana with a blank expression. "My apologies, Miss Carducci, for treating you less than you deserved. You are not my property to do with as I wish, and my disrespect goes beyond just you. Anton has every right to be angry with me for disobeying his orders; please accept my apology."

Was that a ghost of a smile that played on her pretty, full lips?

"You also called me a bitch."

Anton growled from behind Viktor, who cringed at the sound. The brigadier was worried. The boss was even less happy now. "I'd forgotten about that. I'm sorry."

Flattening her hands against the jacket and steeling her gaze beyond Viktor to stare at Anton, she finally nodded her assent. He was a little bit proud, then, given others wouldn't have been so elegant about it.

"I'm sure you will be. Apology accepted."

Anton clicked the safety on his weapon and placed it into the waistband of his jeans. Turning to Ivan, he spoke in Russian, asking his lawyer to handle Viktor when they were gone. All the while, he kept a close watch on Viviana. "Is that clear?" he asked. Ivan only grunted in response. "Good, now leave."

The men exited the room quickly, closing the doors to the office as they went. When the panel on the wall beeped to indicate they were leaving the house, Anton sighed.

"Jesus, Vine ..."

"Oh, I'm not your *Viviana* anymore?"

Surprised at her question, Anton froze. "What?"

"Never mind," she mumbled.

No, he had heard her fine, so there was no forgetting it.

"That was a decade ago," Anton said quietly. "Back when I had some sense of privacy to my personal life and the girl I wanted to share it with. Over the last few years, I've become accustomed to calling you Vine in the presence of others. Maybe it helped to differentiate between the girl I wanted others to know and the one I knew. I've become fond of it, really. That's what they know you as, and they don't know the girl I do. They don't know *you*, Viviana. Not like I do."

"Maybe you don't know Vine."

"Maybe not. I'd like to, though."

She seemed to ignore that. "You're still going to punish him, aren't you?"

He frowned, rubbing a hand over his face in exasperation. "You can't do that again."

"Do what?"

"That!" He waved at the door and then pointed at her. "Come in here like that without even thinking about what you were doing. Do you know how ridiculous that makes me look to them? I'm nearly twenty-seven, a good fifteen or twenty years younger than most of the men I handle. I can't have a woman affecting how my men view me. It's about the respect, Vine, you know that!"

She cringed away. "You were going to—"

"I was going to break his fingers for touching you, and then shatter his jaw for hurting yours. Instead, Ivan gets to take that pleasure now."

Shoot and break were *kind* of the same thing, Anton thought wirily.

"Do you expect me to apologize?"

The aggravation he felt showed when he huffed out a breath of air. "No, what I want is for you to tell me that you won't do it again." She stared back, still silent. His anger overflowed as he slammed an opened palm down to the table where glasses sat. Viviana jumped, surprise and shock flitting through her wide eyes. "*Say it!*"

Color drained from her face and she looked as if she were going to be physically sick. Instantly, he regretted raising his voice. Quickly, Anton crossed the room and kneeled down before Viviana, his hands instinctively finding their way up under the jacket still covering her legs. The heat of her thighs had him aching in a whole new way. The pads of his thumbs rubbed soothing little circles on her bare flesh.

Her eyes swam with unknown emotions; Anton felt his own battle warring.

"Something is wrong with me," she mumbled.

"The sedative was mixed with an anti-anxiety drug. You were out the night before, yeah? The alcohol would have reacted badly with the tranquilizer. Boris should have considered that."

"How did you know that I was drinking?"

Anton looked away. "The Cosa Nostra have their eyes, and I have mine, Viviana."

"You've been watching me? *Why?*"

"I can't tell you that," he admitted softly. "There's a lot of things I can't tell you, but I had good reason to keep watch."

"Why can't you just be honest and tell me?"

Swallowing thickly, he muttered, "You're not my wife; it wouldn't be safe for me to do so."

"You have to let me go, Anton."

His gaze snapped back to hers at the statement. "This was already arranged years ago. *We* agreed when we were old enough to want it, too." A pained look crossed her beautiful face. He grabbed Viviana's thighs once more and said, "You know what Sonny did to the rest of your family just for organizing our betrothal. You know you're not safe. You *have* to know these things, Viviana. Your family will not protect you, but I will."

"He handed over my inheritance; let me go to Toronto

when I wanted. You're lying."

"I am not. I may omit things for your safety, but I have no reason to lie to you."

The sneer she sported stabbed him with a bitter force. "You're a criminal."

"So was your father."

"Yes, but he was *mine.*"

Anton's fingers dug into her thighs harshly. She responded to the roughness by biting her lip and tightening her legs. "And you're mine, Vine."

"Stop touching me," she demanded weakly. "I don't want to marry you. I just want to go home."

"Where is home?" He scoffed under his breath, face growing dark as his eyes narrowed. "With your uncle who is just days away from putting a cheap mark on your head? Perhaps it's the villa in Italy that your parents owned and left for you in their will? Or maybe it's Toronto, with a bull who can't do his job properly." With those words, Anton tilted Viviana's neck up to expose the bright, splotchy hickey. "Look at this, and with your *guard.* You know better than that!"

"You have no right to tell me what I can or can't do." Her hands slapped his away before she bit out, "And who the hell are you to judge me, Anton? How many women do you have climbing into your bed at night? Who I share mine with is not your business to pick apart and chide me about."

Raking his hands through wet hair, he shook his head. God, he wished he had been given a few more minutes to relax before Viktor and the other men showed up. After cleaning Viviana and getting her settled, he'd jumped in the shower. Those bruises on her body just pissed him off something terrible, and it explained the reason why his other brigadier had tried to avoid showing his face when Boris delivered Viviana. He barely had time to get the dried blood off himself before Viktor arrived.

"Vine, listen to me, *please—*"

"No, you listen to me. I want to go."

Anton stood abruptly. "It was agreed. By twenty-five, you were to be married to me. You wanted that. I wanted that. If you back out of this arrangement, the consequences will not be pleasing to you, or your family. The Bratva in New York have wanted to merge with your family for years, and our match would have done it properly. We will not look kindly on this breach—much like how your father handled a traitor, we are the same."

He was lying. She wouldn't know it, but he did. It tasted like poison on his tongue. Every word harder to speak than the last. Even so, Anton couldn't tell her the entire truth. Not yet.

"Don't threaten me."

There was a weakness in her voice. Anton tempered his own.

"It's not a threat, Viviana. Marry me."

Chapter Four

"No." Somehow, her voice had reclaimed its strength. Where had that been two minutes ago? Anton engaged her in a stare down until Viviana turned away from him and said, "You *are* lying to me. And you can't use threats to keep me here, Anton. Tell me the truth, and then maybe we can talk."

"I can't."

She was surprised that those were the words he chose to use. She expected another lie, maybe some crap excuse, but instead he gave her something Viviana could maybe understand in her own way. His fingers raked through his hair once more, showing his stress level was high. Again, she was sucked in by the way he moved, watching as black ink moved with skin she hadn't seen in years, and how the bands of muscle flexed when he moved. Only then did she notice how high he towered over her as she sat there waiting for him to speak again.

"How tall are you?" she blurted out, feeling stupid for even asking. The medication running through her veins was clearly taking its toll. When he looked at her with a raised brow, she rushed to explain. "I'm just ... you seem taller than you were, is all."

"Well, I'm not," he muttered. "But, if you really want to know, I'm six foot two inches."

"You must have gotten that from Nicoli. Your father wasn't that tall."

Anton cringed, his voice growing quiet when he replied, "Probably not, Vine."

"I'm sorry?" His response only served to confuse her further. "Your grandfather was—"

"Wasn't my real grandfather, not by blood," he interrupted shortly. "My grandmother was married once before. He was a useless excuse for a man who beat the hell out of her on a regular basis—well, whenever he managed to stumble home, that is. He was also a lower associate in the Bratva—an old school kind of mobster, I suppose."

Viviana bit her lip, feeling saddened, knowing what that likely meant. "So she was stuck."

Anton shrugged, crossing his arms and breathing heavily, clearly not liking the conversation in the least. "In a way, but he was stupid, too. Making too many mistakes, drinking too much, and leaving sloppy messes behind for others to clean and hide. Nicoli had already noticed his issues work-wise, and my grandmother took a risk by outing his abuse to his brigadier hoping it would help her."

"Did it?"

The corners of his mouth lifted into a ghost of a smile, but the sight disappeared as quickly as it came. "What happened behind closed doors were meant to stay there, but Nicoli had a thing about husbands beating their wives when it wasn't deserved."

"So it was okay if she deserved it, then?"

"It was a different time with different rules," he offered, sounding apologetic. "Nonetheless, he offered to help, if she agreed to his terms."

"To get a divorce, you mean. Was that even allowed?"

Anton's dark laughter surprised her again, given what the sound did to her rushing blood and twisting insides. "Oh, no. He killed him, poured cement in his pockets, cut his hands and feet off, and tossed him into the bay. Then he married my grandmother, who at the time had an eight-year-old son. My father."

Something bothered Viviana. Maybe it was the tone in his voice, or how quiet his words had turned. Either way, his explanation didn't sit well at all. "Why didn't my parents explain your family's history to me? I mean, we were supposed to be married, shouldn't I have known about your family?"

Reaching for a grey T-shirt that had been tossed over his desk, he pulled it over his head, and answered with, "Bratva business, Vine, not family business. He raised my father no differently than he would have his own son. Given my grandmother was unable to have more children, and Nicoli loved her a great deal, he chose not to take a mistress on the side who could give him more. He made the best with what he had in my father."

"He didn't have any *goomahs*?"

Anton rolled his eyes. "Not every man needs a mistress. Sometimes one woman can equal ten with all her nonsense."

"I know, I was just surprised, that's all. It's not uncommon. Dad had a few."

"He had more than just a few. Roman liked his women, or so I was told."

A lump formed in her throat, but that didn't stop the words from forcing their way out. "And what about you?"

"What?" Anton turned to look over his shoulder. "What about me, Vine?"

"Never mind." Rubbing at her eyes, she felt tired and unsettled. The ache in her sluggish limbs hadn't gone away, but at least she'd forgotten about it for a short while. When she looked up again, Anton was kneeling down, his head tilted to the side, watching her with a guarded expression and searching eyes. "What—"

"Women," he interjected softly. "That's twice you've brought it up in regards to me. Do you want a number, or maybe where we met, and how we fucked? Would that suffice your curiosity, hmm? Faceless, nameless, unimportant women who I didn't care for, but they still had their purpose. Is that what you want me to say?"

Before she could bark at him with a nasty comment, she watched as his strong, wandering hands moved the jacket off her legs. "You still have the nicest legs this side of New York, Viviana," he murmured, an eyebrow lifted as he caressed her with the tips of his fingers. Goosebumps prickled up her ankles, crossing over her calves, and trailing up to her thighs. Grabbing tight, Anton moved close enough that she could smell the liquor he just downed, and he opened her legs to move his body in between. His hands came to rest on her hips. "And sweet Jesus, I swear if my men see you half naked like that again, I'll cut their fucking eyes out and feed them to my dog."

Something caught in her throat—air, words, and *want*—the muscles constricting around thick desire that waged a war at his honest, but frightening declaration. "*Anton …*"

"What, you want me to move, quit touching you, or just leave you alone?" He bared his teeth, grinning playfully. "Tell me to stop, baby, and maybe I will."

"You have a dog?" It was the only thing she could manage to think of to ask.

"A German shepherd," he explained while his fingers danced along the hem of her shirt and slipped up underneath without hesitating. "His name is Rocco. We went through a rigorous training program together. He isn't a house pet to be spoiled, but a guard of sorts who is on constant alert. He has a schedule he keeps—one I'd like for you to involve yourself with—and Rocco understands he has a job to do first. He responds to Russian and Italian commands only."

His eyes traveled the length of her legs, appraising them as his palms lay flat on her stomach. Positive the panties she wore were damp just from his touch alone, she attempted to close her legs and hide the proof of how turned on he made her. Anton's body between Viviana's thighs stopped the half-hearted effort.

"Italian, too?"

He nodded slowly, hands rising under her shirt until the tips of his thumbs brushed against the curve of her breasts. The quick rise and fall of her chest betrayed the otherwise calm exterior. There wasn't a thing she could think of to say to make him stop touching her like he was, not that she wanted him to. Instead, she wanted Anton's hands grabbing tight again, with his lips on her skin.

Yeah, something was definitely wrong with her.

"I waited so long for you," Anton whispered, his

fingers digging into her ribcage. Viviana squirmed, needing his heat closer. "Three years ago when your father was killed, Nicoli made it clear we needed to step back for your safety, and I was lost, Vine. Enraged. Destroyed. Just ... *gone.* Sonny was holding you like bait, waiting for us to make a move.

"He had to have known the only reason we weren't declaring a war with the Cosa Nostra was because of you; he'd have killed you in a second, without regret or care. His niece? Nothing to him, a drop in the already full bucket. They would have found your body like they did the rest of your family's, and then where would I have been?"

Her heart clenched painfully, lungs shuddering with an exhale that stung. "Stop it. That's not true."

"It *is*," Anton insisted. He squeezed tighter and pleaded with blue eyes that held such a sober clarity for a man who handled drugs and a dozen other illegal things on a daily basis. "And when Nicoli died a few months later from that heart attack, I was put in the spotlight again. I wasn't ready for their attention, or their expectations, but I didn't have a choice. This is life for me, forever. Between the feds following me, trying to be who the Bratva needed me to be, and your uncle keeping you locked away..."

"I could have left!"

"Could you?" he shot back. "Do you even know why he allowed you to go to Toronto?"

Of course she knew. "Because I wanted to continue with school somewhere where no one would recognize me, or my last name. I wanted to start fresh."

His laugh was sharp and bitter, a stab to her confused heart. "Illegal weapons' charges on my rap sheet mean I can't cross the borders unless my papers are fraudulent. I took a five month sentence and two years' probation for it. He thought with you there, I wouldn't be able to watch so closely. But, the Bratva are not so different from his family, and we have eyes everywhere."

Tears welled behind Viviana's clenched-shut lids. All

she heard in what he said was that he'd watched her struggle for the last three years without ever stepping in. "Sonny will kill me. He'll kill me for this, Anton!"

Anton was suddenly millimetres from her face, his sweet breath washing over her senses in waves. "You're safe here with me. This is only one of my safe houses, with motion sensors on every floor and responding panels in every room that lights up to show where any movement is coming from. Guards are posted at the front and back entrance, and if you go out, you'll have at least three bulls on your person at all times. Rocco is trained to stay at your side—"

"He doesn't know me," Viviana interrupted. "He can't possibly be trained *for* me."

"He will, and he most certainly is trained just for you. The moment I allow you to touch him, he'll understand your importance to me," Anton said quietly, almost reassuringly. "I can't explain everything, Viviana, not yet. But please understand that I am trying to give you safety with some semblance of normalcy in between. My mother and father have the upper level suite in this house because I believe in keeping my family close while there's danger, but I have the basement, ground, and second floors. The upstairs has been equipped to handle my father's medical needs for long periods if it's needed. Ivan or Erik will always be around if I am not."

The fact that his parents were also situated in the same safe house left her with even more questions than answers. If there was a high risk of danger, usually close relatives would be sent out of state to hide out for however long it was needed. Instead, they weren't really in hiding if his statement of giving her some sense of normalcy was true.

"Why all the safety precautions if you're expecting me to live openly here?" she asked. "Doesn't that defeat the purpose?"

Anton cocked a brow. "I'm hoping your uncle will be a lot less brazen if I'm not keeping you hidden." He still hadn't let go of her sides, those teasing thumbs of his rolling gently against the undersides of her breasts in tender motions. "Deny that you want this, too, Vine. You've always wanted me. You want this life because you were meant for it, and I have waited more than long enough to get you here living it with me."

"You're not giving me a choice. I've spent the last three years thinking that this arrangement was over, and then you come in with guns blazing and a house on lockdown, Anton. That's … It's not fair. You signed my death warrant doing this."

Immediately, his hands left her skin. She wanted them back, but her pride wouldn't allow her to admit that fact. "It was already signed."

"*What?*"

Placing his hands to his knees, Anton shook his head and muttered, "He was already getting ready to put out a hit on you. That guard of yours was probably going to be the one to do it to get his in with the family. I was hoping to see you back in the states before I approached you myself, but Sonny didn't give me the chance."

No one likes to off a woman, Vine.

She couldn't help but remember Sam saying that. Would he have done it?

"You can't possibly know that for sure."

The look he gave turned her stomach with fear. "I can and I do, Vine. There are men in that organization who are less trustworthy than a snake. Even *their* eyes and ears can be bought. I stepped in now because I needed to, not because I thought you were ready, or that you wanted me to."

An ache settled in her chest. How was she supposed to trust him?

"Sonny wouldn't kill me simply because I wanted to marry you, Anton. I'm not worth a damn thing to him alive, nothing more than a nuisance he has to look after." Frustrated by his lack of expression, her bitterness rose. "Dead I'm worth even less though, right?"

"Dead you're worth nothing," Anton admitted, hurting

Viviana a little more. "That is exactly what your uncle wants to achieve. For secrets to remain hidden from his family and for his power to remain intact."

That only left her more disturbed, emotions rolling from one thing to the next without ever landing on just one feeling. "Our families won't merge now, regardless if we're married or not. So you lied to me earlier when you said that's what this was about. A marriage is only going to cause more issues. I'm worthless to the Bratva; you practically said so yourself."

"No, you're worth a great deal, especially if you're married to me."

But, why?

"You're hiding something from me," she realized, hurt that he was lying again, even if it was by omission. Viviana couldn't decide which stung worse—that he didn't trust her, or that he thought she didn't deserve to know whatever it was. "What aren't you saying?"

Anton looked stricken, fingers drumming a quick beat on his thighs. "I gave them my word. It was supposed to be them explaining this to you if they desired to—all the reasons and things that happened years ago. It's not my story to tell, and I promised. My word is all I'm worth if you consider the way I live; without it, I have nothing." Reaching out, he cupped a hand over her knee and ran it along the inside of her jittery leg. With his fingers moving so softly against her inner thigh, he pressed his fingertips close enough to her center to make Viviana throb with need. Murmuring, he said, "Can't you try to trust me? Viviana, you know me … you *do*."

She ignored his plea. "Who, Anton?" His fingers pressed harder at her words, grip tightening when Viviana refused to react to his motions. What she really wanted was more. So much more of his hands on her body, but she didn't dare speak that out loud. "Was it my father, or Nicoli? *Who*?"

"I can't answer that right now." With that, he stood and held out a hand for her to take. "Come, I'll get you back in bed for the evening. Let you rest and get the last of that sedative out of your system. I promise you'll feel better in the morning."

Too exhausted to argue, her palm met his. Anton's lips touched down to Viviana's fingers in a flutter of movement. She wouldn't have noticed the quick kiss had she not felt the heat of his mouth brushing along her sensitive skin. She might as well have been sixteen and falling for him all over again.

Viviana couldn't figure out if she was willing enough to let him do it. It didn't help that she wasn't all too sure if she knew this man anymore. Was he the same one she wanted all those years ago? Had his feelings remained the same nearly a decade later … was that even possible? Could someone want another that much?

What was even more frightening was that with his blue eyes watching, and his hand connected with hers, waiting, Anton still felt like hers.

Just like he always had.

*

The light humming of a sweet melody woke Viviana. Wrapped in blankets and curled on her side, she felt no confusion or sickness as shades were opened and morning light filtered in across the floor of the bedroom. The figure singing low under her breath moved to the next window and drew the shades there as well. With her blonde hair pulled back into a messy ponytail, and clothed in jeans and a T-shirt, it took Viviana a few seconds to register who the person was.

"Sasha."

Anton's mother turned, her surprise lighting up a pretty face with familiar blue eyes. "I didn't mean to wake you, Vine," she murmured quietly. Then, waving off to her side, she added, "He likes the light in the morning, is all. It's safer given the time of day. I'll close them if you—"

"No," Viviana interrupted, sitting up in the bed.

In her new position, she could see the sleeping figure on the small couch against the far wall. Wearing only a pair of cotton pants, Anton slept soundly with his back facing the bed and his arm acting as a pillow. She relaxed at the sight, slightly satisfied at the thought of him being close while she slept. Sasha cleared her throat, embarrassing Viviana at having been caught staring.

"I'm sorry. It's just ... been a while, so it's surreal." Her rambling only made Anton's mother hide a smile by looking back to the windows. "Never mind me. Leave the curtains open if he likes it like that."

Sasha shrugged, moving quietly to sit on the edge of the bed. "He'll probably sleep through most of the morning, anyway. The last week and a half has been difficult. You being here puts him more at ease."

Viviana doubted that, considering Anton's gun was still firmly seated in his sleeping hand. With the drug induced haze cleared from her mind, she could finally appreciate the ink work on his broad, muscled back that spiraled down to his elbows. The piece took nothing away from the stars on his shoulders, instead weaving around them. It took her a moment to discern between the marking's loopy pathways and thorny edges just what the tribal pattern was.

Vines.

Vines that covered and entwined with his skin; protecting and touching, dancing across dips and curves as they fell over the sides of his arms and traveled right back up again.

Her heart stopped, she was sure it did.

"Pretty, isn't it?" Sasha asked quietly, her voice barely breaking a murmur. Viviana noticed then that her gaze had followed, too. "He could have went for something a little less...showy...I suppose, but his clothing covers it well enough. I wasn't pleased when he had it done at first, but like a million other things he's done since I birthed him, I wasn't given a choice or the chance to voice an opinion. Anton was always stubborn like that."

Funny, he wasn't giving Viviana much of one, either. "I don't know what to do," she whispered.

Sasha turned, fingering the silver threads on the comforter. "It's not my place to step in or speak against the choices they make, Vine, you know that. If your mother were here, she would say the same. And I wish she were, as this conversation would not need to happen. I can explain things to the best of my understanding so long as it doesn't endanger my family, the organization, or you. Ask me what you wish, and I will make an effort to ease your mind."

Questioning Sasha on the things Viviana had been told the night before would be useless. Asking about Anton's grandfather, her father Roman, or their dealings would likely get her nowhere, also. It didn't matter that nearly ten years ago she was willing to make the choice without fully understanding the weight of her actions because now she did. Anton could preach about safety, family, and the past all he wanted, but it still wouldn't make the situation better.

"Wanting something doesn't make it good for you," Viviana replied, trying desperately to sound indifferent. It came out anything but. "I have to wonder if he understands that."

"What's so different between now and nine years ago?" Sasha asked, not skipping a beat. "You were so taken by him then, has that really all changed? I seem to remember sending you off from Barbados with your mother while your father stayed behind. You never questioned that, did you?" At Viviana's confused look, Sasha chuckled and winked. "You assumed what happened that night between you both went unnoticed, but I can assure you that it did not. Your father wasn't pleased; Anton certainly learned the meaning of respect that day between his grandfather, his own father, and Roman."

A pink blush heated her cheeks. Feeling choked, Viviana asked, "Did they …?"

"No," she replied with a wave. "Just yelled a lot, like men do. Between the Russian, the English, and the Italian, I couldn't keep up. Still, Anton stood his ground, spoke for himself like he needed to when it counted the most. He wanted *you*, Vine, and he told them that. Not because of the things they'd done, the nonsense they agreed on, or because they told him he had to, but because he wanted you to be his.

"You understood Anton, why he sometimes seemed aloof and distanced, how his own life would come later because of the family. You knew how to act, did all the things that would be expected of you, but yet, you were still this happy girl who could make it seem like her father wasn't on the FBI's watch list; like you weren't the daughter of a mafia boss. Anton wanted a girl who could be just her without the rest because he was still trying to learn how to be just him in the middle of chaos."

Zoning in on a loose thread on the blanket, Viviana considered her words. "What would you do?"

"Had my marriage been arranged, I would not have been able to *do* anything." Sasha made a noise under her breath, lips pursing. "How about I ask you something, hmm? Say you married some man, any man—he doesn't have to be affiliated—and went on your merry way. You still have the family to consider, dangerous men who have their necks on a block every single day. You remember what it was like growing up, don't you? As a girl, when something would happen, your father would whisk your mother, brother, and you away for weeks at a time until the dust had cleared and it was safe to come back again. Who will do that for your children?"

Viviana went to speak, but Sasha stopped her by lifting her hand. "Think about what I am telling you. It does not matter that you married a man who isn't involved, or that you no longer speak to your relatives and have no connection to their dealings. It makes no difference to the men who will take you or your children and hurt you while they wait for a payment that will never come because you mean nothing to your family. But your death would, you see? Your death is a slap to their face, an insult to their beliefs and understanding.

"So go, Vine," she said, shrugging. "Marry a man you might eventually love, one who will give you children and a nice home. Hope that you will fly under the radar of the men you aren't protected from, but who are always watching from the shadows. Friends are enemies here, that's what you were taught first. Trust no one and keep your love guarded." Sasha motioned towards the still sleeping man on the couch, her eyes growing soft as she smiled. "It was a good match, you and him. I've seen arranged marriages that destroyed more than you could ever understand, but you and my son ... it wouldn't have been like that. You caught his eye from the moment he understood how easy it would be to love you."

*

Anton grumbled, rolling over and feeling about as uncomfortable as he could on the couch given his size. More grumbles followed, his body shifting again and again to try and find a spot he liked, but coming up with nothing. Defeated, he rubbed his face, eyes blinking as he stared blankly at the sunlight filtering into the room. He cussed low and blinked again, taking in his surroundings.

A form near the bed clouded his tired vision, a hand patting his head as she passed. Anton knew then it was his mother. Sasha was affectionate like any mother, but still quick to give him privacy and space. Had she known Viviana had made it to the safe house the day before, she probably wouldn't have been in his room at all.

"Good morning. Try not to be so loud today, hmm? Your father needs to rest; the infection in his lungs is taking a toll. Take Rocco to the park or something later—you're starting to get cabin fever."

"I'm fine." Placing his gun on the cushion, his mother didn't blink at the firearm. He rolled his wrists, working out the kinks. "I have things to handle today, anyway."

"Ant ..."

"*Ostanovit.*"

Stop, he'd told her. While he let his mother get away with occasionally mothering him in private, he wasn't in the mood for it then.

"Fine."

Without another word, she was gone and the door closed softly behind her. Anton stayed quiet as he stood, stretching out his arms and turning away from the woman sitting back on his bed. "You were crying in your sleep last night," he said to Viviana. "I didn't want to get into the bed and freak you out, so I called Rocco up. You stopped when he laid down by the bed."

"Where is he?"

Anton squinted at the watch on his wrist. "Clarissa is probably giving him food. I told you he keeps a schedule. If you want, I could have her accompany you on Rocco's walk while I go out to the club."

"Is that safe?"

"For now," he replied. "If a breach happens, there's protocol to follow. Ivan can explain that when he comes over later in the week."

"Why not you?"

Anton turned then, meeting her gaze with a cold stare. "I have business to handle. These are things I can't explain outside of a marriage bed, you know that, Viviana."

"Clarissa, she's the maid?"

"She worked in Nicoli's home for many years. They had a close relationship, and she's very loyal to us because of it. She was not a free woman like you are. He protected her from that in his own way. Seems he had a thing for saving the broken."

The choice in wording he used wouldn't be missed, Anton knew. Like the Cosa Nostra, the Bratva was also known to deal in human trafficking, despite his particular branch of the brotherhood keeping their hands far away from all of that.

"Oh."

The quiet tenor Viviana adopted said she hadn't missed his implication at all.

"She's better here with me than somewhere else," he offered. "Her earlier life makes working with others she doesn't trust difficult. Clarissa is free to leave if she wishes, but she likes it here, knows she's safe, and she's good with Rocco, so … "

"You don't have to explain, Anton."

The honesty in her statement struck him silent. His gaze lifted, meeting hers again. "I know, but I wanted to. I wouldn't ever hide things like that from you."

For a brief moment, it seemed as though she couldn't speak, but when she did, she struck him speechless again.

"Okay…I'll marry you."

Chapter Five

Anton stared at her for what felt like hours before he swallowed hard and asked, "Are you sure?"

"Do you think I'll change my mind if we stand here looking at each other for long enough?"

Rubbing a hand over his face, he felt torn. The last thing he wanted to do was force her into it, despite his veiled threats the night before. They had been nothing but a lie. Was marriage really what she wanted with him?

A hoarse sound escaped his throat. "You're sure that this is what you want, Viviana … *Positive?*"

Pushing blankets off her form, she moved from the bed to stand. Anton stood stock-still, watching as she pawed through a small pile of folded clothes he'd placed at the end of the bed. It was her clothing, stuff that Boris had brought back from the dorm. Nothing much, but enough to do her for a short while.

"Thank you for getting these. I don't mind your shirts," she said tugging on the end of the one she wore with a grin. "But, they're a little big."

"I couldn't keep the stuff you arrived in. They needed to be destroyed, so I hope you weren't attached to anything particular. The guys managed to do one thing right when they packed you a bag. It's in my closet, but anything else you need, we can buy. Your dorm was … ruined."

Viviana coughed nervously. "And?"

"You were seen entering your dorm the night before with a friend, distraught and in a hurry. A family emergency called you back to the States. In your rush, you left a small space heater turned on, which set a blanket on fire the next afternoon and then burned down half the wing. At least that's what the report will say. Damages will be paid in full. The university won't want to speak with you as you'll be … indisposed … due to said family issues, and you're not expected to return there."

Anton checked his watch before continuing. "Also, you'll have a short interview over the phone with a fire marshal named Dick Stevens, and an RCMP officer by the name of Ronnie McCloud with the usual questions, approximate times, and whatever other nonsense they feel like handling. During the interview, you'll be properly distressed over what happened, make several apologies for the recorder to hear, and show an appropriate level of guilt in regards to your irresponsible actions."

"Okay," she said, turning to grab the clothes.

"Just okay?" He was surprised she'd take that all so easily. Anton moved to Viviana's side, wanting to be closer. His hand curved around her arm as his thumb swept a line back and forth at the crease of her elbow. Heat bloomed at the touch, saturating his senses with an onslaught of memories and need. "You don't have any questions?"

Automatically, like second nature or an extension of his mind's desires, she covered his hand with her own to calm the clear apprehension in his voice. At her touch, Anton stiffened, his thumb stopping its movements against Viviana's skin. Despite having his hands on her bare legs the night before, this was different. Much, much different. It was intimate, so familiar in how neither of the two hesitated in wanting to reassure the other. As if they'd done this before … maybe.

Old souls …

She seemed to struggle to breathe as they both stared down at their connected hands. "Yes, just okay. I'll do the interviews when I need to, act how you suggested, and give whatever answers they need to hear. Nothing happened, right? A friend, a family emergency, and my forgetful self somehow managed to leave a heater running. How terrible, but nothing more than a mistake. I can handle that, Anton. I can."

"Why?" he murmured, fingers squeezing lightly at the question. She shrugged, clearly confused at what he was asking. Anton moved closer still, lips finding her temple as his free arm wrapped around her waist. With her close to his side, he felt at home. "Why are you agreeing to marry me when last night you wanted me to let you go?"

Turning in his embrace, Viviana faced him. With no men around to see where his weakness truly lay, Anton knew there was an honest vulnerability written in the way he held her tighter. If he didn't hold on, she might disappear. Ridiculous, yes, but he'd waited so fucking long for this girl.

"You were right … I knew I wasn't safe—that I probably wouldn't ever be," she replied quietly. "Like tied down, you know? I felt trapped, so I got to this point where I didn't have to think about it. I was just trying to get from point A to point B without worrying about who was following behind."

"That's still not an answer, Viviana."

She poked his chest with a finger. "Remember that night in Barbados?"

The corner of his mouth quirked up into a small smile, heat rushing through his blood. "Of course I do, can't forget it. Sweet sixteen, tanned legs, and you made me yours so fast …" Anton trailed off with a low whistle. "One of my very best memories."

"I've never been serious with someone." Viviana released his hand and covered the mark on her neck with a frown. While he didn't have room to judge her on those choices, he hated the position she put herself in with that bodyguard. "I've done things—"

Anton's dismissive sound interrupted her. No way was he going to let her feel badly. "Me, too. Who came after and the in-betweens didn't matter. I told you that, and I meant it."

"Two meetings in all those years; that's all we got. We weren't allowed to see each other or keep contact in between. You were just a short drive away. There didn't have to be other people at all."

Two meetings, yes, but there were reasons for that.

And one of those meetings had been when they were just children.

"It wasn't safe," he reminded gently. "Once the arrangement was out in the open, you witnessed how dangerous it turned for your father."

"Regardless, I still felt tethered to something that I knew was out there, but just wasn't with me yet. That's why I couldn't keep someone close to me, or bother going farther than just the bedroom."

"I'm sorry?"

Anton's confusion only led to amusement glittering in the beautiful brown eyes looking up at him. Oh God, those eyes … so familiar, yet so new. Already, he was reconsidering old promises he'd made to dead men.

"Tied down again, tethered to you." She pointed at his chest, smiling as she said, "As if you were exactly where I was always supposed to end up someday. A moth and a flame, that's how I felt—drawn to you. Even after my family was buried and I was told this wouldn't happen, I still couldn't manage to keep a relationship because it wasn't meant to be. I didn't even know you, not really, but all I'd ever been told was that you were going to be mine. It never felt *arranged*, Anton, not once."

Her fingers traced the vines drawing up his arm before crossing the black rose that covered his right pec. He was so enjoying the silky feeling of her touch when Viviana added, "And clearly I've always been yours, too."

Maybe his cold heart stuttered just a bit— missing, skipping beats when he grasped her jaw and tilted her head back up to look her in the eyes. "*Always*, Viviana."

"I'm scared," she confessed softly. "This was intended to be an easy transition for me. Instead, I watched your men shoot my bodyguard, kidnap me, and now I'm in hiding. That's not how this was supposed to happen."

"That excuse for a bull was nothing more than a ruse," Anton muttered unhappily. "I won't regret that choice."

"Nobody likes to off a woman, right? Especially if that

woman is Roman's daughter."

Something struck a chord with Anton at her quiet words. "Why would you say that?"

"I didn't," Viviana answered, "Sam did. That's what he told me. I just didn't hear him like he wanted me to, I suppose. Maybe he was trying to give me fair warning."

"Another reason for me not to feel bothered over it, then."

"Would he have done it, though?"

"No," he said immediately. "I wouldn't have given him the chance. In fact, I didn't."

"Announcements, seating placements, flower arrangements, and all that nonsense seems really ridiculous to think about right now, given everything."

Anton chuckled darkly. "The last day has been rough, give it some time. I want you to feel safe—that this is yours, too. Maybe find a routine for yourself if you need. There's lots to do around here; you won't be bored. School can happen again if you're serious about continuing, but first I want to ensure your safety. If you want, there are two spare bedrooms down the hall. Pick one, it's yours, and when you're ready, you're welcome to mine."

Teeth cut into her lip as she considered his offer. "I liked waking up in here …" Trailing off, Viviana made a face. "I don't think I'd like waking up to another woman in the room again, especially if that woman happens to be your mother. Boundaries, you know?"

Anton choked a little on his sudden rise of mortification at the statement.

"There's a stairwell that connects our apartments with locks on either side. While they have their own entrance, I usually keep my lock turned off so she can come and go as she gets on quite well with Clarissa. I certainly didn't intend to embarrass you, and she likely assumed you wouldn't be in my bed, considering everything. Sasha knows my desire for privacy and that you're going to need time to adjust to things, but she also takes the chance to mother me when I'm close by. I suppose she was so excited to finally see you again, my father, too, though he doesn't leave the upstairs."

"Stop rambling. I want to stay in here. I felt safer the moment I knew you were close, but that ..." she murmured, pointing at the gun on the couch cushion, "needs to stay in the drawer or something, okay? I'll keep sleeping in here; I bet you'll feel better with me close, too."

"With me," he clarified. The husky, suggestive tone behind the words had an immediate effect on Viviana as her pupils dilated and her fingers tightened their hold on his. "Because this room is the only one besides my office and the basement that has responding motion sensors to the whole house. The others are floor by floor. I'm not sleeping on that couch for one more night, Vine; it makes my back ache."

Throwing him a cheeky grin over her shoulder as she scooped up the clothes off the bed, Viviana said, "We'll see how it goes."

Anton's face darkened, want and lust suddenly thrumming deep like the race in his pulse. Eyes narrowed, and taking a step closer to Viviana, he loved how she shivered. "I like lace, satin, and silk. Something that feels nice under my hands and I can tear right off without much trouble. Anything short enough to show those legs of yours off, and heels in every fucking color, hmm? Keep that in mind when Ivan brings over your cards and a new laptop later in the week."

Her mouth fell slack. "But ..."

"Keep it in mind," he repeated thickly.

*

The kitchen looked like a hurricane had passed through. With empty meat and fresh vegetable packages strewn across the counters, pans dirtied from having been used earlier, and no one in sight, Viviana wondered where the food had gone.

Anton seemed to pick up on her confusion. "Rocco is fed a natural raw and cooked diet. He doesn't eat kibble; it's not as healthy. It's a good balance, keeps him happy, his coat looking nicer, and he doesn't eat nearly as much as a dog fed on a dry-only diet as he gets sated faster."

"That seems like a lot of work."

He shrugged, picking up the empty packages and opening the garbage to dispose of them. "Sure, but it's worth the results. He's never sick, he's more aware, and of course the most obvious, he's healthier."

"He sounds spoiled," she teased.

Dishes, pans, and utensils were tossed into a stainless steel dishwasher. She helped in silence, noticing all the shades were drawn throughout the room. With dark, cherry oak cupboards, black granite, stainless steel appliances, and grey tiled floors, the space was modern and comfortable with a table that could seat a dozen people in its high-back, leather chairs.

"Far from it," he finally replied. Then, a quiet beep sounded from a panel on the wall above the light switch. Nodding at the panel, Anton said, "Clarissa is bringing him inside from the backyard. He'll let her enter first, but if it were me—or you—he would make his way in ahead of us to check the space out and make sure it was empty. Always let him do that, no matter if you feel it's ridiculous or not. That's a part of Rocco's job, not allowing him to do it confuses him. He'll always alert you if it isn't safe."

"Does he ever … I don't know, have time off or just a day where he gets to be a normal dog?"

Anton looked up from the paper he'd picked up from the table. "Why?"

"Well, he is a dog, Anton. He should get to act like one, I suppose. You don't agree?"

"No, I do, but for the time being he has to be on high-alert for me. He can hear things we can't, smell things that are long faded, or search you out in a scenario where I possibly couldn't. When he takes his walk to the small park about a mile away, he gets some time to burn off energy, play with other dogs, or whatever else he needs to blow off steam."

"Do you ever take him out?"

The newspaper was forgone back to the table. "Usually. Some days I can't, though, so Clarissa or Ivan does it instead, depending on their schedule. We work it out. Rocco always gets his time for him."

Close enough to read the labeled rooms and spaces on the panel, Viviana saw just how big the ground level of the house really was. With a bedroom, bathroom, and hallway at the back of the house, there was a front entrance with another hallway that led to the stairwell and front entrance to the kitchen. A three level house with a basement and attic meant the home was huge, and she'd only managed to see just a few parts of it.

She wanted to look out the window, gauge where exactly in Brooklyn they were, but Viviana had a feeling she probably shouldn't. "This is too big to be a normal house," she realized.

Anton agreed silently, lifting one shoulder in acknowledgement. "Was an apartment building, but I had it renovated a couple years back to join the separated spaces and put the safety measures in. I wanted the possibility that I wouldn't have to send you out of state somewhere to keep you safe—that we could be together instead of separated."

"How much did it cost?"

"Enough. Five million, though it was closer to seven once I was done with everything."

"And it is safe, right, despite the location?"

Anton looked at her like she'd grown a second head. "Of course it is, Vine! It's not attached to my name. The feds haven't realized this is where I'm staying after I do three car switches before coming home, and your uncle's idiots haven't managed to follow me here, yet. We'll have another week or two at least before someone figures it out, I'm sure."

"And then what?" she asked. "I imagine your clubs keep you out late, not to mention whatever else. Just … will it be safe then?"

He crossed the floor before she had time to blink, his large hand grasping tight to the curve in her waist while the other lifted up her chin. "I'll be home every night, or at the least, I *will* be there for you to wake up to, always. I decided a long time ago that there weren't a great deal of things more important to me than this right here. If I can't be home, for whatever reason, I'll let you know myself. No phone calls from anyone else, only me. A man at both entrances, I told you that last night. Someone capable will always be here. You must know how to shoot a gun, so Ivan will show you where the weapons are located in every room. I thought you were going to trust me?"

"I am," she insisted. "It's—"

A low cough interrupted them both. "Mr. Avdonin, Ivan called a half hour ago to say he'll be a little late getting to the club."

Anton didn't turn around, keeping Viviana's vision blocked. "Where is Rocco?"

"At the back entrance on the mat," she answered.

"Send him in to meet Viviana, please."

"Sure."

A low whistle sounded, followed by two words spoke sharply in Russian. Anton stepped to the side as the sounds of Rocco's nails hitting the tiled floor echoed down the hallway. It was only then that Viviana finally got a good look at Clarissa, and her older age was surprising. She assumed the woman would be younger, but the lines on her smiling face and the grey in her hair said differently. Keeping her eyes drawn to the floor and avoiding direct contact, her hands were clasped to her front. The maid all but melted into the wall, seemingly wanting to be out of sight.

A jogging Rocco entered the kitchen without hesitating to pass Clarissa by. She didn't reach out to touch him, and he didn't stop to acknowledge her presence, either. With a quick snap of two fingers, Anton spoke a low command and rose a palm to the air. Rocco sat, head cocked to the side and big brown eyes looking up, waiting.

He was gorgeous with his short coat, the tan, brown, and black markings brushed and cleaned. With high pointed ears, his body sitting with a disciplined straightness, and a tail that lay flat and unmoving to the floor, he looked commanding. Not at all like a carefree, spoiled house pet, but instead, an animal always on the watch and wait for his next command.

Anton's finger cut through the air; Rocco stood and moved closer at the silent command, coming to sit at his feet. With one hand, he pet the dog's head between his ears, lightly, speaking softly in Russian. Viviana looked up to see Clarissa had vanished from her spot against the wall, the panel across the room beeping to say she'd entered the back bedroom.

"Go on," Anton said with a wave. "Pet him; say hello."

The animal watched her warily as she bent down. With her knees to the floor, her face was level to his chest. A massive beast with muscles that wrapped his every surface, she could see how he would be frightening to some. But he wasn't to her. Viviana thought he was just simply beautiful.

"*Ciao*," she whispered, her hand out to pet Rocco. When her palm met the spot between his ears, the dog pushed back against the hand instantly. Warmth spread through her insides at the action. "You're an awfully pretty boy."

"Pretty." Anton scoffed under his breath. "He's a brute, just look at him." Viviana grinned, sticking out a tongue playfully in response. Amusement spread across Anton's strong features as she scratched the backs of Rocco's ears. "He likes it when you rub the tips."

She did just that, hearing the quiet thumps of the dog's tail hitting the floor behind him. "Hmm, but he *is* pretty."

Anton bent down and rubbed under the dog's muzzle. "He's yours, so he can be whatever you want him to be, I guess." With one word in Russian, Anton lifted the dog's muzzle and murmured, "Viviana, Rocco." He repeated the word again, thumb rubbing at the animal's mouth softly. "Good boy."

The tail stopped thumping on the floor. Rocco's large

head pushed a little harder against the palm of her hand. "What did you just say?"

Anton smiled, making her skin tingle and lungs expand heavily. With her heart hammering, she watched him reach out and stroke her cheek with two fingers. Viviana couldn't help herself when she turned her face into his touch, wanting the heat of his palm against her skin.

Something drummed deep in her blood, rushing fast and hard. Her instinct, maybe, recognizing how easy wanting Anton really was for her, just like it always had been. A term like "soul mate" seemed to fit, especially since she seemed to want him closer, needing the feeling of home nearer. From the very start, that's how he'd always made her feel, scarily so.

"*Tvoyo*—yours," Anton explained, his fingers still stroking, and his voice thick with emotions that underlined his words. "Like me, he's waited a long time to have you with him."

Chapter Six

Anton's eyes popped open and darkness saturated his vision. The low, constant beeping coming from the security panel on the wall was a heck of a lot noisier when the bedroom was quiet. Not that it mattered because even the softest of noises would wake Anton up now.

He kicked the blankets off his legs before sliding out of the bed with as much stealth as he could manage. Viviana turned in the sheets, but her eyes stayed closed and she continued sleeping.

Fuck, he loved having her in his bed, even if all they were doing was sleeping.

Anton grabbed the handgun from the bedside drawer before crossing the room to observe the movement on the wall panel. Sure enough, the sensors were going crazy, showing excessive activity on the bottom floor.

He pressed the silence button to stop the low beeps, but continued to watch three rooms light up one after the other to signal a presence was inside.

That didn't feel right to Anton. Clarissa and the bulls understood they had to key in their codes at night if they woke up and needed something. They had been living in the safe house for a while before Viviana arrived, so they weren't ones to forget procedure. Rocco had a large, metal kennel he stayed in at night, so it couldn't be him.

The security system should have been beeping far louder than what it was if someone had come from the outside in; however, it was that they managed to get in. And no one should have been able to get in because two bulls were at both entrances. Still, if there was anything Anton knew not to do, it was to underestimate someone's drive when they wanted something.

Anton glanced over his shoulder at Viviana and his worry grew. The locks between the floors would keep the intruder from coming up, but once he went down the stairs to handle the issue, it would leave the door opened.

It didn't much matter. He didn't have a choice.

If somebody had managed to get inside, Anton was going to make fucking sure they didn't ever leave unless it was in garbage bags.

The gun in his hand snapped loudly as he cocked the hammer.

"Anton?"

"Shit, I'm sorry. Go back to sleep," he said, turning to face Viviana and keeping the gun hidden. "I'll be right back. Just have to use the bathroom."

Viviana rubbed at her eyes and sat up. "No, I heard your gun. What's wrong?" Anton wished he could lie to her, but the lights on the panel were still blinking brightly on the wall. When her gaze caught the warning from the security, fear welled in her eyes. "Is that ...?"

His heart rate picked up at the tremor in her voice.

"Go back to sleep," he repeated calmly.

"Anton—"

"Don't, Vine. Trust me. Lay your head down on that pillow, close your eyes, and I will wake you up in the morning like I did yesterday, and the day before."

Anton understood he was asking a lot in his simple request. Chances were if someone was downstairs and they had managed to get past the bulls and the security measures somehow, it wouldn't be fun, quiet, or easy when he went down there. He wasn't afraid. It wouldn't be the first time someone had come into his home assuming he'd be an easy kill. However, Anton was worried for Viviana and her well-being, emotionally and physically.

"Can you do that for me, please?" Anton asked.

Viviana bit her lip, nodding. "Okay."

Not wanting to risk the possible intruder having any more time inside the home than he had already been given, Anton grabbed his cell phone off the small desk and left the bedroom. He shut the door behind him, and it wasn't five seconds later he heard quiet footsteps before the door's lock clicked.

Smart girl, he thought with a cold smile. But Anton also knew she wouldn't sleep until he was back in that bed with her.

Dialing the bull who should have been at the front entrance to the house, Anton pressed the phone to his ear and waited.

"Boss?"

"Breach," he said coolly.

"What? No way, Boss. Joe is in the back and I'm—"

"According to the security panels, someone is downstairs and they got in without settling off the goddamn night alarm. As of now, I can't hear anything, but when I get in the stairwell I very well might. If someone got into this house on your watch, I will gut you, Rory. Do you fucking understand me?"

"Yeah, Boss, I got you," Rory answered. "Fuck, I'm sorry. I'll call Joe … if he's back there."

Yeah, Anton wondered that, too. What if someone had taken out one of his guys? It was possible.

"You do that. Ten seconds and I want you coming in from the front and him moving in through the back if you can get him on the phone. We meet in the kitchen. Let's try to keep it quiet. Vine's trying to sleep and Sasha won't appreciate being woken up by someone's screams."

"Got it."

Anton hung the phone up and made his way down the hallway, not bothering to turn on any lights as he went. Once he opened the door to the stairwell, the panel downstairs would notify the intruder that Anton was coming down. He wanted to be ready for whoever it was, not the other way around, so he took a moment to gather his thoughts and calm his raging emotions as he came to the stairwell door.

It took him all of three seconds to blink away whatever hesitation might have remained. Tightening his grip on his gun, Anton opened the door and took the stairs two at a time. Instead of his nerves growing as he neared the bottom door, he only became calmer He could already taste the blood on his tongue.

And now he was just pissed the fuck off.

Somebody was going to bleed for waking him up and scaring Viviana. They'd get even worse if it was an intruder. A soft whine behind the door at the bottom of the stairs stopped Anton from slamming it open.

"Rocco?" he asked.

The animal should have been inside his kennel. He had never escaped, or tried to, before.

The pup barked loudly, but his master knew it wasn't a warning like he'd been trained for, rather an indication of his excitement.

"Rocco, you little—"

Anton gritted his teeth and opened the door to find the German shepherd wagging his tail with his tongue sticking out.

"Boss?" Rory called out from the darkness.

"Fucking Rocco," Joe growled, coming around from the kitchen.

"Is everything okay?"

Anton frowned at Clarissa's groggy voice adding to the mix.

"Everything's fine," Rory said lowly. "Go to bed."

The previous anger and desire to kill Anton had been feeling ebbed away as he stared down at his waiting dog. Clearly, Rocco had set off the sensors from the inside, and it wasn't something they'd ever had to deal with before.

"How'd you get out, huh?" he asked the pup.

The two bulls had come to stand in the hallway, each sporting amused expressions.

"Boss?" Joe asked, hiding his grin with his hand.

Now Anton just felt stupid. Viviana was probably upstairs freaking out.

Perfect, he thought.

"Take Rocco out to piss, and then get him back in his

kennel."

Rory snorted. "Can't. I noticed it on the way in. He must have broken one of the hinges because the side collapsed in."

The dog in question seemed wholly unbothered that he had caused such concern and ruckus. Why on earth was he trying to escape, now? Did he want to be closer to Viviana?

"Viviana?" Anton asked, noticing immediately that the dog perked up at her name. Well, that wasn't going to happen. No way was the dog sleeping in his bedroom every night. "No way, Rocco. You have a bed."

Rocco whined and cocked his head in a lupine way. "No," Anton repeated.

"This is really fun and all …"

Anton tossed a glare at Joe and it gave Rocco all the time he needed to push past his master and jog up the stairwell. Cussing low under his breath, Anton knew there would be no fighting with the dog, never mind Viviana when she found out what happened.

"So, no gutting?" Rory asked cheerfully.

"Shut up."

"Night, Boss," Joe said as Anton turned away.

"The amount of money I spent on that dog's training …"

Grumbling under his breath, he followed the same path the animal had taken.

*

With Viviana on one side and Ivan on the other, Rocco strolled at a comfortable pace between them but never trotted more than a foot or two ahead. His large head stood higher than her hip, ears twitching every few seconds as his nose would drop to the ground to sniff before coming back up again like he hadn't changed his course.

The quiet Brooklyn suburb where Anton had situated the safe house was just that, quiet. She wasn't at all familiar with the area, the roads, or where it was exactly that they were. Ivan had returned to the safe house nearly a week later, and when she gained the courage to ask him, he wouldn't say, simply pointing out that it wasn't important so long as she was comfortable.

And she was, oddly.

Sure, things were a little awkward here and there, but Viviana couldn't ignore the way she enjoyed waking up to Anton's blue eyes or feeling his finger trailing up and down her cheek. Despite her and Anton sharing his bed every night, he hadn't stepped over any boundaries. For all intents, he was a gentleman. Maybe he was just waiting for her to make some kind of move. Hell, he hadn't even kissed her, and she was so wanting for that.

"So ..." Ivan murmured, kicking a stray pebble off the walk onto the street. Rocco's ears perked at the action, but he didn't make a move to go after the rock. "Anton was happier this morning than I've seen him in years. Using his given name didn't get me the automatic, knee-jerk growl it usually does when he's in a morning kind of mood."

She barely acknowledged that he'd spoken. "And how many years is that, exactly?"

"A few," he replied vaguely. "Since he was a young man and me in my early twenties, I suppose."

After a long week that involved Anton taking her through a room by room tour of their multi-storied home, and showing her where she could find anything she needed, he handed over a disposable cell phone with pre-programmed numbers. It included anyone and everyone she might possibly need to call, starting with his. According to him, once every couple of months they would replace the phone with a new one as a precautionary measure. Even though the calls couldn't be recorded, she still needed to be careful about what she said during conversations or texts.

Then, Ivan had finally come around with the things promised, like that laptop and the credit cards. With those two things, she could buy just about whatever it was she wanted. Viviana was still considering all that lace, satin, and silk...

"Anton mentioned something about switching vehicles before he comes home so no one follows him?" she asked quietly.

Ivan chuckled. "Not fun when it has to be done three or four times before you lose the car trailing you. Either way, he has a few drivers waiting throughout the city at different spots and a simple text allows them to move to a new area quickly. The one under the Brooklyn Bridge nearly always seems to work, thank God."

"Do you do that, I mean, before coming here?"

"Of course!" He almost looked offended at her question. "I would never take risks like that, Vine."

"I'm sorry; it's just been a lot to take in. That's all." Sighing, she looked away, enjoying the peaceful streets and trees with leaves just starting to change color. Viviana missed New York, despite Canada's hospitable people and the few friends she managed to make there. "What's he doing today, anyway?"

The chiding click of Ivan's tongue told her that was the wrong thing to ask. "Vine ..."

"Just wondering."

"What I can tell you is that he had an early meeting this morning with many others like us, to inform them of your safe arrival and begin to set a proper watch in place between all the crews throughout the city. Usually I'd accompany him, but he felt safer with Erik going and me staying with you until you've had more time to adjust and settle."

Remembering the older man sitting on the couch the first night she woke up in the safe house, Viviana wondered what his place was in their group. "Erik, what is it he does, exactly?"

Ivan's lips drew a tight line before he answered with, "A bookmaker of sorts, who collects payments, assures the proper enticements for certain people are in place, and whatever else needs to be handled in regards to cash and things. Generally we're considered the two spies, above the Brigadiers, but below your Anton, we keep a close watch on everyone, or try to. In a manner of speaking, we are his right and left hand where he can't always be, you understand?"

"Enticements." She tried hard not to scoff. "You mean bribes."

"You call it whatever you want. I call it what I need to in order for your future husband to stay out of prison."

His blunt honesty silenced her instantly, reminding her that the life they lived daily was no game, it was real, and frighteningly dangerous. One misstep on their part and she'd be stuck like her mother who spent ten out of her twenty-four years of marriage with a husband behind bars. Not all of those years were consecutive, but regardless, it wasn't something Viviana was ready to handle, or think about, for that matter.

With her hand trailing along the back of Rocco's neck, she hummed softly under her breath. Despite the fear he had caused the other night by getting out of his kennel, she still adored the dog. According to Anton, because Viviana slept like the dead and rarely heard a thing, Rocco was attempting to get upstairs more often at night now, too. The furry companion pushed his large head against the palm instinctively, enjoying her contact as much as she liked giving it to him.

"He's glad to have you with him," Ivan interjected kindly, bringing her out of her musings.

"Anton?"

"No," he said, laughing. "Well yes, him as well, but Rocco, I mean. I remember when Anton ordered him from the breeder in San Francisco four years ago. That pup didn't know up from down, wouldn't listen to a thing he was told, shit in every corner he could find, and then suddenly he was gone and came back a whole different animal. Anton still has that chaise he nearly destroyed his first week home. Got it restored, I believe. It was antique, belonged to his grandmother's mother."

The things she knew about Anton's grandmother, or any of his family really, were very little, and she felt ashamed to even admit that to herself. Even though their marriage had been arranged for years, that didn't mean there weren't a lot of things in between she didn't know or understand about him, his upbringing, or the people left behind.

"His grandmother, she died a long time ago, right?"

Ivan nodded. "While his mother was pregnant with him, actually. A stray bullet where there shouldn't have been a gun was the cause, unfortunately. Nicoli always kept her present in the family in some way, and Anton still has his grandmother from his mother's side, but I think he wished he had known this one as an individual instead of just the stories they told. Who wouldn't?"

Viviana had to agree. Her grandparents on both sides had played a massive part in her life growing up, though after her family was killed, her father's parents made a point of keeping her at a distance that Sonny felt comfortable with. It hurt her—still did—but she wasn't about to admit it out loud and give her uncle the satisfaction of seeing her struggle with one more thing he caused. In some ways, she understood her grandparents needed to make that decision, but it in no way meant that she had to agree with it.

It wasn't long before they reached the dog park. Viviana found a bench to sit on quickly enough and waited for Ivan to join her. Surprising her, he pulled a collar with tags jingling from his coat pocket and placed it around Rocco's neck, speaking quietly in Russian before the dog was off, running immediately in the direction of the water.

"He always needs his identifier inside the gates," Ivan informed her as he sat down. "Some of these owners get antsy around an unmarked dog, despite his excellent behavior. They're quick to call animal control and we don't need that nonsense. Anton has a collar he keeps on him, too. I imagine he has one for you to keep as well, but probably forgot, given the excitement over the last week."

Crossing her jean-covered legs and tightening the belt to the tweed coat she wore, Viviana settled into the bench just in time to see Rocco cut through the water of the pond.

He looked almost carefree for a moment, like any dog would, until she watched him come back up. His eyes and ears searched her position out immediately to make sure she was still sitting where he had left her.

"He never gets a second off, does he?" Viviana wondered.

"Rocco knows his place," Ivan replied flippantly. "This is probably the farthest he'll allow himself to be from your person, unless you leave him to go out and do something alone, which you will, eventually. He's all right if someone he knows is still with him, like Clarissa or myself, but Rocco couldn't be left alone for more than a day; he needs his master—*masters*," he corrected quickly, shooting her a small smile, "… to feel as if he's acting—or reacting—properly. He's very much like a furry little child … one who can't speak."

"Why that breed? Not that I don't think he's a good choice, I'm just curious."

Ivan's laughter caused her to grin. "German shepherds are known to be the chosen breed of officials. Anton's method of raising his finger to the police. Imagine how they must feel to know their scenting or search-and-rescue animals can be outdone by a criminal's pup."

She clicked her tongue in mock disapproval, giggling. "Figures. I probably should have guessed that, no?"

He winked cheekily in response. "Maybe, though Rocco is more than just that. His ability to scent is incredible, more so than even the best scenting dogs officials use. They found that specialty of his during training, and it was something Anton demanded they focus on."

"What is it that he scents?"

"Nearly anything that would be of some use to us. Hidden explosives, uncirculated cash or large stacks of handled money, weapons, drugs, bodily fluids, and people, of course. There are a few other little things, like hidden electronic devices, although if there are a lot of those in a room he is unfamiliar with, it can sometimes confuse him as to his purpose."

Damn, *Viviana* was confused. "I didn't realize electronics gave off a specific scent."

His answering shrug was dismissive. "Everything has a scent, we humans are just unable to smell it." A few minutes passed them by in a comfortable quiet while they watched Rocco play his own version of catch with a stick in the water. At that moment, Ivan sighed beside her, drawing her attention away from the playful pup once more. "Is everything a go then, Vine?"

"Pardon?"

"With you, Anton, and the marriage, I meant. Am I free to begin drawing up the proper paperwork and things we need to go ahead?"

Viviana found it odd how her first inclination was to agree without wondering first if she should speak to Anton. She didn't feel the least bit uncomfortable around Ivan, even though she knew exactly what he was, and the things he was capable of. But, at the same time, she also understood his importance to Anton—the situations they had likely been placed in together, the amount of trust and confidence that must have been shared between the two. She had to expect at some level, that Ivan would give her the same respect, given their positions.

"Of course," she finally answered, offering him a smile. Thinking about exactly what he'd asked her, something else fluttered through her mind. "What paperwork needs to be drawn up, anyway?"

Ivan cleared his throat nervously. "Well, Anton's last will and testament would need to be changed, for one thing, as he wants. Any of his possessions—houses, cars, and things of that nature—would be better switched into your name; if an arrest occurred, and fines or restitution was expected to be paid, the government could not seize what is not his."

There was an unspoken *and* at the end of his explanation. "What else?"

"There's also the small issue of a prenuptial agreement

between the two of you," he said, looking away and avoiding her questioning gaze.

"Excuse me?" The noise level in her tone rose a little higher. *Like hell* ... "Why on earth—"

"For *you*," Ivan interrupted, stressing his words for her to understand. "Anton is required to sign a prenuptial agreement for you, Vine."

"Anton is required ..." Trailing off, she scoffed because even the words coming out of her mouth felt wrong. "That is ridiculous. The inheritance from my father's estate was nothing compared to the money we both know he has. He doesn't need to sign a damned thing, Ivan, and I won't be asking for him to, that's for sure."

The lawyer beside her looked awkward, as if he'd just shoved his foot in his mouth. "It would not be for the money from your father's estate. This is money you don't yet have, coming from a different place."

Confusion ran rampant as Viviana tried to process his words. "Shouldn't I have been made aware of this ... money?"

"No, being the executor of the will, I wasn't required to make you aware until certain requirements were met."

"Like a marriage," she managed to grasp, her voice growing quiet.

Ivan glanced sideways from the corners of his eyes, nodding sharply. "Like a marriage," he repeated. "Specifically, a marriage with Anton before your twenty-fifth birthday."

"That's ..." Struck dumb, she fell silent, her mouth growing slack. "Who did it come from?"

"Not really important right now," Ivan offered, sounding apologetic with a frown marring his features. "I'm sorry that I can't explain more of this to you, but it is not in my instructions or orders to do so."

Again, she grew quiet, needing to look anywhere but at the man sitting next to her. Anger was the first emotion to bubble up. They were hiding more things, things that directly involved her that would affect her future beyond her own choices. Not only did she not understand why they were doing it, but they wouldn't give her the smallest of hints to work it out, either.

How was she ever supposed to trust them?

Standing abruptly, Ivan followed suit to her actions. "Don't," she mumbled through clenched teeth, a hand held out to ask him to stay. "I want to go for a walk, to think, or … something." Cry, likely, that's what Viviana wanted to do, but in private. She figured this was a better choice than yelling her anger out at Ivan, anyway. "Surely I can handle going for a walk without someone at my side, right?"

"Yes, of course." He whistled low under his breath and Rocco was trotting back to them in an instant. Shaking water droplets from his fur, the dog waited patiently as his collar was unhooked. With his finger pointed at a dark sedan with tinted windows parked in the visitor's section of the park, Ivan said, "That is the only car trailing you. They are your guards. Two other men are close by on foot, but I doubt you will notice them, and they will not approach you unless they need to. You're safe to walk if you'd like, and I'm sorry that I upset you, Vine. It wasn't my intention."

Without a word, she turned and walked away. With no one at her side, Rocco stayed a good two paces ahead, his nose to the ground and ears twitching at every sound and movement surrounding them. Paying little attention to the pathways they traveled through the park, she only noticed that the deeper they went, the thicker the trees became. Joggers, mothers with strollers, and the occasional couple sauntered past, never paying her or Rocco any mind as they went. The dog barely acknowledged them either.

With a heavy heart, muddled up feelings, and a slow sense of being unsure about her surroundings, Viviana realized she didn't know where in the hell they were. Stopping short, she peered around. Sunlight filtered through the pretty colored leaves all around, her flats crunching against the dried brush underfoot.

A quiet kind of stillness settled heavily on her senses as

Rocco looked back, brown eyes wide and waiting, his tail standing high. Looking around once more, she didn't see a soul following, and there was no way the car Ivan had pointed out earlier could have traveled down the path she took.

Oddly, her first thought wasn't to run. It wasn't that she was free of being watched, or that she was now available to make herself scarce if she wanted to. In fact, she didn't think for a second that running now could be the one way out of the arrangement with Anton she'd agreed to … because Viviana didn't want to.

What she *wanted* was Anton.

And she suddenly felt exposed.

Unsafe.

Unprotected way out in the open.

They'll find me in the bay, she thought, *with a bullet through the back of my head just like Roman.*

Or maybe it'd be more like her mother and brother's death, burned alive in a car that had apparently careened off a small cliff before catching fire, leaving them *trapped* inside. If anything happened to Viviana, she knew Anton would kill every member of the Cosa Nostra he could get his hands on until he felt the slightest bit better, even if that would only lead to his ultimate end.

Air caught in her throat, chokingly so. Turning sharply, her flats hit the ground faster than a walk but not quite as brisk as a jog. Rocco was fast to take the lead again. When the breeze shifted, her dog stopped, ears perking immediately. A tail lifted higher and a sharp, short bark fell from his muzzle, halting her as well.

Fear coursed through her heart, adrenaline spiking as she considered turning around again. Blood rushed her ringing ears, strumming hard and fast, echoing and overtaking the calm sounds of the park. Going back in the other direction would likely lead to her getting even more lost than she already was, but going forward only directed her to something the dog felt the need to alert her to.

Unsure, Viviana froze to the spot, her hand slipping inside her coat pocket to find the semi-automatic .40 Smith and Wesson pistol Anton had handed over earlier in the week. Illegal with the serial numbers filed off and no registration to show ownership, the gun was compact enough to stay hidden in a pocket or purse. She had to admit that the firearm appealed to a certain side of her, despite the initial reluctance she felt to carry it at first.

The small wag of Rocco's tail melted her tension for only a split second. He wouldn't show excitement in regards to danger, right?

A figure entered her vision from around the small bend of the pathway, the blurry form making Viviana realize then that tears had started gathering in her eyes. Blinking away the wetness and breathing deep as she took in the man walking closer to her, relief began to settle through her panic.

Wearing a dark suit with the jacket unbuttoned to show the pale blue dress shirt underneath, a grey scarf hanging untied around his neck, and a fedora tilted down on his face, all of her apprehension drifted away. A cigarette was tossed from his fingertips to the ground, smoke billowing out in a grey cloud.

That wasn't what he left the house wearing that morning.

The very view of Anton's confident, smooth stride as he came closer had the strangest effect on her lungs and heart. Butterflies were fighting their way up from her stomach into her throat, leaving Viviana unable to breathe or speak. Overwhelmed and on a sensory overload, her worry faded a little more.

Anton looked up from under the fedora, the side of his lips quirking into a smile, making her stressed shoulders ease up when he came to a stop by Rocco's side. His hand found its way into the dog's coat. "Lost, Vine?"

"No," she breathed, and feeling stupid, she looked away. "Maybe a little. I thought there were men watching after me?"

"There *are*," he said, smirking. "Ivan asked them to stay a few paces away to give you some privacy."

Anger simmered on low again. "He called you?"

Anton's cocky smirk faded. "No, I was already on my way here. I knew you were walking Rocco with Ivan, so I came to the park first. Ivan was waiting for you to return when I arrived, so I decided to just take a walk and come find you myself. I was speaking to one of your bulls two minutes ago. That's how I knew this was the path you came down."

"Oh." Realizing it was still early in the afternoon, if not maybe a little closer to supper, she wondered why he was even back this early. Usually he strolled into the safe house with just enough time to sit down to eat an evening meal. "I thought you had a lot of stuff to do today?"

The sight of his grin returning made her heart ache in the best way. Anton looked down at Rocco whose tail thumped happily to the ground. The pup was so pleased to have his other master close again.

"I did, and I handled what was most important like I needed to. Then, I realized that I missed you, and so that took precedence. I wanted to see you," he murmured quietly, still not looking back up. "Sending a text or calling seemed really ridiculous considering I have a half a dozen cars that I could jump into and come home to be with you. There are enough people who can handle things when I decide to take a day off. I've been busy this week, I know, and I'm sorry for that. Maybe I'll try taking days away more often … now that you're here."

"You didn't ha—"

"I did," he interrupted, regarding her finally. Bright, blue eyes shined with emotions and want so thick she could feel it; her breathing stuttered. "I've already spent too many years keeping the distance for your safety. Now, I want to be closer. Close that gap for me, Vine."

There was no waver in her actions when she moved fast to meet his embrace. With his strong arms locked tight around her small shoulders, the sense of security and safety slowly faded back into her senses. The slight tremor rocking her shoulders had her understanding just how panicky and fearful she had become.

"Hey, you're fine, okay?" His lips pressed down on the top of her head as he whispered, "They were close enough, baby. Just following orders like they were told to and giving you some breathing room. Ivan was worried you had been the one who called me after your disagreement and that's why I came back early." Anton sighed when she tensed at the mention of his lawyer again. Really, it wasn't something she wanted to get into, but he clearly wasn't going to give her that choice. "Speaking of which, the money he mentioned … all that nonsense, don't worry about it. It's not at all important. It's not mine, it wasn't ever meant to be, and it has no real bearing on the arrangement, anyway. I've known about the prenuptial agreement for a while and already agreed to sign when he had it ready."

"Just …" A huff of breath escaped her. "Why all this secrecy?"

"I missed you," he said instead.

"You woke me up to say goodbye this morning. You were only gone a few hours."

Anton shrugged, tilting her head up. His mouth brushed feather-light kisses on her cold cheeks, warming the flesh instantly. It was the closest he'd come to kissing her lips, and suddenly she was overwhelmed with wanting the heat of his mouth on hers. Shivering from everything but the cold, he held her tighter as his eyes flickered with something she didn't recognize.

"What is it?" Viviana asked, worried something had happened he didn't mention. "You're here, so I'm good now. We can … I don't know, do whatever. Go back to the house if you want, or take Rocco back to that pond he seems to like."

"What I want …" Trailing off, he abruptly kissed her hard with no warning, her mouth opening instantly to taste the sweetness of his.

The taste of cigarettes and the faintest trace of bourbon was heavy on his tongue. It swept into her willing mouth with force. The kiss wasn't gentle, soft, or slow like she expected, but instead he commanded with his mouth on hers, dominating and wanting so heavily with every sweep of his tongue. Tasting, needing, feeling. The ache that traveled from her middle outwards was all-encompassing. When his lips slowed, pecking light touches to the corner of her mouth, his thumbs rolled over her smiling cheeks.

"I missed you," he repeated with a throaty tone that had her muscles constricting. "Didn't take the chance to kiss you, either. The first thing I should have done when you agreed to marry me last week was lay you across that bed and show you how happy that made me. Or just kissed you; that would have worked, too, hmm?"

"I was starting to think you didn't want to kiss me," she teased.

Anton's eyebrow cocked at the statement. "I want to do a lot more than just kiss you, Viviana."

His hand ran down her coat to push against the small of her back. Pressing lightly, he drove Viviana's body into his. Underneath his dress pants, the length of his thick erection pressed to her side, making his point clear. Her throbbing sex clenched at the thought of his suggestion, desire raging a war within her body while she breathed in the smell of him all hot and heavy.

"All week you haven't once—"

"I know," he interjected softly, smiling just a little. "I was battling something, I suppose. Trying to make sure you were doing this because you wanted to …"

"Because I wanted you," she assumed when he wouldn't finish.

Anton sighed. "That, too."

"What is it *you* want, Anton?"

"I want to go home; I think Rocco has played enough, no?"

"Okay." Actually, that was more than okay. "But—"

"No buts, things can wait, others can answer, and doors will be locked."

Driving her frame closer again, his fingers danced along the front of her shirt and down to the waistline of jeans only to slip under the fabric skillfully. Anton hummed low and deep from the back of his throat at the sound of her harsh intake of air. She felt his digits skim the sides of dampened panties.

"Let me touch you. I've waited so long ... I *need* to."

Viviana gave her approval with a nod. The opened jacket he wore hid her trembling frame when two fingers swept underneath the fabric and between her fleshy folds and tapping hard to her swollen, heated clit. The whimper that fell from her parted lips tumbled out loudly, his responding chuckles reverberating down to the pulsing at the apex of her thighs even more.

"Nine years is too long to wait for us. Feel this, you're already soaking my fingers at the thought. I have time to make up for. Home ..." he demanded again, leaning down to nip his teeth on her jaw and removing his hand. "Let's go."

Was she supposed to say no?

Chapter Seven

The lightest sensation of something feathering over her closed eyes woke Viviana. Instead of giving away her awakened state, she relaxed into the pads of Anton's thumbs tracing down over the apples of her cheeks before sweeping over her parted lips. She could still taste the faintest trace of her sex on his skin.

It brought with it a hot, heady memory of his hand grabbing the inside of her leg as he spread her legs father apart. By then, juices had smeared down her thighs; she had been so ready and wanting of Anton before they'd even gotten started.

She could remember his teeth possessively biting into where her hickey had finally faded, his cock buried balls deep into her from behind. A strong arm wrapped her middle, lifting her onto the bed higher, giving him better access to hit all those spots she needed him to with the hardest, deepest thrusts she'd ever felt in her life.

When she'd looked back over her shoulder with teeth biting into her bottom lip, his face had been right there, meeting hers, staring so honestly. With a single fleeting glance, Viviana swore she saw the insides of his soul and back again. Everything and anything he was ever going to want was laid bare in his bright blue cerulean eyes.

"No more marks," he had said, his voice throaty and severe. The words had been punctuated by his hips meeting her ass, the force of the thrust sending her sprawling forward to catch herself. "None on your skin unless I put them there. No man touches you again, Viviana."

The promise from her was a broken sound as his demanding, rough rhythm started. "No … none."

"I'll fucking kill them if they do."

Any other woman might have been frightened by his admission, especially when his hands grasping her body tightened almost painfully. His clean-cut fingernails scratched into her thighs, scoring red lines she'd see for days. His actions only really served to show and prove to her just how serious he was, how much he wanted and needed her, too.

Mob men had a possessive streak over their women. What was theirs was theirs, and that was all there was to it. They didn't marry a woman who wouldn't look good on paper, who wouldn't be appropriate sitting beside them on a pew at church. They didn't speak vows to mistresses. No, they only made public lives with women who understood exactly what was expected of them. Some would lie, cheat, and hurt their wives until the bitter end, but they still expected their women to be as pure as a dove.

And if that woman failed, well, there was a place for them, too. Six feet under. Whether or not that was true, Viviana couldn't say. She'd heard and seen enough things over the years to believe it was, but just like the rest of her life had been, walls could not speak and windows did not see.

She didn't want to be that woman, but she didn't want a husband who had five other women he could turn to at any time, either.

"You're not really sleeping, Viviana. I can see those wheels of yours turning."

At his blackstrap thick voice, her eyes finally fluttered open. Anton cocked his propped up head to the side in an almost animalistic way, regarding her with an intense gaze that set her insides to a fever pitch all over again.

It was the same expression he wore earlier that day when the front door slammed open and his hand was already up her shirt. The same piercing stare he leveled on a bull who was inside talking with the maid before he snarled at them both to, "Get the fuck out."

The doors between floors had been locked, keeping the upstairs from coming down and vice versa. When his cell phone began beeping, she vaguely remembered him leaving her body long enough for her back to meet the bed before he was gone to grab the offending device. The bedroom door slammed closed once more before his phone had even hit the hallway floor and he was crawling back between her open thighs again.

Anton had a purpose with her, clearly, and he didn't want to be interrupted by anything.

"What's on your mind?" he asked.

Viviana caught his thumb on the corner of her lip, turning her face into his palm. Anton tasted distinctly of sex, and her stomach was already clenching with a heavy desire to have him so rough and hard again. The possessive dominance he seemed to own that screamed she was only his. She wanted it all.

"Nothing."

"Mmm, I think you're lying to me. Don't lie to me, baby."

Telling him that she had once again been considering the possibility of his mistresses probably wasn't the best idea. "Really, it's noth—"

Their naked legs intertwined beneath soft sheets. Without warning, she found herself above him, black hair falling over her shoulders in a curtain wave. Straddling his waist, Viviana could plainly feel the length of his hard erection pressing between slick, fleshy folds. With every jostle of their bodies, it rubbed so deliciously sweet along her swollen clit. When his hands grabbed to hold the curve of her hips, grinding his cock up into her harder, she let her head fall back to just *feel* him like that for a single moment.

"Tell me."

"It was ... Oh, fuck, don't stop doing that."

"Viviana. I swear if you don't start speaking, I'll tan your ass to a pretty red."

Would he? The thought might have excited her more than she was willing to admit.

"I promise it was nothing."

Really, it was starting to feel like that, what with the circumcised tip of his cock teasing the hood of her clit the way it was. Every strong stroke as he slid her along his length again and again was making her wetter and hotter.

Bare he felt so much better. Without latex sheathing him, she could feel every glorious inch of him when he was inside. Every vein and ridge was exposed for her to explore. The way she took him in and surrounded his cock like a perfect fitting glove was delirious. Her body was made for his. Given his very clear demand that she keep up whatever appointments needed for her birth control shot, Anton obviously didn't have a desire to use condoms with her.

The heady smell of her arousal hung heavy in the air. The juices spread along the length of his cock and between her thighs, smearing more as he came a little closer to her waiting sex.

"Were you thinking about school?"

"No."

"Your walk with Ivan, then?"

Another stroke and his hand was moving, guiding his cock into her entrance and stretching her full with a single movement. Her fleshy folds parted so easily, taking him all the way in as she sighed, relieved. Goddamn, he felt so good hitting that hyperaware spot inside that made her tremble and had her fists clenching against his muscled abdomen.

"Viviana …"

The tone of his voice was almost a singsong, if the warning hidden behind it wasn't so clear.

"No, not that."

"Are you worried?"

She spread her knees wider under his urging hands, lifting along his length before slowly dropping down again. How could she be worried being with him like this? There wasn't a single thing that could even possibly bother her when she got to have him like this.

"Of course not." The reply from her lips fell like a breathy gasp. "Not worried."

Suddenly, Anton's teasing rhythm stopped. "Me, then?"

Viviana choked on the emotions that built up so

quickly inside her chest. "Please, Anton. I said it was nothing."

Again, she found herself turning in a flurry of movement. On her back, he was still buried deep, leaning high above her to hit a switch over the headboard. Light illuminated his beautiful, striking form better for her to see. The heavy, dark curtains had been pulled closed in the room.

"I don't want you lying to me."

"It wasn't anything I needed to bother you with," she argued, avoiding his gaze.

"Anything that concerns you is my top priority," Anton replied. "I'm not sure if you think it would be nothing more than an annoyance to me, but it wouldn't."

"Yes, that's exactly what I think it'd be. It's not my place—"

"Whoa, stop that bullshit right there." Viviana's head snapped up at his angry tone. Disbelief flitted over the handsome features that she'd missed for so long. "Not your place? Viviana, your place is with me, baby. Yeah, I can't have you throwing a tantrum in public or walking in on me or my associates, but that has nothing to do with this right here."

Didn't it, she thought. Their whole arrangement had come together because of business and family. She was, after all, meant to be the quintessential mob wife. Perfect in every sense of the word. Polite and pretty on the arm of her husband. Appropriate and quiet about what went on behind closed doors. Sadness or discomfort was to be hidden behind with designer sunglasses and lipsticked smiles.

"I don't know what you expected of me, but that isn't it," Anton murmured softly.

"Isn't it?"

For a moment, he looked torn above her. The clenching of his fists along her sides moved fast, dragging down the sheets to rest at her spread legs. Tension was written so painfully clear along the tight line his lips had drawn.

"No."

Viviana didn't want to anger him, but she wanted to make her point, too. "How many homes do you have, Anton?"

"Six. One in Moscow, a small vacation home in Hawaii, two in New York besides this one, and large acreage out of state."

"And how many do you use?"

"All of them at one point or another. Why?"

Viviana licked her lips, trying desperately to ignore the hard, twitching cock still buried deep between her thighs. "How many can I use?"

Again, Anton appeared confused. "What?"

"If I wanted a change in scenery, or if I needed to go on a vacation but you still needed to work … could I take any key to those six homes and leave without you? I asked about homes, but what about apartments or penthouses. How many of those do you own?"

"None. I don't need them. And yes, of course you'll have access to all of my other properties. What are you trying to get at here?"

"How many children do you already have?"

Anton froze, eyes narrowing. "I—"

"Mistresses, too. Maybe you don't own their apartments or flats. Did I not ask the right question to get the best answer? Should I have asked if you bought it for them instead?"

"For fuck sake, Vine. Shut up for a second." Hot, wet tears had snaked lines from the corners of her eyes down over her cheeks and she hadn't even realized it. He brushed the wetness away. "Jesus, stop crying … never cry in our bed. That's the last thing you should ever do here."

Before she could continue with her rant, Anton had spread her knees farther apart, opening her body so damned wide for him. It was a quiet, gentle beat of his hips meeting her slowly rising ones. Watching his hands hold tight to the silky soft skin of her legs, she could see the slight tremors that rocked his arms and he plunged deeper into her clenching walls with every thrust.

Viviana couldn't stop the wanton moans from tumbling out of her fast rising chest. Both of her hands found purchase on the pillow behind her, fisting in and grasping tight as her back rose off the bed. The hottest flames seemed to lick at her nerve endings, a sweet burning hum of pleasure and love rocking through her veins like the best drug.

"No mistresses. No children. Not a fucking one."

The words were growled above her and she found his gaze had sought out hers with that piercingly intense look again. A lump formed in her throat, keeping her ability to speak at bay as he released her legs from his grasp. The weight of his form pressed her into the bed, fingers finding hers in the pillow to uncurl and wrap with his.

"I don't know who you thought I would be, but that is not it. I've got drug dealers on speed dial, guns in the basement, and two strip clubs with women who'd blow any man for the right price. I do bad shit on a daily basis. I dabble in anything that'll buy me another car or house to make you smile."

"Anton," she whispered, feeling him hit just the right spot with the slightest reposition of his hips. Her breath shuddered. "It's—"

"It's not okay," he interjected lowly. "There's no sense in me going to the temple because even I can't buy my way into heaven, so what's the point in pretending. You want to know my secrets, baby? All the dark, bad things I did to get me where I am now? I've got a list in my safe a mile long of women and children I'm paying for because their husbands no longer can. My hand, a gun, and their grave. Do you understand that?

"Answer me …"

Her mouth was dry, words hoarse when she answered, "Yes, I understand."

"Don't act like some quiet mouse, Viviana. Don't stand at my side with your head tucked down in those pretty dresses I buy you. Don't be the weak little mafia princess

your momma said you'd have to be. That's not what I want—
not what I need. Stand straight, meet their stare, and be my
fucking queen. You're the only one at my side because you
can be— because you're worthy and beautiful and mine. Do
you understand me?"

His fingers clenched with hers, pushing her arms up
under the pillow as his lips met her jaw so tenderly. Already
she could feel her body beginning to sing and fly under his
fucking. No one had ever taken her quite so high so fast
before.

"But—"

"No buts. Question me if I'm late. Be angry if I piss
you off. Run our home or hire maids. Go back to school or
don't. Birth me children or enjoy your life the way it is. Those
things don't matter to me; they never have."

She was staring at him again, searching for some sign
of a lie behind the open, truthful gaze with which he regarded
her. He wasn't hiding a thing. For years, Viviana found
herself wondering if the quiet, whispered words he'd
promised and swore under those blankets nine years ago had
been as true as they felt. Now, she knew they were.

Anton loved her. Maybe he always had. It sure wasn't
like she completely understood why, but it was obvious she
couldn't deny the feelings were there, either. Once more, she
was reminded of how much their situation just didn't feel like
the contract it had been made out to be. Whatever they were
together, it was much more than men who shook hands and
decided their fates. Destiny had its own plan.

"I stepped in to take you out of Toronto because I was
terrified I wouldn't get the chance if I waited one more day. I
had men watching you for years. Not once did you lay your
head down and I didn't know where you were. I *always* knew,
Vine. Fuck, don't you know I love you?"

The orgasm that rushed down and swept over her
senses hit like a tsunami. From head to toe, it ravaged and
wrecked what was left of her worries, taking with it the fears
and expectations she thought she had. Viviana twisted in the

bed under the weight of her lover, crying out so broken and high because everything felt alive and awakened all at once. Too much, it was far too much. She didn't have a choice but to let it consume and take her under.

Anton's throaty, muffled groan against her throat followed the release she felt spurt from his cock, coating her core in thick, hot streams. *Tight* ... Oh, God, he held her so tight to his body, letting her feel and take every bit of him he gave. Her name was on the tip of his tongue and the blissful feelings of sex danced across her sensitive skin.

With emotional waves washing over Viviana in choppy bursts, she felt him finally let go of his rough hold and move. His fingers roamed down her sides as their mingling fluids leaked between her legs to the sheets, his cheek turning to press into her stomach before he laid the softest kiss there.

"I'm sorry," she breathed. "I didn't realize or think ... You kept pushing and I thought you didn't understand. I suppose it was me who didn't."

Anton's heavy sigh tickled her sweaty flesh. "I know."

"All this time?"

"Hmm?"

His confusion had her lips curving with a sentimental smile. "I can't believe you held onto that feeling for nine years, is all. People grow up, and we were separated for all of it. I mean, I always held onto you because that's all I ever knew and when it wasn't going to be anymore, I was fucking lost. Just ... why?"

"I told you," he said gruffly, "you're mine. I found who I wanted when I was eighteen. I still got to live, do what I wanted, whatever, but I knew where I was ending up. That's what I was working towards. I fell in love the one time, it was more than good enough for me; I wasn't about to let it go."

Viviana felt overwhelmed again. Like her heart had grown double its size and her lungs wouldn't accommodate the growth. Their attraction had been one thing, and it came naturally, but hearing those statements had all but whipped away any doubts she might have had about the rest. Still, there were people she knew who loved and loved and loved, but time moved all things and feelings changed.

"Can you say you'll never stray, though? Six years, ten years … it could change."

"Not for me. Don't think you're just here to hang pretty on my arm and birth a few kids. I want a wife—*my* wife. And she can be whoever the hell she wants to be so long as she's with me."

She went to speak, but his rising head stopped her words up short. When their gazes met, the faintest smile played on his full lips. "Don't apologize again. You have every right to wonder if you want this, baby. There's very little I expect from you, except for you to follow the rules for your own safety, to get dressed up in something pretty when I want to take you out, and to turn the other cheek when the time is not right for you to step in. That's all."

"Here …" he added, waving his hand to the space they were in, "… is your zone. When it's just me and you alone, Vine, the only thing I want and need is for you to just be you. Normal. Happy. Mine. That's it."

Resting back into the bed, she let his fingers trace pathways over her stomach and sides. There wasn't much else for her to say when he laid it all out bare for her like that. The comfortable silence that enveloped them didn't feel awkward. She wasn't even sure how long they stayed like that before the light hum of Anton's phone vibrating out in the hallway had him sighing an unhappy sound.

"Insufferable *idiots*," he grumbled.

"You've ignored them for hours."

"They pissed me off. You had a terrible bruise on your back and cheek; I've got a massive bill to pay in Toronto, and a shipment is coming in at the end of next week that is probably going to get intercepted by the authorities if they can't get the cargo in after midnight. Given the way the trip has been going, it's probably not going to happen. I need a goddamn break."

Viviana coughed, knowing Anton probably shouldn't

be telling her some of those things.

"Well, I'm here and the bruises have already started to fade."

"True," he agreed, sounding sullen. "But I'll still remember."

"Everything is taken care of in Toronto with all the important aspects, right?"

"For now."

"And this ... *cargo* ..."

Anton's brow furrowed in the sexiest way as he glanced away from her. "What about it?"

"Guns or other?"

"Does it make a difference?"

"I don't know," Viviana replied just as quiet. "You told me, Anton. Does it?"

"Not really."

"So, delay it."

The laugh that barked from him sounded a bit contrite. "It's not that simple."

"Sure it is. A few loose bolts on the ship's mainframe can cause a complete security failure. Engines stop. Ships just float. Maybe it'll float for a few extra hours just out of US waters with a viable excuse to be doing just that while someone else keeps an eye on the docks and coastguard to give a signal. See, *simple.*"

The surprise that registered in his eyes had her grinning.

"That's brilliant."

"I've overheard a few things here and there. Some of it could be useful, but a lot of it really isn't."

Anton was covering her body with his again, lips finding hers as his tongue swept the seam of her lips teasingly. The languid speed he took to taste and love her mouth was a soothing beat to the aftershocks her body was still experiencing from their previous coupling. Before Viviana could try to get his cock rising again, he leaned over and hit the call button on the conference phone sitting on the bedside table. The panel on the wall lit up with an immediate response.

Clarissa's voice suddenly chimed through the panel. "Mr. Avdonin?"

"It's nearly six, yeah?"

"Yes, sir. Supper is almost finished, but if you'd like to take it in your office, I can bring the plates up."

Anton hummed indecisively.

"I'll unlock the door to your stairwell. Allow Rocco up. How many calls have Ivan and Erik pestered you with, Clarissa?"

"Not many."

"Are you sure?"

"A few ..."

"Next time, tell them to stop calling. You're not my assistant and you don't deliver messages. I'll call them back when I can. Otherwise, turn the phones off for the evening. Viviana and me, we still have some catching up to do."

Viviana smiled against the strong arm lying beside her face. She caught his eyes traveling over the length of her naked form with an open brazenness that was filled with want. That lump returned in her throat with a vengeance. Despite her muscles being sore and her body feeling sticky and in serious need of a bath, she wasn't about to complain.

"Oh, and you have all that spa nonsense in the bathroom downstairs, yes?" At Clarissa's quiet agreement, he said, "Bring it up for Vine, and in the next few days you can take her out to show her where she can get some more if she likes it. You can pick up whatever you need also, okay?"

Viviana swore she could hear the knowing smile in the woman's voice when she answered, "Absolutely, sir."

Chapter Eight

"Hmm." Viviana hummed indecisively. "This one is a maybe."

Anton leaned over and sniffed the body lotion as she held it out to him. The slight crinkle of his nose told her he didn't like the scent of the product. Despite him having asked Clarissa to take Viviana out to get some of her own things for the bathroom, Anton ended up going with her himself. She didn't mind, seeing as how it would be good if he enjoyed the stuff she bought, too.

Well, that and Viviana was starting to get stir crazy inside the safe house. A walk everyday with Rocco wasn't enough to make her unrest disappear, and Anton hadn't allowed her to go anywhere else unless she had at least three bulls with her at all times. It wasn't fun, but she understood.

Today, it was just Anton and her.

Viviana loved that.

Anton eyed the lotion. "No. Too spicy. Women shouldn't smell spicy."

Coyly, she raised a single brow. "And just how should a woman smell?"

"Beautiful," he replied, smirking. "Delicate. Soft, like their skin. Silky, like their hair. Sexy."

That hadn't been the answer she was expecting. Something akin to anticipation coiled in her stomach as he stared down at her with mischief in his gaze.

"Those things aren't smells, Anton."

"Nope," he agreed, "but that's how I'd describe you. I think you smell like that naturally. Without all of this other stuff, baby."

"Oh."

When his hand came up to graze along her jaw, Anton added, "But you also smell like flowers because of that perfume you use. Soaks right into my lungs. You should find something like that." Viviana nodded as he grabbed a candle from the top shelf and added it to her basket. "Also, these candles are nice."

"Should I start questioning your sexuality because of this sudden scent love you've got going on?"

Without warning, Anton's arm reached out and wrapped her shoulders, pulling her back into his chest. A dark growl formed in the back of his throat before he nipped her neck playfully while his other hand slipped down to cup her ass over her jeans. At the same time that she melted into his embrace, the door to the spa shop chimed to say another customer had entered. While they were closer to the back of the store and there weren't a lot of people inside, she certainly didn't want to be caught in a suggestive position, either.

When Viviana squirmed in his hold, Anton only chuckled.

"You question my sexuality, Viviana?" She felt his lips form a grin against her skin as she shivered. "That's not what you should be worried about. What you should be worried about is whether or not I can fuck you in the stockroom without someone overhearing you scream my name."

"You wouldn't da—"

The cell phone in his pocket stopped her from saying more. Anton released his hold around her waist before pulling out the phone and turning his back to her as he answered the call.

"Talk," Anton demanded. "They lifted *what?* Oh, those greedy fucking idiots. Are they stupid? Those are loaded with GPS. Get them out of my warehouse before …"

Clearly the conversation wasn't meant for her to hear, or at least she should pretend like she couldn't. Viviana went back to scanning the items on the shelf. A kiss was placed to her cheek, bringing her attention to Anton who was back at her side. Covering the phone's speaker with his hand, he shrugged apologetically.

"I'll be right back. I have to take this somewhere

private."

"Sure," she said, offering him a smile.

With one more kiss, Anton disappeared through the aisles of bath and body products. Viviana appraised the row of pillar candles as the store's front door opened and closed once more.

Slipping down another aisle, she finally found products in the dozens for floral scents. Viviana always did have a thing for roses, so she picked up a bubble bath product with a rose petal design on the label and opened it up to smell. A flash of red hair in the corner of her eye made Viviana nearly drop the bottle.

With her head tucked down to stare at her phone, Cici Carducci stood five feet away from Viviana's very spot. The youngest daughter of her Uncle Sonny, Cici hadn't been especially close with Viviana or her older brother, but they had the same family. Not to mention the girl's father was the same man who was probably planning at that very moment how he could put a bullet through Viviana's brain and get away with it.

Viviana's heart and lungs stopped working as she watched her first cousin type on her phone. They were too close to the safe house, she knew. It was maybe a fifteen minute drive away. Why the girl was even in this part of Brooklyn, Viviana didn't know, but it wouldn't lead to anything good.

Cici could easily report back to Sonny about where she'd seen Viviana. The bratty little bitch that her cousin was known to be surely wouldn't hide it from her father. God knew Sonny spoiled all of his daughters to the nines and back, but Cici had always seemed to be his favorite. How long would it take her uncle to find her after that?

Panic welled in Viviana's gut like a poison.

Where the fuck was Anton?

As if her mind had suddenly shifted gears and started working again, Viviana stumbled backwards to go around into the other aisle and hide. Instead, she just ended up bumping into a shelf in her panic and knocking over a half a dozen bottles and soaps.

Shit.

Sure enough, Cici glanced up at the commotion and straight into Viviana's eyes.

"Vine …" Cici took a step forward, her hand holding the cell phone falling limply to her side. There was something all too nasty in the smile she leveled on Viviana. "Daddy said you were back."

Viviana forced herself not to blink as she said, "Hey, Cici."

"Where's your Russian? Doesn't he know it's not smart for you to be out on your own?"

That was all the conformation Viviana needed for her to know Cici would tell Sonny. She didn't know how much her cousin really knew about what was going on, or even if Cici knew what her father had done to Viviana's family, but the girl had a mean streak, either way. A little taste of power could do that to people, and Cici likely thought she had that in droves, considering her father's status in the mob.

There had once been a time when Viviana was the Don's daughter, and now she wasn't.

Cici was.

And you're the fiancée of a Bratva boss, Viviana thought. *Act like it.*

Exactly.

But she was still fucking terrified.

Lifting her chin to regard Cici as if she was unfazed, Viviana shrugged. "My *fiancé* is around. Where's your father, Cici? Is he around?"

"I'm not the one who needs safeguarding, Vine," Cici replied with a smirk.

She really was a goddamned bitch. It probably wasn't the best idea for her to be poking the beast, but Viviana wasn't about to let Cici see how much her very presence worried and bothered her. "Are you still fucking around with Sonny's messenger boy?"

It would sure explain why or what Cici might know.

Cici's glare turned to ice. "Maybe I should call Daddy and—"

"Cici, look what I found!"

The voice of Lucille Carducci helped to ebb Viviana's panic, but only for a second. Surely her aunt wouldn't do a thing to hurt her, but Cici was another matter altogether. Especially if the way her cousin's eyes narrowed in her direction was any indication. When Viviana's aunt stepped around the corner, the white bag in her hand dropped to the floor. Surprise wrote lines across Lucille's soft features.

"Viviana. Oh my God, honey, you need to—"

"What in the hell is going on here?"

Anton's deep tenor had Viviana turning sharp on her heel to meet his stare.

"We need to go," she breathed. "Right now."

He nodded, but the action was wrought with tension and anger. Anton stared over her shoulder, his gaze blazing as he took in the two people behind her in the aisle. There was no doubt in her mind he was thinking the same thing she was about the situation.

"Sure, baby. Are you …?"

"I'm okay, but please, let's just go."

"Vine, listen to me—"

Anton's short bark of laughter had Viviana flinching. "Lucille, right? Sonny's wife. Tell your husband if we happen to meet up with anyone associated with him like this again, he won't like the result. Understood?"

"Anton, please," Viviana whispered.

"Is that understood?" he repeated through clenched teeth.

"Yes, we understand."

"Good. Be sure your husband does as well."

*

Anton tossed a black gift bag with gold trim across the table. It skidded past Viviana's head and she barely glanced up over the bridal magazine she was knee deep into reading.

Sasha had brought her about ten of them that morning, swearing if Viviana and her son didn't pick a date soon, she would be picking one for them.

It wasn't that Viviana didn't want to, but more she couldn't figure out which would be best for Anton. When they spoke about it together, he also couldn't seem to come up with a suitable date that really worked.

"What's that?" she asked, nodding at the bag.

Ivan slid into the kitchen with a wave at her before sticking his head inside the fridge. Anton didn't seem to care much, instead shrugging and reaching over to grab a carrot stick off the plate Clarissa had brought for dinner.

"Something I thought you might like."

Viviana cocked a brow. There had been about fifty different things that continued showing up at the safe house that Anton said she might like, and she did, sure. The credit cards and laptop she had were only a few. And really, that served her purpose just fine. If she needed something, she bought it, typed in the address Anton wanted her to use, and he'd bring it home whenever it arrived.

The graze of his thumb over the apple of her cheek drew her attention up to him again. "Find something you liked in there?"

"Not really." The answering frown she responded with had her shrugging. "We need to settle on a date then maybe picking out all this nonsense can feel more … fun."

"Planning weddings aren't *fun*," Ivan muttered, still poking around in the fridge. "It's fucking torture. My wife spent two years planning ours and between her father and mine, it cost them close to half a mil for twelve hours of hell. Who spends that much money on a wedding? A nice foreign car, sure. A house, absolutely. A wedding, no."

Viviana suppressed a shudder. "I don't want do that, Anton."

"Hmm, do what?"

Apparently, his hand still curving her cheek had all but distracted him. It wasn't long before those fingers came to dance along the strap of her tank top before trying to dip lower beneath her shirt. She batted his fingers away with a pointed glance at Ivan, who was still trying to find something to chow down on.

It hadn't taken Viviana long to learn that Anton was an insatiable man. From his businesses, to the things he enjoyed, to getting her into the bedroom, his attention focused and his drive began. At that moment, she was thinking his focus had turned to her and sex again. Especially since it was a little after dinner and his day was all but done.

Of course, there was still Ivan, too.

"Ivan," Anton barked. "Doesn't your wife feed you?"

"Sure, but you know she's at her mother's estate for the next few weeks. I can't cook. Your pretty little thing there can, and I'm trying to find out what she made for me today."

Viviana snickered. "Nothing, Ivan. Clarissa felt like I was doing her job and told me to back off."

"She did not," Anton argued.

"All right, so she said it in a politer way, but the sentiment was still the same. What's the in bag?" Viviana asked as her gaze caught the toppled over gift bag again. "Did you buy me something else?"

"Patience is a virtue."

"I'm not a very virtuous woman."

"You can pretend to be," he replied, winking.

She scowled at him playfully. Anton had grabbed the magazine from her hands. Pages were skimmed under his scrutinizing gaze as Ivan finally came to join them at the table. "By the way, I meant to thank you, baby."

Viviana glanced up, surprised. "For what?"

"That shipment arrived without a lick of trouble."

"Oh, well, you're welcome."

"That is horrid," the lawyer said with a nod at a particularly poufy dress with way too much crinoline.

"Agreed." Another page was turned, and then another. Anton's finger tapped down to a mermaid styled, ivory colored dress all done up in lace from top to bottom with intricate pearl work along the bodice. While the capped sleeves and modest cut of the front was sweet, the deep plunge in the back showcased a great deal of skin. There was no denying it was a beautiful wedding dress. "Now, that is something I might enjoy taking off of you."

Viviana cleared her throat at his suggestive tone while Ivan chuckled and gave a short wave before he left their space. "At least you didn't pick something white. Still, it's a little too daring, isn't it?"

"For what?"

"A Catholic service, Anton. What in the hell else?"

"Oh God, no. I am not marrying into that mess. A Justice of the Peace will be just fine."

Viviana felt stunned. Traditionally, men married in the church of the woman if their religions weren't shared. Anton, however, was Jewish and he very well might want her to convert. "You're not Catholic. I'd forgotten."

The low hum that came from somewhere in the back of his throat felt almost dismissive. "So what? I'm Jewish. You're Catholic. I don't go to the temple, and given the reports I've had on you these last three years, you haven't been going to church either."

"Dad wasn't around to make me go."

"And we never quite followed the rules," Anton added gently. "Sex before marriage. Catholics don't believe in contraceptive methods. Living together and sharing a bed. My profession. I already told you I wasn't buying my way into heaven and I don't much care to pretend like I would. Wear ivory if it makes you feel better. Have some Christian readings in the service if it suits your needs. I don't want to be married in a church, or a temple, Vine. Does it really matter?"

*

Anton waited for Viviana's response with silent worry. Looking down at her distant gaze, he wondered if his refusal of her religion was going to be a hard limit for them. Over the last three weeks since her arrival, he hadn't found many things between them that could cause either one of them to kick up a fuss. Almost seamlessly, their lives seemed to intertwine, as if they were always meant to.

He would swear they were extensions of one another. Viviana was his perfect half, and sometimes it scared the living shit out of him. Break someone's jaw, no problem. Step in between drawn guns, not an issue. Sadden a woman who could bring him to his knees and suddenly Anton was a worried, anxious mess.

And damn, Viviana had done so well with everything he threw at her. The interviews with the police and fire marshal went just fine. There wasn't a flicker of hesitation or fear in her voice as she perched up on his lap and spoke to those men over the phone. The bulls who accompanied her on the walks with Rocco didn't have a bad thing to say, and if anything, they were worried her niceness to them would concern Anton. More often than not, she spent her days in the upstairs apartment with his parents until he was due home. Especially after that scene with her aunt and cousin a couple of days ago.

It was obvious a touch of cabin fever was beginning to settle in, though. Viviana had been going to school, she had friends and a life just starting to build in Toronto, and now he had her locked up tight with only the daily walk to the dog park and back with their pup. He sincerely hoped his gift in the black gift bag would help her with that issue.

"Viviana?"

"No … actually, that makes it easier."

Anton didn't know what to say. "Does it?"

"Yeah. We'd have to do those stupid classes, and it's a six month thing that we don't have the time for, or somehow buy our way out of them. I hate the big services for a Catholic wedding. It's always long, the attendance is huge. I didn't want to be in the spotlight like that. Really, it seemed like a hell of a lot of work for us to do in just two months."

Oh, thank fuck, he thought. Relief whisked the sudden weight right off his shoulders. "It would be a lot of work. A smaller service would be nice, given your family isn't exactly on the invite list."

Viviana's lips pursed. "None?"

"I could see about a few, but it probably wouldn't be smart on our end. More like throwing it in their faces."

"But we could send out the invitations to some of them anyway, right?"

"Uh..."

"He should know," she insisted quietly, a finger tracing the line of the model on the page. "I want him to know, Anton."

"Who?" he asked, confused at her statements and pensive expression.

"Sonny. He needs to understand that what he did doesn't matter. The arrangement is being upheld like they wanted. Their deaths were for nothing. His hands are stained red. I still want you."

Without giving her any warning, he turned her chair with a loud screech on the tiled floor. Down on his knees between her spread thighs, Anton found his hands trailing up under that flimsy, flowery skirt she wore.

"If you want, that's exactly what we'll do. I hadn't thought of it that way, but I can understand your motives behind it. Just be sure of the choice because it could very well backfire."

The look on her face told him she didn't think it would. "And as far as this wedding crap, well, it's not all that important. Don't worry yourself into a mess about it. I don't follow my religion like my mother thinks I should, and you haven't been following yours, so why even bother? We can do it however we please this way. Get married somewhere beautiful. Outside if you want, or inside. Have fun with it if we want."

"Have *fun* ..."

"Mmhmm," he hummed.

Anton brushed the raven locks of her hair out of Viviana's face. His hand swept over the magazine, opening it up to a new page just as the lawyer made his entrance back into the kitchen with a bag of chips in hand. He'd forgotten about leaving those in his office.

"Black and gold …"

"Excuse me?"

A chuckle rocked his chest as she turned to look at what he had found in the magazine. Actually, the colors had little to do with the flower girl dresses staring back at them.

"I quite like those colors. Hence the gift bag I tossed to the table. So go from there."

"Classy, elegant," Ivan intoned from the doorway.

"That and I simply like them. Also, this …" he added, reaching across the table to grab the gift bag that had toppled over, "… is something that might make your days a little easier, or just better."

The bag was overturned and a set of car keys fell to the granite table top. The emblem on the keychain was hard to miss, not to mention Anton knew Viviana would know the brand from anywhere. A few days earlier he'd purchased the car and it had only just arrived with his specifications that morning. A bull had picked it up that afternoon, and once it was safe, it'd be in their driveway before the night was out.

"Is that …?"

"A Bentley," Anton murmured. "Sporty little two door thing, all black with chrome wheels and bulletproof glass all the way around. Don't say a word about the cost, just drive it. That's what I bought it for."

For a second, he swore a flicker of fear flit through her eyes. "Vine, what is it?"

"So, you want me to go out, then?"

"Obviously. I didn't mean for you to drive it up and down the street here."

"They'll know where we are."

Anton hadn't wanted to worry her, but the feds already did. It took them a shorter time than he thought it would. If they knew, it was likely her uncle did as well. "That's not the point. You're not going to hide out in fear here. You have bulls for a reason, just like Ivan's wife does. Go out, visit someone. Check out a school. Visit me. It doesn't matter, baby."

Apparently Ivan felt the need to speak up, too. "It's about time you show your face, Vine. And what a way to do it, huh?"

"Show my face?"

"Yes. Don't you think it's important for them to know you're not afraid, you're not hiding, and you're planning your future?" Anton asked with a wink. "Like I said, Sonny might very well be a lot less brazen if we're right out in the open, not to mention this place is on total lockdown at night. You trust me, right?"

She looked exasperated. "You know I damn well do."

"Well, then show it."

"A Bentley, really?" she asked. "Could you give me a little more to go on?"

"Continental GT Speed. Automatic. Five-hundred horse power. Zero to sixty before you could blink. What else do you want to know?"

"Oh, for Christ's sake, Anton. That car is nearly a quarter of a million dollars!"

Closer to three hundred grand once he was done with it. How in the hell did she even know the price of it, anyway? "What'd I say about the cost?"

Her pretty lips drew a thin, mulish line. "That's not fair."

"Consider it an early birthday gift, then."

"A *Bentley*," she repeated.

"Yes, and I quite liked it when I test drove one a few months back. It should be in the driveway before you wake up in the morning. I thought it'd be your kind of car."

"Bentleys are my *favorite* cars."

Ivan snorted. "Figures."

Anton flipped him off with a middle finger behind his back. "So, you're not all that mad about the price, really, huh?"

"Maybe ... no. Ugh, you're horrible."

The smile that curved his lips was wicked. Breaking her down about the car and price hadn't been so hard after all. Now, he just had to get her to his nightclub one afternoon so she could pick out her engagement ring. Maybe he should have picked it out himself, but Anton assumed having her there while his personal jeweler made a special trip into his office would work all the same.

That and he wanted to get her into one of his workplaces just to gauge her reaction.

"I knew you were starting to get cabin fever, that's all. This might fix that right up."

"It might," Viviana echoed.

"And next week ..."

Her head jerked up, eyes meeting his immediately. "What about it?"

"My birthday. The men had some nonsense planned at the club, so they expect me to bring you there as well."

"Which club?"

Ouch. He didn't miss the warning in her tone for a second. "Not either of those clubs, Vine. Seven Lights, actually. Dance, drink, smoke, and eat. They just want a night off, I bet. But, I wanted you there earlier for a little surprise, if you wouldn't mind."

"A surprise like this?"

"Nah, a better one."

With a heavy sigh, Viviana rolled her eyes dramatically and said, "I suppose."

Dropping a kiss down to her forehead, Anton smiled once more. Again, it almost seemed too easy between them. He wasn't about to complain.

"And I say the twentieth of December, by the way."

Viviana coughed, loudly. "For the wedding?"

"Well, it's not for anything else. Sasha called me four times today about your refusal to pick a date and stick to it because I haven't given you a clear answer yet. I swear, if I have to get another frantic call like that from my mother again, I'll change my fucking number."

"That's a day before my birthday."

"That's right. Gives us one day to get it done the way the arrangement was meant to be. No cancellations; we have no do over."

Being it was the middle of October, they certainly had enough time to get the minor details sorted out.

There was no hesitation when Viviana shrugged and said, "The twentieth it is."

Chapter Nine

It was relatively warm for an October day. Warm enough that Viviana didn't need her coat, but she did steal one of the hoodies that Anton liked to jog in so she wouldn't get too cold on her trip to the dog park with Rocco.

While her pup frolicked along with someone's black Labrador, Viviana opened the romance novel she brought along and began reading. It wasn't long before she relaxed, settling further into the bench and losing herself in the words of the book.

Quite a bit of time passed before Viviana thought to look up and seek out Rocco. The German shepherd had forgone the company of the other dog and was back to playing his usual game of fetch the stick all by himself. It wasn't uncommon for their daily trip to the dog park to last a couple of hours, since she liked to get her pup out of the house as much as she could.

With her attention drawn back to her book, Viviana almost missed the shadow of a form that walked behind her. She didn't pay the person any mind as they stopped beside the bench, but she did glance over out of curiosity.

A hood was pulled up over the man's face, blocking it from view. Viviana was quick to notice the dog leash and collar he rested to the ground as he bent down to tie an undone lace on his running shoe.

Unbothered by the presence, she continued to read.

When the man grabbed up the leash and collar and stood, Viviana felt her back straighten against the bench. She wasn't quite sure why she felt off, but something had settled like a dead weight in her stomach.

Perhaps it was because the man didn't walk away. Maybe it was because he didn't look towards the animals, but instead back to where the vehicles were parked. Or, it could have been because he had a collar attached to that black, leather leash that appeared as if it hadn't been used even one time.

All dogs had to have their collars on in the park. She'd been here enough in the last three weeks to know the dog owners here were pretty particular about that rule. Even Rocco, her perfectly trained, always obedient pup, had to wear his identifier inside the gates.

The collar the man held had no tags and it too looked like it was brand new.

Alarm bells began ringing in Viviana's mind as dread washed through her nervous system. Instinctively, she flipped another page in her book, hoping the odd man still standing beside the bench wouldn't notice she had noticed him as his head turned in her direction.

Rocco was accustomed to people being near Viviana in the dog park, and this was his free time, so he wouldn't come unless she seemed frightened or called for him. In fact, the dog was now paddling into the pond with his back turned and his hearing clouded by the surrounding noise.

The parking lot was a good thirty yards away. While there was a car with one or two of her bulls, she knew another one was on foot, somewhere. They rarely showed themselves, actually. Looking around for them or making some move to gain their attention would only serve to alert the man she was fearful of him.

The gun in her purse was useless in public. She wouldn't take the risk of using it.

The cell phone in the pocket of Anton's sweater she wore, however, was a different story.

Viviana slid her free hand into her pocket. Feeling around, she found and held onto the number one button. The device vibrated in her palm to signal it was dialing Anton's pre-programmed number. She covered the speaker with her thumb, and three rings later, she felt the vibrations of his voice coming through the speaker. Not knowing what else to do, she hit random numbers on the keyboard.

Not a pocket dial, Anton, she thought. *Please don't*

think that. Please.

Even her thoughts were panicked.

Like the stuttering beats of her heart, her hands had started to shake, too.

The man sat down on the edge of the bench and Viviana caught just enough of his profile to know she was in trouble. Viviana would never forget the face of a boy who had once been a lowly soldier for her father. No one too important, as he wasn't made then, but it had been three years and a lot could change.

Vito Cavallo.

Definitely Italian. Definitely mafia.

Viviana was *definitely* in trouble.

It was only then that she realized she could faintly hear the dial tone of the ended call inside her pocket. Viviana fumbled frantically to hit the end button, but Vito was already looking straight at her.

"Stop moving and get your hand out of your pocket, right now."

She froze. His voice was cold and calculating. The stare he leveled on Viviana felt like it belonged to a predator.

"Don't fucking look at me," he hissed.

"Vi—"

"Don't say my name, either. Don't beg. I want you to get up, Viviana, and begin walking down the path. Keep walking. Call your stupid mutt and make sure he follows close by. Do you have a weapon?"

Viviana knew better than to lie. "Yeah, it's in my purse."

"Toss the bag when you're inside the pathway and hidden from view. Do you understand?"

"There are three—"

"I know," he snapped quietly, his brown eyes flashing with warning. "I'm not a fucking idiot and this isn't my first rodeo. I've been watching you for a couple of days. The two in the car will stay while the one on foot will give you a three to five minute head start. You haven't walked the mutt today, so let's take him for one."

"They'll see you follow behind."

A quick movement from behind the bench caught her gaze momentarily, but Vito didn't seem to take notice of her distraction.

"I just need a head start to get this done. By the time they realize I got up to follow you, it's already going to be too late. One is at the other side of the pond, the other two are—"

"Right behind you," Viviana whispered.

Thank you, Anton, she thought as the barrel of a gun was pressed into the back of Vito's neck.

"Get up and walk, you piece of shit," Rory ordered.

*

The metal door banged open under Anton's hand. From his head to his feet, the Bratva prince shook. Anyone who looked him in the eye wouldn't like the sight that stared back.

Blackness, like his eyes had drained of color and life.

Coldness, because his emotions had checked out of the equation an hour ago.

Readiness, as his fingers were already fisting tight before he was close enough to hit.

Death, blood, rage, and hunger.

He was so fucking hungry for those things, now.

"Boss," Boris greeted quietly.

Anton nodded his hello, eyeing the squirming man tied to the metal chair. In two quick steps he was in front of Vito. Without warning, Anton slammed his white knuckle fist into the already bloody face of the Italian scum that had failed to hurt his Viviana earlier. Just as quickly, he ripped the gag out of the man's mouth and watched the blood pour as teeth were coughed out.

"Scream," Anton said coldly. "No one will hear you. No one will care. These men want to hear your pain. They like it. This is going to hurt, but it'll be quicker if you talk."

"Like fuck."

Anton landed a solid punch to the man's abdomen. More red spewed from Vito's mouth at the hit as the man fell into a groaning, coughing fit. "Oh, you'll talk before I'm done. And then I'm going to cut out your tongue and let you drown in your own blood."

The three other men in the room said nothing as Anton tugged off the T-shirt he wore and tossed it to the side. Shaking the ache out of his fist, he noticed Vito's flinch at the thought of being hit again.

"I wonder if you'll beg," Anton mused. "I've made bigger and better men than you do it."

"For no man," Vito bit out.

"Would you for God?"

Despite the bloodshot eyes, matted, bloody hair, and the bruises and cuts marring up his features, Vito still appeared to be determined and arrogant.

Anton would enjoy breaking him.

When Anton reached for the ballpoint hammer, a flicker of fear passed over Vito's features.

"Pray."

"Wh-what?" the Italian asked.

Sweat dampened Vito's forehead, the beads of perspiration running lines down his face. Staring up at Anton with wide eyes and a bloody mouth, he didn't seem to have a clue what the Russian wanted. Anton stayed quiet as Boris snatched up the pliers and paring knife and moved to his Boss's side, taking the knife when it was passed to him.

With the sharp tip of the blade pointed out, Anton held the knife under Vito's chin. He greatly enjoyed seeing Vito's nervous swallow as he twisted the weapon slowly. The smallest amount of blood rose to the surface of Vito's skin, sliding down the metal blade.

"Pray," Anton repeated. "It's the only thing that might save you."

"P-praying?" Blood sprayed from Vito's mouth as he stuttered over the words. "You're going to let me go?"

"No. But, you tried to hurt an angel today, so God

might."

Finally, Vito understood. The lines trailing over his cheeks were no longer created by his sweat, but by his tears. They drew pathways through the blood, spit, and dirt, marking him clean in only those salt-touched spots.

"Th-the Lord is my shepherd ..."

"Good," Anton praised. "Like I said, this is going to hurt."

The hammer in Anton's grasp swung to and fro. The Italian's eyes watched the movement with terror choking his words out in a breath. "I shall not want ..."

"Boris, when we're done, keep the tongue," Anton said. "Perhaps Sonny would like a gift."

*

Viviana stayed quiet as Sasha paced the space between hospital waiting room chairs. It had been a rough day, to say the least. Anton was on his way. She called him without thinking he might have been handling something and just sending a text instead. Lucky for her that he wasn't, but now he was in a panic and that wouldn't lead to anything good.

"He's going to be terribly angry," the older woman said, shaking her head sadly.

"Anton?" *Not for a minute*, Viviana thought. Heartbroken was more like it. He adored his father.

Sasha chirped out a bitter laugh. "Oh, no. I meant Daniil. He despises the hospitals. I can only imagine how hard of a time he's giving them while they take x-rays of his lungs."

"How long?" Viviana asked.

"What?"

"Daniil. How long has he been this sick?"

It wasn't like she hadn't noticed the medical supplies and the doctor who came and went throughout the day. She had, but Viviana just assumed that they were treating Anton's father, not waiting out his failing health. They didn't talk about it, and she could understand that because for one thing, it hurt the family to do so. And secondly, maybe Daniil didn't want the grief of others over his sickness to be the last of what he witnessed for his final months.

Sasha's sadness turned into a teary gaze. "Awhile. He's far too sick to continue with chemo. It's only killing him instead of helping. The pain has been getting worse the last couple of months, but he's lasted longer than his doctors predicted and a constant morphine drip helps."

That was the worst thing about having the lifestyle they did. Sometimes having everything you ever wanted at the simple drop of a hat could come back and bite you in the worst way when there was something you finally couldn't have. Life, for example. Sickness couldn't be bought away. Sure, the best doctors and medicine would be brought in without hesitation, but death would still come if there was nothing that could be done. No amount of money could buy health.

Up until then, another week had passed Anton and Viviana by in an almost blissful silence, minus Vito showing up and scaring the living hell out of her. When Anton came home that night stony and silent, she decided she didn't want to know what became of Vito.

Sasha had been happy they picked a date for the wedding and didn't say another thing about it, let alone pester her son with more phone calls. Planning for the wedding suddenly seemed a whole lot easier with a date officially picked and Anton's declaration over what he'd like to see used as a color scheme. It wasn't going to be big, so a lot of little nonsense could and would be crossed off their lists.

With Anton's influence and a few phone calls, The Plaza Hotel's entertainment, dining room, and spa on Fifth Avenue had been booked for their wedding, dinner, and reception with practically no notice at all. Viviana didn't dare ask the cost of that one, or just how much money he shoveled out to the owners and management to save that date. Given the price just to rent a room for a night, which Viviana's mother had done more than once when her father was alive, she knew it had to be quite an expense.

The pretty black Bentley was waiting the very next morning after Anton's show with the keys. The cutest red bow sat perched up on the hood, just waiting for Viviana to get in and make those tires squeal. Which she did—all the while Anton had his hand on her thigh sporting the most devious, sexy smirk as it trailed a little higher, making her breath catch.

It had been an easy, quiet week. Nothing to worry about during her walks with Rocco after Vito, though her bulls were sticking closer to her than ever. The bulls weren't giving her warnings or signals about something that might have concerned them now, though. Whenever she ventured away from their safe house with her car to visit a few shops for wedding things, or just because she could, Viviana hadn't once felt unsafe, even after the dog park fiasco. Although much to her displeasure, but not surprise, she was made aware on her third trip into the heart of the city that a federal car was now on detail with her. Anton had been in a particularly good mood for the week when he was home as well.

Simple, so damned simple.

And then it wasn't.

Sometime in the late afternoon, Sasha called over the intercom in a panic. The doctor had been to the house earlier in the day with a promise to be back after supper just to check if Daniil's cough was getting worse. When the coughing fits turned up bright red blood in a tissue, it was clear something else was going wrong beyond a little chest cold.

Nothing was little when it came to cancer.

The phone in Viviana's hand dinged with a text. Sighing with just a smidge of relief, she said, "Anton is coming up from the underground parking garage now."

It was the softest, most heartbroken sob from Sasha that all but did Viviana in. Almost as if Sasha's heart was being ripped from her chest and torn apart, because if the way she looked at Daniil on daily basis was any indication, it most certainly was. With her knees drawn up into her chest, Viviana hugged her legs and hid her face, not wanting to watch a stronger woman than her cry.

*

"One second, Boss," Boris muttered, slamming shut the car door. "Just give the others a moment to catch up."

Anton fought back his rising urge to bark at the brigadier. It was his father after all, so if he wanted to rush up through the garage without waiting for the other men to arrive, he had every right to goddamn well do so. Of course, that was the irrational side of his brain, which at times, still felt like he was that twelve-year-old kid who thought his father and step-grandfather ruled the fucking world.

Being who he was now, Anton knew it wasn't just about him anymore. Daniil had more than earned his place and respect in their world. He didn't have biological brothers, but he had four dozen Bratva brothers scattered across Brooklyn with their phones on constant dial. At least eight of them were in cars on their way there.

"Boss, heads up. Sixth row down, second lane in, black car with hats down."

At Boris's quiet warning, Anton made quick work of finding the unmarked car with an almost predatory gaze. Two federal agents. They looked to be the same ones who continued following his Viviana around, although they had yet to approach her. Anton was more concerned with just why they were tailing her more than the actual fact that they were.

"Fucking cockroaches," he growled darkly. "Here with my dad sick, really?"

Boris shrugged. "Maybe they just followed her car in."

"She jumped in the ambulance with my mother."

"What'd you think it is, then?"

Anton swallowed the heavy lump in his throat. "Roman, maybe. I know Sonny had her locked up tight after her dad died, making sure the feds couldn't get to her when she was grieving."

"You gonna let her talk to them?"

As three cars slid into the underground parking garage one right after the other at a speed too fast to be regular civilians, Anton kicked his car door closed and shrugged. While the cars began to unload with older Bratva members, Anton and his brigadier began making their way to the entrance for the elevators.

Crossing directly in front of the federal car, just to let them know they weren't fooling a soul, the younger man stared straight through the windshield before flicking them his middle finger as a silent fuck off. They'd only get the one warning.

"My fiancée is a grown woman who knows what she can and can't do without me needing to tell her. If she's got something to say to the feds regarding her father's death, that's her choice. It has absolutely nothing to do with the Bratva. We all know she isn't going to speak a word about me. That's what's most important."

"The Italians—they'd kill her for talking about family business."

"They could sure fucking try."

*

Viviana looked up as a pair of hands squeezed her shoulders soothingly. Anton's tired, sad expression stared back down at her. "Hey."

"Hey, babe," she answered back, seeing the slight curve of his lips at her sentiment. "Missed you."

"Missed you, too."

The moment Anton's gaze met his mother's form coming over to greet him, he released Viviana's shoulders. She looked away as he embraced his mother in the suddenly quiet waiting room, knowing they probably needed that moment together. It was only when his hands came in contact with her body again that Viviana felt it was okay to speak again.

"I didn't realize he was ..." Emotions lodged in her

throat. "I'm sorry about Daniil."

There was the briefest flicker of wetness shining in bright blue eyes before the man above her blinked it away. "He's got a little while left. Already planned his own funeral, sad as that is. We don't talk much about it because it makes him angry. I just assumed you would have figured out how bad it was on your own, but I suppose I should have sat you down and really explained it."

Viviana didn't have a clue what to say.

Looking around, she was quick to notice the many men who suddenly swamped the waiting room. They all chatted in English and Russian, their voices far too low for her to really catch onto anything they were saying, not that she would have understood their mother tongue. A few had gathered close to Sasha, one with an arm wrapping her trembling shoulders tenderly, and she nodded in response to whatever the men were saying. Even still, Viviana couldn't help but feel awkward under some of their scrutinizing gazes as they, too, watched her.

The following day was Anton's birthday. It would have been the first time she was properly introduced into their very private society at the party they were throwing for him at his club. There was no doubt in her mind that they were all too aware of just who exactly she was, and all the trouble she could be very well causing them, so it only served to make Viviana that much more uncomfortable.

"What's wrong?"

"There's a lot of Bratva here," she mumbled, feeling silly. Zoning in on a loose thread, she picked at the fabric, avoiding Anton. "They're all looking at me."

"Of course they're looking at you. You're beautiful, and they're probably wondering where your engagement ring is."

Viviana choked back her laughter. Yes, with teary eyes, a sweater and jeans, and hair that had just been tossed back into a loose ponytail before the ambulance arrived. Sure, beautiful. The engagement ring was a whole other matter altogether that he wouldn't even talk about, for some reason.

"Come on, Anton."

"I'm serious. Some of these men haven't seen you since you were a drooling two year old. Imagine how big of a surprise it is for them to see you all grown up, and with me no less."

Now, Viviana was wondering just how many of them had been a part of the agreement and which men in the room he was talking about exactly. "Really, who?"

"Never mind that. They wouldn't talk about it anyway. Business, baby."

With a disgruntled hum, Viviana found her knees being drawn away from her chest under his urging. In Anton's strong hold, she was picked up as if she didn't weigh anything more than a feather before he rested back down in the seat with her curled up in his lap. An arm curved around her shoulders, his hand stopping to rest on the pulse in her neck.

For a single moment, she stilled in Anton's hold, listening to the quiet rise and fall of his chest and the beat of his heart. Without a doubt, she knew that beating organ was breaking. Strong and stony on the outside, but shattering to pieces on the inside.

"I don't want to lose my father," he whispered. The words were so grief-stricken and heavy in her ear that Viviana shivered under the weight. "I don't know what I'd do. First it was Nicoli, now Dad … Fuck, you think I'd be used to death by now, given everything."

"It's not the same kind of death. But when it is, and it's someone else's grief, don't you feel guilty?"

That hold on her shoulders tightened. "You shouldn't ask me—"

"I should," Viviana interjected, keeping her tone quiet and calm. "I want to know."

She felt his mouth press to the side of her temple as his lips parted and he exhaled heavily. "Ever since my first, yes. I always feel guilt for their grief, even if it was deserved. I was taught to respect the life I took, no matter what it owed. At some point that life was worth no more or less than mine."

Viviana decided she loved him even more because of that. There had been no respect shown to her father, mother, or brother. There had been none for her when she was made to hold Sonny's hand at her father's funeral, probably the same hand that was used to hold the gun and pulled the trigger to end Roman's life. It made her weak and unsure, taught her that even blood didn't hold a flame to greed. Her learned respect was created from nothing more than fear. She didn't want to be that girl anymore, and she sure as hell knew she wasn't, but it had taken a lot to get there, starting with Anton.

"I didn't want to lose mine, either," she heard herself admitting. Reaching down to find his hand holding her knee tightly, she uncurled the fingers and weaved them with hers. Viviana allowed them both a moment to breathe before she spoke again. "I didn't want to be scared; I was so tired of crying. It won't matter if I'm thirty or eighty, it'll never really go away. It's always going to hurt."

Viviana swore she felt wetness smear from his cheek to hers, but she didn't acknowledge his tears. It was more than likely he wouldn't want her to anyway. His grasp on her leg released just long enough to rub his face.

Anton cleared his throat, voice turning hoarse when he said, "So, on Sunday ..."

"What about it?"

"There's a baker that's always made the cakes for our family whenever we had special occasions. He's opened up his shop to us personally for that day. If you want to go with me at noon, we'll have one more thing crossed off your list."

"I can do that," she agreed, settling back into his hold with a sigh. "So I guess there won't be a party tomorrow, huh?"

"Oh, there'll be a party, and we'll still have to go. Actually, it'll give them a chance to celebrate my father in one way or another, too. All the more reason to drink good vodka. Like they need an excuse to drink."

Out of the corner of her eye, Viviana noticed a very

mousey looking nurse standing with a clipboard in her hand and staring wide-eyed at the sudden influx of men in the small waiting room. With a nod in the woman's direction, Anton coughed to gain her attention.

The woman startled at his simple look. Viviana guessed then that the last name on the clipboard probably spoke volumes as to who the woman thought she was dealing with, and everything she thought, well, it'd probably be right.

"Immediate family for a Mr. Daniil Avdonin?"

Every Bratva man who wasn't already standing did. Viviana couldn't help but snort under her breath at the sight. More than once she'd spent nights like this in the hospital when she was younger, watching her father's men rush in with wives and children bundled up. The Bratva was not the Cosa Nostra, but they were still a family in every way that counted for them.

Sasha was back at her son's side in a flash, her hand resting atop his on Viviana's knee. "I'm his wife. This is his son."

"Could you come with me for a moment, ma'am? A more private area—"

Anton spoke up, tone gruff and low when he interrupted with, "Here is just fine. Whatever you have to say, they'll be told regardless."

The nurse was once again looking like she wanted to bolt. Viviana was left wondering where in the hell the doctor was. "Yes, okay then. Uh, so a viral infection has settled in his lungs. There's a lot of fluid that they're attempting to remove, but we had a collapse. By the looks of the x-rays, there is a good chance pneumonia has started in as well. He can go home …"

"Go home?" Anton growled.

"In a few days," the nurse finished quietly. "If everything goes fine with removing the fluid and getting rid of the infection. Otherwise, he'll probably be here for at least the next few months."

Two sets of hands squeezed painfully tight on Viviana's

leg.

"A few *months*."

"That is the best time frame the doctor could give, considering his current state. He has a good appetite, has gained weight since coming off the chemo, and besides this, health-wise Mr. Avdonin has done considerably well. But yes, a few months, and at the most if his health remains somewhat well, a year. The cancer is beginning to spread through his blood if the latest blood work is any indication. We think it is best that he does go home, and repeatedly, he's voiced that very wish."

Sasha's broken laugh hurt Viviana to hear. "I would like to see him, please."

The nurse nodded. "Absolutely, they're just moving him into a private room now."

When Anton didn't immediately move, his arms still locked tight around Viviana while his mother followed behind the nurse, she turned in his grasp. In his eyes, she could see the pain, all the things he didn't want to say or admit, but she also knew he didn't have a choice.

Sometimes, those strong men needed an even stronger woman to make them see it.

"I can't—"

Viviana shook her head, steeling her emotions and frowning. "Go. Right now."

*

"You should tell her."

Daniil's voice was so low that Anton strained to hear his father above the beeping monitors. The tube in his lung had been removed two hours before, and after a brief nap induced by something a little stronger than morphine, the sick man was once again awake. Anton's mother, on the other hand, had finally fallen asleep in the lounging chair in the corner of the room.

Anton had spent the last bit of daylight moving back and forth between his father's room and the waiting room, allowing the few visitors the hospital agreed could go in. No one who was sick, had been sick, or had come in contact with someone else who might have been sick was allowed in. That cut out well over half of the men.

"Dad …"

"You *should*," the older man insisted, before he fell into yet another coughing fit.

Knowing his father wouldn't want him to fuss over the cough, Anton settled back into his chair with blurred vision and stared at the wall. "Is this Daniil, my father speaking, or Daniil, the man raised by Nicoli and the Bratva?"

"I am one and the same, Ant."

No, he disagreed. Too many times he'd seen his father's personality flip a switch when it needed to. Just like his did. Just like Nicoli's had. There were separate men who lived inside them from the time they walked out of their homes with a gun in their waistband, to the time they walked back in it. The men who handled money made from laundering, drugs, prostitution, trafficking, and anything else illegal were not the same men who laid their wives and children down at night. At least, not in their hearts.

"That's bullshit."

"Right now," Daniil said softly, "I am the same. Dying, yes. Hurting for you, yes. Thinking of the difference it may make to the Bratva, yes. And I do not think telling Viviana the truth will hurt them a bit. The Cosa Nostra are a different story. It may make her reconsider a few things—"

"*Me*," Anton interrupted sharply, ignoring the wince his father responded with. "It will damn well make her reconsider me, Dad."

Once more, wetness slipped down his cheeks, betraying him. Anton didn't cry. He just didn't. Fuck, his chest hurt like nothing else at just the thought of what could happen if Viviana knew the truth that had been hidden from her for years. It damn near killed him when he found out, but it didn't make a difference to the things he already felt for her.

"He was clear on his instructions," Anton muttered, wiping at his face and hiding it from view. "Nicoli didn't want her to know for her own safety and because she already loved Roman. If she figured it out, that was different. Don't tell me she wouldn't stop and think for a moment if that was the only reason why I wanted her married to me; she absolutely would."

"You're not giving her enough credit."

"I love her. I won't have her believe my desire to marry her is based on whose blood runs through her veins and past mistakes. I won't fucking do it, and you better not, either."

Daniil's chest rattled and Anton immediately felt guilty for pulling the boss rank on his father. This was the time when he should have been nothing more than a worried, saddened son.

That didn't matter though, because switches got flipped.

They just did.

He would always be Boss first, and Anton second.

*

Golden whiskey swirled in the glass as Anton placed the tumbler back down to his desk. After his mother refused to come home and midnight began to approach, he'd found Viviana sleeping with her head on the shoulder of one of her bulls before he took his love home.

They didn't say a thing on the drive. He white knuckled the steering wheel while pretty brown eyes watched him, all wary and concerned. At his insistence, she showered and readied for bed, but Anton hadn't joined her when she slipped under their sheets well over an hour before.

The time on his cell phone 2 AM. The device crashed into the wall seconds later, glass from the screen splintering to the floor. Too much time and too many things on his mind led Anton to the worst place possible.

One glass of whiskey followed two, then three. Three quarters of the bottle was downed and the heavy buzz had settled around his heart and senses. When his fists cracked into the oak of his desk, teeth clenching, the quiet whine of Rocco outside of the office told him he wasn't quite so alone anymore.

"Fuck," Anton hissed, watching red bloom so painfully sweet across his knuckles.

Then, the softest knock had him sighing. Despite his rules about the office, Viviana opened the door and slipped in without his permission. Crossing the floor in silence, he found her hands curving up under the suit jacket he still wore. Her mouth trailed gently over his shoulder before her lips pressed to the side of his throat. He swallowed thickly.

"What is it?" Viviana asked. "I've been listening to you for the last hour and a half."

"Nothing. Go back to bed."

"Are you coming, too?"

Anton scowled at the ceiling, avoiding her gaze. "Not right now."

"Are you coming at all?"

That stopped his breath up short. "Excuse me?"

"You'd always be there with me in the morning, that's what you said. But you're just about ready to drink yourself to sleep in here by the looks of it, and I'll wake up alone. What's wrong, Anton? It's more than just your dad, right?"

"I said it was—"

"Stop lying to me!"

The hurt in her tone rang so clear to him, but his anger had risen, too. Anger for lying, anger for hiding, and anger for not being strong enough to tell her the truth because of his own selfish fears.

"What do you want me to say? You don't know what it's like to hide this shit from you. I acted like a shitty son to my father earlier when all he wanted to do was help me! To help *us*!"

At the widening of her eyes, Anton realized what he had blurted out in his drunkenness. "What? What are you talking about?"

"Nothing. I'm just … tired, Vine. Really."

"Bullshit. I thought you were upset over Daniil, but clearly it's something else, too. This isn't the first time you've hid something from me. Do you think by omitting it, it's not a lie?"

"You don't know a damn—"

An opened hand struck his jaw with aimed precision. Fire burned through those beautiful eyes of hers. The faintest trace of blood skimmed over his tongue. Oh, fuck, her slap stung like a son of a bitch. That was just about the last thing Anton expected her to do.

"Don't tell me that. Don't ever tell me what I don't know when you won't speak to me. You wanted me just as I was, remember?"

Fists clenched at his sides, anger exhaling from the strangled breath he released. The air seemed to turn a little thicker when she looked up at him so openly unhappy with tears brimming. "You going to hit me back now, put me in my place and show me how to behave, Anton?"

"No."

Never, his mind screamed, but he was awfully goddamn angry.

His dick was as hard as a rock and his mind was hazy with whiskey, so when her fingers started loosening up those buttons on his dress shirt, switches just flipped all over again. He had her ass up on the edge of his desk in a second. The glass of whiskey and opened liquor bottle skidded across the desk before falling to the floor, sending glass shards scattering and golden liquor pooling at his shoes. A laptop and lamp crashed to the floor as well.

Sweet kisses dotted the side of his mouth before her teeth cut into his jaw, her fingers scoring lines down his throat with sharp nails. Fuck, he'd take feeling anything from her at that point. If it was hurt she wanted him to feel, Anton was already filled.

"This is what you needed?" Viviana demanded, popping the buttons on his shirt. When his mouth came dangerously close to hers with a growl forming at the back of his throat, she bit out at him. "Come on, then. *Fuck me.*"

Anton ached. From his chest, to his cock, to his heart,

it damn well throbbed. "Jesus—"

"There's no God here, only me." Tears slipped over her trembling lips as Viviana looked up through her lashes and frowned. "But that's just what you want, right?"

Another drag of her nails across his bare middle had Anton shuddering. And he gave it back just as hard, forcing her thighs wider, knowing it had to have burned. She only tilted her head back to expose the silken flesh of her neck and sighed. That shirt of his she wore had nothing underneath it, just her bare sex on the wood of his desk, wetness seeping from her pink pussy, and she reached down to spread those silken lips open for him.

"You're not even sorry, are you?"

"What do you want me to say?" he ground out, teeth gnashing on the words.

Her gaze met his bluntly. "Don't treat me like the woman you don't want me to be."

Raven hair twisted in his fist, tugging her head back so he could watch her face for just a moment. There wasn't a lick of fear there, no hesitation or worry. A ragged exhale left his lungs in the most painful way. The smell of whiskey washed over her lips and jaw as her hands started working at the belt and zipper of his pants.

"Can you even say it to me?" Viviana said, voice wavering.

"Sorry. I'm so fucking sorry."

When his cock was buried balls deep, her nails clawed into his back, and glass crunched under his shoes. Finally, he felt like he was home. Viviana whined a sound that was so full but airless at the same time, her lashes fluttering along his neck.

"Love you," Anton whispered. "You know I do."

Their love was the only thing his lies didn't own.

Chapter Ten

Viviana woke to warm lips trailing a burning path from the corner of her mouth across to her cheek. There were fingers between her thighs, teasing lines over the sensitive lips of her pussy, making her body feel alive and revving to go. The scent of stale whiskey and lingering cigarette smoke hung heavy in the air.

Ignoring the way her body wanted to respond to Anton's touches was an impossible task. When her hips rolled into his hand almost involuntarily, and fingers slipped in between her folds to thrust up knuckle deep, her gasp couldn't be contained. With skilled precision, he found her g-spot and curled his digits, making fluid gush between her legs at the touch. A thumb flicked up to press at her aching clit, rolling gentle circles over the nub and making her jerk into his body.

"Mmm, you're so fucking wet and ready for me," he hushed in her ear, burying his face into her neck. He suckled and kissed, teeth nipping with a faint sting determined to bring Viviana from her sleeping stupor. "Wake up just a little more for me, baby. Open those pretty eyes so I can watch them when you come."

Unfortunately, the couch they'd fallen asleep on in his office wasn't the most comfortable spot, considering something was digging into her back in the worst damned way. It made focusing on his motions and voice a little difficult.

"Stop."

He froze immediately, withdrawing from her sex. "I just thought ..."

Viviana's eyes popped open at the barely hidden quake in his voice. More than once he'd woken her up in that very same way, heating her body to a fever, chuckling dark and deep when she shook and came so surprised and relieved.

Their frustrations from the night before weren't what urged her to stop him, but she could understand how he would misinterpret it in that way. She found his cheek pressed to hers, gaze trained downward, and those wet fingers of his were now grasping roughly to her thigh with a shake he couldn't quite hide. Whatever he must have felt, it was a little more than disappointment at her refusal, and it probably tasted a lot like shame.

"No, that's ... I didn't mean it like *that*."

"You'd have every right to."

Yeah, she probably would. If the night before was any indication of the kinds of arguments she could expect in the future, she hoped to hell she'd get a decent time lapse in between them. The physical tax it took was nothing compared to the emotional toll. In fact, while her scalp still stung from where he'd grabbed her hair, and every muscle in her body was screaming for a hot bath, none of that made a difference to the heavy weight on her heart.

"Look at me, please." Those blue eyes of his lifted, but she sensed how hard it was for him to do it. The bloodshot gaze he leveled on her said he likely wasn't feeling too well, either. "Do you even remember how much you drank or what you said? Did you mean it?"

He wet his lips, drawing her gaze to the bob of his Adam's apple as he swallowed with an audible sound. "Mean what, because I said a lot of things."

"Any of it. All of it. Give me something, Anton."

The afghan blanket that covered them was twisted in his hands. He tugged it up around her shoulders a little tighter. Wrapping his naked legs with hers, it caused the hard length of his erection to press to her stomach, and made his morning desire known.

"A lot of my business is done under the influence of strong liquor with men who could drink me under the table. I try not to say things I don't mean, even if I'm acting like a stupid fool. Otherwise, it could lead to nowhere good."

"Try not to," she echoed quietly.

"Yes, *try*. And most times I failed miserably, so I've taken to using one of Nicoli's old tricks where my alcohol is watered down significantly without anyone else knowing. While others are stumbling drunk by the end of the evening, I still have my head clear when I need it most. It might break our code, but drinking too much often leads to guns being brought out when they don't need to be, or fists flying. Makes for messy situations I only have to clean up later."

Viviana wanted to smile at his admission, but the sadness in his eyes and tone rang clear. "But?"

"Mistakes happen," he said. "Would you like to know why Nicoli began having his liquor watered down?"

"Shoot."

"Exactly, shoot. Or, a *shooting* to be precise. One that took away his wife."

Air caught painfully in her throat. "Oh."

Anton hummed a miserable sound, frowning. "My grandmother used to enjoy being a part of whatever dealings she could that he would allow. Usually it was the loudness and Russian culture that kept her going with him. The atmosphere gets a little rowdy, especially with the older generation. He always said it reminded her of home."

"You drinking out of anger isn't okay. Especially if it'll lead to another repeat of last night. You were hiding things and I let it go, but I expect and explanation Anton. Last night … that bothers me."

It truly did. More often than she could remember, too much liquor led to issues in her own family. Everyone always felt things needed to be celebrated with some kind of alcohol, be it babies, dealings, or whatever. No one ever seemed to know their limits. Things were said that couldn't be taken back. Grudges were held. Stupid, little things that led to bigger issues. Viviana didn't want to handle that with Anton, too.

"I keep any social drinking at home, and only with people I most trust, like Ivan. Last night was brought on by something else entirely."

"That's not my point. And you didn't explain yourself."

"I know," he replied, just as softly. "I understand what you're saying. I'm telling you I hear you, Viviana. I need you to trust me when I say I will tell you. I'm not hiding it purposely, I just can't right now."

"I'm not okay with that, either."

"I know, but it's the best I can give." Anton sighed before rubbing a hand over his face. "There's also the issue of drugs, I suppose. They float in and out of my businesses more than water, but I haven't touched a chemical in years, not since I was doing my rounds as a brigadier and in need of something to keep me awake and aware for Nicoli's calls and nonsense. It didn't matter, though, because every single time Nicoli noticed the high in my eyes, his disappointment was the first thing to be voiced."

"Years?" Viviana asked, wanting his confirmation on that again.

"Like I said, chemical wise, no. Remember that night in Barbados with my smoke kissing your lips? You took my shotgun hits like a pro."

Oh damn, just the way he voiced that old memory sent her lust in a tailspin. Viviana managed to nod; a little bit of weed was the last of her concerns. Something akin to memories and excitement skimmed over her skin like a dancing, rolling hum. That night was the first time she'd ever tried pot, but certainly not the last. Many of her firsts had been given to the man beside her.

"That's a rare pleasure, and I keep it very private," he said.

"I'm okay with that, on occasion."

He grinned slyly and she felt her own form in response. "Good to know."

"And thank you," Viviana added, her voice above a whisper.

"*Fucking hell.* For what? After last ni—"

"For explaining yourself without making excuses. For telling me the truth about the rest. We could have just ignored what happened and went about it differently." Without warning, Viviana found her body rolled over. Anton was behind her then, his steel hard cock sliding deliciously along the crack of her ass. "What—*oh*."

Tender kisses started at the base of her spine while his hands rounded the globes of her backside. Eventually, his mouth moved upwards, hot breath touching down to her flesh as his tongue peeked out to lick and taste. Already, she wanted to beg; was so ready to plead for his cock and love; needed him to take her like only he could, despite the things hanging in the air like an anvil ready to fall.

"Yes, I remember exactly what I said to you last night, and I meant every word. I said I was sorry, and I am," he murmured darkly against the blade of her shoulder. "I said I love you, and I do." A broken sound tumbled from her parted lips as he brushed hair over her shoulder. "I was being a coward and did you wrong. Acted like a jerk when you couldn't possibly understand because I wasn't giving you a thing to go on. I'm not so much of an asshole that I can't admit I have faults, Viviana. Some of them are sure to bleed onto you, whether I mean for them to or not."

"Won't you explain what brought it on?"

A kiss touched down to her cheek. "Eventually."

That was enough for Viviana. It was more than enough. If Anton was anything, it was a man of his word.

With one hand gripping along the curved arm of the couch, her free hand found purchase on his bare thigh. Airless and wanting, she pleaded for his touch as his strong hand rolled over her back and shoulders. The most tender and fond words whispered in her ear. The tip of his cock rubbed along her slit, only entering her pulsing sex just enough to tease and stretch the sensitive tissues of the entrance.

When Anton's hand hooked around her throat with the gentlest of grip, she felt his cock finally slip through the wet, swollen lips of her pussy and begin taking her like she so wanted him to. He took his time working her clamping muscles, thrusting in halfway before slowly withdrawing and plunging right back in to reach a bit deeper. Three sweet strokes and he fitted her to the hilt, the head of his dick hit her cervix in the best way—he had her filled so wholly, stretched her like no other.

Only him. It was only ever him that did that for her.

Viviana burned with pleasure, blood singing and nerves humming. Leaning over her back with an arm wrapped around her middle, he was close and covering, protecting and loving, but still not nearly close enough. Her arms trembled as she buried her face into the soft leather of the couch and cried his name when the slow moving rhythm of their hips began.

The sounds of his cock fucking her pussy filled the room, skin slapping, heavy pants turning fast and ragged. Anton pulled their bodies up, propped on their knees with her back tight to his chest. His hand still held tight to the base of her throat and sweat started to bead along her pebbled flesh. His hand around her middle moved up over her breasts, his calloused thumb rolling over her peaked nipples.

"Touch, Vine ... My God, baby, touch and feel *us.*"

When she didn't—because she couldn't think to move—he was fast to force her hand downwards with his. Between her thighs spread so wide, their joined hands found her sensitive folds and his cock soaked with her arousal. The vein in his shaft pulsed at her touch, hips slammed a little harder, cock reaching her a little deeper.

There was unrestricted power in every thrust of his body. Viviana let her head fall to his broad shoulder, feeling his lips open and press to the side of her face with a shuddering exhale. It was too much and not nearly enough; her nerves turned into live wires that snapped with electricity ready to bite and sting and burn. Viviana was sure she was dying in the best way. His name in her mouth was a broken record on repeat. Every slow, measured stroke of his cock stretching and filling her pushed wanton, rolling cries from her lungs faster and higher.

"Goddamn," he ground out as she felt her inner walls begin to clamp down. "Come on, give me all you got. Don't hold that back from me."

The orgasm had already sent her flying. A cattish cry ripped from her throat, leaving her feeling raw. Twisting against his hold, her body jerking from the force of pleasure and lust raging through her system, but Anton kept his hold on her throat tight. When his movements turned harder, more frantic and desperate, Viviana knew he was right there, too. The strangled groan he buried into the back of her neck was punctuated by his hips meeting her backside one hard, last time.

Tremors rocked, the ecstasy of bliss slowly washing away. Seconds ticked by, the cool air washing over her skin and making her shiver. Viviana needed a moment to breathe, and by the quick rise and fall of Anton's chest, he clearly needed one, too. She could feel their mingling fluids dampening their fingers, but he didn't make a move to release his hold or remove his softening cock from her body.

"Happy fucking birthday to me."

*

Viviana rubbed Rocco's belly, giggling a happy sound when his tail thumped a fast beat on the floor. Anton had been so preoccupied in his office that she had been left to her own devices for much of the morning and well into the afternoon. After a long, hot bath, warm breakfast, and a short walk to the park with her pup, she was finally becoming bored.

Some of her morning had been spent preparing part of her gift for Anton's birthday. A gift that left her backside a little tender, but her body raging with anticipation. Given his distractions upstairs, she was grateful he had yet to notice her sudden aversion to sitting down. It was just one more first she wanted to give him, in her own way, and she was so damned thankful some of those things she ordered online came in packages that were purposely marked to hide the items within.

"You're spoiling my dog."

The deep voice came from the kitchen's entrance. Viviana looked up at the sound, surprised to see Anton dressed in a sharp black suit that hugged his body handsomely. The top two buttons on the silk shirt had been left undone, exposing his throat and part of his chest. As he attempted to button the cuff of his jacket, Viviana laughed before deciding to help him with his plight. With the cuff done up properly, she patted his middle teasingly.

"I thought you said he was *my* dog so he could be whatever I wanted," she mocked.

Anton raised a single brow. "You're turning him into a puppy again. I already paid for his training once. He's supposed to be an attack dog and now you've got him practically begging for snacks and tummy rubs," he grumbled.

The dog in question was already on high alert as Viviana glanced back at him. With eyes sharp, ears pointed, and his tail straight, Rocco was in no way distracted. Anton was making a bigger deal out of it than it really was. The dog still took the lead when she walked into a room, accompanied her on all her trips away from the house, and she'd even taken to cooking his food the way his special diet required instead of having Clarissa do it.

"You're just jealous that I get to spend all day with him when it used to be you he followed after."

"Viviana, he whines to get upstairs with us at night."

"He does not."

Anton huffed a breath, making her look away guiltily. "More than once his chirping woke me up. I can't help it that you sleep like the dead and I don't."

"You let him up into the bedroom that first night I was here, so that makes it your fault by default."

For a moment, the man staring down at her seemed flabbergasted—totally speechless. The giggles caught in her throat were just barely held back. One of the biggest mob bosses in North America was wrapped around her finger. Viviana had to wonder if he truly realized just how much he let her get away with sometimes.

"Is this how I can expect the next seventy years of our life to go down?"

She smoothed out a wrinkle in the silk, white shirt he wore, cocking her head to the side with a sly smile. "Yes."

"Great."

He didn't seem to mind all that much about it, especially when she felt her chin being tilted up in strong hands. His lips melded so smoothly to hers, and for once, Anton didn't dominate the kiss like he usually did. Instead, she found herself probing gently against the seam of his mouth, wanting it opened. When it was, their tongues moved a slow, lazy rhythm, taking time to explore, taste, and feel the sweet kiss. The lingering taste of tobacco, mint, and heat danced from his mouth to hers.

"Happy birthday, Anton."

The hum he sounded against her lips rocked Viviana straight to the core. "Thank you."

"Do you feel any older?"

"Ancient. Three years off thirty. Arthritis and Alzheimer's will be setting in soon."

"Ah, you have jokes so you must be in a better mood."

"A little."

"And Daniil?"

Anton's quiet sigh held both relief and sadness. "Better, too, but they're keeping him sedated a lot while they continue to drain the remaining fluid from his lungs."

"Are we going to the hospital?" Viviana asked, wondering why he chose to wear such a smart looking suit.

"No. I spoke to Mom for well over an hour a little while ago, and she was pretty insistent that I just let you enjoy the surprises in store for you today."

"It's your birthday."

"Oh, well," he replied with a wink. "Like I said, Sasha insisted."

"I wouldn't mind going."

"I know, so we'll visit first thing tomorrow morning.

We have a lot to do today."

"Just the party, right?" She assumed that was the surprise, considering she had yet to see one of his businesses up close and personal.

Anton's grin had a whole lot hidden behind it. "Maybe a little more. I had something special brought in for you."

"Something like what?"

"Something you don't have yet, but need."

With his forehead resting on hers, Viviana smiled as his thumbs rolled over the apples of her cheeks. "I don't need—"

"You haven't bought a single dress, baby. Nothing fancy. No pretty shoes to make your legs look a mile long. How on earth am I supposed to show you off tonight if you haven't a thing to wear?"

Viviana eyed his suit. "I am feeling sorely underdressed standing next to you."

"Well I need to fix that. Can't have my fiancée feeling that way now, could I? Arrangements were already made for you in my office at Seven Lights. Nothing too big, but you'll have a decent choice to pick through. You haven't been to Brighton Beach in what, ever?"

"Something like that," she agreed. "Wasn't a smart move for the daughter of a Cosa Nostra boss to be slummin' it in the Russian territory, or so I was told. We don't mix well."

Anton laughed. "We do now."

Viviana caught his gaze traveling down to her fingers spread across his chest.

"And this …" Anton added quietly, a finger tracing where an engagement ring should have been resting, "…is something I need to rectify before tonight. You're off the market, and I damn well plan on having everybody else know it, too."

"I was wondering when you planned on doing that."

"I was trying to not stress over it, honestly."

Viviana suddenly felt a whole lot more nervous. "Do

you have it?"

"Ah, now, now," he murmured, smirking. "That is for me to know, and you to find out."

Well, she could play that game, too. "Would you like your birthday gift—part of it," she corrected, grinning wickedly. "The rest may or may not come later, depending on a few things."

"Vine, you didn't have to get me anything."

A small palm-sized remote was placed into Anton's hand before he could say another word. Staring at the oval shaped device, she was positive he was unsure of what he should say. It wasn't like he could know what it was he was looking at. With a single power button, and two speed buttons, it simply appeared to be nothing more than a remote for a massager.

"Care to explain what this controls?"

Viviana turned quiet under his gaze. "You'll figure it out."

"I'd rather you just told me." Heat flooded her body, a blush of pink reddening her chest and cheeks. "Viviana?"

"Like I said, you'll figure it—"

Anton hit the power button on the small remote then proceeded to push the first speed button. A strangled cry escaped as the vibrating anal plug was suddenly activated, stimulating her freshly stretched tissues, and sensitive nerve endings with the most intense rush she'd felt ever.

Her fingers clenched into the lapels of his jacket, her knees damn near buckling as the gentle speed of the first setting hummed inside her tight hole. Viviana was straight up lost in the sensations traveling straight through her ass, into her pussy, and up the base of her spine.

"What—"

"Shit," Viviana hissed, unable to speak much more than that.

The plug shut off, giving her just enough of a moment to breathe. The slight sting of pain was nothing compared to the sweet singing pleasure rocking her most sensitive area.

Juices leaked into her thong, soaking the fabric. Anton breathed a heavy sound and when she stared up at him, she could see his eyes were slightly glazed.

The sound of her voice was high and airless, totally unknown to her, when Viviana said, "Try it again."

"What did you do?"

When she wouldn't answer, the sudden buzzing hum of the plug in her ass was turned on again, sending her spiraling right back into that gasping ache once more. Muscles clenched around the plug instinctively, holding the silicone toy inside. Anton pressed on the small of her back, driving lower until he'd reached the elastic waist of her sweatpants. A little lower under the fabric, and she knew he could feel the soft vibrations tickling against his fingertips when his mouth opened and another sexy sound rolled from his lips.

In one fluid movement, Viviana found herself turned, her chest sprawled over the countertop as her hands grappled to find purchase. The pants and black thong she wore were pulled down to her knees, making her legs tremble at the force of his roughness. Two of his fingers slid down the crack of her ass, and Viviana shuddered when he came in contact with the remnants of the lube she'd used to help insert the toy.

The plug was suddenly ramped up to the second speed, causing her shaking to increase. Teeth clenched as Viviana pressed her forehead to the granite counter. "Pl-please … Fuck, it's … that's to-too much."

The toy shut off immediately at her words. Not a second later, the cheeks of her ass were spread and his fingers came in contact against the flat, silicone end of the toy. With the softest pressure, she felt him pushing against the plug, the tapered tip reaching a delicious spot that sent another soft cry forcing its way from her lungs. His teeth bit into the tender flesh of her ass. Viviana jerked in surprise when the vibrating began once more on the slower setting.

A growl formed in the back of Anton's throat, echoing in the silent kitchen, making her body respond to the want in his tone instantly. "Oh, baby. How… *why?*"

When the toy abruptly stopped again, Viviana could finally speak, albeit still feeling a little overcome. "A healthy exploration of my own body." She swore she heard him swallow behind her. "Lucky for me that certain stores allow their packages to come in the mail with privacy labels so that no one knows what I've bought."

"I've never checked your cards or packages."

Viviana chanced a glace over her shoulder, but his face was turned away. Even so, she could see the tension in his hands as he grabbed her ass and the tick in his tight jaw. If it were any other situation, she might have thought he was angry, but given his cock was hard and pressing into the back of her thigh, she knew he wasn't.

Not once had he brought up the topic of anal to her, never mind approaching it while they were in the midst of something sexual. With her own private trials, Viviana knew it was something she might like, and she trusted Anton enough to give her that experience, if he wanted.

"I know," she said, still trying to catch her breath. "I've never …"

Anton did look up then, his eyes piercing into hers with registering surprise and desire. "Never?"

"No one, *ever*. Like I said, a healthy exploration. I've tried some things, so I know what I like. And today, you're the one with the remote."

"I am, aren't I? *Shit.*" He fixed her thong and pants before letting her stand up again. The remote was slipped into his pocket as she turned in his embrace. Viviana could see the battle raging in Anton's eyes. "I don't know what to say."

"You don't want that with me?"

"No … God, no, it's not that."

The quiet murmur of anxiety crept up her spine with a cold grip. "I just thought—"

"Shut up. Shut those pretty lips of yours right up," Anton muttered, eyes flashing down at her in warning. "Of course I want that with you, yes. I just … *damn*. What happened to that innocent girl in Barbados who hadn't even kissed a boy until she met me; where did that girl go? I'm not saying it's not okay she grew up, but sometimes this is a serious mind fuck for me, okay?"

"Okay. I get that."

"Not that I'm complaining, but where did she go?" he repeated, lips curving with the most sinful grin.

Viviana returned the gesture, letting her fingers dance up the silky material of his shirt before replying, "She wasn't all that innocent. After all, she agreed to marry you."

Chapter Eleven

Anton chuckled as Viviana's eyes widened at the sight staring back at her. The upstairs office inside Seven Lights had been all but turned inside out for her the evening before. It had taken some serious wrangling on his part, and Ivan's wife, to get what they needed, but it had come together, despite the craziness over the last few days. Now, the entire office was filled with clothes, shoes, and whatever else his lover might like.

The office was a good twenty by twenty in size. Anton liked it a little bigger than usual, seeing as how when his men came in to pay their tributes, they always seemed to stay and chat. Another would arrive, and the same thing would follow suit. A dozen cigars later and the club would be closed, but the raucous, loud laughter would still be banging out from his office above.

There was no denying he liked it. Of course he did, it was all he ever knew. Even at five years old with droopy eyes and little understanding as to what was happening around him, Anton could remember sitting perched on his father's or step-grandfather's legs. He learned some of the dirtiest Russian slang before he even understood English completely.

"What do you think?"

Viviana gaped a little more. "It's ..."

"Vine?"

Still, he got nothing.

Unable to stop himself, Anton found the little remote hidden in the inner pocket of his suit jacket, and pressed the first gentle speed. Her jerk of surprise as the toy turned on did the wickedest of things to his insides.

"Anton!"

A shrug fell flippantly from his shoulders and he turned it back off. "You wanted to play this game, baby."

"I'm ..." Her eyes closed as she breathed heavily. "I

will take that remote away from you."

Anton grinned slyly, turning away. No, she wouldn't. Viviana had a dirty streak he hadn't even thought to consider, but now that he knew … well, the boss was going to have some fun. The sexiest of sights had been in his car as they drove through the city on their way to Brighton Beach. It was clear that with every little jostle or bump of the tires, Viviana was just barely hanging on to the ledge of control. He desperately wanted to see her lose it, but Anton wanted it to be his cock that did it to her, too.

"How does that feel, having your own body fucking you like that?"

Fuck, the way her quiet moan couldn't quite be hidden when he pressed that button on again just about did him in. How he hadn't already shot off a load inside his pants, Anton wasn't quite sure.

"Are you going to answer me, now? Do you like the clothes?"

Viviana simply looked around again. Anton understood it was a little much for her, probably. In fact, he might have overdone it a bit, but he really had no clue as to her personal preferences and styles when it came to clothing. Especially dress wear.

So, he had just about a little bit of everything brought in from shops across New York. Only the best names with price tags that would make someone's heart stutter. She could pick what she wanted for the evening, but the rest had already been bought and paid for by him. His office had suddenly turned into a clothing store. Garment bags hung off several dress racks, boxes of designer shoes sitting opened on leather couches and chairs, and the glittering gems of crystals reflecting light off the many clutches on the desk.

Underdressed she would not be. The only thing he wanted her to do was enjoy the night. And if that meant dropping a few thousand dollars—more like twentyish—so that she could pick through whatever it was she wanted to wear, that was exactly what he would do.

Anton was a giver, after all.

"I'm not even going to ask how you did this," Viviana murmured, voice still hot from his escapade with the toy in her ass. Just the sound was giving him a hard-on. There was no doubt in his mind that he'd have to stop himself from bending her over something and ... "Can I just pick whatever?"

"It's all yours," he said, grabbing that tote bag of hers and dropping it into the chair.

"*All* of it?"

"Every little bit, baby. The sizes should be spot on, but if something's not right, we can have it returned and replaced."

Anton could see the question burning in her eyes before she even asked it. "It's not ... *hot*, right?"

It wouldn't be unusual if it was, he had to admit. Bratva brothers on more than one occasion would pick up a load of something and the spoils were distributed as Anton saw fit. From all kinds of electronics to jewelry to high end clothing, it had all passed through his hands at one point or another. Some brought in more money than others, but that wasn't really a part of the business that he wanted to discuss with Viviana.

Sometimes the less she knew, the better.

"No, it's not. And that's about all I'm willing to say in regards to that topic."

With a small nod, he knew she understood. Anton stayed quiet as she moved over the rows of heels in opened boxes, reaching out to linger over the leather pumps, then a particular pair of silver peep-toed stilettos with shimmering crystals embedded from sole to tip. Viviana's gaze lingered on those for a while and Anton knew then he had her caught. In a second, his hand was back inside his pocket.

"Anton! *Dammit ...*"

The sweetest cry tumbled from parted lips as she staggered in place, a hand bracing on the arm of the couch. Anton simply lifted a brow and looked back at his open office door, knowing the four employees downstairs wouldn't be coming up anytime soon.

"Those," he said, turning the toy off. "Pick them."

Air hissed through her teeth, but the pink blush staining her cheeks as she regarded him over her shoulder said more than Viviana ever could have. Her pupils were dilated, lips bitten a rosy red, and he had little doubt her thong was absolutely soaked with arousal. Good God, his dick fucking ached.

It was teasing him just as much as it did her.

"Could I at least look at the dresses before I pick a pair of shoes?"

"You've got to start somewhere. Build from those. I like them. Think of what it'll feel like to be standing in them while I fuck your ass, Viviana." The audible sound of her mouth clamping shut had him smirking. Anton brought the remote out and waved it as he added, "That was your point in this little show, right? You had a goal in mind, I'm just promising to follow through on it. But, I really like those shoes, so I couldn't very well let you pass them up."

"You should. They're five hundred dollars a pair. You have expensive taste."

"I have good taste," Anton corrected, almost wanting her to challenge him. "And so do you considering they were the ones to catch your eye. Pick those shoes for tonight. The rest is all yours to do with as you like anyway."

When he turned to leave the office, Viviana asked, "You're not going to stay and help me pick a dress, Anton?" There was a little sarcasm hidden beneath her tone. That and a bit of her lust was coming through awfully strong, too, coloring her words. "Here I was thinking you'd press that button every time I came to something you might have liked, but nope. That's too bad."

"I have some things to do, so you'll have a bit of time for yourself to go through it all."

"But—"

"I'll send Jen up in a while once she's done with her

liquor order. She has a good eye for fabrics on bodies."

Anton didn't miss the flash of something unknown in Viviana's eyes. "Who is she?"

"The head bartender here. She also keeps the books on the legal side. The girl doesn't have a bit of Russian in her, but she can drink like a fish and not be any worse for wear. Some of the younger guys like her a little too much, which got me to put her behind the bar instead of working the floor. They tend to leave her alone that way."

Viviana tapped her sneaker to the floor, glancing away. "Anything else I should know?"

Ah, there it was. The question he figured she was eating but wouldn't spit out.

"Yeah ..." he said, turning to leave again. "I've never fucked her."

*

Viviana was on sensory overload. There was much too much for her to choose from. Between the knee high dresses to the shorter, tighter ones, to even the lingerie that could be worn underneath them, and then the fifteen garment bags that only held the most expensive fur coats she'd ever laid eyes on, she was so lost.

The very least she had managed to do was to narrow the color scheme down to black. It seemed that was Anton's favorite color when it came to dressy clothing, considering nearly all of the dresses were exactly that shade.

A soft knock on the closed office door drew Viviana's head up. "Yeah?"

"You decent in there?"

The feminine voice had Viviana sighing. Apparently her earlier question about Jen to Anton hadn't exactly been as vague as she meant for it to be, considering his response. The fact that the girl wasn't some old flame of his was a relief for Viviana, but she still felt a bit childish for even having brought it up. Of course there were women she was going to meet that had been with him, and pretending like there weren't any out there was only going to be more difficult when she did come face to face with one.

Or shit, she could just go down his path and shoot one of his past lovers.

Quit it, Viviana thought bitterly. *You're not even the jealous type.*

"Um … Vine?"

"Yeah, come on in."

The girl that opened the door was not what Viviana had been expecting. Jen was pretty, yes, but in a really unassuming way with a warm smile and bright eyes. At least in her early thirties, she was dressed in jeans and a T-shirt, seemingly relaxed as she looked around the office.

"Wow, he really did go all out for you, huh?"

Viviana cleared her throat, feeling a bit embarrassed about the mess she'd made in the office. "I have no idea what to wear."

"Well, something clubby but not whorish."

A bubble of laughter burst from her lips. "Is that even possible?"

"Yeah, and by the looks of it, Anton had somebody helping him. He's a man; there isn't any way on earth he knew what to order. Oh, here …" Viviana barely caught the remote before it could have flown by her head. With a squeak, she hid the device in her tote bag. "He said something about leaving his coat lying around, so you needed to have that for now."

Oh, God. The heat that crawled up her cheeks couldn't even be hidden. "I—"

"Don't want to know," Jen interrupted with a soft laugh. "I just do as I'm told, honey. I don't see, hear, or know a damned thing. My paycheck is always better for it, too. Of course, explaining some of those bonuses at the end of the year always hurts come tax time."

Viviana shook her head, smiling. She liked this girl already. "Can you help me?"

Jen nodded. "Yep, I sure can. And we've got some time seeing as how he has visitors downstairs and I needed to make myself scarce for a while."

"Okay."

A too-short dress was picked up by Jen, the black, slinky fabric shimmering under the office lights before she dropped it back down with a disgusted sound. It wasn't long before she had pawed through half of the articles Viviana had already dismissed as being a little much, given the occasion. Before long, Jen laid four black dresses across her legs then moved towards the rack that held the coats.

"My, my ... what do we have here?"

Viviana scoffed. "I have no idea what those are for. The tweed coat I have is more than dressy enough for this, to be honest."

Jen smirked over her shoulder. "I do."

"Care to enlighten me?"

Jen opened up one of the bags, rubbing her hand along the fur in silence. Another bag was opened, and then another. While Viviana wasn't exactly against wearing fur, she didn't have a whole collection of them, either.

"I don't think he meant for these to be worn tonight, but more for you to just have them period. These men have a thing for it. Gets them bothered in all kinds of naughty ways."

"Excuse me?" Viviana asked, more confused than ever.

"Maybe it's a Bratva thing ... or a Russian thing. Furs, they like them a lot."

"*Oh.*"

Jen winked. "By the looks of these, I'd say Anton has a preference for minks."

With Jen's help, it didn't take Viviana long at all to find the right dress, undergarments, and purse to go with those shoes Anton decided on. The dress fell to her mid-thigh, hugging the curve in her waist with a perfect fit. Elbow length sleeves and a modest V-neck plunge in the front, the article was more than sexy enough to be worn in a club, but with the right accessories and coat, it was also quite appropriate for just about anything else, too. Even those silver heels didn't detract from the dress, adding a bit of freshness to the dark color.

Fixing the strap of the white lace brassier underneath the heavy, black fabric, Viviana finally felt like she might not be so under dressed standing next to Anton in his suit. Of course, she was pretty sure that was exactly his motive, too.

"Okay, look."

Jen turned with a smug grin, arms spreading wide as she appraised Viviana from all angles. A low whistle cut through her lips. "Damn, girl. Look at those legs of yours."

"Too much leg."

"Not enough, if anything. Oh, he's going to love this."

Viviana sighed. "Good."

Jen perked up a brow. "You don't sound happy."

"Just nervous, I suppose."

"Honey, for the last few weeks you're all that man seems to think about. His head is not in the game here like it usually is, but thank God I'm the only one noticing at the moment. With that being said, he's a damn good boss … in *every* aspect, you know?"

Viviana swallowed thickly, glancing away from the woman and wondering just how much of the behind the scenes business she actually witnessed day to day. "Yeah, I know."

"So, it's your turn. Smile and let him love you. He's got you now, Vine, all that's really left is to show everyone else just how much."

*

At Jen's insistence, the woman all but pushed Viviana out of the office to go find Anton. There was no question she wanted his approval on the dress. With the remote for the toy hidden safely in her palm, Viviana left the small upstairs of the club to find him.

Rounding the staircase, loud laughter brought her attention over the railing. Down below with dimmed lights shadowing the two men who greeted each other, she watched as a manila envelope nearly three inches thick was passed between hands. Anton slipped it under his coat resting on a table where paperwork was spread out.

"If I had to guess by the size, I'd say that's a better turnout than last month," Anton said, reaching out to cuff the other man on the shoulder.

"Last month I was a week late."

"And you're two weeks early this time around. You're not forgiven, but I am impressed."

Anton leaned against the wall so he could survey the large expanse of the club's floor. It wasn't hard for Viviana to recognize her lover's posture or choice in seat. It gave him ready access to move if he needed to quickly, and his line of vision had nearly everything in its path.

"Sit," he ordered, before his head dropped down to survey the paperwork in front of him.

When the man did, Viviana finally got a look at his shadowed profile. She didn't recognize him, but his age surprised her. In his early twenties at the least, she figured he was a bit young to be having direct contact with a Bratva boss, especially where what she assumed was money was being exchanged. Usually those men's ages reflected their time served in the business, but given Anton's status, maybe there was newer, younger blood taking over, too.

"I took a big risk on you," Anton said, not even looking up.

Viviana felt her fingers wrap around the edge of the banister, knowing she should probably turn around and leave. More than once she'd overheard conversations that weren't meant for her ears, and it left her heartbroken because of it. There were things no daughter wanted to know—to *hear*.

"I know, Boss."

"No, I don't think you do. I don't think you truly realize the weight of my choice. I despised your uncle, but everyone else said you were much too young to take over his spot when I wanted him gone. Sure, I covered for you last month, but I will not be doing it again, Bo. It doesn't look well for me to do so, and shorts won't be overlooked. Do that to me again and I'll break every one of your fucking fingers."

"I—"

"Shut up. We had this discussion once. I don't want to have it one more time."

Silence passed between the two men as Anton scrawled ink on a piece of paper.

"Steph is giving me shit again."

"No wonder. She's eight months pregnant and likely questioning why you're coming home late every night. Marry that girl and explain it to her. Unless you have someone else on the side that's keeping you away. If that's the case, you're just being an asshole and I'll break your fingers for a whole other reason altogether."

"No. Steph is enough."

"Good to know. I'd hate to see my mother's niece being done wrong," Anton said lowly.

"And what about yours, Boss?"

Anton jerked his head up, meeting the other man's gaze. "What do you think?"

"Just wondering how the honeymoon phase is coming along for you, that's all."

"It's coming ... every damned night."

Loud, masculine laughter echoed through the club's empty floor. Before long, the conversation below had turned to Russian mutterings Viviana couldn't understand let alone hear. When a black case was pulled out from beside the younger man's feet, Anton seemed to turn a little excited at the sight.

"Bo, you didn't have—"

"I absolutely did, Boss. Besides, after last month, I kind of owe you, okay? Happy fucking birthday and all that stupid crap. This piece cost me a fortune and took some serious wrangling to get. I might have heard you were looking for something with a specific set of specs, so take a look and tell me what you think. If you like it, I can get a good order in for more—*lots* more. This one is all on me."

"Yeah?"

"Yes. Stop your bitching and open it up."

With both men standing again, Viviana watched as the case was set down carefully on the table. Locks were unlatched, the top of the case popping open with ease. Anton ran his hands over the inside, whistling a quiet, appreciative sound under his breath as a cuss left his smirking lips.

"Goddamn, Bo. This is something else."

The weapon that was plucked up from the case had Viviana's heart racing.

Under the lights, it shined with brushed, blue metal from the very tip of the barrel all the way to the wood grain of the butt. Clearly the rifle wasn't meant to be just any ordinary gun, considering the level of scopes it sported. It was a custom gun, even she could see that from her hiding spot, and one Anton seemed to thoroughly enjoy as he shook his head again.

"We've never gotten them like these," Anton said.

The gun was raised a little more, the butt coming to rest at Anton's shoulder as he took an aim to the wall and glanced through the scopes. Viviana couldn't deny the strange sensations that passed through her at the sight. It made her hotter than it should have considering her fear of guns, but who was she to deny his pleasures, or hers?

"No, this one is just for you. The blue is specially manufactured, and that snake skin design costs one hell of a dime to get done, but it looks fucking sweet under the sunlight."

"I bet. All Russian, too. Shit, we're looking at a sniper here, yeah?"

"Like I said, I heard you needed something particular. This is very *particular* with a bit of pretty to liken it up. Can't have our Bratva prince handling something unworthy of his attention, now could I?"

Anton cleared his throat, placing the gun safely back into the case. Viviana stayed hidden at the top of the stairs as he turned and gave the younger man a one-armed hug, whispering words into his ear.

He raised a hand, patting Bo on the back of his neck before their eyes met and a nod was exchanged between both men. Then Anton released him just as quickly, his stance straightening.

"You're forgiven, Bo. Don't let last month happen again."

"Not a chance, Boss."

Chapter Twelve

As the young man disappeared from the club, Viviana heard Anton's heavy sigh from down below.

"I know you're up there, Viviana."

Shit.

She couldn't even have tried to move fast enough if she wanted to. Anton was suddenly at the bottom of the metal stairs with that gun case tight in his grasp.

"I'm—"

"What, baby, sorry for eavesdropping? You know better, Vine."

A dreadful feeling settled in her stomach as he climbed the stairs with a painstaking slowness. It almost looked predatory as one hand slid over the metal banister and a grim line drew his lips tight into a frown. Her fingers tightened around the remote. Viviana hadn't meant to walk in on his business, but he was correct when he said she knew better.

"I know. I shouldn't have—"

"You're goddamn right," he interrupted, words coming out like a dark growl. "Where is Jen?"

"Um ..."

Words failed to form as he finally came to stand toe to toe with her at the top of the staircase. Viviana practically felt three inches tall under his angry gaze. There was no way to excuse what she had done by continuing to listen in on his conversation after she knew what was happening.

"Jen?" Anton called out loudly.

The woman in question poked her head out of the office doorway, a dress stuck halfway inside a garment bag. "Yeah?"

"I'll get the rest. Finish up that order and begin getting the bar set up for later, please."

"You sure? I thought you said Richard—"

"Right the fuck now, Jen," he snapped sharply.

The tone in his voice seemed to do the trick. Jen quickly dropped the bag inside the room before pushing between Anton and Viviana to get down the stairs.

"You didn't need to kick her out, Anton."

"In my office, Viviana."

"But—"

Her wrist was suddenly in his grasp as he led her down the short hallway to the opened doorway. She was damned lucky she didn't stumble or fall in those four inch heels. When the door was slammed shut, Viviana turned in his grasp, ready to give him a verbal lashing for the rough handling, but the piercing gaze that met her own stopped the words up short.

"Tell me what you should have done."

"Pardon me?"

"When you walk in on something like that—what should you do, Viviana?"

That godforsaken lump in her throat had returned. Suddenly, she was hyperaware of that anal plug in her ass again, the jostle of his body pressing closer to hers sending sparks of pleasure licking through her ass as arousal dampened the white lace thong she'd changed into.

"And I like this dress. It was a good choice," he added, a finger skimming over the V-neck to move the fabric off to the side. At the sight of the lingerie underneath, he hummed appreciatively. The slight bite of fear that had nipped at her heels from the thought of him being angry was all but gone. "Come on, tell me."

Viviana forced herself to swallow. "I'm sorry."

"I don't doubt that, but it's not what I asked."

"You're giving me whiplash."

"You scared the fuck out of me," Anton bit back, blue eyes darkening. "Thought you were going to walk in on that."

"I wouldn't—"

"I know. Still, you shouldn't have stayed there and listened, either."

Viviana breathed a shuddering breath, handling the

silky fabric of his shirt where he'd rolled the sleeves up to his elbows. Anton's stance softened at her motions, but she knew she still had a hell of a lot of explaining to do.

"Jen figured all your guests were gone, so I wanted to see what you thought of my dress."

"It was a last-minute call and he was already outside when I received it. I couldn't very well send him away."

"I didn't mean to come in on it like that, and I should have turned around as soon as I knew what was happening."

"And what was happening?"

A beat of silence passed before she answered with a solid, "Nothing."

The gun case dropped to the floor, Anton's foot kicking out to move it aside. "You sure, baby?"

"Yeah, nothing. It was dark, so I didn't see very much."

"Good to know."

Viviana couldn't help but enjoy the change in his demeanor. In fact, it had shifted like a switch going off when they left the safe house. It might have been his birthday and his party, but it was clearly just another workday for Anton. Very rarely did she get to see him acting like the mob boss he really was, and it hadn't been something that turned her on like it was now.

"It won't happen again," she promised quietly, looking up to meet his gaze again.

"Actually, I'm sure it will, and the next time, I can expect you to turn around and ignore what you're seeing, yes?"

She wet her lips with her tongue, letting her fingers dance along the black licks of his vine tattoo that barely peaked out from under his rolled-up shirt. The defined, rock hard muscles of his forearm twitched under her touch.

"Yes …"

Anton raised a brow. "Are you playing coy with me right now? This isn't a joke, Vine."

"I know—"

"No, I don't believe you do. This is Brighton Beach,

Viviana. The men that walk in and out of here aren't going to be like Ivan digging through our fridge or Erik drinking us out of vodka. They are not my spies, they are my soldiers. This is my territory. I run these fucking streets and more so here than anywhere else, my last name draws attention. Here, I'm not Anton, a friend, or anything like that. I am just *Boss*."

"Okay."

"I need to know you understand me. That you're hearing this."

Fuck, it would be so much better if she weren't so goddamn turned on just by the dominant sound his voice had taken on, not to mention the tantalizing toy in her rear that was keeping her body awake and ready with every slight movement. No, there was no forgetting that, either. Maybe his birthday hadn't been the best time for the toy, considering everything. Even so, Viviana couldn't deny the lust that raged through her veins like an inferno intent on destroying what little control she had left.

"I'm ... I hear you. I *do*," she insisted when he grunted a disbelieving noise above her. "You know how much I hate to use the term *behave*, but this is one of those situations, right? I mean, you can't come in here and be just Anton, so why should I expect to come in here acting like I'm just Vine. It's not ... we can't. I understand that."

The slightest tilt of her head under his urging had his lips meeting hers softly. She could taste the remnants of bourbon so thick on his tongue when it probed gently inside her mouth. She let her fingers twist into his shirt, wanting him just a little bit closer.

"Thank you." Without another word, the remote that had been tucked into her hand was back in his, a wicked gleam playing in his eyes. "Had to send it up, but I think I'll take it back for a little while now. Couldn't chance it, you know?"

Viviana swallowed, letting her forehead rest on his cheek. "You have pockets in your pants."

"It might get turned on accidentally. I am being

discreet, Vine, or trying to be ..." For that, she was grateful. "For now."

Oh, God. "You wouldn't."

"I might, if I catch my future wife spying on me again. Seriously, it's not so much that it pisses me off as it's terribly unsafe for you to be in positions like that." Again, he lifted her face, his thumbs rolling over her jaw tenderly. "And what would I do if something happened to you, huh? Locked up in my office while you're aware there are people here is a different story. *They* don't know you're here and I prefer it that way. Some of these men ... you don't even know, baby."

"*You're* one of those men, Anton."

Instantaneously, his spine turned ramrod straight, but she didn't even have the chance to apologize. Catching her off guard, a hand slipped under that short dress of hers, the heat of his palm cupping her sex as his fingers slid against the crack of her ass. The toy jerked to life inside her rear on the second speed, nearly sending Viviana to her knees from the shock, pleasure, and vague hum of pain that burst through every nerve ending she had.

"Oh—"

His voice was a dark sound in her ear, growled through clenched teeth and enough to make her shake. "So, I can go on assuming you're so fucking wet because of that young man who just left, instead of believing it might have been because the sight of me with a gun on my shoulder got you so damned hot you couldn't think straight, right?"

Jesus, Viviana couldn't even speak. His fingers moved her thong aside with a skillful movement, finding where the vibrating plug was driving her absolutely insane inside her ass and pushing the toy a little further in.

Once more, he thrust the toy inside her ass a little harder, giving her the best burn and the sweetest pleasure at the same time. The harsh rhythm of his fingers and the plug fucking her ass had her legs trembling and an orgasm ready to crash onto her like a tidal wave. The heady cry was muffled into his neck as Anton drove her close enough into his hips

157

that she could feel the growing erection pressed to her middle.

"It's … it-it's …"

She wanted to say too much, to tell him he needed to slow it down, but Viviana realized it wasn't true. In fact, her ass backed into his hand, wanting it harder still. The sound of her voice turned high as she begged him for more, only getting low chuckles in response.

"Tell me, Viviana … is that what got you so hot, baby? I quite like that young man, but it wouldn't be too much of a drop in my bucket if he needed to go." When his teeth bit her neck, he muttered, "I'm a jealous motherfucker when it comes to what's mine, or haven't I told you that yet?"

"No-no … not him," she stuttered, so fucking close to falling off that peak he held her on.

"The gun, then?"

"No, yes … Oh, fuck, Anton, *please.*"

"No, or yes. Which one is it?"

"Both," she somehow managed to breathe.

Before she could speak again, he impaled her with the toy even deeper, opening the clenching ring of muscles that held the toy tight. Immediately, it sent her spinning into an orgasm so intense tears slipped through her clamped-shut eyes, spilling against his neck. As her knees gave out, every muscle in her body relaxed at the rush of relief and euphoria that soaked her like a bucket of ice water.

Slowly, her panting breaths decreased as Viviana whined brokenly from the aftershocks.

Never had something hit her so strongly.

"There, hmm?" he hummed darkly, kissing along the raging pulse in her neck. "I think you needed that. Bend over my desk."

That sobered her instantly. "What?"

"I believe it can come out, given how well you opened for me just then. If you can handle that, well…" He trailed off with another one of those throaty hums of his that sent her sex clenching. "I know you brought the kit for it, so pack it away in that purse of yours and we'll keep it under my desk until we leave tonight. Clean it at home, whatever. Besides, I think you need to show me what else you bought when we get back. Sound good?"

Her throat was so tight that she could only nod in response. On shaky legs, she moved from his embrace, letting his hand find the small of her back. Anton grabbed her purse off the back of the chair, quickly finding the plastic box inside for the toy. With her palms lying flat on the edge of his desk, she sighed a heavy breath as he bunched the dress around her waist before laying a kiss to the rounded cheek of her ass. Her thong was hooked to his thumb and moved to the side.

"So, both. Care to indulge me here?"

Embarrassment slipped through her emotions like a slow moving killer. "I didn't—"

"It turns you on, doesn't it? Admit it. Guns scare you. Me and a gun is a different story, however. Gets you hot and bothered like nothing else. I think I like that more than I should. Come on, Viviana, is that it?"

"Yes."

Once more, a tender kiss touched down before his teeth nipped painfully sharp to the same spot, sending a jolt of need through every inch of her aching body. At the same time, his fingers slipped inside to wrap along the flattened end of the plug before it slipped out of her rear.

With the toy packed safely away and her dress fixed, Viviana found herself rotated beneath his hands, the small of her back pressing into the edge of Anton's desk as he leaned over her form. Their kiss was slow and lazy, the heat of his mouth overtaking hers as his fingers curled around the small of her waist. Pulling away, her nose skimmed the strong line of his jaw and she watched his eyes close at the motion.

Closed doors gave her him, she knew. No matter where they were. Anton flipped his switch like nothing, but she always got the very best ones when they turned on her.

"Both," she murmured, nipping tenderly at his bottom lip. Blue eyes opened at her voice, the striking gaze he leveled on her making Viviana's heart speed up. The very sight made her feel weak and overcome all over again, so she lowered her head. "You were right, it's both. But, it won't happen again …"

"Good."

"*Boss.*"

At the harsh intake of air, Viviana chanced a look up at him once more, only to see the hard swallow in his throat and hooded eyes. His fingers tightened almost painfully on her waist, but she didn't mind a bit.

"Oh, baby. You're playing with fire, now."

Viviana pretended like he hadn't said a thing. "So the dress is good then?"

"We're back to coy, huh?"

"Anton …" she said, reaching up to tap his chin with one finger, "the dress?"

"I love this goddamn dress."

That was good enough for her.

*

"Mr.—"

"Anton," he corrected automatically as the intercom turned on. Viviana's legs on his lap was keeping his attention semi-diverted from his work. "Just Anton."

His earlier moment when he'd snapped at his favorite employee had clearly given her a frightening shock if she was reverting back to using his last name.

"Right … um, Richard is here," Jen said quietly over the intercom.

Viviana's finger poked his ribs. "Richard?"

"Great. Send him up."

The office had been cleaned—all of the clothing, shoes, and accessories removed from the space in little to no time at all. At his order, one of Viviana's bulls had taken what she wouldn't be using for the night back to the safe house. And damn, he could barely keep his eyes off her sexy curves as she moved around his office with a comfortable ease in those heels and dress. Jen needed another raise for getting her to wear it; that was all he had to say about it.

That and he probably owed her an apology for acting like an ass earlier. The apology wouldn't come, because Jen knew better than anyone to turn her cheek at his moods and odd visitors, but the bonus on her paycheck always said more than he could, anyway.

Anton wasn't expecting any other visitors besides his personal jeweler, so he spent most of the afternoon hidden in his office with Viviana by his side. Spreadsheets were a hell he tried to avoid at all costs. Having businesses that were on the legal side of things meant he had to do crap like this more often than he wanted to.

The loud knock on his office door had Viviana's questioning gaze turning on him again. "Who's Richard?"

The confusion in her voice was almost cute, considering he hadn't given her any indication she would be a part of his dealings for the day. In all honestly, Anton just wanted to surprise her again, because the thunderstruck look it created on her face was quickly turning into something he lived for.

"A very good friend of mine," Anton told her quietly, bringing up her left hand to kiss the suspiciously bare ring finger. "Come on in, Richard."

The man who entered his office was sporting a smile, eyebrows lifting with a suggestive lift as Viviana attempted to move her legs from Anton's lap without her dress rising up. In his late sixties, Richard was a gentleman through and through, averting his eyes until she cleared her throat. He'd been around the Bratva organization long enough to know he could expect just about any kind of scene when he opened a closed door.

With the two silver security briefcases placed safely to the floor, Richard crossed the room and leaned down to place a kiss on Anton's cheek as the younger man patted the back of his neck in response. It was a common sign of respect, one he knew Viviana would have seen before with her father, but not one she had gotten to witness properly played out with him.

Richard cocked a brow, meeting Anton's gaze as the paperwork was tossed aside. "Are you slacking again, boy?" The thickness in his accent hung off every syllable. More often than not, he'd use Russian to speak to Anton, but because of Viviana's presence, he chose to use a language she would understand, too. "Nicoli would be in a terrible fit seeing his little prince slumming it in the office with his fiancée instead of doing actual work."

"I am working …"

"*Sure.*"

"On more important things," Anton finished with a smirk.

"Ah, well, at least your priorities are getting straightened out. I can assume that's because of this pretty little thing, here? It's Viviana, yes?"

"That's me."

Richard's steel-grey eyes turned on the woman who had crossed her legs and kept quiet while the Bratva boss was greeted. For a single moment, Anton knew what the older man was doing. Searching those eyes and features like he had done so many times before, looking for the clue that gave away who she really was behind the Italian name and mob boss father. Being the friend that Richard had been to Nicoli for all those years, he knew his step-grandfather wouldn't have held back that secret from him.

The quiet exhale of Richard's breath as he straightened was enough for Anton. The lump in his throat disappeared. "Very pleased to meet you, sweetheart. You've had this lazy prince here making me run for three weeks."

Viviana glanced at Anton out of the corner of her eye as he brushed her wavy hair off her shoulder. "Three weeks?"

"This …" he said, waving at Richard with a smug grin, "is my jeweler, Viviana. And I do believe he has only the best for you, right, Richard?"

"Absolutely."

The slight drop in her jaw had him chuckling. "You

didn't."

"I did, baby. I thought I was clear when I said I had things planned for you today."

"It's *your* birthday," she said pointedly.

Anton hummed, shrugging as he lifted himself off the couch. "Yeah, but making you smile is my greatest gift. Come, it's time to pick out a ring for me to put on that finger of yours."

One of the silver briefcases was propped up on the oak desk and opened with a set of keys. Viviana's soft gasp whispered in Anton's ears. He didn't blame her a bit. The engagement rings Richard had brought along certainly outdid just about any he could have personally picked. There hadn't been many requests from Anton regarding the rings, and he'd left the rest up to the older man to decide. And decide he had. Ranging from simplistic designs to some of the most intricately laid pieces he'd ever seen, Anton was quite literally struck quiet, too.

Twenty rings sat resting in black velvet, the shimmer of light reflecting off the carefully cut diamonds and gems. Between the rows, a particular piece caught Anton's eye. In the middle of a white gold band sat a blue sapphire, five carat princess cut gem, encased with a solid crown of clear diamonds. He hadn't asked for color, but there was something about that ring that drew his attention above the others.

"Very nice," he appraised quietly. "I quite like these."

Richard's hand hit the spot between Anton's shoulder blades and the older man laughed. "I hoped you would."

"Never failed me before," Anton replied. Viviana made a sound under her breath, almost turning into a skittish deer at the sight of so many jewels. "See anything you like?"

"Um ..."

"Pardon me, Vine?"

" *Yes*. Oh, they're beautiful."

That awed look had replaced her initial shock as her fingers hesitantly danced over the sides of the case, but never once coming near any of the rings.

"You can touch them, sweetheart," Richard said gently. "They are meant for you to wear, or at least one of them, anyway. All sized specifically for you, so you needn't worry about that. Take your time if you need to."

Once more, Viviana looked back at Anton, and he could see the battle warring there. It was quite a selection, and if he had to guess, she was probably wondering which ring he wanted to see on her finger.

"I really wanted you to choose without my input," Anton murmured, hoping she'd understand. "Sometimes it might seem like you have so little control on everyday things, and you have to wear this ring, not me. If you want something small, go with that. If you want something that looks fit to be on a queen, go ahead. It's all on you, Vine."

When her trembling fingers ghosted over the case once more, Anton sighed, moving to her side. An arm wrapped around her waist, pulling her close as his lips met her temple and he added, "We'll leave you to go at it."

"What? No, you can't let me choose alone, Anton."

"I've already chosen the bands. They'll arrive next week. Just … do this for me, okay? It'll make me incredibly happy, and that way, I know the ring you'll wear is one you truly love."

Viviana didn't say a word, simply shook her head and glanced down with an audible swallow. The second, unopened case was passed into Anton's grasp before the men left the office. When the door was shut, Richard laughed a low sound when another one of those quiet, disbelieving noises came from inside the office.

"You'll spoil that girl if you keep up with all this sweet nonsense," he said with a joking spirit. "Doesn't she have the slightest clue of the kind of man you are beneath the charm, Anton?"

"She does, not that it matters. Couldn't hurt her if I tried."

"Ah, I see. Knowing Nicoli like I did, well … That

makes me a very happy old man."

"The sapphire band, you chose that one for its likeness to this, hmm?" Anton asked, lifting the silver case in his hand. What lay inside was a gift that had been held in the jeweler's trust for many years, under instructions Anton hadn't been privy to other than the basics of when he was to give it to Viviana, and why. The older man didn't deny his claim about the similarity statement. "And you placed it just so, I think, hoping it would catch my eye first."

"Not just yours," Richard said, smiling slyly. "If I know women like I think I do, she will pick that band because it was where your gaze traveled first. She will pick it because when her hand touches your face, the piece will compliment your eyes. And, it is more than appropriate enough in style, size, and design to be worn on the hand of your wife, Anton."

"A ring that by extension compliments me. I hadn't even considered that."

Richard nodded, expression darkening with pensiveness before his words turned to Russian. "But her eyes, my boy, they're all his."

His suddenly shaking fists hid inside his pockets. "I know."

Chapter Twelve

"What is this?"

Anton smiled at the confusion in his lover's voice as the car slid to a slow stop in a paved driveway. "My ... *our* home."

"It is?"

"Yep. I tried to buy it not long after I turned twenty, but Nicoli ended up giving it to me instead. This was his gift, I suppose." That, and a dozen other things he wasn't about to mention. "The locale is perfect."

That surprised look was back on her face, cheeks sweetening with a touch of pink behind the carefully applied makeup. Anton couldn't exactly blame her. The two level, modern house in the gated Brighton Beach community of Oceana was quite a sight. It was bigger than most on the block. A stone wall fence kept the corner property from having unwanted guests walking over the manicured grass, and not only was the location beautiful, and expensive, but it was also smart. Given the large bay windows on the top floors, Anton could see just about anybody coming for miles.

On the lower floor, windows were suited with triple latched locks. Only two entrances donned the home, also equipped with high tech alarms and locks, making it that much more difficult for an intruder, or police, to get in without him knowing in plenty of time to make whatever move he needed.

For all intents and purposes, the safe house located right in the heart of Brooklyn had been the perfect residence and spot for the Bratva boss to do his business and keep Viviana as safe as possible. But with the danger slowly beginning to ebb and his desire to return to his own home rising, the draw of their pseudo-home was starting to fade. She had yet to see where they would be living after the wedding, and considering they had a couple of hours before they needed to return to the club for his birthday party, he figured now was as good of a time to show her as any.

"I need to change my shirt. It doesn't match your shoes," he said, glancing down at the heels in question. They still had his body and mind in all kinds of turmoil, so just as quickly, he looked away. "And I didn't want to drive all the way back to the safe house. Come on, Vine."

The hand that touched his wrist stopped Anton from exiting the vehicle. Sunlight caught the glittering blue of the sapphire ring she now wore. It reflected a dance of light across his shirt. He'd kissed her deeply as he slid that band down her finger. His nerves only grew as he realized his hand had been trembling. But damn, doing that, and then seeing it, hadn't been at all what he was expecting. It was so much more.

Now, the torn expression she sported had his heart beating into a worried frenzy.

"What is it?"

"I ... well, is it like the safe house?"

It wasn't. The home in Oceana had a great deal less in the safety feature department because it was his personal residence. Anton tried to keep as many weapons out of the home as possible, though there were a few handguns hidden in choice spots just in case. Little to no Bratva business was done inside or around the property, as all the phones were constantly tapped by the feds, and a federal car was usually close by monitoring his private activities.

"No, not really. That's why we've stayed elsewhere for so long, because it's safer for the bulls to keep an eye on you there while I'm working away from the safe house."

"No, I meant business-wise, Anton."

"*Oh*," he drawled softly. "No way. Nothing in this house is off limits to you, not a single thing. There is a safe in the basement and one in my office that really don't concern you, but you'll have access to them if you want. None of my associates other than Erik and Ivan will make an appearance here. On a private scale, this is, in every way that counts, our home. The business will not intrude here, and I have kept it that way for as long as I can remember. That's why there are other places, like the safe house, where certain precautions are already in place for other … *things.*"

Her brown eyes lifted to meet his as she asked, "Promise?"

"Yeah, of course." Then Anton felt the need to explain a little more, wanting her to understand just how much of a distance he kept between his home and outside life. "Also, no one else was invited here, Viviana. I didn't share this space with anyone other than family and close friends."

The befuddled look had him sighing. "Women," he stressed. "I did not bring a woman to this home. Ever."

"No?"

"Not one."

In fact, he never took another woman beyond wherever it was she caught his eye, honestly. The backseat of a car, in a dirty alleyway, or the hidden hallway of a club. No, Anton was quite clear with all of those women about just what he wanted or needed from them, and it wasn't to invite them back to his home to spend the night. He simply assumed if he didn't give them any impression that he was searching for more, they wouldn't come knocking. So far none had, and he was grateful.

Viviana Carducci had been the first and only woman to sleep in his bed; she would be the last, too. None could ever look quite so good under his sheets with her head resting on his arm and her eyes closed, so he wasn't going to try and replace that feeling with someone who wasn't her.

The faint scent of her perfume had all but coated his car and lungs with its floral smell, overtaking him in the best way. That pink stain on her lips popped with the same color that naturally rose to her cheeks when she was happy, loved, or sad. Sometimes, it was the small things with her that caught him up in emotions he wasn't used to experiencing. Without thinking anymore about it, Anton leaned over the console of his Mercedes, cupping her jaw in his grasp and pulling Viviana in close to his face so lips grazed over hers as he spoke in low, hushed tones.

"I love you and you love me, yes?" An almost dazed nod had him smiling. "That's all that matters, then. I've been dying to see how you'd look walking through our home. That little dress you've got on, that ring on your finger, and those shoes are going to be the death of me if I don't get you out of this car so I can think and breathe for a moment, so let's go."

"All right, you insatiable man. Let's go."

*

"So, what do you think?"

Viviana jumped in fright, not having realized Anton returned from the master bedroom's attached bath. Turning away from the large window where she was looking down on the quiet, fenced backyard, she offered him a fake scowl for scaring her. Anton only grinned teasingly in response.

Basically, he left her alone to search out the basement, ground, and upper floors while he went to change his shirt. And explore she had. There was no doubt about it; she absolutely loved the home.

Fresh, white walls in every direction with high ceilings and bright lighting, it felt open and clean. Where the safe house was equipped with barely any personal touches on the walls, this home held artwork, family photos, and mementos of years gone by everywhere she looked. Instead of high priced, modern furniture that suited a group or gathering, the rooms were filled with comfortable pieces that fit the house and person inside it.

Spacious enough, but not ostentatious.

Relaxed, but not lazy.

Professional where it needed to be, sweet where she would want it to be, and homey in all the spots in between, Viviana was struck speechless. It felt like ... *home*. It had been so damned long since she felt that. Despite not having been directly in his life when the property was purchased, she had to wonder if she had somehow been considered in its choosing, too.

And then there was the matter of what she had been learning about her future husband during her travels through the home. Anton liked baseball, and she'd come to find out he played his first three years in high school. He had a propensity to collect knickknacks, take candid photos, and there were at least three stashes of candy she'd found so far. The basement was fully furnished, equipped with an at home gym in one area, and what Viviana would consider a man cave in another. Several entertainment systems, a flat screen TV, and a massive DVD collection told her it was likely one of his favorite spots in the house.

"Hey, the house?" Anton asked again, taking a step forward as his mouth curved with a gentle smile. Viviana turned back to look out the window again. "You've got me nervous over here, baby. I'm not used to feeling that way."

"Well ..."

"Well?"

"What did you mean when you said you wanted to buy it, but then Nicoli gave it to you?"

"I was starting to look for a house ... was just made a brigadier. Looked for months because I wanted it to be perfect, you know?"

"Yeah, and it kind of seems like it is."

"It is. But, when I finally found a house—this one— the owners refused to sell to me."

"What?"

Viviana turned on her heel, staring at the man leaning in the small entranceway of the master bedroom that had her all worked up into an emotional mess. The tiny cubby that looked like it may have once been a second walk-in closet had drawn her attention immediately when she entered the room, considering there was nothing in it but sheer curtains covering the window and two white leather chairs.

That certainly wasn't what that room should have been used for with its miniature vaulted ceilings, natural light, and quiet setting compared to the rest of the house. While the room had its own attached bath and a decent sized walk-in closet, Viviana knew exactly what the small, comfortable, intimate cubby inside the master bedroom was meant for.

"They wouldn't sell to *you*, specifically? Why?"

"Nope. Told the realtor there was no way they would sell their house to a gangster." Anton scoffed, rolling his eyes upwards. "Didn't matter when I offered two hundred thousand above their asking price and then doubled that again. Just no—real fucking simple. I was outright devastated about it. You were just turning eighteen, your father was getting ready to make the arrangement between our two families public, and I wanted you with me so badly by then."

"How did Nicoli get it, then?"

"The bastard planned it," Anton said, laughing. "Made me find the house I wanted, paid off the realtor and the owners to keep their mouths shut, and then bought it for me as a birthday gift. I was pissed off like nothing else, but he just sat there and smiled as he handed the keys over. Made his year."

"I really like this house."

The smile that lit up his face had her heart skipping beats. "Yeah?"

"Yeah," she admitted, shrugging a single shoulder. "I don't know. I guess it feels like home. Ours, really, even if I haven't been living in it. I didn't expect that and it scared me for a second."

Anton's teeth bit into his lower lip as his fists hid in pockets. It was an action she now recognized as him being nervous. "Why? Shouldn't that be a good thing?"

Viviana didn't know how to respond, instead avoiding his gaze and fingering the sheer curtain's fabric between her forefinger and thumb. There were so many things about the house that reminded her of the home she grew up in, and a million and one other things that screamed it was entirely different. Soft blankets on a California king sized bed that brought back heady, hot memories of similar bedding in a Barbados beach house.

Ready, that's what it was. Ready and waiting for her to

simply make herself at home, and Viviana didn't even have to do a thing. She couldn't bring herself to understand how it could feel that way; how Anton knew her so well. Knew that she wouldn't want something so massive it needed maids to clean it; knew that windows needed to be opposite to the beds so morning light would touch the sheets; knew ...

Knew that she would want a tiny cubby in her bedroom just waiting for a baby's crib to be placed inside.

He couldn't possibly have known those things, but instead wanted them, too.

So, maybe it had scared her for a moment. Because how else could someone react when their life, wants, and thoughts were being reflected in someone who could only know what they'd learned in one short week nine long years before? Finding her soul mate had been a scary thing when she was only sixteen, but finding him all over again when she was almost twenty-five and not expecting it was heart-stopping.

Viviana breathed through her nose, blinking at the hardwood floor. *Speak*, her mind ordered. *Say something*.

"I like this ... cubby, too."

Anton hummed a sound, staking a step forward into the room. "It was a second walk-in closet, but the room had more than enough storage space. It's nice to just relax or whatever, especially in the morning."

Something stuck in her throat. Words, likely, and overwhelming feelings.

"You didn't put it in for that, though, did you?"

"No, I didn't," he admitted, staring straight at her and seeming wholly unashamed. "And I hope it doesn't have you frightened."

Suddenly, Viviana was rambling, words spilling from her heart and mind. They wanted to get out; had to be said. Fought their way from her chest to tumble straight out trembling lips. Anton needed to hear them, she knew.

"I asked earlier about the business in the house because my father didn't keep it out, like at all. The garage was off-limits, his office, the library, and fuck, once we couldn't touch the freezer in the storage for a month and a half. I don't … damn it, Anton, I don't ever want that for my children. And what's worse is that I never wanted children because of this," she muttered, waving between their bodies.

"I don't understand."

"You and me before we were … you and me. I just thought of it as an arrangement—a duty. I knew I wouldn't get the choice. My husband would want children, so I'd have to do that, but that didn't mean I wanted them, okay? Why would I want my children being woken up to someone's screams, or God forbid, finding *teeth* in the fucking driveway while they rode bikes? Roman was a great father, but he was Boss first. He was the *Don.* I loved my dad, loved him so much …"

"I know you did," he whispered. Viviana hadn't realized how close he'd come to her until his hands were rubbing her shaking shoulders then cupping either side of her face. "Don't cry, baby. Not today, Viviana, please. Not in this room, not with me."

Always so soft and caring with her when she needed it most, it was just another striking contradiction to the man she thought he could have been.

"I didn't want children, Anton."

"I told you I wasn't expect—"

"I know what you told me," she interrupted, a little too sharply if his wince was any indication. "And I said *didn't.*"

Air cut through his teeth like a hiss. "Oh."

The heavy weight of what she confessed hung in the air and Viviana could only stay silent and let him absorb it. Children had been one thing, but the possibility of children with him had turned into something else entirely. Something so passionate and terrifying that it hurt her lungs when she breathed and made her heart kick-start all over again. A little voice said it wouldn't be the same as her life had been growing up, while another had a dozen and one reminders of just how it could be exactly that.

And it didn't even matter because standing in that almost bare cubby and thinking about what could be there felt so much better. Thinking about the three other bedrooms on the second floor that needed to be filled was scarily stirring. Her birth control shot would stop the moment Anton asked her to, and she knew it. There wasn't any question in her mind now, but fuck, it still ached.

Outside of the walls they called home, the two of them could be whomever they wanted or needed to be, but inside … inside was a different story altogether.

"If you want children someday, you have to understand what that means for us. Please don't do that to our children, okay? *Please*, Anton. Don't be that man first and their father second. If you give us a home, you need to make it one, too."

Anton cleared his throat before he murmured with a husky tone, "Okay, Vine."

*

There was a brief period where Anton simply didn't know what to say or do; he was still so damned wrapped up in the realization that Viviana wanted children. And not just children, no, *his* children. Sure, the thought has crossed his mind; he'd be flat out lying if he said it didn't, but he hadn't expected her to convey it the way she did, either.

Now that she'd brought up the topic, his mind was running rampant. Viviana wasn't the only one who had things to share. Especially on that front.

"This little room brought on all that, huh?"

"Yep."

Anton nodded, his hands still cradling Viviana's face as he said, "I'm not him, your dad, I mean. That's not to say he was doing wrong, either. By his … *family* … that's just how they roll. Sometimes things can't be helped and shit gets brought home when you don't intend for it to. Us—the bosses—we have to clean up after a lot of stuff that I can't even begin to explain, nor do I think you really need to know. But it happens; we manage, deal with it, move on …"

"I know," she whispered.

"And hope to fuck you'll forgive us in the morning," he finished even quieter. "I was fourteen the first time I walked in on something I shouldn't have. Daniil, his eyes were blank and black. No emotion, no fear, nothing. I didn't recognize him at first. He just handed over the jug of bleach and a bag of rags and told me to help after everyone calmed down."

"Jesus." A shudder rolled over her shoulders.

Anton shrugged. "It was also the first time I realized how groomed I had been from a really young age to accept what was going on around me. I didn't even blink; got down to the floor and cleaned the mess like he told me to. Scrubbed my fucking hands red raw, couldn't look my mother in the eye the next morning, and aced my English exam that afternoon.

"Like it always does, life went on," he said, trying not to sound as indifferent as he truly felt about it. Anton had a lot of time to pick apart his upbringing and the whys of the way it happened. "I finally understood why Dad and Nicoli's guys kept calling me the little prince then, too. Daniil never wanted to be the boss, he just wasn't meant to be one."

"But you were?" she asked.

"Yeah, I was. It was something about me, like I was reflecting Nicoli from the time I was small. Called me dangerous and magnetic—*significant*. I could focus it all when other guys couldn't. That didn't mean everyone wanted me to be the boss; the first year after Nicoli died was probably the most dangerous of my life. I made a lot of choices I didn't want to make and said goodbye to men who watched me grow up, but I did it because I was supposed to. That's what it took to make me what they knew I always would be."

"You shouldn't tell—"

Anton smiled grimly. "I'd have to be a little more specific than that to get myself in trouble, baby. My point, though, was that I never wanted that to be my boy. I don't want to teach him how to clean up a scene, never mind

175

having him see me as anything other than his father. Grooming my child to be like me? I can't even consider it."

"I hear a but in there," Viviana said, eyes lowering from his.

"Yeah, there's always one, right? *But*, sometimes we don't get the choice, Viviana. Sometimes it's just in his blood, so he seeks it out and once he's in, well, he's in. I'd so much rather he knew what to expect than stumble into it by mistake."

"I don't want to think about any of that. It shouldn't even be like that."

Anton licked his lips, sighing. "I'm sorry if it hurts you to hear, but whether you like it or not, it is something I have to think about should we ever have a boy. That's reality for me. It might be a rough one, but it's one nonetheless. I won't fault you for drawing comparisons, but don't fault me for knowing what I have to do … and I will do it, Vine. I won't lie about it."

Lines sometimes had to be drawn, Anton knew. It might be the limit that pushed her to say no children, and he'd accept that, but he wasn't about to lie to her. If Viviana was ready to take a hypothetical leap into the future, he was going to damn well make sure she understood just what it meant.

But the words she said next weren't the ones he thought she'd say, either.

"Don't tell me, okay? If we ever … It might not happen, but it doesn't matter. Never tell me."

Could he even? Would he be able to tell her the first time their son pulled the trigger; when he learned what it was like to enjoy the spoils of being the son of a boss; when he came home with the tattoos of a rose on his chest and stars on his shoulders? Or would he just let him always be her son?

No, Anton knew what he'd do. It'd be the same thing as his father did; his hand grasping tight to his son's jaw, forcing him to stare into blank eyes when he said the words, "Don't you ever tell your mother about this. Never."

Once more, he rolled his thumbs over her cheeks to soothe and wipe away tears. It hurt him to see her struggling, especially if it was with something that should been an exciting, joyous topic, but nothing about their lifestyle was really simple in the end. Everything was double edged.

"That a rule to remember?" he asked.

"That's a rule."

Anton nodded, leaning down to catch her frown with his lips. "Understood."

Chapter Thirteen

Cool air whispered along Viviana's bare legs, pebbling her skin at its passing with goose bumps. The quiet sounds of the Brighton Beach boardwalk hummed around the pair, but neither seemed to notice the passersby. With Viviana up on the hood of Anton's Mercedes, he stood on the ground between her legs with his arms wrapped around her shoulders. His chin rested on the top of her head, and they were quiet. Somewhere along the line, one of them decided they had spoken enough and the comfortable, close silence ensued.

"Too heavy," he'd told her before they left the Oceana house. "It's my birthday, and we made this day way too heavy with all this nonsense. Between last night, this morning, the ring, and this? We need to take five minutes away from all of it and chill out."

And so, they ended up at the boardwalk. With the sky just beginning to darken and wind picking up from an oncoming storm, most of the people at the pier had left. The few stragglers that were there were also making their way home, so despite the cold as October was coming to an end, Viviana was happy … content.

"We're going to be late," she mumbled, not even bothering to try to move out of his strong grasp. The party started at eight, and the club would open at ten for regular services.

"We already are."

"Oh. Damn."

His broad shoulders shrugged. "They expected me to be late. It's fashionable, or so I've been told."

Well, she was quite relaxed, so it wasn't like she was going to complain. "Okay."

"*Ya lyublyu tyebya*," Anton murmured.

The sweetest feathers of his kisses dotted down the

bridge of her nose as Russian rolled off his tongue like dark molasses. Very rarely did she hear him speak it, and usually he only conversed in that language when it was a conversation she wouldn't want to be a part of anyway. Still, there was something about those unknown words that called to her, drawing Viviana closer into his embrace and body. Anton held her a little tighter, repeating the same phrase again as his mouth brushed over hers.

"I don't understand."

"I know," he said, laughing deeply. "You should learn, even if it's only a few choice phrases."

"Italian and English is enough," she replied, nipping at his cheek playfully. "What did you say?"

"I love you."

"Oh." Viviana tried to repeat the words he'd said, failing miserably and getting another round of his laughter at the lame attempt. "Ugh. Never mind."

"*Ya tozhe tyebya lyublyu*. Try it."

"That's not what you said first." Now she was starting to wonder if he was just fucking her around. "Are you being smart?"

Anton winked. "No. But good catch. It's the reply, working in both feminine and masculine forms, *katyonak*."

"*Kat* ... what?"

"Cat is close," he teased. "Kitten, actually."

Viviana made a face. "No thanks."

"Well, I wasn't about to call you a pussy. There's about ten different ways to say it and none of them mean nice things in Russian You're going to hear a lot of this muttering tonight, although it'll be nothing you'll want to learn, but you might as well get used to it. Come on, try it," he urged, hands slipping up under her coat to splay against her stomach. "Say it slowly. *Ya. Tozhe. Tyebya. Lyublyu*."

Viviana tried the words again and again until she'd finally managed the pronunciations to his satisfaction. At the sight of his smirk, she knew he liked hearing Russian in her mouth a lot more than he was letting on. Tugging on the collar of his buttoned-up suit jacket, she brought him back to her level again.

"I love you, too."

That smirk curved into a brilliant smile. "All right, it's better like that. You ready—"

The sudden sheet of rain stopped his words up short. She shrieked at the cold droplets splashing down over her head, keeping her face hidden and hoping to God the bit of makeup she still had left on wouldn't be ruined.

"Shit … get in the car." Anton groaned, pulling her down off the hood and steadying her with one arm. "Go, go, go."

Heels slipped on the slick pavement, but it wasn't long before Viviana found herself shoved inside the dry vehicle. Of course, where she landed wasn't quite where she expected, either: across the back seat. Anton was right behind her, slamming the door hard as his chuckles echoed inside the cab.

"Well, damn it."

"I think you messed up where we were supposed to go," she said, struggling to get upright, her voice still breathless. It certainly didn't help that large hands were gripping both of her thighs up under the short skirt of her dress. "We need to get to the club."

Anton made a dismissive sound. "Take your clothes off, Vine."

"Excuse me?"

He waved at the sopping wet coat she had on. It was already seeping through to the dress. "Hurry, before it wrinkles the hell out of your dress. We'll lay it over the seat, let it dry out a little and then go."

"Anton, we're in a public parking lot." The words came out slowly, as if she were speaking to a small child. "Anybody could just walk right by and see."

"Nope, glass is tinted too dark."

Viviana groaned. "I'm not—"

"Take it off."

He didn't give her another chance to refuse, snapping open the buttons to her tweed coat and pulling it down her shoulders before it fell like a heavy lump of wet wool to the floor. Under his influence, she turned to let him unzip the back of her dress, too. When the black garment was slung over the front driver's seat, Anton made quick work of removing his own. The grey silk shirt, black tie, and jacket hung off the passenger's seat.

After staring out the window and watching the few cars left in the parking lot zoom out, Viviana was satisfied no one would notice her nakedness. The cool leather of the back seat met her back as she lay down across it. Leaning between the two front seats, Anton dug for something up front before she heard the low purr of the engine starting. Quickly, he was back between her thighs with a cell phone in hand. Warmth blew through the heaters almost instantly.

"Seven forty-five," he informed her. Hot kisses danced from the line of her thong up to her navel. She weaved her fingers into the hair on the crown of his head as he looked up and grinned a wicked sight. "We might be more than a little late."

With the heat of his hips pressing into the lace of her covered sex, Viviana wasn't really sure she cared anymore. "You just wanted to get me naked and in the backseat of a Mercedes."

"Maybe. The dress would have wrinkled, so it was a perfectly plausible excuse to get you out of your clothes."

"You don't need an excuse."

"Sometimes I like to think I have to work for it, okay? Let me have this."

Viviana snorted. "All right, work for it, *Boss*."

Anton growled a hoarse, sexy noise that had her soaked from the sound alone. Just as his lips lowered to kiss the sensitive flesh at the inside of her thigh, that cell phone he'd dropped to the floor began ringing. There wasn't anything quite like bad timing, and by the specific ringtone that was chiming through, she knew it was one of her bulls.

Anton cussed and grappled for the device, holding it up to his ear. "What?" A beat of murmuring passed on the other end before he huffed. "Yes I know what time the fucking party starts and no, I don't care. Where are you, anyway?"

"We can go," Viviana piped in, but the shake of his head had her sighing.

"Three rows down?" Anton asked. Pushing his frame up, he squinted out the back window. "Yeah, I see you now. Are you holding anything?"

Viviana's heart sped up at the question. Once she'd asked about her guards beyond just who they were and why he'd chosen them for her, and Anton hadn't given her much to go on other than he trusted them more than some. When she wondered about drugs, given the occasional smell of pot coming from the back end of the house, he'd shrugged and said he didn't care so long as they weren't using anything chemical-wise. It wasn't like she did, either.

"Shit, *yeah*. Cali grown … Bring that to me, would you?" At her light tap to his bare chest, Anton only grinned in response. What in the hell was he planning on getting? "Yes right now. The rain isn't going to kill you, Rory. You're not made of fucking sugar. Stop acting like a whiney prick."

Oh God. Crass would be an understatement. His mouth only got worse when she did understand what he was saying. Viviana could only imagine the words he spit in Russian when somebody irked him into a shouting match.

"Anton!"

He ignored her completely, keeping all of his attention on his phone. "You have thirty seconds or I'm coming over there and I can promise you won't like it. I bet it costs one hell of a buck to replace a damned headlight in that SUV. And keep your fucking eyes out of my windows, got it?"

Before the phone was tossed back to the floor, Viviana swore she heard the younger man mutter, "Got it, Boss."

"What did you do?"

"Nothing too bad. Might as well have a little fun before we have to go and be serious, right? Now, quiet that pretty mouth of yours and let me work here."

Her lover's lips found their way back to her thigh before she could say another thing, trailing a burning path over the crotch of her panties where his teeth nipped gently. Sizzling sparks burst along her already pulsing sex. When his hands pushed her thighs wider, they skimmed down her legs lightning fast. The throaty hum that built in her chest only urged him on, until two raps on the glass interrupted his wandering fingers.

The window lowered only a single inch when Anton pressed the button behind her head with one quick tap. Two fingers popped inside the car, a pin-sized joint dangling between the digits before it disappeared out of Viviana's sight into the hand reaching above her.

"That all, Boss?"

"Yep."

Just as quick, the bull was gone and the window rolled back up. Anton's heated blue gaze leveled on Viviana with a sinful gleam as the joint was waved almost tauntingly, his head lowering enough for a pink tongue to strike out and lap at her stomach.

"You gonna smoke with me, baby?"

"Should I?"

"Oh, you definitely should."

*

Anton's parted lips skimmed up Viviana's neck as he held the harsh hit he'd just inhaled inside his lungs. He could feel it, the smoke, tumbling through his chest and making it ache with the best burn as he bit the trembling line of her tilted up jaw.

Her hips straddling him shifted in the most tantalizing way, muscles constricting and the sensitive tissues of her pussy fluttering around his cock that was buried balls deep inside her hot core. The action made him groan loudly, allowing just the faintest billow of smoke to escape his mouth. The wisps curled over her face as her lashes blinked and fluttered, fanning over her cheeks. Another roll of her body and his hummed in response with a high induced by her and California grown bud.

The pungent, thick scent of weed in the Mercedes soaked straight through everything, including his very skin. It wasn't often he got high, but when he did, he preferred a certain kind of smoke to get him there because it simply fucking electrified his nerves like nothing else. Mix that sensation in with Viviana riding his cock above him with a slow, teasing rhythm and he was just about ready to explode.

Nothing ever felt so damned good.

Anton had been a little more than surprised to watch her take hit after hit off the joint and never once choke on the smoke, never mind how goddamn sexy it was to see it roll off her lips. He'd dragged the straps of her lace brassier down her shoulders, kissing and biting her collarbone until it blushed with a pretty pink under his rough motions, just before he removed the item from her body completely.

"Hmm … *there* … yeah, right there," she breathed, shifting to rock on him again. Her one hand was lifted, fingers brushing against the soft roof of the car as she tilted her head back farther, giving him better access to the hollow of her throat. The other scratched down the black inked rose that covered his pec with shaking fingers. "More, *Boss*."

Oh, he heard that title three dozen times a day, but nothing quite compared to the way it dripped like silken honey from her sinful little tongue. Fuck, her airless voice had him throbbing. From his fingers, to his toes, to dilated pupils, he burned. With the hand that wasn't holding the small blunt, he pinched her chin between his forefinger and thumb to draw her head downward.

She shot-gunned the smoke he gave without even hesitating. Anton felt the heavy pressure build inside his middle a little more, causing his heart to stutter and begin to race. It wasn't just the situation or the smoke that had him feeling so damned sentimental, but the woman above him always trusting and willing.

"Right there?" he asked, bracing his one foot to the

floor and the other to the seat as he flexed his hips up into hers. Viviana shuddered on top of him, eyes flying open as air and second-hand smoke blew over his cheeks. "You love my cock, huh? Who fills you like this, Viviana?"

"You. Only you."

He was thankful his pants had joined the rest of his clothes because her juices had soaked him beautifully. They'd been teasing and touching for only a short while, but he had her just about wet and ready enough to take her like he knew she wanted.

"Who gives you this feeling?" he asked.

Another rock, another roll, another lift of her body on his shaft and she trembled with a cry. Achingly full, that's how he felt. Damp from sweat, sticky with her, high with smoke, and topped with *love*. It dripped down every nerve in his body like liquid gold.

"You."

"Mmm …who's yours, baby?"

Pink lips curved around the half inch roach he offered, sucking in a good puff before she whispered, "You."

Sixteen and curious she wasn't anymore. Hesitation didn't flicker in brown eyes, hands moved with knowing yearning, and words fell like a beautiful song. She was so far from the same it hurt, but she still wasn't any different, either.

It was the third time in less than twenty-four hours that he'd had her body, and it didn't feel any less intense than the last time. Anton wouldn't ever tire of the way it felt, or how she pulled him deeper inside than he ever thought possible. Overwhelming and wholly gone, she had him broken to pieces and put back together again in one swift motion.

So close, he was so fucking close to telling her everything he'd been hiding. Anton didn't want to keep the things he knew that she didn't inside any longer. Beyond the way she had him tied all the way around her like a protective, wanting bow, he also knew the secrets he held felt like personal bars of a terrible prison he shouldn't have ever been inside.

Smoke billowed again, twisting in thick spirals to the roof, clouding his vision and the car.

"Feel me. Always." It came out soft and torn, almost like an admission forced from a ripped open heart. His thumb rolled over her lips, down her chin and throat, between perky breasts and the flat expanse of her stomach. Viviana swallowed a gulp of nothing when the tips of his fingers slipped deftly over the hood of her clit and drummed a circling beat. "Almost, yeah?"

A lazy nod answered him back, her body tensing and gently rocking hips still moving. "Yeah."

The rhythmic clenching of her walls around his dick had him moaning. Her orgasm was so close he could practically feel it clawing its way through his veins himself. But, Anton wanted her sweating more, panting harder, with her body, nerves, and sex singing from smoke and bliss before he filled her in a whole new way.

Still, Viviana didn't make the move to quicken her riding pace, keeping it unhurried and delicious in the most provokingly lustful way. Anton's head fell back to the seat as her breath caught on the exhale. Removing his hand from between her thighs, those fast-rising breasts of hers caught his palm one after the other, his thumb rolling over taut nipples that felt hot to the touch.

One light draw off the roach and he blew a perfect line of thick smoke from her neck down to her stomach, letting the sharp-tasting weed roll over her skin in billowing waves. Her teeth cut into her bottom lip, reddening the plump flesh to the same hue as her swollen, wet sex. Viviana mewled with the quietest whine of need that said she was so close to toppling under the building pressure that her spine was beginning to curve and her head drew farther back.

"God, yes. I'm creeping up so hard. We gonna do this?"

Oh, she'd been so surprised when he waved a condom he brought back from the front console before they'd really gotten started. They didn't fuck with them, didn't have to, and he wouldn't ever so long as she was only his, but he'd use one this time and she got his point in wanting to straightaway. There wasn't fear in her voice when she agreed, but he heard the quiet waver even so. It wasn't like he blamed her; despite the toy they'd played with earlier, his cock was longer and thicker and sure to make her ache.

Anton hummed his assent, feeling that heat sizzle in his blood as a buzz roamed his mind. "Yeah, just wanted you rolling hard first."

Her fingernails dragged along the ceiling, waves of her hair tumbling down her back, and he caught her free hand curving his jaw with a quick turn of his head, laying a loud open-mouthed kiss to her palm. A shiver rolled over every muscle in her body as two of her slender fingers slid between his lips. His tongue swirled around the digits, tasting the weed and her arousal on her skin.

"Oh … almost," she sighed, lips smacking as the trembling in her legs grew a bit more.

"One more, just the one. Take it and give it back," Anton murmured, reaching up to tug on the few strands of hair that had fallen over her shoulder gently. "Come on, I want to taste it out of your sweet mouth."

With her face leaning down close to his again, his hazy line of vision cleared enough to watch her drag that last hit off the joint hard. Viviana let the smoke roll from her lips upward, French inhaling the final pull from the joint as their gazes met. The pelting rain outside had dimmed to practically nothing at all, but the thundering storm clouds remained, keeping the car dark. The humidity in the air mixed with the heat of their sex and the whispers of smoke fogged up the windows.

"Hold it hard, don't let it out until I want it, hmm?"

Again, her teeth bared to his cheek when he pulled her close to kiss her eyelids. When his mouth found hers, a tongue was quick to spear into wet heat, allowing the exhale from her lungs to inhale into his. The harshness of the weed was lessened with her taste and he burned all over again.

Their lips moved a leisurely speed, slow enough to taste and relish and seek.

Then, her high and broken cry of his name caught in his mouth. The walls of her pussy clamped down tight with the sudden sweep of her orgasm, holding him in as his hand grasped her hip. When her eyes glazed and hands shook, she gasped another one of those sighing sounds. He let her roll out the waves of bliss.

"Just like that, baby. Up, raise up for a moment."

"*Now?*" Viviana asked breathlessly.

"Mmhmm. Right now."

"It's going to *hurt.*"

"Some," he said, not wanting to lie. "Not for long, I promise."

With a quick movement, Anton had the window rolled down just enough to toss the stub out. At the same time, Viviana had lifted up, her still trembling-thighs straddling his sides. In a flash his hand was between their bodies, grasping his shaft at the base as her hips tilted upwards and forwards and her spine arched to give him better access to her back entrance.

He needed her steady, wanted her movements controlled and careful. Given the toy had prepped her a little and she had soaked him with more than enough of her fluids to give them plenty of lubrication, it could be an easy go for her first time … or if she went too fast, took him too hard, it might not.

Viviana didn't give him the chance to get her steady or careful. The moment the latex-covered head of his cock slid against the tight hole of her ass, she was pressing down on his length all over again. Damn, he could feel her vibrating under the hand that was splayed to her back … muscles practically shuddering with want and need, so beautifully harsh.

Beads of perspiration had dampened the valley between her breasts. That pink stain she'd applied to her lips earlier was all but gone, but they were kissed and bitten so red she didn't need to put on any more. The dark kohl that had lined her lids was smudged at the corners, making her eyes look deeper and smoky.

Anton went to speak, to tell her to take it slow, to breathe, to calm down, but the ring of muscles and walls of sensitive tissues that flexed and stretched to take him in had his throat tightening like a vise. The channel of her ass felt like velvet gripping steel.

The fit of her ass around his shaft *was* tight. Tight like his teeth gritting between parted lips. Tight like his fingers squeezing to dig into her waist. Just fucking tight and hot. Too goddamn tight. So tight it hurt and his eyes flew open, flicking up to seek out hers.

Before he'd even really knew how it happened, Viviana had sunk down his length totally, taking in his cock completely. The pulse in his shaft increased. Anton swallowed, blinked, and forced himself to breathe again so he could think for a moment.

The flicker of pain that flitted over her features had his grip tightening. "Baby …"

Viviana whined under her breath, air rushing from her nose as her eyes screwed shut. Suddenly, her hands clenched into balled fists on his chest. It was clear she couldn't quite find words to say, or she wasn't able. Either way, the last thing he wanted to see in her eyes was *pain*.

Finally, his voice was working again as he slid those hands up her spine and drove her forward into his embrace, shushing a low sound in her ear. Gently, he rolled the tips of his fingers over her trembling shoulders. Her face buried into his neck with another noise that had his heart racing and guilt rising. He could feel her bearing down.

Shit, he should have slowed her the fuck down.

"You all right?"

"*No.* Jesus Christ." Air blew in a huff against his neck before she whispered, "Out, I want it—"

"Okay, okay."

Keeping his hands splayed open on her back, Anton urged her body upwards much slower than she had lowered herself onto his length. With the feeling of muscles rippling around his cock, he found himself biting the inside of his cheek to ignore the sweet burning hum that swept throughout his entire nervous system.

Fucking hell, she was still tighter than a fist and hotter than fire.

Then, Viviana sighed shakily, her legs almost relaxing. Her fists unclenched and the pads of fingers pressed down softly to each of his pecs.

"*Wait.*" The word didn't even sound like it came from her, but more like built up pressure that burst from somewhere inside. Raw and aching, that's how it felt caressing his senses. "Just … oh God, do that again."

Anton swallowed thickly. "I didn't do anything."

"That … I-I don't know … *that*, Anton."

Still not knowing what it was she wanted, he pressed a kiss to her temple, smoothing out her hair and waiting for the turmoil of emotions running through his soul to simmer. He flinched as she lowered onto his length once more. Again, her teeth clenched, air hissed, and her fists balled.

But when she raised … Oh, fuck, when she raised, her chest expanded with a tumbling moan that rocked him to the core. It almost felt like the inside of her channel was grasping even harder on the withdrawal, wanting to keep him inside. Warmth created by her and the buzzing high still creeping around his senses licked like flames over his skin.

"*That,*" she repeated in a breath.

Anton nodded. Releasing his hold on her back, he untangled her curled fingers on his chest and weaved them with his own. Pressing feather-light kisses to her knuckles, he let her stretch and open around his cock, feeling muscles relax ever so slightly with every single slow rise and fall. Pants of her breaths turned a little faster against his neck. When her fingernails bit into the skin of his hands, she moaned a deep noise as the tightening in his groin increased.

"That," Anton echoed.

Her mouth ghosted over his cheek, searching out his as

the air turned a little thicker, a little damper. Bright eyes with darkened, widened pupils met his own as her forehead pressed down to his and lips curled back with another low whine. The desperate expression taking over her features was the most beautiful sight.

"You got this, huh?"

"Yeah," she said all airless but still full. "I got this."

Chapter Fourteen

"*Oh*. Look at you, grinning like a goddamn fool," Ivan said, grabbing the back of Anton's neck with a tight grip to pull the younger man forward. Their foreheads met, both men smiling as his lawyer sighed. "Forty-five minutes late to your own birthday party. I think that's a new record. Be extra nice tonight to the older ones, yeah? They were in a right fit about your tardiness."

"You told me to be late," Anton muttered when Ivan released him. "And besides, I had things to do."

"Oh yeah? Things, someone, same difference."

"No, *things*." Another disbelieving look crossed Ivan's face before Anton chuckled. "Fine, asshole. That, too."

Ivan's finger ticked up under the boss's chin as he regarded him with a cocked brow. "I called Rory, just to make sure everything was good at eight and guess what he told me? Not that it matters," he said quickly with a sly smirk. "Because I can smell the smoke on your jacket and see it in your eyes. *Zhopa*. I've been asking him for months to give me some of that bud. Boss gets all nasty for a moment and he hands it right over like a scared boy."

Anton glanced over Ivan's shoulder, watching as the bull in question leaned over the bar to greet Jen. But, his bartender wasn't having it, ignoring the man's advances but offering him a wink instead. Viviana, on the other hand, was given a hug over the bar top, her chin picked up in Jen's hand as she forced her to look in her eyes. Both women laughed. When Jen spotted Viviana's new engagement ring, it was hard not to notice how fifteen other gazes turned to watch as the jewelry was appraised and shown off.

"*Zaebis'*. Can't keep your eyes off of her for more than a minute, can you?" Ivan asked, shaking his head.

"No. No, I really can't."

Damn, he wasn't even ashamed to admit it.

"You've had her at your side all day, Anton!"

A flippant, lazy shrug fell from his shoulders. His mind was still running high with a sizzling buzz while his body, blood, and heart were still singing with an awe-worthy tune. He was outright fucking exhausted, physically and emotionally. Even so, he was nearly revving and ready to go all over again, already wanting to take her back to the safe house and get her between soft sheets.

Only his girl could do that to him like she did. Only her.

Anton had kept his word to Viviana after all when it came to her first time trying anal. It only hurt a short time, and then she calmed, her body adjusted, and with her bottom lip caught between his teeth, fingers weaved with his, and her name in his mouth, she broke in the most beautiful way. They took their time cleaning up, getting dressed, and then making their way to the club.

Now, he just wanted to simply *watch* her.

His birthday. His party. His people.

Anton didn't give a shit. All he wanted was Viviana.

He watched the seven spotlights that worked on a mechanical system above do their slow crawl over the club's floor. White light pooled at her feet where she stood still chatting animatedly to Jen. The crystals embedded in her heels reflected colored prisms up the backs of her legs and she leaned a little farther in to hear what the other woman was saying. That only served to drive her tight-as-fuck dress higher around the curves of slightly swaying hips.

Oh God, she was so beautiful it hurt. Even though her makeup was all but gone from the rain, even with her hair mussed from his hands and the damp weather, and even in a club's darkness, she was *beautiful.* From his spot in the corner, Anton had the perfect line of vision for her profile. High cheekbones, a straight-edge, tiny nose, pink lips with the top a little bit fuller than the bottom, and almond-shaped eyes pooled with a deep, chocolate brown. The plains of her face fit so well in the hold of his hands, too.

"I'm …"

Ivan's brow furrowed at Anton's loss of words. It wasn't often he was rendered speechless, and given his status, he nearly always had to be saying something. And usually it had to be important. Anton's best friend clapped his shoulder and his hand squeezed gently.

"You're what, man?"

Anton swallowed the lump forming in his throat. "I'm so fucking in love with that girl."

A cough covered the fleeting surprise in Ivan's eyes. Anton had made the admission with the company of several other Bratva brothers close by. He'd said it without care, open and bared. It didn't even matter because it was so damned true it hurt. Sometimes it wasn't safe to admit where your heart and feelings lay, no matter who you were. Anton couldn't help it.

"Yeah, just … crazy in love, Ivan. I'm not even here right now, not in my heart. I'm over there."

"You smoked too much, clearly. You always said you loved her."

Anton nodded, shoving his hands in his pockets to hide the slight tremble that rocked them. "I know, but I was remembering a different girl at a different time, you know? This girl … God, she's *mine*. That's all there is to it."

"That's … okay, Anton. More than, even. It's great, especially for you. People grow up and shit changes, so you and she might not have clicked again like you did the first time. It just so happened that you two grew at the same pace again, even separated like you were. Maybe old Nicoli had seen something no one else did when you were four and she was two. God knows that fool had a knack for picking out gold in dirt and he did it more than once."

"Did he ever tell you it was me who called her Vine first?" Anton asked quietly, blue eyes flitting up to stare at Viviana again.

"No, he didn't."

Anton sighed heavily, forcing himself to look at his

friend.

"Yeah. When I asked about her name nine years ago, she told me the nickname came from her brother. Her *brother*, Ivan. They told her *he* couldn't say it properly. They didn't tell her it was really me. I couldn't speak a word of English when I was four, and I guess when they told me her name, I couldn't get it to roll off my tongue right. So Vine it was.

"Nicoli said she pointed at her chest," Anton said, voice turning into a whisper as his hand raised to his own chest and fingers splayed wide open. "Right where her little heart beat and repeated it, just like that. It stuck her whole life. I gave her that name. I fucking marked that girl as mine when she was just two years old in my own way. She's always been mine."

Ivan cleared his throat, his foot tapping a nervous beat to the floor before he asked, "What's bothering you right now. I mean, this is a good thing, yeah?"

"Yeah, so good. Spending the rest of my life with her seems like the most natural thing next to breathing. It's absolutely fucking terrifying to hand that feeling over like it's nothing. Loving her every day; watching her live; holding her hand when she gives me children; weaving together through this life … I want that so badly and it would be the easiest thing to do because she's already got my goddamn heart and soul right there in her hands. No one has ever had that from me."

"But?"

But his heart was aching and his soul was ripping. Strings were pulled taut as something plucked a painful rhythm to the beats. Anton felt guilty as fuck. Shame was eating him alive and he never felt like that about anything he'd ever done before. He didn't have the right to share those feelings and have those profound expectations for her and him if she didn't *know* what he did.

"I have to tell her, Ivan. I *need* to."

"Shit."

Apparently his friend had decided their conversation was no longer appropriate to be had in the presence of others, because Ivan cussed harshly again before looking over his shoulder. With a jerk of his head, both men slipped through an employee only door that led to the kitchen. The club didn't offer a huge variety of items on the menu when it was open, but it made a few easy things and there was a cook who worked only in the daytime for Anton and his business associates.

"Out," Anton snapped at the chef who peeked up over the metal stove. "Now."

"Uh … kind of busy—"

"Get the fuck out," Ivan hissed.

The man rolled his eyes before turning a burner off and taking his sweet time wiping his hands on a hanging towel. When he was finally gone from the kitchen, Anton snapped the lock on the swinging door, effectively preventing anyone from coming inside before locking the other swinging door as well.

"I know you're rolling right now," Ivan said quietly. "It's not like you roll often and when you do, you get all thoughtful and whatnot. So, is this your heart talking or the boss talking? Because it's important for me to know the difference and right now, Anton, I can't tell."

"Maybe both."

"What do you need from me? Tell me what you need from me. I can't do this if you don't."

Anton chewed on the inside of his cheek, refusing to meet the other man's stare. It was times like this when he was glad Nicoli had given him the insight he had before his unexpected death. His step-grandfather could have just as well let Anton slip and stumble through finding the right Sovietnik to guide him, to be his partner and friend, but instead, Ivan had all but been placed at his feet.

Sure, Ivan was five years older with a wife he loved and two little girls, and another on the way, who were his whole world … the men were leaps and bounds apart from each other in the world at times. But when it counted—when it *really* fucking counted—Ivan just knew Anton. He knew what to say or what to do, he knew how to ask or when to back off. They were brothers beyond the Bratva, beyond the titles, and beyond DNA. They just were.

They were one hell of a pair. Unstoppable when they wanted something. Anton and Ivan respectively held the two highest titles in their organization and some thought it wouldn't be a good match, but they were fucking brilliant together. It was yet another one of Nicoli's gold in the dirt findings.

"Fuck … just be my friend, okay?"

Ivan made a noise under his breath. "I don't think I can. Not if we're talking about what I think we're talking about. I have to be yours and Nicoli's lawyer. I have to be the Sovietnik. You have to be Boss. You know this. I have his wishes to carry out just like you do, Anton!"

"We are talking about that, and I know where your mind is going," Anton murmured, swallowing hard and finally looking up. "If this was Eva, wouldn't you want to tell her the truth?"

"Don't bring my wife into this. It's not the same. You gave him your word."

"He's dead. They're all dead!"

"Lower your voice, man," Ivan snapped, shooting a fleeting look at the doors. "Tell me why this is coming up now."

Anton gave himself a moment to breathe, flexing his fingers into fists and cracking his knuckles before he felt able to speak. "This doesn't make a difference to the will. The money Nicoli left for her isn't mine to touch, and the prenuptial agreement keeps it safe. She'll always be taken care of in that regard. It doesn't hurt the brotherhood. If anything, the ones that know respect her more because of who she is and the rest would think the same. It won't affect Nicoli because he's gone, and her mother, may she rest in peace, no longer needs to be protected from the secret getting out.

Roman is six feet underground and Sonny is a breath away from losing his life. Who does this really hurt, Ivan?"

"Viviana," Ivan whispered, almost pleadingly. "You know that. It would hurt her."

"I know. I *know* it would, but I think … I think she deserves to know. Vine could see from the start that we were hiding something and she asked. She *asked*, okay? I told him if she found out, I would tell her, and I said that never would I tell her directly before she figured it all out, but I also told him—"

"That you wouldn't lie if she asked," Ivan interjected. "Yeah, I remember."

"I don't want to lie to her anymore. I never want her to find out that I kept on lying when I could have told her the truth. She talked about Roman today, and I could hear it in her voice—she loved that man. I just … shit, why can't she have the chance to love the one she didn't know, too?"

"Anton—"

"I love this girl, Ivan. *Love* her more than anything. She makes my heart beat like nobody else. I can't keep doing this."

Ivan blinked up at the ceiling before he asked, "So what are you going to do?"

"Tell her. Put it all out there. Let her choose what she wants. I'll protect her no matter what. I'm going to love her until the day I die, and it won't make a difference if she chooses me or not because she owns me regardless of the rest."

"Okay." And just like that, Ivan seemed to understand Anton like he always had. Crossing the short distance, the older man offered opened arms and Anton took the embrace with a quiet sigh. "Happy birthday, huh?"

"It's been a great fucking day, actually."

"Because of her?"

"Always," Anton confessed. When Ivan pulled away with a sentimental looking smile, he offered a shrug as his only explanation. "She makes everything so much better.

Managed to keep my mind off Daniil, not to mention the bullshit going on with the Italians."

"And you want to risk giving that up just so she'll know a truth that's never really affected her before?"

"Hasn't it? An arranged marriage. Lost out on a culture and history she might have loved. Never knew her fath—"

"She had Roman."

"She had a *dad*," Anton stressed. "She didn't know her *father*. There's a difference and she missed out on a great man because of it."

"That was how he wanted it."

Anton refused to accept that. He never would. Good men didn't work that way.

Deciding to change directions, he asked, "Were you going to visit Daniil tomorrow?"

"Yeah, of course," Ivan said, looking confused. "Why?"

"I was going to first thing in the morning, but I got a call about an issue with the restaurant over on the east side. I need to handle that immediately. I'm supposed to be at the bakers at noon with her, and I won't miss it if I go early. I think I'll sit her down and tell her after that, but maybe she could go with you to the hospital if you have time to stop by."

"You're going to tell her tomorrow?"

Anton shrugged indifferently again, but even the action felt as heavy as his heart. "Yeah. Not tonight. I can't do it tonight."

"Not tonight," his friend echoed softly.

"No. She gave me a beautiful day, Ivan. One amazing day with just me and her. I'll give her this tomorrow."

"Okay."

*

Viviana squealed as arms caught her around the waist, pulling her body into his. Lips pressed to the back of her neck with loud chuckles. Instantly she melted into Anton's hand, sighing a quiet breath of air when his nose skimmed behind her ear.

"Sore?" Anton whispered.

Viviana shook her head, feeling heat crawl over her cheeks. "Not really. Starting to get tired."

"Good to know. I need to get you home, in a hot bath, and in bed so I can crawl between those fucking legs again and get you making all those pretty sounds of yours."

"Holy hell," she breathed. "Haven't you had enough yet?"

"Nope. You have no idea what you do to me, Viviana."

Going back to the safe house didn't seem like such a bad idea. "How much longer?"

Anton shrugged. "We were late, so maybe we leave at ten-thirty just to make sure our faces have been seen enough. We're just about to open for regular business, so a lot of people are going to clear out anyway. Everyone being good?"

"Yeah, great."

"Okay." He hummed a dark sound, letting her hips sway with the heavy bass in the music. "Love you."

Viviana reached up and patted his cheek. "I know. *Ty nuzhen mnye*. Always, Anton."

He froze behind her, his arms tightening their strong grip. His fingers dug deliciously into her side, drawing her backside harder into his groin as the bass picked up a little more. Lights flickered around them and people kept talking, but Viviana knew they were being watched. The choked noise he made told her she got the pronunciation perfect.

I need you.

And she did, in more ways than he knew.

"Oh, baby. Who taught you that?" he asked.

Another quiet laugh fell into the air. It was funny that he asked, considering all the conversations she'd had in the last little while. It could have been just about anyone, but Viviana only trusted very few to actually give her the right translation to use.

"Why, you going to go all boss on them for it?"

"No. Thank them, maybe. That was just … *fuck*."

"Rory. I couldn't find Ivan."

"His wife arrived a little bit ago. She wasn't supposed to come because she was at her mother's and she's quite pregnant. Ivan was just getting her to go back home ... Rory as in your bull *Rory*, really?"

"Yep. Blushed like a schoolboy when I asked. He was hitting on Jen again. Girl should give him a shot. She could totally pull off the cougar thing."

"She could, but I have a rule about employees dating my guys."

"You should bend it."

"I'll think about it."

She tried to ignore the dozen curious gazes that watched their near silent interaction. They couldn't hear his low, sexy words in her ear, but they could clearly see his lips skimming her neck as he spoke, the way his body pressed into her back to fit them tight together, and the way her breath had picked up just by his close contact. It seemed anytime she moved during the evening, someone was always watching.

She'd already had a dozen and one conversations with people she didn't know from Eve. Sweet drinks were constantly being brought over from one of the three girls working the floor with a wink stating this was from another so and so. Viviana was overwhelmed. It wasn't that they weren't nice because everyone was very respectful, but it was a lot to take in all at once.

"Where'd you disappear off to, anyway?" Anton asked with a smooth, black molasses tone. Those lips of his ghosted behind the shell of her ear, teeth nipping at a sensitive spot. "One second you were at my side, and the next, gone."

"Someone wanted to dance."

Ouch.

His fingers squeezed tighter. Viviana's breath caught as a dark sound rumbled in her ear.

"Who?"

"Anton." Turning in his grasp, she met his cocked

brow. "Stop it."

"I told you. Jealous motherfucker ..." he warned, pointing at his chest with one finger, "who is no way afraid to cut a fool for putting hands on what's mine."

With two fingers, she reached up and tapped his lips gently to shut them up. The last thing they needed was him going all possessive right there because it served to do nothing for her self-control, of which she had little to none as it was when it came to him.

"All the guys have been super respectful, or they're just really terrified you'd bite their heads off if they even suggested I dance with them. So, while you were talking with Ivan ..."

Anton cringed. "Sorry, it was kind of important."

"Erik's wife asked me to dance."

"Oh, well ..."

"Not so bad if it's a woman, then, huh?" she asked, jokingly.

As she looked up, she caught the fleeting sadness in his eyes that usually looked so happy whenever he was holding on to her. That was the very last thing she expected to see. Especially after the day they had, and considering how well his party was going, Anton should have been radiating his usual calm, pleased attitude.

"What's wrong?"

When his blue eyes glanced down again, the brief emotion she witnessed was all but gone. "Nothing, baby."

"Anton, did something happen?"

A tick in his jaw caught her notice before he shook his head. "Nope. Nothing."

"So everything is good, then?"

"Yeah, of course. Why?"

He was deflecting. Now, Viviana was positive there was something wrong.

"I just thought—"

"Boss!"

"Where's the prince of the hour?"

Anton's head turned at the voices calling from behind them, but she didn't miss the frown that pulled at his mouth. With a nod over his shoulder, his gaze was back on her with a soft smile. His thumbs stroked the apples of her cheeks as he held her face up to meet his eyes. Viviana found herself forgetting what she was worried about all of the sudden.

"I'll be right back, okay? Don't go too far. Maybe we'll sneak out of here sooner if that's who I think it is."

Just the fact that he didn't want her to join him in greeting whoever was demanding his presence told Viviana it was likely a conversation he didn't want her to be a part of. Or one she probably wouldn't want to hear. Either way, it didn't offend her. She hadn't been given much of a chance to sit down and relax since they'd arrived at the club and her feet were already sore.

"Sure. I'm in need of a refill, so go say hello ... or *yeah*."

"No business," Anton said, turning quieter. "I made it clear I wasn't talking business tonight with anybody."

Viviana shrugged, leaning up to kiss his jaw. "Whatever, *Boss*. Go."

With another squeeze of his hands and a warning under his breath that had her body spiking up to a fever again, Anton was gone. At the bar, Jen was waiting for Viviana with a glass of ice water and a smirk. Viviana perched herself up on a stool, crossed her legs, and searched across the darkened room through the mass of people to see if she could find her lover.

When she couldn't right away, she turned back to Jen. "I was told to cut you off."

"Wow, thanks. Wasn't like it was me who was buying those drinks."

"You don't sign my pay check," Jen joked.

"Ah, true that. He's probably just worried."

The older woman wiped the bar down as she asked, "Why?"

Viviana shrugged. "I drank a lot while I was in Canada.

It was becoming more of a habit than a social thing. This is the first time I've really partied, or had the chance to, since being back."

"It's good he watches out, though, right?"

"Yeah, it is."

And it was. Viviana didn't mind a bit. After all, it had been her that morning who'd questioned his behavior with alcohol. It wasn't all too surprising that he'd be keeping an eye out on her drinking, too, considering the fiasco her life had turned into back in Toronto. Sure it'd seemed great at the time, but now she could tell she'd been spiralling out of control, partying more than she studied. Like Anton had said, he'd been watching ... somehow.

"Hey, I'll be right back," Jen muttered, her eyes narrowing on someone reaching over the bar at the other end. "Ugh, fucking guys thinking they own the place sometimes because Anton owns it."

"Sure thing."

Jen wasn't gone but two seconds before a body dropped into the stool beside Viviana's with an almost feline sort of grace. The shine of a red heel caught the glint of a light. It drew her gaze to the slender calve it rested on.

Pale, smooth legs were crossed as a clutch was tossed onto the bar top. A feminine sigh echoed. Viviana turned to stare into ice-blue eyes that all but glared back. Full, painted red lips tugged into a sneer. The woman was beautiful, no doubt about it. Plenty of curves from her hips to her waist, and a bust that filled out her short, red dress. With pixie-like features and blonde hair that fell halfway down her back in perfect waves, she oozed self-confidence and sexuality.

Still, the last thing Viviana felt in her presence was insecure. She didn't know the girl from a hole in the ground. However, what she did feel was the burning resentment behind the stare. The woman's first words sure didn't help, either.

"Well, if it isn't the Russian whore."

Chapter Fifteen

The light Russian accent to the woman's voice didn't escape Viviana's notice. The woman reached out with her hand, brushing over the engagement ring on Viviana's finger.

Instantly, Viviana jerked her hand away as if she'd been burned. Many people had looked at the ring, their gazes appreciative when they asked how exactly Anton proposed, but not one had openly touched it like this woman just had.

"Pretty. But I bet I could have gotten a much nicer one out of that man. Is that all it took for you to roll over in his sheets and moan his name, girl? Just a pretty ring, a fast car, and a big house?"

Viviana felt air lodge in her throat, but the woman didn't give her a chance to reply before she continued. "I mean, they all know you're practically bought and paid for as it is," she said with an indifferent wave to the crowd behind them. "But I want to know what it took for you to put on a show like you just did out there on the dance floor. He was holding you tight, making it look awfully sweet … like he actually fucking cared. And he's so good at pretending, you know? Men like that, they can't be caught. They don't love."

"That wasn't a show." Viviana's voice had finally came back, but it sounded a lot quieter than she wanted it to. "Far from it."

"*Sure*," the other woman drawled with sarcasm dripping thickly over every word. "I'm Tatiana, by the way."

Viviana scoffed. "And I don't care."

Placing her glass back on the bar before she left the woman's space, she heard Tatiana's soft, vague reply. "Oh, you will."

"Listen, *girl*," Viviana muttered, forcing herself to breathe and be calm. The very last thing she or Anton needed was some kind of drama going down on his birthday with so many Bratva around. "I don't know who the hell you are, or what exactly this stunt is meant to prove, but you don't bother me. Not a single bit. Sure, you're pretty, and I bet you spread your legs like a pro. Have you screwed around with him, is that it?"

Tatiana raised a brow. "I have. Many times."

Viviana nodded; she'd assumed correctly, then. "Honestly, I don't much care to sit here and have a chitchat with some used up, back alley former *fuck* of my fiancé's. Because *I'd* be the one to bet that's just about all you're good for, and that's why he hasn't come calling back. Don't take offense, he's just got someone much more worthy warming up his bed. But, oh, wait … Anton didn't actually share his bed before me, yeah?"

The anger that blazed in steel-blue eyes had Viviana smirking. "Right … that's it, isn't it? Couldn't resist checking out who got what you didn't?"

"Wrong. One: my daddy is just as good as yours, girl, making me just as worthy. And two: you're pretty, but you're sure not me."

Viviana's fingers curled into fists at her sides as she stood gracefully from the stool. There wasn't any way on earth she was about to let some flighty twit from Anton's past ruin her night. For a brief moment, she searched the crowd of people for him again, but like he had warned, the club's doors were now opened to the public and in just a matter of minutes, it seemed like the floors were packed full.

"He's busy," Tatiana said, drawing Viviana's attention again. Those red lips curved with a nasty smile. "Having a moment with my father, I believe. Friendly Pakhans are rare, but our families have good history. Their territories are very close and business tends to intermingle."

Shit. That didn't help Viviana at all. Dread climbed up her spine with punishing steps.

"Mmhmm, been *friendly* for years," Tatiana continued, turning on her stool to face the crowd in one fluid movement. "I nearly had him, too … nearly. We were quite young then, though."

"Shut up," Viviana spit through clenched teeth.

The woman laughed sharply. "I suppose you could say we grew up together. When that grandfather of his was having troubles with whatever nonsense, Anton was spending time at my family's estate. Damn, didn't he grow up good, huh?" The taste of bile saturated Viviana's mouth. She refused to even look at the woman. "He didn't want you then, Viviana. In fact, he didn't want you at all."

Ouch. Something painful sliced into her heart with wrecking force.

"It's Vine. To you, whoever the fuck you are, it's just Vine."

"We'd have been a much better match. Powerful, too. He knew it when he was seventeen, but someone didn't quite agree. Nearly had him," she repeated a little more vehemently. "Anton didn't want some pretty Italian pussy waking him up in the mornings and sucking his cock at night. No, he wanted a *Russian* girl. Someone who spoke his mother tongue and bled the blood of the Bratva. Of course, he didn't know about you, then ... not really."

Viviana felt her lips quirk into a condescending smirk. "Yet look who he chose, hmm?"

There was a brief silence before Tatiana chirped out a high laugh.

"Oh my God."

"What?"

There wasn't a thing about their conversation—if you could call it that—that was funny.

"You don't know?"

Viviana exhaled through her nose, turning on her heel to stare with open hatred. "What are you going on about?"

"*You don't know!*"

"Again, what—"

"I didn't believe it, you know? When my father told me why the marriage had been arranged all those years ago, I just couldn't believe it. Such a stupid mistake for a woman of your mother's status to make, and with a Russian mob boss no less. She was lucky her husband didn't put a bullet through her fucking brain. And Anton … my God, he loved Nicoli so much it wasn't such a big shock to see him following along with whatever plans he made. But I was so sure you would have known … I thought they must have told you …"

Viviana's heart was pounding, blood rushing her ears. Nothing the woman said made much sense, but that dreadful feeling was back with a vengeance, eating away what patience and rationale she had left.

"Oh my God," Tatiana said again though her tinkling bouts of sardonic laughter. "It makes so much sense, now. It isn't any wonder why you think he loves you. How could you possibly think any different, you stupid, ridiculous girl? You don't even know *why* he's marrying you."

Yeah, all of the patience and calm she had remaining left her body in one fell swoop. Viviana turned to grab her own clutch off the bar top before making her move to leave. Tatiana's painful grip to her wrist stopped the desire up short.

A harsh exhale shuddered from Viviana's lungs as she stared at the hand on her body. "Remove your goddamn hand before I cut it off, Tatiana."

"You really don't know …"

Something a little softer had colored the woman's tone, like she may have felt badly. Viviana wasn't having it.

"I said—"

Tatiana's fingers squeezed harder, her nails cutting into Viviana's skin with enough force to make her bleed, but she refused to flinch or show proof of the pain the woman was causing her. For a split second, her brown eyes met steel-blue, a fire raging behind both women's orbs as they openly glared.

Pretty, yes, it was no wonder Tatiana caught Anton's eye. She might have had the looks, money, and father to back her up, but so did Viviana, and not once did she feel the least bit frightened or unworthy standing next to the man she wanted to marry.

"*Let me go.*"

"Jersey Girl … hey!"

Oh, for fuck sakes. She was from Jersey? Viviana never had any luck making friends from Jersey. No wonder they were like oil and water … or better yet, gasoline and fire.

Boom.

Jen's cheery voice, though Viviana was sure she heard the tension hidden in there as well, had Tatiana letting her death grip go. "You shouldn't be here, chica. You know what the boss said the last time you swayed your pretty ass up in here."

"Jen." A radiant smile curved her red lips, but it wasn't meant to be sweet. "Daddy came to wish Anton a happy birthday, and insisted I come along to meet the soon-to-be wife. We were just getting acquainted, right, Viviana?"

"It's Vine," Viviana spat.

Jen sucked air through her teeth, scowling. "Okay, so Sergei was your ticket in, and I'm your cue to get gone. If Anton sees you in here, he'll have a righteous fit. It's his birthday; you really want to ruin this party they threw for him by being a jealous bitch again?"

"Ouch," Tatiana said, pouting with wide eyes. "And I thought we were friends."

"Yeah, like a snake with a mouse, honey. Now, out."

Viviana assumed Jen had the situation handled, so she chose that moment to make herself scarce without bashing the blonde's teeth in. Once again, Tatiana wasn't having it because her fingers curled into the side of Viviana's black dress and pulled roughly to stop her from leaving.

She'd taken just about all she could. Viviana swung around and hit the arm holding her with an opened palm, smacking it away from her frame with a painful slap. Jen made a noise behind the bar and jogged to the partition where she could get out from behind the space keeping her confined.

"If you touch me one more time, I will ruin your face."

Tatiana not only looked surprised, but just a tad bit frightened as well. It was an honest threat, and one Viviana

209

wasn't afraid to carry out. The warning in her tone said it all. Tatiana wouldn't be the first woman she laid out, and she probably wouldn't be the last, either.

"Let's be clear on this. Our fathers might be bad fucking men, but I bet there was one hell of a difference between mine and yours. You're nothing more than a Bratva child. I'm a *principessa* of *La Cosa Nostra* and he raised me like one, too. He didn't keep me coveted on a shelf and hiding in the dark. No, I was taught how to bat my lashes at the same time I learned how to wield a knife."

Viviana took a measured step forward, making Tatiana draw back closer to the bar. "And did you know, *Jersey* ... just a single slice on your pretty thigh at the right spot, depth, and length would have you bleeding out to the floor before anyone even had the time, thought, or care to call an ambulance? Because I sure do."

"You would—"

"You're not in Jersey anymore, honey," Jen said quietly, her voice threatening. She'd come to stand behind Viviana, blocking the view of anyone behind them. "You're in Brighton Beach. This is Anton's territory, and this pretty thing here, she's the only thing he gives a shit about now. She's got one hell of a man backing her up, unlike you. My one and only suggestion is that you get off that barstool and leave, right now."

Viviana tilted her head upwards, looking down on the blonde with revulsion when she murmured, "Don't come back here, Tatiana. If you do, I won't be so forgiving. And for the record, if you're going to insult me, the least you could do is get it right."

"Excuse me?"

"It's not the Russian whore, it's the *Russian's* whore."

That snide smile crossed the woman's red lips once more. "Oh, but that's where you're wrong, *Brooklyn*. I said it right, you just haven't figured it out yet."

*

A finger tapped on Anton's shoulder forcefully.

"Boss, we gotta problem. A *big* one."

Anton tried to ignore Rory's voice behind him as he continued to chat with Sergei. It wasn't that he liked the man or wanted to converse with him because in all honesty, he didn't, but a Pakhan was a Pakhan in the Bratva world and Anton had to be appropriately respectful or it'd lead to nowhere good.

"*Boss.*"

The word was all but hissed.

"Rory, shut up," Anton warned quietly, not even glancing back, "and go find my girl."

"You're already shipping from Africa," Sergei muttered, dropping his glass down to the table. "Diamonds aren't any different, boy."

Anton fought the urge to roll his eyes before he banged his head on the table repeatedly. It didn't matter how many times the discussion was had, no one got the point. There were some things Anton simply didn't want to put his hands into. Human trafficking was one, for obvious and moral reasons, and diamonds was another route he didn't want to take.

Personally, he did pretty fucking good with his guns and narcotics in the trafficking department. A lot of the time, it kept him under a lower profile because he wasn't so big of a fish on the fed's lists.

"Boss," Rory whispered again.

Anton sighed. "I said—"

"Diamonds," Sergei repeated, tossing his arm over the back of the booth. "You've got good contacts over there, much better than I ... we could work it out together, Anton. Nicoli would have been the first to jump on that ship."

No, he wouldn't have. There was a reason he wanted to stay away, after all. Anton wasn't about to correct him.

"Okay, listen ..." he said, leaning forward to grab the beer one of his waitresses had brought over, "I promised my girl no business tonight. I want to make good on that, so Monday I'll get Ivan to set something up with just you and me. Neutral spots, no toes are being stomped on, and I get to go home tonight in lots of time to still save this evening from turning into a total shitfest. Sound like a plan?"

"But—"

"*Boss!*"

"Don't your boys know when to back the fuck off?" Sergei growled, glaring up at the bull behind Anton. "Because that one needs a swift kick in the tee—"

"No, he doesn't," Anton interrupted darkly. "He just doesn't answer to you. Now, I have to get going. Thanks for stopping by, and be sure to remind your daughter that she still isn't welcomed anywhere near Brighton Beach."

The sound that left Rory had Anton's spine straightening. He tried like hell not to react to the younger man, but it was damned near impossible. With a tick of his chin, his lover's bull was down near his shoulder, words whispering fast into his ear.

"Tatiana is *here*, Boss, and Vine went straight-up Brooklyn on her. I mean, girl spoke about slicing and dicing like she knew what she was saying, okay? Tati said some stuff, and I don't really know because I didn't get to her in time, but Jen said it wasn't anything all too good. Something about her mom and you and the arrangement. Anyway, Viviana's in the bathroom taking a breather, but the blonde is in the back alley having a smoke with Felix. So, your choice. Pick one."

Oh, for fuck sakes. Anton couldn't even hide his cringe.

Tatiana was something casual. It happened when he was seventeen and pissed off about being forced into a marriage that he was positive just wouldn't work. Then, he reconnected with Viviana and all of the stunts he'd been pulling and the nonsense he was going on with just quit. She had literally been his turning point, like finding his soul all over again.

Yeah, he'd messed around with the Jersey girl a few times in his early twenties at different clubs under random circumstances. It wasn't like either of them had actively

searched one another out, or maybe she had for him …
Either way, he was sure she understood that they weren't
rolling together like that. A quick fuck or Tati on her knees
blowing him off was just about as far as it went. Nicoli had
warned him, though. Anton should have listened when his
step-grandfather said she was no good … just a spoiled boss's
daughter who wanted the title with her money.

Fuck, he should have *listened.*

Anton clicked his tongue chidingly at Sergei. "You
brought your daughter along."

At least the man had the decency to look ashamed.
"She assured me your … issues … had been resolved."

"Far from it," Anton spat. "The bitch tried to burn
down my club the last time she was here because I wouldn't
let her suck my dick. Quite the child you raised, *Boss.*"

That probably wasn't the best choice in words, but
Anton was a little too pissed off to calm down. What in the
hell had Tatiana said exactly? His mind ran with all the worst
possible scenarios he could think of, and all of them collided
with the same conclusion: the truth. Of course she would
have known, her father did, after all.

"Mind your tongue, prince," Sergei warned.

Something flashed in the older man's eyes and Anton
felt the heat flare through his blood in response. Ivan, who
sat quietly beside him, coughed to draw their attention away
and defuse the situation, but neither man moved his gaze
from the other.

"That girl of yours," the older Pakhan continued,
sneering a grim smile. "She must have a hell of a lot of Italian
in her, doesn't she?"

Anton spoke through clenched teeth. "You know she's
only half."

"Given what we both know her mother did, aren't you
the least bit afraid she's going to do the same to you?"

Air sliced into Anton's lungs like a hot knife through
butter. It literally fucking ached.

"No, I'm—"

"Raised by a *byladina*, Anton. Your pretty little wife might just turn into her mother the first time you find yourself behind steel bars. After all, you've managed to keep yourself from doing any real hard time so far, but how long is that going to last? Every one of us does our time eventually, my boy. Will you come home to find her knocked up with your Sovietnik's child?"

"Fuck you," Ivan snapped beside Anton, speaking totally out of place but his boss wouldn't correct him.

"Or maybe she'll run to another boss like her mother did."

Byladina was by far one of the most offensive terms in Russian for the English equivalent of slut. It was regarded as an even worse title in their language, to be sure. Women who were worth less than even the stale air that left their lungs were graced with that insult. Never had Anton used it in his life. For Sergei to even remotely consider letting that word roll out of his mouth and compare Viviana to it was just about the worst thing he could have done, especially in Anton's presence.

There was no way for his bulls, or Ivan, to stop the fast movement of Anton's fist reaching over the table. Clenched knuckles slammed into an unsuspecting face, crushing the bones of the other Pakhan's nose on impact.

Anton packed one hell of a punch.

It carried a heavy price, and he knew it.

He did it, anyway.

The knuckle in his pinkie popped out of joint, but he drew back his fist again and landed another solid hit. When his fists grabbed at the broken man's collar, blood was already pouring. His knuckles were cut up but the pain didn't even register. He could hear the shouts of both languages beginning to rise around him, but his fury was swelling by the second. Russian spit from his mouth like poison when he was in Sergei's face.

"*Durak! Ty troop*, Sergei!" Close enough that he could smell the heat of the man's blood, Anton's voice turned to a dangerous whisper as he muttered, "Say it again, motherfucker, and it'll happen. I fucking *dare* you."

"Damn it! Anton!"

"*Boss!*"

"Shit, get off, Boss …"

The click of a gun's hammer being pulled back just barely registered to Anton's ears.

"Shoot and every fucking Jersey boy in this room is dust," someone snarled.

"Man, come on," Ivan hissed, arms circling his waist to pull him back.

"You're dead," Anton repeated in English, swinging out with another hit that landed hard on the man who was just being pulled away. "Get that piece of shit out of my fucking territory before I paint the walls with his brain matter!"

Anton slammed Ivan off of him, sliding off the table and fixing the arm of his jacket. When he realized there was blood stains on the cuff, he cussed and tugged the damned thing off. Tossing the offensive item at Rory, Anton turned to walk away. Sergei was still laying prone on the floor with the men who had escorted him in attempting to bring him out of the semi-unconscious state.

"I said *get him out!* Make sure that he wakes up in the parking lot of a hospital in his territory so he gets the goddamn point. His daughter will be right on her way to meet him, too. And get rid of that jacket, Rory."

"Sure thing, Boss."

One issue down, one more to go. Anton's previous buzz was all but gone. He was just plain and simple pissed off, now. People on the floor separated without looking the Russian boss in the eyes. It wasn't the first time something bad had gone down in the club and it wouldn't be the last. With a predator's gaze and a smooth, fast stride, he found the back entrance to the club with Ivan close on his heels.

"Shit, you just caused a big issue, Anton."

"You heard what he called her."

"I know … I know."

"Yeah, you fucking know. And if that was Eva, you'd have cut out his tongue."

Ivan huffed. "Not the point."

Anton turned fast, his hands coming up to slam into Ivan's chest hard. "Then what is the point, huh? I let him call her that because her mother made a mistake—one she probably paid a dozen times over for—and then everybody else assumes it's okay for them to label her with that title, too?"

"No—"

"He said it like the fact that Nicoli is her father didn't even make a difference! Never mind that she's got more Russian in her blood than his own daughter, or that she's going to be *my* wife … a *Pakhan*'s wife, no, only because her mother *birthed* her. That's why he called her that. No fucking way, Ivan. Not on my watch. Not in my territory. Not about her."

When Anton turned around to continue his trek to find Tatiana, he came face to face with his beautiful Viviana. His heart stopped just like his feet. Panic, grief, remorse, and fear roared through his veins. Pain throbbed from his dislocated finger but it didn't even register to the ache that suddenly took residence in his heart and soul.

That's not how she should have found out. That was the last way he ever wanted to tell her. Viviana deserved so much better than it to be blurted out in his anger with his back turned and blood on his collar.

Anton damned near stumbled when he jerked forward. "Baby …"

"I want to go home."

"I'm so sorry."

"*Home*," she repeated quietly.

Anton nodded, but he knew there was still something he had to deal with. "Just give me five minutes, okay?"

Viviana blinked, but there was water in her gaze.

Not here, he wanted to tell her. *Please don't do this*

here.

She could yell and scream at him anywhere but not at the club with all those people watching. A breakdown she deserved if she wanted to have one, and he'd take every punishment she had to give, but not right then.

Anton didn't have to worry. Only a single silvery tear escaped the corner of those familiar brown eyes before her hand swiped it away. She walked past him just as fast and he watched to make sure she was finding one of her bulls.

Even still, his heart cracked.

"Fuck," he breathed. "I ... I just ..."

Ivan swallowed audibly behind him. "Anton, breathe."

Hadn't he been? "What did I do?"

"It's—"

"Don't say okay, Ivan. It's not okay."

There was a hand on his shoulder squeezing painfully tight and it was the only thing keeping him rooted to the floor. Anton was grateful, because his heart and soul just walked on by like he was the last thing that she ever wanted to see again.

"You've got to deal with the fire bug, man."

Again, Anton found himself nodding dumbly. "I fucked that up."

"You love her," Ivan whispered, sounding torn and pained. "That's not nothing. It's just *not*. Take a breath, deal with crazy, and get Vine the hell home like she asked. Give the girl some credit; her heart just shattered and she didn't even say a word. Anybody else would have thrown a terrible fit. She walked away."

The throb in his hand reminded him of his other pain. Anton blinked down at the injured pinkie. Without thinking about it, he grabbed the digit with a stinging twist, grit his teeth, and forced it back into place with a painful pop. The damned thing came out of joint nearly every time his fist cracked into something.

"She walked away," Ivan repeated calmly. "She's got nerves. So while you take a breather, let her have hers to think about whatever."

Nerves, yeah. That was one way of saying it. Another was being honest and stating it like it really was. Viviana Carducci had been raised a true mafia princess. She might have had Bratva in her blood but she was born into a Cosa Nostra world. She knew how to walk, when to talk, and the second she needed to blink it all away.

And she was supposed to be his ... only ever his.

Anton shuddered with another breath as his heart splintered a little bit more.

"Let's get this done."

The exit door slammed open under Anton's hand. The heavy metal banged on the side of a dumpster as he stepped out into the alleyway. Instantly, he met the waiting gaze of one of Viviana's bulls and the very frightened stare of Tatiana.

"You made a big mistake, Tati."

He pulled a cigarette from his pocket, lit it up and took a puff. Ivan closed the exit door, keeping a hand in to make sure it wouldn't latch closed completely. Really, he just wanted to get this done and over with. Tatiana wasn't even important to him; she hadn't ever been. Now, he just needed to make it clear.

"What, you going to hurt me for making your pretty little fiancée cry, Anton?"

"Nope." Another inhale off the cigarette burned painfully sweet into his throat. He felt raw and ripped open. "Apparently my girl can handle herself just fine, and by the looks of it, you didn't make her spring a leak. I don't hit women, contrary to popular belief. What I will do, however, is pay a mighty price to knock you off. You understand that, Tati?"

Her eyes dropped from his sight. "You wouldn't dare."

"Oh yeah, I would. Wouldn't even blink when I got the call to say it was done, too. I don't know what you said, and I don't give a shit, but if I ever see you walking the streets of Brighton Beach in the next forty years, I promise you won't breathe long enough to leave them, girl."

"Fuck you."

The words were as good as a punch, but they didn't sting a bit. Still, her defiance only served to piss him off further. In a flash, Anton had crossed the space of the alley. He had her throat in his palm as he forced her back into the wall and made her eyes meet his. The choking sound of air only had him cutting off her oxygen supply even more. Tears slipped through her rapidly blinking eyes. When her fingers clawed at his arms, Anton looked down with a severe expression.

"I don't *hit* women ..." he repeated, resting the cigarette precariously between his lips with a careless flair, "but I'll sure as fuck make sure to get this clear so you won't misunderstand me and come knocking ever again. I don't want you. I've already had you and it was more than enough. Find some other man to spread your legs for because it won't ever be me again. If you even *think* to dare look in the direction of Viviana one more time, I will pay that price and have your blood spilling on Jersey ground, Tati. Are we clear?"

"Anton," Ivan warned quietly. "Ease up a little."

No fucking way. His grip tightened instead.

"Are we clear?"

The hard swallow and single nod was more than enough. Anton let go.

Chapter Sixteen

Anton's forehead rested on the bathroom door. The throbbing beats of his heart coursed through his veins with every aching thud, making it that much harder to breathe. With his hands splayed wide open against the wood, he begged once more for Viviana to let him inside the bathroom. The silent response he received was more heart-wrenching than if she would have screamed at him.

Because she didn't…not at all.

Viviana hadn't said a single word.

Not a fucking one.

Their car ride home had been so unbearably tense that Anton eventually yanked the car over on the freeway and whispered the apology he had been wanting to give her the movement she walked back into his life.

Again, Viviana said nothing.

She wouldn't even look at him; wouldn't grace him with the knowing that she had simply heard him *speak.* Her shaking hands had stayed limp in her lap as she watched cars blink by their stopped vehicle on the roadway.

Frustration had overtaken his pain in that moment and he had grasped her jaw roughly, turning her head to look at him. Just the tears that streaked over her cheeks at his handling should have told him more than enough, but Anton just couldn't *not.* That beating organ inside his chest was ripping apart.

Convulsive swallows followed his action before she looked on past him, refusing to meet his gaze. More tears slipped down her trembling cheeks. All he wanted—*needed*—for her to do was just say something.

"Goddamn it, won't you even look at me?" he had shouted.

Nothing.

"Viviana…please."

Silence.

A freight truck passed them at an alarming speed, causing the Mercedes to rock.

"I didn't—"

"Don't say you didn't know, Anton."

The words hadn't even been a whisper, but more like painful, stinging air that forced its way out from her center cavity. There was a heavy exhale that rattled from her chest, and he mimicked the action. Even the words she spoke felt riddled with pain and grief.

Oh, God, she *hurt,* too. He did that.

"Let me explain, that's all I'm asking."

"Please remove your hand."

"Vine…"

"Now."

When Anton noticed the blooming red forming around the spots where his fingertips were digging into her beautiful skin, he was quick to release his hold. Shame bit at his heels. Again, he rushed to apologize but she was already turning away like it didn't make a difference. Those switches he was so good at controlling were suddenly taking over him in the worst way.

And so, they ended up back at the safe house.

Without a word she walked past the three waiting bulls and Clarissa. Viviana reached down to graze over the tips of her pup's twitching ears; he was quick to trot behind when she left their space. The panel on the wall beeped with the indication that she had disappeared to the second level of the three floor building. Anton didn't know what else to do but let her go.

Rory had been the first to ask, "Is she going to be okay, Boss?"

How was he supposed to answer?

Clarissa's quiet voice, the one they rarely heard, was the only one to speak up. "If I understand what happened correctly, I believe she will, but it's a hard thing to learn who you thought you were, isn't really the person you are."

Anton's eyes flitted to the maid's, trying so damned hard to keep the rising tears at bay. "What do I do?"

"You give her time," Clarissa replied, smiling sadly. "You let her breathe. You hold her hand. You apologize. And I know you may not understand, but you forgive. Her. Them. Yourself. It's been many years, and you've had a great deal of time to absorb all of this."

"I know," he said faintly.

"It is all on her, Anton, to learn that blood doesn't make the person. Nicoli understood that when he made the choice to let her grow up with a different man as her father, because she would always be his, even if she wouldn't think the same, no matter where she lived. Just like you not sharing his blood didn't make you any less important or loved, because you were."

Another splintering crack settled somewhere deep inside.

Anton flinched. "Rocco, *ostanovit.*"

The order for his pup to stop didn't even register as the dog turned and clawed down the door once more. Fresh marks appeared where his nails had dug into the wood. Jesus, his dog had never outright disobeyed him like that after his training.

"*Rocco!*"

Anton raised his hand to pet the animal, but the dog's gentle nip of teeth on his two fingers stopped him. The bite was released. The animal lowered its head again only to push up under his lifted hand.

"Oh, buddy. *Vverkh.*"

Quickly, Anton pulled the dog into his lap, wrapping his arms around the animal and burying his face into the clean smelling fur.

So, he curled the animal tighter to his midsection, letting his dog rest over his sprawled out legs. Anton's hand ran a continuous cycle from the very top of the dog's head, down its trembling back, to the tip of his limp tail.

Eventually, Rocco's eyes drooped, breaths turned to

quick pants, and he slept.

Anton only wished he could do the same.

When Clarissa made her hesitant approach to take Rocco downstairs for his final outing in the backyard for the night, Anton damned near refused to let him go. Still, the dog had a schedule and it was important that no matter what, he keep it.

Anton couldn't help the tug in his chest as Clarissa asked if he would like for the doors between the floors to be left open. "Just in case he wishes to come back up and find you, sir." He didn't say no. It was painfully obvious trying to keep the dog away for the night wouldn't be an option.

With them gone, Anton was once again alone.

Desolate in the silence of his own hell, the empty hallway, and the door behind him. That was how he found himself pleading with the woman inside to just let him in.

The heart inside his chest that rarely ever felt was feeling *everything*.

Anton didn't know *anything*.

He didn't know if she had fallen asleep; if she had gotten clothes from their bedroom; if she was physically hurt from when he'd listened to her hit the walls earlier.

"Please, Viviana, please…let me in, baby."

The knob wouldn't turn under his hands, and despite the fact that there were keys in his office that would open the door, the very last thing he wanted to do was force his presence. After everything and all the choices she hadn't been included in, Anton knew he needed to give her that option. It had to be her choice…*had* to.

"I didn't know," he whispered to the door. "I grew up thinking I was being married off to some spoiled Italian princess. I watched my mother and father love each other, Vine. That's all I ever knew, okay? Daniil didn't have mistresses. He made it home every night to sleep beside my mom. I never heard their voices raise and not once did his hands hurt her."

Anton was rambling, and he knew it probably wouldn't

make a difference if she wasn't willing to listen, but he had to talk to something, or that pressure in his chest was going to explode.

"How was I supposed to love a girl who was just picked for me? I can't tell you how many times I asked them that question. Over and over. That's what they wanted for me? Exactly what they had, I wouldn't ever get it. It hurt me, Vine. I was so fucking angry. I pulled some bad stunts and messed up a lot of things when I was just seventeen and stupid. Pulled the trigger before I ever should have and nearly got myself killed over it; screwed girls with fathers who wouldn't have blinked to put a bullet through my brain.

"I was made the day before my eighteenth birthday, but I was so screwed up by then. Drugs, drinking myself dead, not coming home at night and then not knowing where I was when I woke up in the morning…" A lump formed in his throat before he cleared it with a horrible sound, once more resting his head on the door before he continued. "Nicoli just up and said it was enough. I had to stop. Took me away to get my shit straightened out. Told me I needed to find my *old soul.* I thought that trip to Barbados was just a ploy for him to get me away from the drama I'd started back here; none of them told me we were coming to meet your family. I didn't know when he said that, he meant I was coming to find you all over again."

Anton swore he heard a movement inside the bathroom but the stilled quietness that followed made him think he was just creating what he wanted to hear. So, he steeled his raging emotions with another ragged breath and kept talking.

"I didn't know," he repeated thickly. "Not then, Viviana. I found the most amazing girl and it took me one day to realize how wrong I'd been. Just *one.* I watched this girl with sober eyes, happy laughs, and innocent smiles who didn't know a thing about me or the shit I'd done and *she didn't care.*"

"Stop."

The word was all but hushed through the door, but his heart broke all the same.

"No, I can't. I'm sorry, but I won't." Once more he tried the doorknob under his hand, but it wouldn't turn. "Maybe I should have seen something then, Vine. Like the way Roman and Nicoli tolerated each other, but they wouldn't really speak. Or how your mother chose to keep her distance and stayed off of the property for most of the trip.

"And twice...twice when Nicoli called you his sweet girl in Russian," Anton murmured, thinking back to the way he'd let those comments roll off his shoulders so easily. "I should have known. I should have seen the way your lips quirked off to the side when something angered you was the same way his did when I pissed him off. I should have noticed yours eyes were the carbon copy of his. I know I should have. I know, baby, but I didn't. I was so damned caught up in *you*."

Once more, tears welled with a stinging burn as he tried to hold the inevitable back. When the drops slid through his eyes, Anton said, "I was too busy realizing I'd spent so much time hating a girl who'd be so fucking easy to love. I didn't fall in love with the daughter of a boss, no matter which boss it was. I fell in love with the girl who stole my favorite T-shirt, made me eat healthy crap, snuck past an entire house just to climb in my bed, and who wanted me only because I was supposed to be hers. That was the girl I knew. She was the one I wanted, too.

"I didn't fall in love because they told me I had to," he continued through clenched teeth. "I did it because you didn't give me the choice. Everything I didn't even know I wanted was being reflected in a girl who didn't know me from Adam. You were the best thing that ever happened to me. You saved my life in six fucking days and you didn't even know it."

The lock turning to unlatch echoed in the deepest part of his blackened soul. Anton literally stumbled away from the door like it had burned him. It wasn't an invitation for him to go in, but it was a clear indication that she was finally starting to hear him—that she was *listening*.

Then, the door swung open. Viviana stood in nothing but a thigh length, wool sweater that hung over one bare shoulder. Her wet hair hung loosely over the other shoulder, while she kept her eyes lowered and chin tucked down.

"Look at me," Anton pleaded.

"My Wikipedia page says I was one month premature."

Confusion settled in him like a dead weight. "What?"

"My Wikipedia page. You have one, too. Except yours is a lot more involved than mine is. But that's not the point...the point is that my page says I was born one month early. Apparently there's hospital records to show proof of my mom going into early labor."

Anton didn't have a clue what to say, but if it got her talking and kept her that way, he didn't care. "Okay."

"I wasn't premature, Anton. More than once my mother told me I was just as stubborn before I was born as I was after because I made her wait two extra weeks before I came, and even then, they had to induce her."

"Uh..."

Viviana didn't give him a chance to find words. "Roman has a Wikipedia page, too. Funny, our whole fucking lives are just recorded right here," she said, waving her cell phone mockingly. "People who don't know a thing about me can go on here and find out I'm thought to be the daughter of a deceased Cosa Nostra Don. Alleged Don, because you know, he never admitted it in court. They can learn my middle name is Christina. That I had an older brother who died in a car accident along with my mother, although it's still under investigation."

Her voice had turned sour, but she still wouldn't look up. "And then they can click on my father's name. Roman, I mean. His page, like yours, is quite extensive. It talked about his arrests for drugs, and for the weapons. It describes the circumstantial evidence to other crimes he was never charged for. And your page... The lists on the dealings your thought to be handling, how you rose to your respective positions, and the years *served*."

The final word had all but been spit from her mouth like poison.

Anton finally found his voice. "I've spent a few months in jail, but nothing serious. I'm careful with anything and everything I do."

"Not my dad, though," she said pointedly. "He wasn't so careful. It's no wonder my page says I was a month premature. Considering if I wasn't, he would have still been in prison when I was conceived."

The way the word broke coming out of her mouth had him rushing forward. It was soaked in pain and truth, wrapped in sorrow and hatred. More than anything, Anton just wanted to hold her. Viviana wouldn't let him, taking a quick step back.

"Please don't, Anton. I *can't* … I need to breathe and I can't do that when you touch me."

Something lodged in his airways. Didn't she know what she did for him?

"I need to, though. *You* make *me* breathe."

Viviana ignored his grief-stricken confession. "How long?"

"I don't—"

"How long did you know that my mom had fucked around with Nicoli?"

Anton blinked in disbelief at the harshness in her tone. "It wasn't like that."

"Really?" she bit out bitterly. "How was it, then? How was it, that Christina Carducci ended up pregnant with another man's child when her husband was just one month off his release date from prison? How was it that to hide who my real father was, they arranged a marriage to put me in his path another way? They lied to me my whole life. Given what my mom did, it's no wonder he had so many *goomahs* and—"

"That's why he forgave her," Anton interrupted softly.

Finally, Viviana's head jerked up. Wide, red rimmed eyes stared brazenly open with pain and confusion reflecting back. "I don't understand."

"I only know what I was told," he explained with a shrug. "And from what I understand, Roman put her through the ringer, too. They married young. He was running with women from one side of New York to the other. Your brother was just a newborn when he went back to prison, leaving her alone to raise him for those first two years. Their relationship was bad. One of those destructive things where you know it has to stop, but you can't find the strength to do it because when it's good, it's so fucking good—"

"That's not an excuse."

"You're right, it isn't, but that's not how they saw it. They believed what they'd been taught. Once you married, you were married for life. You accepted the spouse you chose. When I was able to ask Roman why, because any other boss would have put her six feet underground, baby, all he could say was that he loved her. She made a mistake—one he made several times over—and he couldn't punish her any more for it."

"She conceived another man's child."

"*You*, she conceived you," Anton pointed out.

"That's great. I'm the product of some ridiculous revenge my mother decided to enact by fucking Roman's enemy. I bet she had the best time running around with Nicoli right up until she found out about me. That's just *great*, Anton."

Again, he was stunned speechless. It took him an entire minute to regain his thoughts so what he said didn't hurt her more than she already was. The last thing he needed was her running to hide again.

"It only happened once. Nicoli gave me very little details because he was a private man in that regard. Just the once … bad timing and random circumstance. They didn't see each other again until you turned two."

When Viviana didn't speak, Anton took it as his chance

to keep talking. "No one knew but a few choice people that you weren't Roman's. Christina told him the moment he returned home; he wanted you, despite the fact that you weren't his blood. She didn't know, and neither did he because she couldn't give him a last name, who Nicoli was. They didn't meet under circumstances that led her to think he was a high ranking member of the Bratva. It wasn't anywhere near Brighton Beach. Like a perfect storm, that's all."

"But that doesn't make sense."

"The only thing Roman wouldn't do, Viviana, was risk having you marry a Cosa Nostra man because your children wouldn't have been full Italians," Anton finished quietly. "He couldn't do it because he believed, respected, and followed his creed."

"How?" she asked, brown eyes daring to flick up to meet his.

"How, what?"

"This ... us," she said, waving.

"Sonny. A mix up happened between trucks and Nicoli's guys stepped in to take what wasn't theirs; Sonny's guys got in and some lead was tossed. A meeting was set up, and because they didn't want it to end violently, the wives were brought along. Or the ones that were alive, anyway."

Anton felt his chest grow with that painful pressure again. God, he wanted so badly to reach out and touch her, but he was terrified that wouldn't do him any good. He settled for shoving his shaking hands in the pockets of his pants, instead.

"Again, the perfect storm. Shitty circumstances. Christina could have just not told Roman and he wouldn't have known the difference, but they'd changed a lot in those two years after your birth. They weren't the same people. She wouldn't lie, so she was honest, and Roman ... he was good man, Viviana. Decided to give Nicoli the chance to know he had a daughter."

"And then this happened," she assumed, her bare shoulder lifting before it dropped back down.

"Basically. Nicoli didn't want to take you from the man you already loved, but he did want the chance to someday know you as a different woman. When he noticed how well you and I seemed to take to one another, he was quick to throw the arrangement on the table. It served to fix Roman's issue of not marrying you to his side, but instead, the one you were more suited to because of your bloodline. And, it served Nicoli's purpose of having you close to him at a different stage in your life. Not everyone was happy with that."

"No?"

Anton shook his head. "Sonny again. Everyone already thought you were Roman's, so what difference would it make? He didn't want to be mixed up with Russians. By Nicoli and Daniil's accounts, it was pretty clear those brothers weren't on good terms even then. I think Sonny was planning a long time before you came along to get rid of Roman, he just needed a reason to."

Viviana sucked in a harsh breath. "I was that reason."

"It's not your fault, baby."

When tears slipped over her cheeks, she was quick to swipe away the glimmering wetness. Anton stood stoic and silent as he let her digest everything he'd said. He knew it was a lot and that she'd probably have a dozen more questions, but what he really wanted her to do was just sleep. The dark circles under her eyes and tremors rocking her small hands had him worried.

"Come to bed, please."

A simple shake of her head had him sighing. "What about you, Anton?"

"I'm going to shower and then, if you want, I'll join you."

"No, that's not what I meant."

"Oh."

His heart kick-started with another painful rhythm.

"Just ... when did you know?"

His lips wet under his tongue. It was the truth he'd been avoiding even more than the history of her paternity.

"That morning you left Barbados. I couldn't figure out why Nicoli was so fucking mad at me. Roman, I got. He was your dad and there was that tiny spot of blood on my sheets that said what I wouldn't. But, Nicoli? I couldn't get it to click. And he slipped … in his anger, with his Russian. I heard my father kind of choke and my mom just made this awful sound. I got it then. His *princess*, he'd said. My dad called me the little prince my whole life, Vine. I knew what he meant when Nicoli said that about you.

"And then he went really quiet, but I finally recognized the eye color when he just sat there and stared at me. Nicoli didn't ever show his emotions, but the pain in his eyes was unbearable," Anton admitted, frowning. "He was so torn because I was finally getting it together. I was happy, healthy, and I wanted you, but I'd disappointed him because I'd taken something from his *daughter*. It didn't matter that you were going to be my wife, in his eyes, what you gave to me wasn't mine to take at that time."

Her voice was just a breath when she said, "That long."

"It didn't matter to me," Anton rushed to say. "I already wanted you. I wanted you because I loved you. But Nicoli was clear and so was Roman, I couldn't tell you. Neither of them wanted you to know, unless there was no other way around it, but there was the big issue of safety, too. They just wanted you to love the life you already had, not the one you could have had. I decided after Sonny made it pretty obvious that he wanted to all but eradicate the truth of his involvement in hiding your paternity that when the time was right, and we were safe, I would tell you."

"But … I do."

That time, it was his head that jerked up. "What?"

"My life, I did love it. Loved Roman so much. And I love the life I'm just beginning to build with you."

Anton felt frozen at her words, and when Viviana finally stepped close enough to pat his chest, all that pressure and pain he'd been fighting off ceased to exist. He could breathe. His heart continued to beat. When her fingers fisted

231

in the blood-stained silk shirt he wore, she stepped to his side.

"I'm going to go to bed now."

"Okay," he murmured, not sure what else to say.

"Please be there for me to wake up to in the morning. You promised."

Chapter Seventeen

"If he is, that means something's about to happen, man. You need to keep a keen eye out and be careful. Get those bulls of hers on a closer detail for a little while. Rocco shouldn't be left at home, ever. You know the drill."

"Yeah, point being *if* he's gone into hiding, though," Anton said, tilting his head back to blink up at the ceiling. "And we don't know that Sonny has, Ivan."

"Hard to say," his lawyer agreed, "given his wife didn't follow along. I'd take my fucking wife."

"Do you think he loved me?"

The phone nearly fell out of Anton's hand as his boots dropped off the shelf he'd propped them up on. Slowly, he turned to face Viviana who stood looking almost resigned in his office doorway. The nervous action of her hands wringing had him swallowing back rising emotions.

"Ivan, I need to go. Call me back immediately if you find out more."

"Everything okay?"

Anton didn't answer the man. He dropped the phone with a loud clatter to its receiver. One week. It had been one week since the crapshoot his birthday had turned into, and Viviana hadn't said a single thing about anything come the morning after.

Those early morning hours after he'd crawled into their bed, however, had been a different story. Over and over again she'd stirred, her tears falling and soft cries waking him up. Anton hadn't known what else to do but let her cry it out and hold her all the while, and when she reached for him in a whole different way, he gave her that soft and slow, too.

Then, she'd finally fallen asleep. In the morning, she went on like nothing was amiss. When asked, everyone had the same report: Viviana wasn't talking about it.

Anton didn't know what to think.

Maybe he thought she wanted to move on, forget it. That didn't mean he thought it was a healthy way to go, but it was up to Viviana to figure out what it was she wanted or needed from it all. So, just the fact that she was standing in the doorway asking a question like that was a huge leap forward.

"Who, baby?"

Viviana took a hesitant step into the room, pursing her lips. "Roman. I mean, would it be so terrible to believe that he did?"

"No, that wouldn't be a bad thing at all. Of course he loved you, Vine. Why would you think that he didn't?"

"Because I was the child of another man. Every time he looked at me, how could he not see someone else staring back? It wouldn't be a crazy assumption on my part to believe he might have resented me in some ways. Sure, he and Mom put on a good act all those years we were growing up, but that had to have been all it was."

"It wasn't. They very much loved each other, it just took a while to get them both to a healthy place. I don't know how that all came about; that's their own story, I suppose. One Roman didn't share with me when we sat down and talked in Barbados, but I think that might have had a lot to do with the fact that the man who slept with his wife was just feet away."

The heavy sigh she released sounded shaky. "How could they even stand to be near one another? Roman was a jealous man who would have put you to shame, Anton. I don't get it."

"Nicoli knew he'd done wrong. He took another man's wife to his bed, even if he hadn't known she was married. When it came to Roman, he took a step back and let him be because what the hell else was he supposed to do, really," Anton replied, laughing bleakly. "There was a lot of respect that went around when so much disrespect had already been slung out. It wouldn't have worked between them otherwise. Both of them were dangerous, charismatic, and intelligent men. It couldn't have been easy to just sit there like Nicoli did and swallow his pride, just like it couldn't have been easy for Roman to sit across the table from him and not kill him. They fucking deserved medals."

When she didn't speak again, Anton drummed his fingers on the oak desk.

"I know he loved you. You, out of everyone in the whole situation, were the only innocent one. Didn't ask to be born. Didn't choose your parents. Are you going to fault him for never wanting you to feel like you do right now?"

The saddened look that widened her eyes and had her plump bottom lip drawing between her top teeth had Anton backtracking instantly. "Shit, that's not what I meant, Vine."

"Yeah, I think it was," she whispered.

Anton scowled when she refused to meet his stare. "You're right. It was."

"Ouch."

"That man loved you. The one you didn't know loved you. Your mother loved you. I won't sit here and let you try to convince yourself otherwise. That's ridiculous. I don't know if this is your way of dealing with all this crap, but screw that. I've sat back and let you have your self-imposed gag order about all of this, Vine, but in no way will I allow you to believe that kind of bullshit. Not going to happen."

"Where do you get off—"

"Because I love you, too!" Anton shouted, standing from his desk instantly.

She flinched from the level of his voice. His knuckles that were still sore from the week before cracked against the hard oak, splitting the healing wounds open all over again. It barely even registered over the thrum of anger that simmered under his skin.

"That's not fair to them. It's not fair to Roman after he raised you and never once gave you any indication you were worth any less than your brother. Or Nicoli … not after he sat back for all those years he knew you were alive and let you be raised by another man, one he knew would love and raise you well. While I'm at it, I ought to just shove Christina in the bunch, too. She could have aborted you before anyone even knew you were there and simply went on like nothing was different, but she didn't. Don't do that; don't assume that of them. That's not okay, Viviana."

Her eyes flickered with emotions. He didn't even think she'd taken a breath since his voice raised, considering her chest wasn't moving and she all but stood like a statue with shaking hands.

The silence that ensued had his lungs hurting. Not five seconds later she turned and left the office without even glancing back. The quiet clatter of Rocco's paws down the hallway followed instantly.

"*Fuck.*"

Once more, his fists hit the wood, splitting the wounds wider before blood seeped to the surface. At least the sting of the old injury opening up was enough of an ache to let him forget about the sudden rise of remorse in his heart.

But only for a moment.

Just as quickly, he was jogging around his desk and following the path she took down the hallway. She hadn't barricaded herself inside a room again, considering their bedroom door was wide open and Rocco sat in the entrance, his tail wagging. Leaning in the doorway, Anton placed his hand on the pup's head, scratching gently as Viviana paced inside the room.

"I'm sorry," he muttered under his breath. "I shouldn't have done that. It was insensitive of me."

"And downright ignorant."

"Okay, now that's arguable. I think out of the two of us, I have a bit more insight to all of this than you do, considering you won't even speak about it."

"I meant ignorant of my feelings, Anton. You're being an asshole. An *insensitive* one."

"Stop trying to pick a fight," he snapped.

"You already did!"

Damn it. Why couldn't she just listen to him?

"Is that what you thought I was doing, Viviana? Instead of listening to what I said, because it damn well made sense whether you liked it or not, you turned tail and ran again. *Again*! You don't want to hear it. None of it. You just want to pretend like none of it even happened and you can't do that."

"No, correction, Anton, you only want me to hear what you have to say. You don't want me to feel anything that might shine one of them in a bad light because heaven forbid I be angry at people who just chose all of this for me instead of letting me decide for myself."

Instantly, he jerked at the accusation she tossed back at him as if it'd been a knife she threw in place of words. They stung like nothing else. Was that honestly what she thought?

"I didn't mean—"

"Well that's how it feels!"

Anton forced himself to swallow back the anger he'd previously felt. Maybe she was right. His view on the whole thing had been one-sided. He'd never stopped to consider that everything she thought before about the arrangement and her parents would be totally turned upside down and ruined, leaving her in the same state. Of course it would … who wouldn't see it that way?

"Okay."

Taking one step inside the room, he turned to hold a hand out when Rocco tried to follow, stopping the animal up short. When he was sure the pup would stay out in the hallway, he closed their bedroom door and turned to face a teary eyed Viviana. The confused look she gave him had Anton offering her a small smile in return.

"What are you doing?"

"Okay," Anton repeated, his tone turning thick as he nodded at the bed for her to sit. When she did, he leaned back into the door and crossed his arms. "Whatever you need, baby. Whatever you want to say. It's just you and me. Fuck them, my opinions, the outside world, the crap I have to handle for my guys before we go to bed … fuck it all.

Right now, I just want to hear you talk."

Viviana looked up through wet lashes, finally starting to look more like his girl. "Yeah?"

"Yeah."

"Why now?"

Anton crossed the space, kneeling down and placing his hands on both of her jean covered thighs. Straightaway, she sunk into his touch. Tears slipped down to her wet trembling lips, but for a moment she seemed calmed.

That was why, he thought sadly.

Viviana might have not been speaking, and when he talked, Anton thought she wasn't understanding. But he had been the one who wasn't *listening.* All week she'd been stuck in silent screams that all but begged for him to just listen to her, and he hadn't.

"Because I wasn't hearing you. I am now."

Her voice was just an echo when she hushed out a quiet, "Thank you."

*

"Did you like your childhood?"

Viviana didn't miss the surprise that flitted through his eyes at her random question. They'd been quiet for awhile, given he let her talk so damned much without barely saying a thing back. And when he did talk, he managed to keep those opinions of his out of it. She was grateful; she didn't know she needed it until he gave it.

"What do you mean?"

Crawling up to his spot against the headboard, she was quick to find herself in his opened arms and leaned back into his muscular chest. Anton used her propped up thighs to set his weapons magazine on. Flipping to a new page, he hummed an appreciative sound in her ear over a vintage revolver that had one entire spread in the centerfold.

"I only have one of these," he said offhandedly. "I need another few and I'd be happy. They're mighty hard to get a hold of, though."

"You like guns far too much for it to be healthy."

"I beg to differ. It's very healthy given my lifestyle. I know guns better than most. After all, I am a weapons tra—" Anton stopped short suddenly. His next statement could be something Viviana would be forced to use against him in court if they weren't married. "Yeah, I have a *thing* for guns, baby. Don't judge me."

"So, my question …"

"Again, explain."

"Just your upbringing in general. How do you think it was, good or bad?"

"How do you think yours was, Viviana?"

He'd stumped her there. She wasn't quite sure how to respond for a second. It was a loaded question in more ways than one. Did she see or hear things she shouldn't have or didn't want to along the way? Sure. Had she been given some of the best moments of her life with a man who, when alive, had been known as one of America's most notorious crime bosses? Yes.

"It was … different, at times. Good, but different."

"Mine, too," Anton admitted. "I wasn't just raised by my parents. I was raised by many men. Bratva men. Gangsters. But they were gentlemen, too, as hard as that is to believe. I heard 'try this, boy' more times than I can count and probably should have said no more than I did; I learned to disassemble and reassemble an assault weapon by the time I was twelve; school pretty much bored the hell out of me because I was leaps and bounds ahead of everyone else in the maturity department, at least in my own mind. Sure, I had a lot of normalcy in between, but I was a mafia child all the same."

"Didn't that bother you?"

"No."

The answer was so simple. It struck a chord with Viviana.

"I loved having so many different personalities around me to grab onto. I quite liked my life, just the same as I do now," Anton continued when she stayed quiet. "I respected the values I was taught. And it wasn't just about this crime world I deal in, either. A lot of those guys were the first men I ever really knew besides Daniil and Nicoli, and I was quick to watch them … to want to be them. I was grateful they'd been put in my path; I wouldn't be who I am now had they not been."

"So, who are you exactly, or have you figured it out yet?"

Viviana hadn't meant for her tone to turn so silky and demure when the words tumbled out without her even thinking about them, but they had anyway. By the way he swallowed a rumbled sound behind her, she knew he didn't miss the change in her voice, either.

"How am I supposed to even answer when you're not looking at me? Turn around."

"What—"

Before she finished her sentence, Viviana found herself turned in his strong arms, the magazine forgone to the bed sheets. Darkened blue stared back under the lamp's light, a mix of desire and curiosity burning behind the irises. Given that she was wearing nothing but a pale pink, silk camisole with matching panties and he was in only his boxer-briefs, she was all too aware of how her question had affected him.

The hardness starting to stir under the thin fabric had her heart rate picking up at an alarmingly delicious speed. It didn't take much time at all for him to get going, and once he was, so was she. Anton had that lustfully swirling effect on her every goddamn time.

"Hey!"

A devious grin answered her back before his hand was slipping under her camisole to trail an aching path straight up to her breast. A teasing thumb rolled over her pebbled nipple, flicking the sensitive bud and getting it a little tauter with every rough, calloused stroke. Viviana was quick to melt into the heat of his hand as the other curved to her back and splayed wide open.

"So, who are you?" she asked again.

"I'm me," he said huskily. "Anton. Boss. Son. Prince. Sir. Asshole. A different mask covers my face every day of the week. A lover. Awfully jealous at times. Quick fists when someone pisses me off, but a calm head otherwise. I like bourbon more than vodka, but I wouldn't dare tell my father that. I hate to sit still unless it's with you. I have a thing for guns, fast cars, and good music. Preferably all three mixed together. A girl with brown eyes and an Italian last name owns my heart. What else do you want to know?"

His lips had come to rest dangerously close to hers. She could smell that dark roast coffee he'd been drinking not ten minutes before dancing on the edges of his mouth. With one hand pressing at the black rose that covered his right pec, Viviana had him pushed back to the pillows as she shifted just enough to straddle him.

"There's always more to learn, Anton."

"What is it you want to know that you haven't already been told?"

Viviana grinned, rolling her hips over his groin and watching his dark lashes flutter closed at the action. Air cut through his teeth as a thick groan fell into the quiet room. Juices leaked from her overheated sex as her hands grabbed tighter to grind his hardened length against where the silk covered her crotch.

"Won't you tell me about the kind of man I'm marrying?"

"Oh, I think you know," he replied darkly.

"No, not always. I see too many faces and sometimes I wonder which one you really own. Not that I don't like them all in their own way, but still. Sweet as sugar and charming as a snake. That's a dangerous combination. I'm not all too sure at all of just what I've gotten myself mixed up in."

For a brief second, he seemed to consider her words. Despite how turned on she was, body hot and ready, sex already throbbing with the need to have him deep, hard, and fast like only he could give it to her, she wanted to hear what he'd say, too.

"Is this really about me, or is it about you?"

Viviana pressed her hand to his chest again. "A little bit of both. I feel like I don't know who I am now, and your upbringing was similar to mine, in some ways."

She tried to look away, embarrassed at her own admission. With a chiding click of his tongue, he gently turned her face so she was staring at him again.

"Yes, you do. You're the same girl with a little more past, that's all."

A sigh passed her lips as she replied, "Your opinion, Anton."

"Sorry."

Not wanting to start another argument, she decided to drop it. Her body was still hyperaware of his thick erection sliding gently along her silk covered sex, rubbing beautifully over her swollen clit. Anton was good at keeping her mind distracted, anyway.

"So, a dangerous combination for my sensitive heart …"

"You're right; it is because I'm a risky kind of man. I'm not a good one and I don't pretend to be. I've got stars on my shoulders and a rose on my chest for a reason." His hand left her shirt before he spread his thumb and pointer finger to give Viviana the view of an inverted cross tattooed between the digits. "Marked for a worthy hit," he added, not sounding smug or prideful, just honest. "But, I'm a better man than others. I love you best and hold you tight at night."

"So, my man, then?"

"Always and only."

"And what's this man of mine like, anyway?"

Anton laughed a dark sound. It rocked her straight down to the pulsating ache between her thighs. While her question hadn't meant to bring on their suggestive banter, she didn't mind the change. Again, Viviana found herself shifting on top of him to relieve some of the tension in her body.

"He's pretty fucking sinful and downright dirty when he wants to be."

With a lifted brow, not even bothering to hide the way his words provoked her desire a little bit higher, she leaned forward into his body. Getting right up close to his ear as her wandering hands slipped lower to the spot where Viviana wanted them connected, she couldn't miss the catch in his breath when her fingers grazed over the bulge in his boxer-briefs.

"What's that?"

"He likes waking you up with his name in your mouth and hearing those sounds you make right before you break, because when you come it fucking soaks him totally. Nothing ever tasted so good on his tongue. Those juices of yours get so damned tart and heavy when you burn through your orgasm like it's a fever."

"*Mmhmm.*"

"He's not going to always say the right things. He might even disappoint you more than he wants to admit, and sometimes he acts like an ignorant, insensitive asshole. " Anton's lips curved with a wicked smile as she pulled away. "Like I said, he's not always a good man, but he's a better man in a lot of ways, and he's yours."

"Well, I think I like him just fine the way he is. This is who all those men raised, huh?"

"This is him," he agreed with a shrug. "My raising might not have been perfect, but it worked just fine for me. Gave me everything I needed in one way or another. I learned exactly who I wanted to be, and who I didn't. I'm quite pleased with the outcome; in the end, after all, it got me you."

When her hips rose just enough to allow her hand to slip underneath his boxer-briefs, Viviana whispered, "That it did."

*

Anton let her shift and move enough for her hand to get a comfortable, tight grip on his cock while her other one lay flat on his abdomen, keeping her hovering above just high enough. His fingers dug into her waist as she pumped his shaft slowly, a teasing burn licking from the base of his cock straight up through his spine.

When his own hand released its grip to find the heat between her thighs, Viviana sighed. She had soaked right through those panties she wore. More of her sex's fluids gushed as he stroked her slit, feeling the strained bud of her clit through the thin fabric. The prettiest pink stained her chest and neck when his two fingers were quick to sweep the fabric aside and thrust inside the silken wetness of her pussy.

Knuckle deep, he watched her body sink onto his hand and Anton swore he could feel the pulse of her heart thumping against his palm. Her hips rolled, and he could see it in her blinking brown eyes that she wanted him moving those fingers of his to get her revving and ready to go.

Anton had other plans. "Get your hand down here, baby."

"What?"

He had the best view of her sex. All wet and swollen, juices dampening his hand with the best scent of her arousal. She was slick, hot, and tight. When his cock was buried balls deep, there wasn't anything quite like the feeling of her muscles and walls holding him inside her soaked heaven.

"Let go of me and get your hand down here," he repeated, his voice coming out darker than he intended it to.

"You want me to stop … right *now*?"

"I want you to play a bit before I fuck you hard. Hurry up, I'm a fickle man and I've had a long day. Maybe we'll just go to sleep, hmm? My mind could change at any moment."

Her clear exasperation had him chuckling. That didn't stop her hand from slipping off his cock, though. Anton waited her repositioning out, watching her legs spread wider as her backside rested on his thighs. His thumb opened up the lips of her pussy with feather-light touches, making her shudder. Settled, Viviana fixed him with a stare that came off a bit too challenging for his liking.

"Now what, Boss?"

"Don't start with that," Anton warned. Jesus, his throat

tightened and his cock got harder every fucking time she said that. He wondered if hearing that title in her mouth would ever not give him that reaction. "I haven't got the self-control for it tonight, baby. Unless you want to be bent over the bed with your ass a cherry red, begging like I know you can for me to fuck you good and hard."

"Don't tease me with idle threats."

"Maybe that is what you want, huh? Damn, all you had to do was ask."

Viviana's eyes widened. "You *wouldn't*."

"Spank you? Yes, I would. And you'd like it."

Just the way her sex pulsed and clenched around his two fingers said much more than she was willing. Anton used that to stroke against the fleshy spot inside her walls with the faintest hum building in the back of his throat. Her velvet walls turned wetter, fluids smelling so much like that heady sex he loved as he coaxed her g-spot with tender motions.

"You'd never spank me," she challenged quietly, mischief glinting in her eyes as she looked down. "You can't *hurt* me, Boss."

In a flash, his hand was gone from her sex. Just his sharp movements had her squeaking in surprise before she scrambled to get out of his reach. Her lame attempt at an escape was all but lost when he grabbed her around the waist and jerked her back into his hold. Another switch of his hands and her body, and Viviana was spread over his thighs, one hand digging into the sheets as the other grappled onto the side of his leg with surprisingly hurtful force. He kept her pinned down with his arm lying flat on her bare back where the camisole had risen up.

"What did I tell you?"

"Don't you spank me," she breathed, nails scratching into his skin with a delicious sting.

Chapter Eighteen

Her nails bit into his thigh a little rougher. "Don't, Anton, I swear to God."

"That feels quite good, so if you're worried it's hurting me … it's not. You know how much I love getting your marks all up and down my back. Left a bite on my shoulder that stayed for days, girl."

She whimpered a lovely sound as his palm came to lie above the line of her panties, rubbing under the fabric with a slow speed that was sure to make her nervous. Anton laughed lowly when she hid her face from his view.

"You want me to, don't you?"

"No …"

"*Viviana.*"

When she refused to respond again, Anton dragged her panties down low enough until they rested on the backs of her thighs. Viviana shifted and tried to pull away again, but the attempt was a half-hearted effort. If she really wanted him to let her go, she'd say so, and he would have instantly. It was just another one of those moments where she was embarrassed by her enjoyment, and he refused to let her shy away.

An opened palm snapped down and cracked her olive-toned flesh just above where he'd bunched the fabric up. Viviana gasped. Her muscles tightened and back straightened, her fingernails cutting into his thigh as the locks of her hair tumbled down to hide her tilting face from his view. His hand slapped down with another marginally harder tap above where he'd previously hit, and her back just barely curved off his legs.

With his fingers traveling down between her thighs and slipping in between her folds, Anton found her wetter than ever. Another one of his quiet hums released as he leaned forward and let her go just long enough to crawl up behind her. Pressing his lips down to the base of her spine, Viviana wasn't making a move to get away.

"You're so fucking wet, baby. Ask me to do it again." The faintest shake of her head was all that answered him back. "That's how you want to play this? You don't even want to get away now."

"You're such an asshole. A *bossy* one."

"Deny it turns you on. Beg for it."

"Fuck you," Viviana uttered, turning her face just enough for him to get the sight of her smirk. "Make me, *Boss.*"

Jesus, he all but growled as his teeth bit into the blade of her shoulder. Instead of jerking away like he thought she would, her body pressed back into his mouth. Blood rushed to the spots where his hands had previously spanked, turning her skin a pretty pale red. He rolled his thumbs over the handprints. She all but vibrated under his motions, backing into his palm every time it swept over the rounded cheeks of her ass.

"I'm warning you, Viviana. You keep that up and watch what will happen."

"You don't have the ba—"

Anton didn't even let her finish that statement before a fistful of her hair was entangled in his hand, pulling her up with his frame so her back was flush to his chest. Reaching around, he let his fingers dance along the curve of her throat before they gripped tightly there as well. When her air caught, he sighed and kissed the spot behind her ear.

"You want to finish that sentence, *katyonak*?"

Without a doubt, Viviana didn't like to be called kitten, no matter what language it was in. Claws came out every time he let that pet name cross his lips. Sure enough, her fingers dug into his side with damning force.

"Why, is the boss gonna come out to play with me?"

Anton wasn't going to give her that one, because that was exactly what she wanted.

"You know what I want to see?" he asked darkly.

"What's that?"

Anton swallowed the thickness that had suddenly built up in his throat, letting his teeth graze against her. "You bent over, fingers fucking that pretty pussy of yours while I spank you. I think you'd come so hard like that, Vine."

"*My* fingers?"

"Mmhmm," he purred. "Don't even try to say you've never touched yourself. After that show with the plug, we both know better. I've been dying to see you get off on your own."

Viviana shuddered with another roll that seemed to start from her delicate shoulders and go all the way down to that ass fitted so nicely against his groin.

"That's not fair, Anton."

"Bad men don't play fair games. You picked me and I always win, but I bet it'll feel so fucking nice for you, too." With another nip on her neck, Anton released his grip on her throat and hair before she caught herself with her palms opened up to the bed as she dropped back down to her hands and knees. The lightest snap of his hand cracked across the back of her thigh with a force he knew would only hum with a sting. "Now, beg me."

Anton leaned back against the headboard, cocking a brow and waiting for her to make a move. He crossed his arms behind his head. Again, he was graced with the best sight of her ass lifting a little higher, showcasing her sex off in the sweetest way as her thighs widened and her knees pressed into the sheets.

"You lie," she whispered, looking back over her shoulder. He didn't miss her hand coming down to rest between her legs, either. Two fingers spread the lips of her pussy while a third swiped across the slit, gathering wetness to take up to the sensitive bud as the middle digit rolled with quick circles. "You've seen me."

"No," he said, shaking his head.

"Liar, liar."

A flutter of confusion and aggravation bit at his heels.

"Again, no I haven't. Stop pushing me, baby. It isn't going to work."

"Oh wait ..." Viviana said in a murmur, head dropping back down out of sight. When two fingers slipped into the entrance of her pussy without hesitating, her hips dropped into her own hand at the action. His dick was throbbing as she started a teasing rhythm with her own fingers. "No, that was me."

Anton's mind turned into a chaotic mess as he tried to figure out exactly what she meant. "Excuse me?"

A sigh, all wanton and thick slipped from her lips. Her fingers withdrew from her sex, wetness glistening, digits spreading to stretch her hole. Damn, his mouth turned dry as her legs shook when she didn't answer right away, instead bringing another finger out to roll over her clit.

"Did you watch me jerk off, Viviana?"

When her shoulders dropped down into the bed, her other hand joined the first. Anton couldn't even speak as Viviana took her time spreading fluids, fucking her body with two fingers on one hand while the other circled quick beats to her clit.

"Answer me," he managed to hiss out.

Anton didn't realize his teeth had clenched that hard behind his jaw.

A soft, muffled moan fell into the bed. Her shoulders tensed as her fingers fucked a little harder. Anton didn't even know how close she was, but he hadn't wanted it to quite go like that; after all, he did intend for his hand to be lying flat out to her ass ... repeatedly.

She was winning. He was fucking letting her.

"Viviana!"

"Yeah, Boss?"

"Oh, you little ..."

Clenching his fists at his sides, he tried so fucking hard to ignore the way his cock was aching to either be in his own palm, or shoved so fucking deep in her that he couldn't breathe. A harsh Russian curse fell from his lips before he was slipping a hand under his boxer-briefs to relieve some of the tension filling him up. Slow, measured strokes down his length matched the thrusts of Viviana's two fingers inside her sex. Sparks lit up behind his eyelids as they clenched shut then flew back open again.

After all, he so badly wanted to watch her, too.

"Like this, then?"

The question came out huskier than he intended because of his own hand on his cock. Pre-cum swept across his thumb as the digit rolled over the circumcised head, pleasure biting through his groin with a delirious tightening sensation.

When had she spied on him?

"You watched me play like this?"

Just as quick, one hand was gone from her sex. Viviana propped up on her elbow, just enough to turn back and stare at him with dark, hooded eyes. "No. Not quite like that."

"Tell me."

"Why?"

Anton forced himself to breathe, hand tightening around his shaft.

"Because ..." Something caught in his throat. He wanted to be buried inside of her before he came, but just the sound of her voice alone was doing him in. "Because I want to know."

"I'm so fucking wet," she murmured, withdrawing soaked fingers that spread her wider and tapped at her clit all at the same time. "Burning right up here, Anton. Singing from head to toe. So damned hot. Bet you could get me raging right through it, huh? Oh, this feels so good. You don't even know."

Fuck, she was avoiding his question like nothing else. He all but ached to know, now.

"Please ..."

The word hadn't even fully formed out of his mouth before he realized his mistake, but her satisfied laughter filled the room anyway.

"Check mate, *Boss.*"

"Goddamn it, Viviana."

When her fingers started to leave the only place he wanted to see them, Anton was quick to move. Crossing the small space between their bodies, he had his arm around her waist to hold her back in place while he leaned over her back. His hand laid flat to her ass instantly, the sound of the slap echoing into quiet room.

Viviana hissed at the hit. It had been much harder than the previous ones he landed.

"You're going to tell me," he said, the words coming out sinister and desire-fueled at the same time. "And I'm going to get you back for that trick, baby."

"Come on, then," she breathed. "Do it."

That pretty little ass of hers backed into his hand. Anton rubbed circles a little lower on her stinging flesh. His cock pressed against the small of her back, giving him just enough pressure to relieve that tension filling him back up again.

"Get that fucking hand back down there, Viviana. I want to hear those fingers sinking in and out of that pussy while I spank you again."

Finally—*finally*—the word he wanted to hear forced its way out of her mouth.

"Oh, God ... please."

"Are you going to tell me?"

Anton's hand slipped down between her thighs, meeting her own hand that was suddenly working a fast beat to her clit.

Wetness soaked his fingers more. Letting go of his hold on the bed, he leaned back enough to get her ass opened back up for his taps again.

"Are you?" he asked once more.

"*Yes.*"

"Tell me."

"I-in ... in the shower," she whimpered.

Anton cocked his head to the side, brow furrowing.

251

"You watched me in the shower." It wasn't even a question, just a crazy, hot realization that flooded both his mind and cock with the same lustful ravaging wave of need. A tiny nod answered him back. Jesus, why did that turn him on so fucking much? "Why?"

"Because—" Without warning, he released her ass before landing another solid smack to the back of her left thigh. Her fingers stuttered along his, stopping the rhythm to her clit instantly. "Fuck, *please* ..."

"Don't stop. Get that pussy of yours good and wet for me. Now, answer."

"I ha-had to grab ... the hair ... hairbrush," she managed to get out. "You didn't even know. Just cau-caught it out of the corner of ... my ... my eye. I'm—"

"Next time join me."

Her thighs trembled as heat saturated his palm when it laid down flat to sooth away some of the sting he'd created on her flesh.

"Come on, come for me. I want to really get started. This was nothing."

And she did ... broke so beautifully, high cries muffling into the sheets. She might have won, but he was still right. It felt awfully fucking good for him, too.

*

A week later, Viviana was on edge. She hadn't been expecting to be.

"Are you going to make that tasting with me today?"

Damn, she tried so hard to keep the tension out of her voice. It didn't work.

Anton walked past the bedroom for the second time without saying a word. He'd been attached to his cell phone all morning and it was starting to irk the fuck out of her. When he passed again, still not giving any indication that she'd even spoke, she threw a pillow out into the hallway. Finally, his steps faltered as his eyes glanced over his shoulder with a flashing warning.

"The tasting?"

Anton pointed at his phone and mouthed, "In a minute."

Viviana sighed, frustrated. Nothing bothered her more than when he ignored her.

They had a tasting scheduled for not only the wedding dinner, but the engagement party someone decided they just had to have, as well. She could have done without that, since they had enough to worry about, but Anton agreed without even asking her. Not only that, but the invitations were ready to be picked up and sent out, too. Then there was the party planner ... designer—whatever the hell she called herself— who needed confirmation on the choices for linen, flowers ... and so much more. That was another thing Viviana didn't know if he was handling, or her.

Considering he was still on his fucking phone.

Viviana didn't really know what was going on, but it had to be something serious because from five o'clock in the morning on, Anton wasn't at her side like he usually was before he left to go to the club. When she asked, he wouldn't say.

Irritated was an understatement.

"Anton, hey, are you going to make that tasting or not?"

Nothing.

"No, that's good. I don't like that that's where he wants to go, but I can't say anything about it. He wants to be comfortable, right?" Anton paused in his spiel, his fingers coming up to pinch the bridge of his nose as he shook his head. "I don't know, Ivan. I was lucky they stayed here as long as they did, honestly."

Viviana looked at the alarm clock on the nightstand as she put the clean sheets on their bed. Their time was running short and she still didn't know anything about the day's plans. Both of them needed to be out of the house within a few minutes or she wouldn't make her doctor's appointment. She had just managed to get that appointment an hour ago, too.

Damn it, her heart was stuttering just thinking about it.

In the midst of everything going on, Viviana had *forgotten* about something she shouldn't have. She felt so incredibly stupid. They drank, and smoked …

What if?

Her thoughts were all but screaming.

Finally, the conversation out in the hallway ended.

"*What*, Viviana?" Her words seemed to catch in her throat at his exasperated voice. "Yes, I'll make the tasting. We can pick up the invitations together after. You'll have to go to the designer's alone because Daniil got confirmation for his release from the hospital and he convinced Sasha to go back to their home. I promised to be there to get him settled. What else is there?"

She blinked back at him, her hands splaying out to the comforter. Tears threatened to make an appearance, but she forced them back as a deep breath shuddered into her aching lungs. More than anything, she just wanted to blurt it out and see what would happen, but her nerves weren't quite strong enough then.

"Okay, thank you. That's all I wanted to know. I'm going to the clinic first, so I might be a little late for the appointment with the designer. Can you call her and let her know; she likes you better and probably won't bite your head off."

Anton didn't move for a minute. "Why?"

"I just said—"

"No, why are you going to the clinic today? You should have told me you weren't feeling well, Vine."

Something painful rolled through her stomach. One thing they had made clear between them was no more lying. Ever. If he couldn't tell her something, he just wasn't to say anything at all and she would get the point. This wasn't even close to being the same thing and Viviana knew it.

"I forgot to take my birth control shot."

The words were breathed below a whisper but they seemed to reach his spot, given the phone slipped out of his grasp with a clatter to the hardwood floor. Frozen like a statue, Anton didn't even blink. In fact, Viviana was sure she didn't see him breathe for a whole thirty seconds.

"Say something, please."

A noise ... that was all she got. A single noise.

Viviana felt the need to explain. "I used to get appointment notifications from my doctor's office in Toronto on my old phone, but Boris destroyed it. I'm so, so—"

Another noise interrupted her, his heated gaze blazing into hers with a burn that had her aching.

"Don't apologize," he said quietly.

Relief washed over her. "I know I was supposed to get something set up here, but it just slipped my mind. I thought I'd have time."

"Stop."

"What?"

Anton exhaled through his nose. "Just ... stop. When did you figure it out?"

"This morning. I was trying to work out the dates for the rehearsal and all that ... then it clicked. I should have started my cycle two days ago. I'm pretty damned regular. Most girls don't even get their period on the shot."

"We fucked last night. We've fucked every night for the last week." A nod answered him back. That was about all she could give. Viviana didn't need a verbal reminder of just how often they had sex; she was more than aware. "So, even if nothing shows up, it might still ..."

"Yeah."

The silence that answered back was almost painful. Anton's gaze had turned to the wall behind her. Viviana finished making their bed and tossing the pillows back up in place before she grabbed her purse from the couch. She didn't have time for him to let it sink in. The appointment was in thirty minutes and she would just make it in time.

She bit her lip and shrugged. "It's more than likely that nothing is going to come up. Chances are pretty slim. The shot is weird like that." Even she didn't believe what she was saying. "Anyway, we can talk about it tonight. I have to go, Anton."

With a nod, he stepped to the side and let her leave the bedroom. Viviana had just made it to the stairwell when she heard him clear his throat.

"Wait …"

Viviana turned to find him staring down at the floor where the phone had dropped. "Yeah?"

"Do you not want to be?"

"At all, or at this moment?" she asked back. "We talked about my feelings when it came to kids."

"No, I know. I just meant—"

"Yes, eventually that'd be awesome. And even right now, if you were okay with it. There's also the issue of smoking up and drinking. That kind of stuff isn't okay when you're …" Oh God, she couldn't even force the word out. "It's just not okay, Anton."

He opened his mouth to speak, but nothing came out. She understood the confusion he must have felt, because turmoil had wrapped her heart all morning.

"It's a bad time," Viviana said, waving like that was the best explanation she could give. "It's great Daniil and Sasha want to go home and that you're allowing it. I've asked you repeatedly to make accommodations for us to leave here and move into the Oceana house, but you refused. That tells me you don't think it's safe at all."

Anton swallowed, his fists dropping into his pockets as he looked up to the ceiling. "It isn't. I haven't been talking about it, but there's a good chance Sonny dropped off the radar because something's about to go down and he doesn't want to be found after it happens."

"I don't care."

Exasperation wrote lines over his face as he stared back. "This would be even more of a reason to stay here where security is in place."

Viviana pointed at a door three feet away that had been locked the entire duration of their stay. "What's behind there?"

"Nothing." Anton cringed, eyeing the door before he corrected himself, "Nothing that's for you to bother with."

"Don't lie to me. There are two other rooms in this house that I can't enter, too. Do not shovel bullshit at me. Sure, when we leave this place it will go to the Bratva and it'll be out of our hands, but right now, it's not. I want to go home. If you want to get serious about this ..." she muttered, waving at her midsection because the word just didn't feel okay to say, "then talk to me about going *home*."

Scooping up the phone off the floor, he dropped it into his pocket, and made his way down the hall. It didn't matter now that she was likely going to be late for the appointment, not with the soft smile that played on his face filling her sight. Coming to stop beside her, a single finger found its way under her chin. His lips pressed softly to her cheek.

"Okay, we'll talk about going home."

"Just talk?"

Grazing his thumb along her bottom lip, Anton said, "No, we'll figure it out."

"I can't get the shot today ... in case, you know. We'll have to wait a little while."

"I'll pick condoms up." Turning her face, she met his tender kiss. "I'm sorry I was being difficult this morning. Daniil is ... stubborn. Mom just wants him to be happy and comfortable."

"And so do you," she pointed out gently.

"Yes, but I want them safe and close, too. That's why they had a private suite upstairs, despite the awkwardness at first. I had them close so I could keep my eye out in case someone got crazy ideas. Just like I keep you close." Anton sighed before he added, "Please don't do anything rash. Give me time and I'll do whatever the hell you want. Shocked the fuck out of me for a minute ... I wasn't expecting to hear that for at least another couple of years, baby."

"I might not—"

"But you might be," he interrupted, his hand touched

comfortingly on her back. "You're trying to soften it like we're teenagers here. I'm twenty-seven, not nineteen. This is okay."

"Just okay?"

The feel of his mouth curving against her cheek told her more than he would say. Anton was ecstatic, he just wouldn't admit it outright.

"Great, Vine. Go to your appointment and call me the moment you find out anything. I promised Sasha and Daniil, plus I have to pick up something from one of my guys. Otherwise, I'd drop everything and go with you. I'm sorry. I'll let the designer know you're going to be late."

"I feel stupid," she whispered. "I should have been keeping better track."

Again, Anton shrugged dismissively. "You were, but I came in and upset your life and the schedules you were keeping. It just happened. We'll figure it all out. I'm not going to complain."

Thank God for that.

Viviana was shrugging on her coat and opening the front door to the safe house when she heard Anton calling behind her.

"Hey, you know how this goes. Rory needs to escort you and don't forget Rocco."

"Anton, I don't want him going in," she said, eyes narrowing as he came around the corner of the hallway with their pup on his heels. "That's private business. Rocco, on the other hand, can wait outside with him."

Crossing his arms over his broad chest, Anton's challenging stare meeting her defiant gaze. "Rory can stay in the waiting room. Everything remains private. Rocco will wait outside with the other two."

Viviana stared at him in total disbelief. "Come on, please?"

"No. No one is going to know a thing, but you have to have at least one of them close by."

"No one is going to shoot me in broad daylight,

Anton!" Just the look of pain that crossed his features had her backtracking. "I'm sorry, I just … fine. I'll take Rory inside but I swear to God if he makes a move to go in the room with me I will cut off his balls."

A faint smile curved his lips before it disappeared. "You know why I'm doing this."

"I know." Turning to grab Rocco's collar off the designated hook, the pup was already bounding over and letting it slip over his thick neck. He took off out into the wide driveway when Viviana allowed him to, hearing the whistle of a bull outside. "I won't be difficult if you promise to make good on your promise about going home."

"I'm a man of my word."

"Come on, princess … we haven't got all day out here," Rory said.

Viviana frowned over her shoulder.

"I'll be happy when I can go somewhere without babysitters."

"Probably never going to happen; you just won't know."

"Yeah, but I could handle that."

"Go," Anton said, leaning down to kiss her mouth soundly. "You're going to be late."

Outside, Rory waved at the SUV parked across the quiet street. Far too excited for her liking, he began to make grabbing motions at Viviana's car keys. Rocco sniffed between her car and Anton's with a vengeance. Sharp huffs of breath panted from the dog like he was catching something, drawing her attention in.

"Let me drive, please," Rory pleaded.

"No way."

"You haven't opened up that pretty thing in days. Let me be the one to do it properly."

That was sadly true. Despite how much she loved her Bentley, Viviana didn't get to drive it as much as she wanted.

"No."

Viviana unlocked the car just as Rocco came to sniff

her leg. A sharp bark fell from his curled back muzzle, stopping her action up short.

Rory opened the door on his side, not even thinking about the warning the pup had just given off. Anton was out the front door shouting her name fearfully. Rocco bit down onto her wrist with damning force. Then, she heard the slight hiss before a tick ... tick ... tick echoed.

Viviana hit the ground, all breath gone at impact.

It was heat ...

Screams ...

Pain ...

And then nothing.

Chapter Nineteen

Anton stared with unseeing eyes at the emergency room lobby. All he could picture was Viviana, lying pale and slumped on the pavement. Dimly he registered that Ivan was talking to him, but Anton barely heard, unable to stop his mind from replaying the terrifying events, the horror and helplessness he'd felt when that car bomb exploded.

"Please open your eyes, Viviana … look at me."

"Call the ambulance!"

The lowest, most achingly pain-filled whine from the pup curled around one of his arms was the hardest thing Anton ever had to hear, next to the total silence of the woman in his other. He'd take anything, even air, to pass her lips.

"… time relay, gave it a five-second lapse before the pipe blew. Someone screwed it up when they set up the wires because it shouldn't have had a delay like that at all. The blast wasn't as big, either."

"Rory, you good? Rory!"

"Yeah, I'm good. Shit. Knocked the wind out of me for a minute. Cracked my head on the pavement."

"The second floor and basement needs to be cleaned the fuck out. We've got three minutes at the most."

"Did they clear out the safe house?"

"Just in time before the cops showed," someone else piped in.

"Boss?"

"Call the goddamn—"

"I did … I did."

"Rocco took most of the hit. She didn't get a burn on her, thank God. They're performing an emergency operation at the vet. Burned half of his side to nothing."

"Get that vet on the phone for my dog!"

"Somebody get the vet on call for Rocco!"

"I'm sorry, Boss ... I didn't know."

"Ambulance is here ..."

"When was her car left unattended?"

"Does that really matter right now?"

"Turning tachycardic... Blood pressure is dropping"

"No ocular reaction ..."

"Anton?"

"Possible head trauma ..."

"Anton?"

"Severe blood loss. Have two liters of type-O on standby ..."

Anton blinked up at the face staring down at him then looked around. The emergency room seemed to go on like nothing was amiss.

Like his heart and soul hadn't almost fucking died two hours before.

No one would give him answers, he wasn't immediate family. No one would say a thing.

"What?"

The sound of his voice was nothing more than a raspy breath of air. Panic and pain had all but saturated his entire nervous system. Never had he shut down so totally before. There was something to be said for a body that responded to shock in the way his did, and for a moment he was grateful because he hadn't even noticed the time passing him by.

His fists curled and fingernails bit into the palms of his hands as the memory of her blood staining everything red filled his mind again. The thuds of his heart turned louder, adrenaline rushing through his widening veins like a drug.

Ivan rubbed a hand over his face, chancing a glance over his shoulder.

"Her aunt just arrived."

Anton was out of his chair instantly. "Who in the hell—"

Ivan's hands landed on his shoulders, keeping him in place. "This is important, Anton, so shut up for a minute. Sonny's wife is considered her immediate family. You wanted info, now here's your chance, okay? Even the bastard's cousin showed up with her. The one we paid off the first time. They're either really stupid, or they're looking for something. Take a breath and decide how you want to go about doing this."

A beat of silence passed before Ivan asked, "Shit, have you had your neck and arm looked at yet?"

"No," Anton growled.

Glass had embedded into his shoulder and arm the blast of the amateur pipe bomb. It didn't even register over his anger and anxiety. More than one nurse had approached him, but he made it clear if they weren't there to tell him about Viviana, he didn't want to see their faces.

Eventually, they stopped.

"Man, this one is bad …"

"Don't touch me," Anton spat, jerking out of his friend's hold.

Several heads swung in his direction, given it was the first time he'd spoken that loud in hours. Too many of his men to count. They all just stared and waited. He didn't know what to fucking say. So many precautions had been put into place. Rocco had done just was he was trained to do.

Unfortunately, things slipped his eye.

Given her car was left unattended whenever she traveled with him, the device could have been placed at any time. Someone suggested it was likely done during a rain that happened three days before because the wiring hadn't gone off right for the timer. Maybe water screwed it up.

Anton didn't care.

It still *happened.*

"Goddamn it!"

The hard plastic chair met his back again. Ivan was quick to find a seat beside him while Anton studiously avoided the eyes watching his every move. There was nothing worse than feeling like you were under a microscope. Of course his whole life had felt like that, but this was so much different.

How would he react if someone came out and said she was ... was ... *gone?*

Oh God, he couldn't breathe again.

Ivan's hushed voice brought him out of the panic attack. "Tell me what we know."

"What?"

"Come on, Anton. We've seen this kind of crap before. Tell me what we know."

The lump in his throat ached. "Superficial wounds. A possible head injury. Bad cut above her eye. A lot of fucking blood."

He'd seen more, caused a lot of others to bleed, but he didn't ever want to see *hers.*

"What else?"

"Heartbeat went crazy in the ambulance and then her blood pressure suddenly dropped."

"What'd they give her?"

"Huh?"

"Didn't they say?"

"Probably."

"You weren't paying attention?"

Anton shook his head. "I couldn't, not well enough. She was ... she was ... *fuck.*"

"Mr. Avdonin?" The sound of his last name caused Anton's head to jerk up. A tired nurse with a clipboard waved a single gloved hand with a faint smile. "Hi. I just received confirmation from the family that you are Miss Carducci's fiancé and they've given me permission to divulge her current state, so we can speak now, if you're ready."

Anton's mouth went dry. "Okay. Yes, sure. Here is fine."

The nurse gave a snort nod before she went over the charts in her hand. Anton barely heard anything over the thrum of his heart and the anger that surged through his soul.

Several lacerations and wounds, and contrary to what the bulls had thought, Rocco didn't take all of the hit, as Viviana had also sustained a few minor burns on her left arm.

The dog bite where Rocco had taken her down before the blast was minor compared to everything else. Only one transfusion of blood had been needed, her heart was stabilized, and the lung that nearly collapsed was doing fine. They were going to keep her sedated for a while longer until all the wounds were cleaned and they were positive the glass shards were removed. No unnecessary pain that way. If she woke up and showed no visible signs of head trauma, she could be out within a couple of days with the understanding she needed vigilant care for her wounds.

Despite all the good news, there was one more thing he wanted to know about.

Again, Anton felt like the pressure in his chest was making it hard to breathe.

"What about … her blood work?"

One would have been done, he knew.

"I don't understand what you mean specifically."

He was all too aware of Ivan sitting beside him.

"Did anything show up in her blood work pregnancy-wise?"

Ivan coughed and sat back in his chair. Anton ignored the surprise that flitted through his best friend's eyes as the man met his gaze. What did he expect him to say?

"I'm sorry, that's related directly to the patient and not her current state of injury due to the accident. Confidentiality laws state—"

"Yeah, we know the law," Ivan interrupted shortly. "When can he see her?"

"Once she's set up in her private room and they're ready to wake her up, it'll be great if Mr. Avdonin can be in there. Someone she'll recognize. So far, everything is going remarkably well. She's a very strong, lucky young woman."

Without another word, the nurse was gone.

Anton leaned back into his chair with a heavy sigh.

"She's pregnant?"

"We don't know. It's just a possibility."

"You work fast," Ivan mused quietly.

"I didn't intend to."

"That's how it usually happens."

Despite the seriousness of everything, Anton found himself chuckling. Unfortunately, even the sound of it was cold. A slow rage was beginning to build in his blood, turning him raw and red from the inside out. A strange calm seemed to overtake his previous panic, settling deep in his gut like a poison ready to kill.

And he found that he was ready for exactly that.

"If she is, are you sure—"

"Do not finish that question, Ivan. I'm warning you. You're mighty fucking lucky you even got that much out before you sported a newly broken jaw."

"Well …" The lawyer coughed, looking about as uncomfortable as he could possibly get. "It's just that bodyguard of hers. You told me, so I have to ask. As your friend, I have to. Anton, that wasn't very long before you, okay?"

It'd be a damned lie if Anton didn't admit he had considered that for a brief moment when Viviana said her being pregnant was a possibility. It also took him thirty seconds to do the math when she said four weeks late for her shot and a couple of days late for her cycle. He also knew she'd had it last month, considering he had to go out at the crack of dawn to pick up the stuff she needed. Which in and of itself was embarrassing for her and him enough. That would be the last goddamn time he ever picked out tampons. There were some things men shouldn't have to be subjected to and that was one of them.

"I'm able to count just like you can. Your fancy schools didn't do anything more for your common sense than a lack of higher education did for mine."

"Ouch. That higher education keeps you out of jail, asshole."

"S'mine if she is," Anton mumbled, rubbing a hand over his face and ignoring Ivan's comment. "I know it is."

"Good enough for me."

Anton stood, turning up the cuffs of his dress shirt until they rolled around his elbows on either side. The one side of his shirt was soaked a morbid reddish brown. A sting started to hum in his neck and arm where he himself was injured.

"Let's go."

"Huh?" Ivan glanced up.

"We've got some Cosa Nostra to speak to."

*

Lucille Carducci wouldn't meet Anton's gaze.

"You've got a lot of fucking nerve coming here," he ground out.

The man at her side leaned into the wall, crossing his arms and keeping his mouth shut. That was a better choice for his health, in Anton's honest opinion. He wasn't above laying a beat down on somebody inside a hospital. It just meant they were that much closer to getting help when he was done.

"After what your husband did, you'd think you'd know better."

Lucille looked up through her wet mascara lashes, tears streaking down her cheeks. "That, Mr. Avdonin, is exactly why I'm here." Ivan was ten feet away, keeping watch for intruders while they spoke in a private hallway that had dimmed lights and practically no activity at all. "After all, the feds will be around, no doubt. They very well might stop to wonder why his wife is here if he is the one involved, and in the morning ..."

"In the morning, what?"

"Perhaps they won't look to you when I'm at the hospital again, yes?"

Air cut through his teeth like a hiss. "If you knew—"

"I didn't," she rushed to say. "Neither of us did."

The man—Conrad—who had been keeping quiet finally spoke up, but he kept his gaze averted to the wall behind Anton. "Had we known, we would have brought it to your attention. Sonny has been making a lot of decisions like that lately without giving anyone notice. Sonny doesn't trust a soul anymore. I overheard some of your boys talking."

"And?" Anton asked.

"By the sounds of it, this was probably somebody's *in* into the family, and it screams of amateur work."

Anton had to agree. "The bomb wasn't packed right for the blast to get maximum impact. Whatever relay they had on the timer fucked up because my dog had more than enough time to take her down to the ground before it blew. Her bull only got a few scrapes and bumps. Amateur is saying it lightly. We were lucky her car's gas tank was just about running on empty or else it might have been much worse."

"Sonny offered the job to somebody young, likely." There was clear revulsion coloring Conrad's tone. "Some of the younger boys who want their button mentioned Sonny was looking for a pipe maker. Any idiot can Google that shit, but it takes someone with a little bit of experience to get it right."

"Which bothers you the most—that it was someone young, or that it happened at all?" Ivan asked from behind them. "Because let me tell you, I know which one pisses me off more."

"We certainly don't think Viviana deserves to die because Sonny has a mistake to fix. His work is always sloppy."

Anton was confused. "What mistake? If this is about the paternity again, that's a pointless, dead horse he's beating. She already knows and it doesn't make much of a difference now. The Bratva who know aren't making any fuss and they won't while I'm alive. Fucking pointless," he repeated.

"No, not that."

"Then what?"

The words were all but breathed into the air as Conrad said, "Roman's death."

Ice slipped over Anton's heart as the cold grip of reality climbed his spine. "Explain."

"It's only an assumption," Lucille interjected gently.

"We don't know for sure."

"Not what I said," Anton all but snarled, making the woman flinch. "Explain!"

"Anton," Ivan warned. "Lower your voice before somebody comes down here."

"Someone needs to explain this *assumption*, or I'm done with this chitchat."

"He's a shitty boss." Conrad finally regarded Anton with an indifferent gaze. "I've worked alongside him and his brother ever since we were teenagers in this business. There was a reason his father had Roman ready and willing to take over as the head of the family when he was gone. Sonny can't do it because he's too fucking greedy; his choices lack intelligence; things slip between cracks too often; he's got a mighty temper …"

It was only then that Anton noticed the yellowish bruises that barely peeked out above Lucille's high collared blouse. It didn't matter how much he hated her—all of Viviana's family, really—no woman should be touched by her husband in that way.

"It's not so far of a stretch that he might have screwed up something with Roman, too."

"Like what?" Anton muttered.

Lucille heaved a sigh. "Viviana was staying at my home the night Roman was suspected to have been killed. Her mother and brother were out somewhere, but he had them staying with us for safety reasons. Vine was calling her father just as she was leaving my house to return home. She'd forgotten something she needed for the next day. I can't remember what it was. It wasn't five minutes later that she was back in the house, white as a sheet. Wouldn't answer a thing when asked."

"Anton, you okay?"

Anton ignored his lawyer. The moral compass he tried so hard to keep a firm grip on was suddenly spinning with no desire to stop in sight.

"Are you telling me she might have been on the phone

when—" Pulling his lips into a sneer, the words cut off. Anton wouldn't say it out loud for his own peace of mind. "Is that what you're saying?"

Conrad shrugged. "It's a good possibility. The paternity was nothing more than a reason for him to get Roman gone. Tony and Christina were just fodder to make sure no one talked. Viviana, on the other hand, was a whole different ballgame. Take her out, and he risked having the wrath of the Bratva coming down on him. He very well might have stuttered in that choice. And then when he had her away in Toronto and you weren't making a move to take her, maybe he figured you didn't want to anymore. If you were letting it go, then he was fine to give an order for her to be gone. That bodyguard of hers was begging for an in, anyway."

"That would have been a very bad choice," Anton said. "A terrible one, actually."

"If I'd known what he had done … I never would have told him about Viviana calling Roman and coming back into the house like she did that night," Lucille whispered, her ashamed gaze turning away.

Conrad's arm draped over the woman's shoulders, his fingers squeezing with the compassionate touch of what Anton considered to be a lover's. When the man's eyes turned softer, Anton didn't doubt they were involved for a minute.

"It's all right, Lucy. Not your fault," Conrad murmured.

"I wish we would ha—"

"But you didn't." Fingernails bit into Anton's palms again. The only thing he wanted to do was end the person responsible for everything that had happened. "You haven't done a thing for her since her family was killed. She's been alone. No fucking thanks to you, she's a hell of a lot better off now. I'm going to leave this hospital, and I expect you to as well. But before you go, make sure the front desk knows Ivan is her lawyer and the only one with control of who enters and leaves her room. Is that understood?"

"Not you?" Lucille asked, appearing confused.

"No, I have things to do. After all, you said it first. When you're called back to a hospital tomorrow, perhaps the feds won't look to *me*."

*

The sky was quickly darkening. It was the only real indication for the Bratva boss as to how much time had passed him by. He was ignoring the green glow of the digital clock on the dashboard. As it was, he'd already been gone far too long.

Anton glanced out of the SUV's tinted window. Constantly on alert. He checked and rechecked behind, around, and in front of their vehicle more times than he could count. Sure, he'd lost whoever was trailing him before he even left the hospital's underground garage thanks to a switch of clothes and a well-placed fedora, but that didn't mean he wasn't on edge.

"What do you think?" Bo asked quietly. Anton's youngest brigadier checked his own mirror.

Because Anton couldn't risk being seen at his club, he called Bo to pick up his weapon of choice. The particular set of scopes he'd been looking for that the man had previously delivered to him as a birthday gift were going to come in handy sooner than he thought.

Anton's hand came to rest on the steering wheel lazily. The pain simmering up his arm only served to fuel his low lying rage. The cuts crisscrossing his neck were nothing compared to the wound on his shoulder. One of the bulls had hastily dropped superglue along the jagged tear before wrapping it up with some gauze. It was sealed tight. Still, the injury seemed to lick with an excruciating burn every time he moved, so that needed to be looked at soon.

An infection was nothing more than a bitch he didn't need.

"Boss?"

Anton ticked his chin up in the direction of the

apartment building.

"Right there. One of his mistresses, I guess. Ivan's been trying for days to find out where the bastard was staying, but I got it from his wife like it was nothing. Woman wants him gone; she just won't outright say it. I think she's screwing around with the cousin, actually. Sonny's got his head shoved so far in the sand it's crazy. Everything he touches turns to shit. He's a walking, fucking disease."

Bo cleared his throat, taking a heavy drag from the cigarette dangling between his fingers. "You're taking this remarkably well. If it was Steph …" The younger man trailed off as he exhaled the smoke into the SUV's cab.

Anton disagreed. He wasn't taking it well at all. Whatever care or concern he might have had left for anyone in the direct vicinity of Sonny Carducci was in no way his problem when the scene went down. The quiet, stillness of his own person was just a by-product of his own anger and anxiety, one he learned to control with near silence and little movements.

Ethics? Gone.

Lungs? Breathing.

Heart? Aching.

Viviana? Alive.

Anton felt robotic. As if he was just moving through the motions for the time being because that's what he had to do. He just fucking had to. Despite the city moving around them with a gentle, humming flow, sounds didn't register. The only thing he heard was rushing blood in his ringing eardrums.

Stony.

Calculating.

Seething.

Anton was *pissed.*

And there wasn't anything quite like a Russian boss with a vendetta.

"You could say that," he finally replied indifferently.

Red hot and ice cold.

The man inside that building had damn near taken away Anton's entire life with a horribly placed, substandard bomb. The damned thing could have been a how-not-to-do manual for any pipe maker. That wasn't to say it hadn't gotten his point across, but the Bratva prince had a much better one coming. It was sure to turn a few heads and make headlines.

When it came to Viviana, lucky was a downright understatement. Had she been just inches closer to the blast, had Rocco not taken her down like he did, had the medics not gotten her heartbeat to regulate—there were too many variables that slipped into place for her.

Maybe Anton should start going to the temple like his mother kept bothering him about. Considering some God was up there looking out for one of them. It was probably Viviana. The girl was a goddamn angel while he was nothing more than a well-dressed sinner.

"What'd they say about Rocco?"

Anton flinched at the question. His tongue peeked out to wet his lips as he considered the phone call he'd received a little over a half an hour ago.

"Operation went okay, he made it out which was more than they thought he'd do. Covered with seventy percent burns. Three broken ribs. The blast likely ruined his scenting ability, or most of it. Pup's going to be in a lot of pain for a long time."

There was a choice he had to make ... one that damn near killed him. Put Rocco down or see how he fared in the next few months. It'd be rehab, constant pain medication, and skin grafts. Costly, but that was the least of his master's worry.

"I'm going to have him put down in the morning," Anton managed to say, ignoring the thickness that built in his tone. "They're keeping him sedated so he doesn't wake up. Vine isn't going to be happy about it, but I can't let that dog suffer. There's no respect in that."

"And Vine?"

Anton breathed, letting the pain from the action soak him from head to toe. He hadn't spoken to his lover on the phone, but from Ivan's account, she was doing okay. After she'd calmed down about him not being there, of course. And when he asked again about the blood work, he hadn't gotten a response because his lawyer was too much of a fucking pussy to ask.

"Awake, talking, being her usual self ..."

"That's good," Bo said, shrugging.

"And pissed off like nothing else because I'm not there."

The younger man chuckled with a nod. "No doubt."

With his arm reaching back into the SUV's cab, Anton's hand came in contact with a gun case. Agony rocked him from the action, but he didn't care a bit. The boss had business to attend to and his own issues could wait.

Only a few more hours, and he'd be right where he needed to be: beside Viviana.

"I made a promise to be there with her every morning. I need to make good on that."

"Get it done, then. Let's smoke this rat out."

Chapter Twenty

"You didn't tell him, did you?"

Ivan, resting back in the comfortable leather chair in Viviana's private hospital room, shook his head and grinned like a fool. "No."

"But he asked?"

"Yep. You do know he's going to kill me when he finds out I knew before him, right?"

Viviana sighed, resting back into the pillows meant to help ease the pain in her back. Holy hell was she sore ... and tired. She was also terribly worried and had little to no memory of the last forty-eight hours.

Maybe the memories would come back slowly, the doctor said. And maybe they wouldn't.

Viviana wished they wouldn't. She didn't want to remember any of it, but she swore she could hear Anton yelling her name. Or maybe that was just her muddled brain creating the recollection. She also wished that little drip of morphine she had finally accepted to take when it was offered for the fifth time would actually do something.

Not long after the sweet nurse and quiet mannered doctor woke her up, one of the first things out of their mouths was the fact that she was pregnant. Not very far along, and from what they understood, everything seemed okay. The mandatory blood work that was done on all new patients shown her hGC level was at twenty-eight mlU/cc.

A definite positive for pregnancy.

They then proceeded to calmly explain the accident, her injuries, and what happened after. It didn't matter how soft they kept their voices, or how quick they were to say it most likely wouldn't affect the pregnancy, Viviana still cried herself into an anxiety worthy mess. She couldn't figure out when it had happened and she'd been so worried that maybe—oh God, just *maybe*—it had been before she was back in New York.

That all disappeared when she was able to remember her last menstrual cycle, and the doctor guaranteed her conception date would have been between the last fourteen to eighteen days, given the level of hormones doubled with every passing day and hers was still showing a low enough number to be an early pregnancy.

It might have gone better if she'd woken up to Anton in her room with the nurse and doctor instead of Ivan.

"He'll get over it," she finally replied, wincing on the last word when her fluid IV jostled.

"The doctor said all you need to do was ask and the nurse will up the dosage. It's safe."

"I'm fine."

"Said no one who survived a blast from a crappy bomb ever," Ivan joked.

"How old are you?"

Ivan gave her a cheeky smile. "Old enough to ignore your dirty looks when I say it. It *is* safe, Vine. Just ask."

Didn't matter to her. Studies this and studies that. Viviana heard enough of it from the nurse when they were changing her bandages. It was bad enough the time she got pregnant was likely right around the point she drank half a night away and smoked up. Of course, the doctor had rushed to assure her those little slips probably hadn't done any damage, either.

Oh God, he'd taken her so good that night, too.

Soft and slow.

Tender and sweet.

Like loving her was the easiest goddamn thing for him to do.

And he did it *so* fucking well.

Coming deep and hard enough that she'd felt his release. Holding her body connected with his as she gasped her way through an orgasm. Wrapping her tight in blankets and limbs before his fingers splayed wide open above the spot where her heart thundered like a drum.

Yeah.

Viviana couldn't remember a bit about the past forty-eight hours, but she remembered that night two weeks before like nothing else. She had to wonder if ... *somehow* ... that had been the one to do it.

Turning to look at Ivan out of the corner of her sore eye, she asked, "Where is he?"

The older man sighed. "Please stop asking."

"But—"

"Stop."

Viviana scowled, the action causing pain to ricochet from the cut above her brow to the side of her face. Tears fell without her permission, air sucking into her lungs like a cat's hiss.

"Okay, that's enough of that," Ivan muttered.

Not thirty seconds later, the nurse was in. Pain medication was doubled. Viviana slept.

*

"So, the police were here again," Ivan informed. "Left an hour ago."

Viviana had only been awake for a short time. Just long enough for the nurse on duty to come in and wake her up to ask if she was feeling well enough to eat. Another dosage of antibiotics in her IV drip later and the woman was gone just as quickly as she came. Viviana couldn't swallow pills, so liquid form it was.

"And?"

Ivan shrugged as he handed over a plastic cup with a bendy straw. "Same as this morning, sweetheart. You don't have any recollection of the actual event or the hours leading up to it, it's been verified by the doctor, so what can they do. They've gotten more than enough statements from the bulls and the medics that arrived on the scene. I imagine they'll want to speak with you in a week or so when you're feeling up to it."

"And?" Viviana pressed again.

"And nothing. There's no set rules for this. You say

what you know."

There wasn't very much for her to tell, then. The apple juice felt like heaven sliding down her raw esophagus. Never let it be said that an impact, no matter how little, didn't affect someone everywhere it could possibly reach. Because it damn well did.

"What about ..." She trailed off, forcing the pain in her throat to subside before she could speak again. "Anton. Surely they want to speak—"

Ivan's gaze traveled to the door of her room that was only opened a crack. "As far as they know, they've been missing him on and off all day. He's come and gone. There isn't a sign-in sheet for your room, the security cameras are horribly placed and could have missed him easily. You've slept most of the day now, and otherwise you've been medicated, so you couldn't possibly be a reliable witness to his presence."

"Has he?"

Ivan wouldn't answer.

"Has he called again?"

"No."

Viviana swallowed the emotions rising up. Crying only served to hurt. Everything made her hurt, really. Unfortunately, holding it back caused painful sobs to catch in her throat.

Then something else pricked at the back of her mind.

Like a memory trying to form. One she couldn't bring up but knew was there.

A simple glance down at her wrist had the memory bubbling up. Suddenly, she was almost feeling Rocco's jaw clamping down on her bones as sharp canine teeth tore into skin.

"Oh, *Rocco* ..."

Ivan made a noise that fell somewhere between pain and concern. "Viviana?"

"Is he gone?"

"Rocco?"

"Yeah," she whispered, taking slow measured movements to turn on the bed.

"No, he's alive, but hurt awfully bad. The vet said he was doing all right, given everything. It's certainly not going to be easy, and I think … Well, Anton is seriously considering having him put down."

Anguished was an understatement.

Instead, it was more like a knife had stabbed into her heart. It had been vaguely explained of Rocco's involvement of getting her out of the way of the blast, and taking a great deal of the shrapnel and damage himself. Even so, Viviana hadn't really remembered, let alone felt what that meant to her until now.

Yours, Anton had once said. *Like me, he's waited a long time to have you with him, too.*

"But-but … he *can't*. Ivan, he just can't do that."

"Vine, listen to me and think. Rocco isn't going to be the same animal. He's going to need specialized care for the next long while …"

"I don't care! I'm *his*. He's mine. Anton can't do that!"

"He's going to be in a lot of agony. I know you care a great deal for him—"

"Stop trying to convince me otherwise," Viviana snapped, surprised at her own vehemence. She didn't even care if she sounded like a brat, not when it came to poor Rocco. "Call him. Call him and tell him I said no, Ivan."

"But—"

"*Do it.*"

His hands flew up, a signal of surrender. The trembling in Viviana's body barely began to subside at the sight. She was quiet as he picked up his cell phone and waved it between them with a soft expression.

"Okay. I'll try to call him, but there's no saying he'll answer right now."

The black darkness outside the windows caught her eye.

Where was *he?*

"Then leave a fucking message."

*

The ear buds from her iPod blocked out all noise. Slow, throaty tones that reminded her of a forties Americana type music hummed from the tiny speakers in her ears. Viviana didn't notice the time passing by after Ivan had left the room. The emotional, deep blues soaked her right to the core, reminding Viviana what it felt like to be ten-years-old and watching her mother in the mirror as she readied for a party.

Christina Carducci had once had the raspy hum of a smoker when she sang, but she never actually smoked. The low notes crawled from her lungs with the same ease and expertise as the higher ones, but she never took lessons. It was one thing Viviana wished she had taken from her mother … that ability to sing … but she couldn't carry a note to save her life.

Blues aren't about the sound of a voice, her mother once explained. *They're about feeling the emotions and the words where it hurts and making it echo from the heart and soul.*

So, when Rory had peeked into her room a little while ago with a bag in hand, Viviana had all but clawed through it to see if her iPod was there. Thank God it was. That and comfortable ass pajamas. Hospital gowns were not only indecent, but useless and itchy.

It had sucked for her to see Rory with a gash on his cheek and a large bruise up along his hairline, but he was quick to comfort that he'd faired even better than Anton. For a bit, Viviana felt better … but the sentiment didn't last long when she realized exactly what he said. No one had mentioned the injuries Anton suffered, and that only sent her worry right back up to spiking levels.

The bull didn't stay either, not after he handed over the bag and an unopened bottle of her favorite vitamin water, with the promise he'd be waiting to open up the next car Anton brought her home.

Damn, the Bentley was probably *dust.*

Or … tin scraps.

With the iPod in her ears, she didn't realize someone was in her room until someone gently touched her blanket-covered ankle. It didn't matter how lightly they approached, Viviana still shrieked like a banshee, tugging roughly on the IV in her arm as she flinched away from the intruder.

Her lungs ached as she tried to catch her breath and forget the pain.

No, it didn't work a bit.

Two men stood at the end of her bed. Tall, with faces shadowed by the dim lighting in the room, they almost looked menacing. Well dressed in similar black suits, ties properly tied, and badges on display in opened hands, Viviana swallowed her fear and felt a whole different emotion rise.

"Agents Todd and Danover from—"

Federal agents.

"Yeah, I know who you are. Get out of my room," she rasped. "I haven't a thing to say to either of you. I don't remember what happened, so we have nothing to talk about."

"Now, now, Viviana." Agent Todd on the right raised his brow in a chiding manner. "We both know that isn't true."

"We're not here for what happened today," Danover said quietly. "The police have their own investigation and it isn't considered our issue, yet. And even if it ever is, it won't be our team dealing with it."

"Then what?"

Her shaking fingers reached up to move the strands of tangled hair out of her eyes. Only twice had she been approached by federal agents in the past, and both times she had managed to get out of their vicinity quickly. This was a whole different ballgame, given she was all but forced to stay in bed for the next little while, and her lawyer was nowhere in sight.

Before either man spoke again, Viviana muttered, "Ivan wouldn't have let you in my room."

"No, but a badge does wonders for a young nurse," Todd replied just as quick. "Can't you speak without Anton's dogs attached to your ass?"

Ouch. That hurt a little more than he understood.

"Okay, now you can get the fuck out."

"No, I don't think we can. June sixth, two thousand and ten. Where were you around ten o'clock that night?"

It could have been so easy for Viviana to just up and say she couldn't remember the date. That was, after all, three years ago. It would also be the biggest damned lie she ever uttered in her life. It wasn't like she could ever forget the night before her father's body had been found in the bay with a bullet hole in the back of his skull.

"You're just coming around here to ask me this, now?"

Deflection was one tactic to use at least until Ivan returned. That was her piss poor plan, anyway.

"Seems like as good a time as ever," Danover answered, shrugging. "No uncle keeping you locked away. No crossing country borders for school. You certainly have nothing to hide, right? Just us, a room, and you. So, why not?"

Nothing to hide, sure. They had no idea. Speaking about family business—Cosa Nostra business—was a very bad thing. Especially if it was to federal agents. For Viviana, her silence had nothing to do with honor for her father's family, but the safety of her own self. Death was the only punishment acceptable when someone started talking to officials.

"Where were you that night?" Todd repeated.

Viviana swallowed again. "My Aunt Lucy's."

"Lucille Carducci, you mean."

"Yeah. Was there all night. Woke up to a news broadcast about Roman, and my mother called crying when she found out over the goddamn radio on her drive home. Now, if that's all you—"

"It isn't." Todd tossed a stack of white papers on the bed, but Viviana didn't make a move to look at what it was.

"Phone records between your father's office phone and your cell phone shows you were on the phone with him from nine-fifty that night until five after ten. Care to share what that call was about?"

No, she certainly didn't care to fucking share.

"How many times do I have to ask you to get out before you get the hint and go?"

"Where's Mr. Avdonin?" Danover asked. "We've stayed around watching and he's been MIA for a great length of time. Seems like people hear of him coming and going, but no one has actually seen him for themselves. That strikes me as odd, what about you, Stan?"

Agent Todd nodded with a severe expression. "Certainly. Wouldn't be like a mob boss to leave his pretty fiancée all alone like he has, unless he has some important business to attend to. Something he isn't worried about coming back on her because he's going to take care of that all by himself. On the streets, right, Viviana? Men like him, they don't deal with waiting for police to handle a little nonsense like a bomb. After all, no one can handle a situation quite like an Avdonin could. They have something of a flair when making a particular point clear. Would you like to hear some of his?"

Viviana flinched inwardly. *Shit.*

"I was arguing with him about wanting to leave my aunt's. The phone call, I mean," she was quick to say, hoping it'd keep them away from the topic of Anton. "I needed some clothes and was going to pick them up, but he wanted me to stay there for the night. We'd already been there three weeks. I was getting sick and fucking tired of it. I was young ... stupid. Didn't really understand the severity of what he must have been handling, or trying to."

"Because of the arrangement between the Avdonin family and yours," Todd said, expression not changing in the slightest.

"If you know, why ask?"

The man smiled a grim line. "You know why. We'd like

it confirmed."

"I *assume* that was why," she bit out.

"Your father was killed—"

Viviana snorted indelicately. "My father died of a heart attack. My dad was killed. If you want the facts from me, you might as well get your end right."

Both men's brows flew up to their hairlines.

"What?"

"I am the biological daughter of Nicoli Avdonin. Roman Carducci, however, was the one to raise me. See the difference?"

"That's … very interesting," Todd muttered, eyeing his partner.

"And odd," the other man echoed, "given who she's about to marry."

"Not really," Viviana butted in, feeling indignant and pissed. "Anton's grandfather was killed when his father was a young boy, which anyone with access to the internet would know. I think that's enough on that, though, so if we could finish this up, that'd be great."

"Yes, fine. Again, the phone call. Given the coroner's report, it's likely your father—*dad*—was killed that evening. Water mucked up the exact time of death a bit, but they narrowed it down to late evening hours to very early morning. Several reports from neighbours stated your uncle wasn't seen around his home that night. The car trailing him earlier in the evening lost him. I'm sure you're aware we're looking at him, especially since right after Roman's death, he slipped right into the Cosa Nostra throne like he was born for it."

Viviana forced the rising bile down. "Are you asking if Roman mentioned something to me? Because if so, he didn't."

"No," Agent Danover replied, "we're wondering if you *heard* anything. See the difference?"

"Shit, Vine, sorry that took me so long. The nurse from this morning just came back on shift and had your engagement ring packed away in a safe spot. Figured you'd want it clean …"

Ivan's voice trailed off as he pushed the room door all the way open. The disgusted scowl that covered his features as he exhaled harshly at the sight that met his eyes only caused Viviana's nervousness to intensify. She understood all too well how it looked for her to be alone with federal agents.

The lawyer was fast to surprise her.

"Might I remind you both that given my client's current medical state, any and all questions you ask, along with the answers she may give, are irrelevant and inadmissible for any public record." His finger pointed to the beeping machines when he added, "She's medicated. Dealing with immense trauma and stress. Liable to be considered under duress, which her doctor will be quick to point out first, should you take anything said farther than this room. Not only that, but she's in a much more delicate state than either of you possibly understand, not that it's any of your business to be properly informed. Under no circumstances is this an appropriate time for you to be accosting her with questions."

"Relax. We're not here for Anton," Danover said, not even bothering to turn around.

"And I don't care," Ivan barked.

"Miss Carducci … the call, that's all we want to know."

Viviana hid the shaking of her hands under thick blankets.

"There's nothing to tell. Roman made his point clear. I hung up the phone."

The stare-off that commenced between the two agents and Viviana lasted longer than she was comfortable with. Neither of them were budging and clearly she wasn't either. If they knew she was lying, they didn't call her on it.

"Your fiancé …"

Ivan huffed under his breath. "Get out."

Todd lifted a single shoulder as he asked, "Do you really know the man you're marrying?"

"Probably better than you," she retorted hotly. "If you

want to throw out some Freudian worthy bullshit about how I must have daddy issues because I'm marrying a man just like Roman, then you can go to hell. Yes, Agent Todd, I'm very aware of whom I lie down beside every night. And I wouldn't ask for anyone different."

"He's a dangerous man, Viviana."

Viviana shrugged. If they thought that bothered her, she had a news flash coming.

"Funny, the last thing Anton ever makes me feel is unsafe."

When the agents were gone and the door was closed, Ivan leaned against it and sighed with an exhausted noise. While Viviana was relieved they were gone, she was also waiting for the backlash from her lawyer.

"I'm sorry, Ivan."

"Don't be," he muttered. "We figured they'd be around."

"We?"

"Anton and me. Chatted about it for a little while. Nothing you say really affects him in regards to Roman, but if you don't want to talk, you're not required to. I wasn't about to let the bastards bully you into it."

"I'm hiding knowledge of a crime. That's punishable by law."

"You didn't hang up the phone, did you?"

"No," she whispered. "Dad had this new conference phone. Didn't matter how many times we told him he needed to hit the end call button after he hung the receiver up, he never remembered. Sonny was there, but he didn't know Dad had been on the phone with me ..."

"Sonny, what the fuck are you doing? You don't realize—"

"All you had to do was kill the bitch, Roman. That was it," Sonny spat.

"And the baby, too, right? Because let's not forget her. You gonna fucking kill me, now? Your own brother? Blood never mattered in this life. But unlike you, I followed that

creed. Come on then … do it."

"Turn around."

"No," Roman said.

Viviana blinked out of the memory, hearing the snap of the handgun's chamber being loaded in the background of her mind. She'd never forget that sound. And that's all it was … just a fucking sound.

That sound brought death. Always.

"Viviana?"

"He shot him in the back of the head, Ivan."

Ivan licked his lips and stared at her sadly. "To dishonor."

"No …" she said, shaking her head, "because Sonny couldn't look him in the eyes."

Chapter Twenty-One

The SUV's door silently closed shut. Anton didn't move his gaze from the front windshield as the younger man beside him nodded shortly and lit up another cigarette. Anton probably smoked half the man's pack before he even got back.

"It's done."

"You managed to get it all the way in?"

Bo shrugged. "Heard it hit something, Boss. Wasn't all that full so the flames aren't going to be huge. Now, we just wait for the alarms to start ringing."

So wait they did. Anton had the SUV sitting a little awkwardly in the parking space, but it wasn't bad enough to attract him a violation ticket. Like he'd told Viviana … careful. That's what it was all about for him when he did a scene. Anyone else could do theirs however the fuck they wanted, but Anton made sure he left nothing behind.

Vehicles were dumped. Weapons and clothes destroyed. No souvenirs kept.

Just memories and broadcasts.

Sure enough, not ten minutes later the building's fire alarm began to ring. They could hear it echoing through the near silent streets.

Bo meant what he said by smoking the rat out. It wasn't like they could just call the bastard on the phone and get him to make his merry way out, and Anton didn't want to risk the chance of going in. There was no promising that cameras wouldn't be around, not to mention the amount of possible witnesses.

That just screamed messy.

Anton didn't do messy.

A good twenty minutes passed before tired, bundled up bodies started filing out of the apartment complex. Bo had tossed a glass bottle filled with gasoline, plugged off with a burning rag, into the building's dumpster shoot that led to the can in the underground garage. It wasn't likely to do any real damage to the apartment, or the people inside, but it was one hell of a way to wake them up in the middle of the night and get them all out.

With a single tap of a control button, the sunroof slid open. Anton moved his seat back as far as possible. The weapon on his thighs was picked up and placed in his calm, waiting grip. Plucking up the ammo cartridge and clicking it into place with an almost satisfying sound, he was near ready.

No shaking. No worry. Nothing.

Business as usual.

The SVD rifle was only about ten pounds of lightweight metal and wood. Nothing like the stock model, considering they usually came equipped with polymer furniture instead of the slick, blue-brushed snake skin that covered Anton's gun. Accurate with its scopes for up to thirteen hundred meters, he only had one bullet in the cartridge to use.

Anton didn't miss. Not once.

When he took the shot, he got it.

It didn't matter that it was dark as tar outside, the scopes were specially designed for night use. Sonny only needed to fuck up once and he was done.

Dead man walking.

"Ready?" Anton asked gruffly, taking one last drag from his smoke before it was flicked out the opened window.

"As I'm ever going to be," Bo said.

With the younger man settled back into his seat, Anton took care to get his frame out of the sunroof with near silent movements and careful wrangling of the gun. When he and the weapon were sitting on top of cold metal, he noticed the wind was all but dimmed to nothing at all from the tall buildings around them, keeping it out. Cocking his foot up to the edge, he waited for another moment. The roads were silent with no cars, no people, and the surrounding buildings dark from the night. Not a soul would notice them parked where they were in the darkness.

More people left the apartment building. Anton could hear their rustling movements and murmuring voices carrying down the quiet street. As it was, he could also hear the sirens starting to screech from somewhere close by.

Time to get to work.

"Phone, Bo," he said.

Bo handed him his cell phone. Anton readied his weapon quickly, resting it on his shoulder so when the kickback came, it was going to hit hard into that already bruised spot. No incriminating marks to find if they were already looking over a wounded canvas.

With the night vision scope attached and the sights turned on, he surveyed the green and black landscape until different colors bloomed, indicating movement. The warmth of the bodies showed in bright reds and yellows.

Anton hit the pre-set button on the phone and hit speaker.

"Where'd you get his new cell number from?" Bo wondered down below.

"The wife."

"Ah …"

Anton hummed, but he didn't share anything else.

Four rings later and the phone finally picked up.

"Christ, yeah … *Ciao?*"

That smooth, blackstrap voice of Anton's carried like dripping honey into the phone. He rested the barrel of the rifle to his propped up knee and started surveying the crowd of yellow.

"Sonny, we've got a little problem here."

There wasn't a response. Not even a breath. Given Anton still had a slight Russian accent, he knew it wouldn't be mistaken by the man on the other end as to who the caller was. There also wasn't any change in the line of swarming bodies he was keeping a close eye on.

"Who the fuck—"

"You know who," Anton said, his lips curving wickedly

as a lit cigarette was handed to him through the window. "Let's not play stupid."

"The Russian scum, I assume. Did you like my gift this morning?"

"Liked it just fine," Anton replied coolly, ignoring the obvious jibe. "Liked it even better when it fucked up something awful and didn't blow right. I thought it'd be an obvious thing, Sonny, but I guess not."

"I beg your pardon?"

Anton gave Sonny a moment to let the words have their confusing effect. That was the point, after all. Once more, Anton lined up his sights and gauged the crowd. There still wasn't much change. Certain bodies had swarmed together, families and friends likely. He was looking for two bodies out of order from the rest, or at least slightly off from the others, considering Sonny wouldn't want the phone call to be overheard.

"You know what the difference is between you and me, Sonny?"

There was a certain biting acid when the Italian scoffed out, "What's that?"

"When something needs to be done, I fucking do it. I don't wait around and ask questions. I don't expect my boys to frolic along like a bunch of idiots who just know what they have to do. No, I'm me because I'm goddamned good at what I do and they know it. They have a boss for a reason. I get my hands red just like they do. They call me Pakhan and respect it. And you know what else comes of that, Don?"

"Don't you—"

"I don't fuck up," Anton interrupted darkly. "I don't mess up hits, or takes, and like hell would I accept anything less than perfect craftsmanship from my guys when it comes to their work. Bombs don't get mucked up; we keep it good and clean, and toes don't get stepped on. Also, I like to think I have a pretty good internal indicator on when to back the hell off of something. Clearly yours is broken, given the gift that blew up in my driveway this morning.

"Important bulletin, Sonny ... your work was terribly shoddy in more ways that I have time to explain." Anton chuckled, keeping his gaze locked through the scope. "That the kind of guys you have working under you now? Or would the regulars who do your hit work just not take the minuscule bait you offered to off Viviana for you?"

"Wasn't me who offered that."

"Bullshit."

In no way was Anton going to keep the train of questioning going if it wasn't working to his gain. He'd already spotted ten different pairs of people and he had his scope pulled back at a far enough length in sight to have all of them loaded in so he could watch their movements closely. So far, nothing.

"Your daughter, Cici ... right?"

Sonny went silent again.

"I'd suggest you don't hang up the phone on me, Don. You won't like what I do next," Anton warned quietly. "The very last thing you want is for me to go in on her angry, trust that."

"I have three daughters."

"Mmhmm, and two sons. But your youngest girl is just twenty-one. Cici," he repeated, drawling the name out on an exhale of ashy smoke. "Shit, you even got that girl in etiquette school. I have to say, her bull is a downright idiot, though. You should get on that one. He might be fucking her like Vine's was. Sorry about that, by the way. It was better we do it than you, of course, because you would have if I let him live, but still. They made it quick. Apologies nonetheless."

The bull comment might very well have done what Anton was looking for. Sonny was murmuring on the other end of the phone in what sounded like Italian while a particular movement from the far left of his scope caught his keen eye. A bigger body was moving away from a tall, female-looking figure.

Again, Anton's mouth curved into a smirk, his tongue already tasting blood.

"You wanted to make your point, so I'm going to make mine now. You're a stupid man, but you're an even worse boss."

"Fuck you, Anton."

"Ouch, try a little lower. You should have killed her when you had the chance, idiot. Lucky for a lot of people that you didn't manage to get the job done. You want to know one more difference between you and me, Sonny?"

"Not really. Your opinion doesn't add any merit to my life."

Anton watched the figure move in sync with the sound of muffled voices being passed by, sirens getting closer, and grass shuffling underfoot over the receiver.

"I'm going to tell you anyway. Figure this will be a life lesson you might want to take from here, you know, should it ever happen again ..." There was a goal to Anton's rambling madness. The last thing he wanted Sonny thinking was that he was in his vicinity. "When you go into hiding, the rest of your family does, too. Third row building, first floor, eighth apartment down from the left side is Cici's bedroom window at her school. The building doesn't have electronic security for room break-ins, so why on earth did you think it was okay for her to be situated on the bottom floor?"

Other than the background noise, all of Sonny's sounds and movement had stopped.

Just like the figure in the scope.

Anton had him.

So damned easy.

Snap, click ... *boom.*

"Don't—"

"Yeah, because you get to make all the fucking calls right now, asshole."

Zoning in to ready the shot, Anton felt himself grow cold all over again.

"Before I finish this off, there's one more thing, Don."

The voice was choked on the other end of the phone.

"*What?*"

"The last thing you should have ever done was stepped in my way. Contrary to the old tale, there's no honor among thieves, especially our kind. Your biggest mistake was picking up your phone tonight and saying hello …"

"Wh—"

"Because if you haven't figured it out yet, you're nothing like me," Anton finished.

The trigger pulled back under his finger.

It'd be a clean hit. Through and through.

This boss wasn't one to miss and he didn't second guess.

The body dropped.

The phone's speaker went silent as screams cut through the dark air.

Anton slid down out of sight.

*

A nurse slipped into Viviana's room in the early morning hours. Anton had damn near fallen asleep, but even her quiet footsteps had his eyes snapping open. Nothing like natural adrenaline to keep someone alert.

"Lemme wake her up," Anton mumbled, rubbing his face. "If that's what you're here to do, I mean."

The nurse faltered, two little white cups in her hands nearly spilling whatever medication they had in them. "Um, it is what I'm here for, Mr…?"

"Anton Avdonin. Her fiancé."

Again, the nurse just looked surprised and confused. He tried to look unbothered by her reaction. It had been a rush-rush night for him and Bo to dispose of the SUV at a scrap yard, along with the phone and gun. Needing another vehicle, he'd finally made face at his club, though he didn't notice anyone trailing him. Then he'd made a quick trip to his Oceana home where he showered and changed clothes before throwing the ones he had worn into a random dumpster on his way back to the hospital.

Finally making it back to the hospital around five in the morning, Anton was let in a back exit door where no cameras could see him returning. Ivan slipped out just as quickly.

"Is it done?" his lawyer had asked.

"All done," Anton had replied.

That was the extent of their conversation. Nothing else needed to be said. Of course, he hadn't slept in fucking hours. Anton was exhausted, but there was no way on earth his girl was going to be waking him up.

"I was here yesterday, most of the day. You didn't see me?" he asked the nurse.

"No, sir."

Anton shrugged. "Ivan went home late last night. Maybe we just passed you girls by. We know you're busy."

"Yes, very busy. I'm sure she'd love to have you wake her up. Just be careful of her bandages, and make sure she takes her antibiotics and vitamin with the breakfast they're about to bring in. It won't be long before she'll need her bandages changed and burns cleaned, and she seems to get a little prickly about the pain …"

"She's not being given medication for that?"

The nurse pursed her lips. "Very little."

Anger pooled in Anton's gut. Viviana had survived a shitty bomb, sure, but she'd still survived it. Did they expect her not to have pain at all?

"Who's the doctor on call?"

"Dr. Kinley."

"Okay, so when he or she, whatever, gets around to getting here, make sure they're aware that my fiancée nearly died yesterday. If she wants pain meds—"

"She did have them for a while, and the dosage was upped a little yesterday. Before bed last night, however, she refused the drip again, sir."

"*What?*"

The nurse cleared her throat before placing the little cups on the nightstand. "You were here yesterday, correct?"

He cringed at the slip, before turning away to look out the window. He didn't want to be in the woman's sight. "Thank you. I'll wake her up."

"Remember, prenatal vitamin and antibiotics *with* her breakfast."

Prenatal vitamin?

Anton stood in shocked silence for longer than he must have realized because when he turned to ask the woman to repeat herself, just for his crazy mind's sake, she was already gone. Instead his gaze zoned in on the figure curled up in the bed.

With a pillow under her head, one tucked into her back, and another keeping her arm elevated, Viviana's side rose and fell with quiet breaths. She seemed content, despite the pain. Turned towards him, he could see the cut they'd stitched up above her eye. They did a damn good job, despite the swelling. It was a reminder that he still needed his arm looked at. The side of her neck was bandaged quite heavily, too, making him wince. Scratches dotted her cheekbone and jaw, splattering a reddish discoloration up to her brow.

Damn, his heart was aching.

Of course he'd seen her injuries right after it happened, and between the flurried movements in the ambulance, but now ... now it just fucking *hurt*. It was a sickening reminder that he'd somehow managed to let someone slip past his eye.

It wasn't like Anton to mess something like that up.

Fuck, she had him in a right mess in a whole bunch of ways.

Prenatal vitamin?

Again, he couldn't wrap his mind around those words.

Chances are slim, she'd said.

And he'd been de-fucking-lighted.

Yeah, Anton would have let her wade through the next couple of years of their life until she was ready for kids. Whenever that was, but that didn't mean he wasn't already ready and revving for one ... or two. Especially with her.

Now his hands needed something to do because his lungs were taking in air too fast and his heart was racing. He wasn't any less excited, but suddenly the weight of just what it meant for her to be in that state while she was recovering kind of snuck up on him.

Reality sucked.

They had so much crap to wade through.

It certainly didn't help that he needed to wake her up and talk about Rocco, either.

Ivan's late night message about Viviana's wishes for the pup hadn't been expected, but maybe it should have. Her love for the dog went deeper than he thought if she was willing to watch him go through all the pain and suffering on the possible chance he might eventually be okay. Anton wasn't going to say no, but he wasn't going to sugar-coat that for her either.

Oh God, she was pregnant.

Pregnant.

With *his* child.

All over again, his heart kick-started with love.

Like he'd been lifted, wrapped, and suffocated in it.

His.

He'd waited so long to be able to safely say that. Now, it overwhelmed in the best kind of way. The feeling was so similar to the way he felt with her in that car on his birthday, all slow and muddied up, rolling over his skin like velvet and dripping over nerves like gold.

It took and took and took more than he had to give and Anton didn't even care.

Nothing compared to that.

Nothing at all.

So he stood there and grinned, letting that love she made him have soak all in.

*

"Wake up, baby."

Anton moved the chair a little closer, trying not to let the legs scratch too loudly against the tiled floor. Once the morning meal had been brought in, he decided it was finally time to get her brown eyes opening. The doctor had managed to come around as well with a dozen and one questions for him that Anton wasn't quite comfortable answering but succeeded well enough.

The man said she could be out within a couple of days, too. Best news ever.

Next to hers, of course.

Anton wanted to get her awake so she could fucking say it.

There was also a worried call from his mother that he ended up having to take out in the hallway, given Sasha's voice rose to an octave not even sleeping beauty could have ignored. Daniil eventually took the phone away from her, thank God. Despite his father's sickness and him needing rest, they'd be around later in the day. Anton nearly told his parents right then.

Proud was maybe an understatement. The excitement had more than taken over again.

"Come on, Viviana, open those pretty eyes of yours."

She seemed to react best to his hand trailing along the curve in her waist down to her hip and back up again. Snuggling deeper into the nest of blankets and pillows that she'd created, her face hid from his view as she groaned.

"Oh, God. It fucking *hurts.*"

Anton flinched. "I know. Second day out of any kind of recovery is always the worst. That's when it catches up to you the most. You're going to take that morphine at the dosage they recommend today, right? It's not the time to be acting like a hero because you think you need to."

Finally, Viviana's head peeked up over the blanket. Her eyes locked on his like heat seeking missiles. The grin that split his lips matched hers.

"Hey, baby."

Viviana sighed. "You're here."

"Yeah. Man of my word. Always."

Her IV clad hand reached out and smacked him on the injured shoulder with a force he didn't expect from someone who'd lain in bed for the last day, was medicated, and just barely survived a bomb blast. Goddamn that fucking hurt. Anton couldn't even try to hide his yelp of pain or the way he jerked away from her, scared for a possible second hit. "What the hell was that for?"

Her gaze narrowed. "What did you do?"

A lump formed that he swallowed back.

"Don't make me lie, Viviana. Don't ask me those questions. It's over, that's all that matters, now. When we leave here, we're going *home*." He had to give her credit, she didn't cry. "Love you, hmm?"

"You could have called me yesterday, Anton. I was a downright mess here without you."

"You muddle me up," he replied just as quiet.

"What?"

"Muddle me up," Anton repeated, shrugging. "Like crazy in ways I can't explain. Fucks with my head and heart. You make me go into a different headspace. It's not a bad place, but it's your place. I'm not going to wreck and ruin that with crap."

"Not an excuse."

"Still love you." She blinked away from his face, but he was quick to lean close enough that his lips brushed over hers when Anton murmured, "Say it back. Tell me good morning. Ask me for a kiss. Anything, Viviana. I've missed you something awful. And I feel terrible. I know you wanted me here, and I'm sorry I wasn't."

"Did you get Ivan's message?"

Anton leaned back in his chair. "I did."

"And?"

"I don't agree, but you're right, it's not my decision to make. I said he was yours."

"Don't agree—"

"No," he interjected calmly. "Rocco did just what he needed to do. Do I think it's fair to let him suffer out the next year or two because I'm too selfish of a man that I don't want to say goodbye for my own sake? Absolutely not. But, I'm not you, either."

Tears did well up in her gaze that time. "That's not fair."

"I know, but that's it. That's the truth. Sucks, but it's honest."

The silence that covered the room felt heavier than he wanted it to. That wasn't how Anton planned for her to wake up, not to mention feel.

"Eat something, hmm? They're going to be in soon to change your bandages."

Viviana scowled at the mention of food. "Not hungry right now."

"If you're being difficult because of Rocco, that nonsense can stop right now."

"I'm …" she said, struggling to sit up, "just not hungry. Between being tired, the pain, and the rawness in my throat, I feel like total crap."

Anton licked his lips, his gaze falling down to her midsection.

"You need to eat, Vine. Something, anything. I don't care if it's just pudding for Christ's sake. I know you don't feel well, but you're car—" Anton swallowed the words. "Eat, please."

Fuck, he just caught himself.

It was kind of crazy how his heart outright skipped and a flurry of something unusual stirred in his gut at the thought all over again. Her abdomen was as flat as ever, and it probably would be for a while, but there was something about knowing his child was right there … *thriving* … that had him, his heart, and his dark soul all spread out in a variety of ways.

Terrified. Happy. Lustful. Content. Overwhelmed.

None of them really fit well together, but damn, he still felt it all.

Viviana caught his staring and coughed. Anton didn't even act ashamed.

"You going to tell me, baby, or do I need to keep pretending? I'm a straightforward man. I never was any good at being vague. In reality, I suck at it."

"You really do," she said, laughing. "Did Ivan tell

you?"

Anton's brow furrowed. "No. Why, did he know?"

He'd kill the bastard.

"Are you happy?"

The sudden worried expression she sported had his air catching.

"My God, yeah … so happy."

"Okay." Her tiny, scratched-up hands grasped for him all over again, touching down with feather-light love and a heavy want. "Come here, please."

"Always." Anton reached back, his fingertips tracing the contours of her bruised cheeks, shadowing over the spots he knew must have been sore. "I am sorry."

"I know."

"You do know I'm going to be even worse now with the over protectiveness, right?"

Viviana smiled against his mouth. "Yeah. I'm okay with that."

"Good to know."

She did what he had asked then, too. Let him kiss her, said good morning, and whispered quiet love against his cheek. With his encouragement, she finally did manage to stomach half of the easy-to-swallow foods the hospital staff had brought her for breakfast.

Anton crawled up into the tiny bed and moved blankets and pillows around until she was comfortable and cradled in his arms. Heat danced along his palm when he laid it flat to the smooth contour of her pelvis. They didn't move until the nurses knocked on the door to clean her injuries and change her bandages a half hour later.

And even then … he buried his face in her neck, held tight, and didn't let go.

Chapter Twenty-Two

The mirror was taunting Viviana.

Behind her reflection, she could see the beautiful ivory lace spread out on the bed. Sure, she'd gotten in front of one since the accident, stood there more than long enough to take a list of all her injuries and scars, but this was something so much different.

"Come on, child," Sasha said, smiling tenderly. "How can you possibly know that it won't look good if you haven't even put it on yet?"

How could it look good at all?

That was the real question.

Even though the superficial second degree burns on her arm had healed, there had been a slight discoloration in the scarring. While the rest of her was olive toned, from her elbow down was a mixture of garish white and a sore looking pink. The minor burns on her neck, however, had all but healed with little to no scarring at all.

How on earth she'd managed to forget about the capped sleeve, lace mermaid style dress after the accident, Viviana didn't know. It had already been ordered. Given Anton hired two planners to take over what they couldn't handle while managing her healing and Rocco's— well, either of them could have picked it up and not mentioned it.

Viviana was blaming it on the pregnancy. All of her forgetfulness was the baby's fault.

It was a perfectly viable excuse to her.

Not to Anton.

He assumed her tiredness weeks later, mixed in with the sudden absentmindedness, had something to do with the aftereffects of the accident. Viviana barely held herself back from sticking out her tongue at him like a child when the doctor explained it was likely just the pregnancy.

The dress, like several other things, had simply slipped

her mind. Or, maybe she hadn't wanted to go shopping for another one and she forced herself to forget about it. After all, Anton had been the one to pick that dress out and Viviana wanted so badly to let him take it off like he promised.

In the mirror, Viviana's reflection had gone pale. Stress had that immediate effect on her now. There wasn't any such thing as morning sickness. That was a goddamn myth, and the man who made it up should have been shot. It was more like morning, noon, night, and whenever the hell in-between sickness.

"Oh God," she mumbled, turning away from the mirror as her stomach rolled. Viviana didn't know if she could make it to the bathroom. "Sick … gonna be …"

Sasha was at her side, producing another one of those ginger suckers, pulling the plastic off and popping it into her soon-to-be daughter-in-law's mouth. Viviana hated the way they tasted, but the damned things worked like nothing else.

With another soft grin, Sasha's hand patted gently on top of Viviana's still flat stomach, whispering quiet words in Russian before she asked, "Better?"

It was such a motherly action that Viviana felt her heart clench in the most painful way. More than anything, she wished her own mother was there. She loved Sasha like nothing else, but every girl deep down inside wanted their mother and father on their wedding day.

"Getting there. Thank you."

"You're welcome, now put the dress on."

Viviana scowled around the lollipop.

Deciding to try and divert Sasha's attention on the dress a little longer, Viviana asked, "How's Daniil doing today?"

Sasha smiled faintly. "Much better. Even the doctors are surprised at his sudden energy and excitement. I think that may have something to do with his first grandchild being born. I know he's not going to …"

Viviana frowned as Sasha trailed off and wiped at her

eyes. There was a chance Daniil wasn't going to see the baby. That was just the sad truth they were all trying to swallow. But just a few short weeks ago, his doctors had given him the possibility of a year, too. With careful monitoring, a good diet, and a little bit of luck, he very well could be there to meet his first grandchild. At least for the start of the baby's life, anyway.

"He might, Sasha," Viviana whispered, knowing that's what Anton's mother was thinking about, too.

"I hope so. It certainly seems like the news of the pregnancy has made him happier for the moment."

And just how had hiding the pregnancy for the first little while gone?

Well, not terribly fucking great. It might have helped if Anton could have left her midsection alone for five minutes, but no, his hand or fingers were always waywardly traveling in that destination even if he didn't realize it. The biggest shit-eating grin took hold of his features every time, too. Not to mention, he damn near had a fit every time someone bumped into her for the first month after she was out of the hospital.

More than once she had to remind him she wasn't a glass china doll.

It didn't work. Anton still had a thing about too many people crowding her.

Tonight should be fun, Viviana thought with a sigh.

Of course, none of that gave it away to Sasha. Oh no, the woman knew the moment she walked into Viviana's hospital room. Somehow ... Daniil had been completely oblivious to the way his wife's eyes scanned her son and his fiancée before she smiled, kissed Anton's cheek, and whispered her congratulations.

When Viviana asked how she could tell, Sasha shrugged and said, "It's a mother thing."

"Put the dress on. Now," Sasha repeated, snapping Viviana back into the moment.

"But—"

A heavy exhale fell from behind Viviana. "Talk to me."

Her scarred arm lifted as an explanation. The low plunge in the back of the dress would show some of the scarring over her right shoulder. Thankfully makeup had all but made the deep slice above her eyebrow disappear.

"I know the doctor said it might take a couple of years for the discoloration to go away, but still," Viviana said, frowning. "I'm the bride, right? Everyone's going to be looking at me."

"Everyone looks at you anyway; you're beautiful."

Yes, but Viviana could wear long sleeves to hide the burns. She didn't even have a sheer cover-up to put on today. There were over sixty guests starting to arrive downstairs with their respective plus ones, so that was more people putting her in the spotlight all at once than she'd had in a long time.

Her stomach was rolling again.

Sasha seemed to pick up on that right away. "Okay, you sit tight. I'll be right back."

Viviana didn't argue.

Not ten minutes later, her hotel room was opening, but the person who slipped in certainly wasn't who she'd been expecting.

"You can't be in here!"

"I wasn't supposed to be in your bed this morning, either, but somehow I was. We're not traditional, and we're never going to be, so get over it, baby."

"But ... still," she sputtered, trying horribly to cover the dress that lay on the bed.

Anton cocked a brow and crossed his arms. Something delicious and heated washed through her body at the sight of him half dressed, his shirt still unbuttoned and hanging loosely open while he stood in nothing more than white boxer-briefs. It did the most terribly naughty things to her insides, turning them all out and around, making her sex turn wetter with every rise of his chest.

She couldn't even think straight.

And it always slammed down on her like that every damned time.

Stupid fucking pregnancy hormones.

"What's wrong, Vine?"

"Can't think," she managed to whisper, a blush crawling over her cheeks and neck.

Anton smirked as he glanced up at the ceiling. She wanted to hit him for being so smug about her sudden lustful tendencies. Okay, so maybe it wasn't so sudden, given how often they fucked before she got pregnant, but now it was a whole different ballgame.

Now, every time he touched her, even in the most innocent of ways, her body lit up like fireworks. Electricity burned through her blood just as much as her mind. Sex wasn't just physical, no, it was downright fucking expressive. Suddenly there were nerves in places she didn't know existed, and he seemed to find every one without having a lick of trouble.

And oh God, *licking* ...

She squeaked a noise under her breath.

The pretty white lace panties, trimmed with silk bows, she wore under her sweat pants were likely ruined.

"Vine, that's not what I meant."

"Oh."

"Yeah. I mean, we could do that, but we might be a little late. So, ceremony starts in forty-five minutes. I need to be down there in thirty. Again, what's wrong?"

Viviana stuck the lollipop back in her mouth, hoping the taste would distract her mind enough to speak. Instead, her words just came out mumbled around the disgusting candy.

"I'm going to look horrible."

"Because of your arm?"

She shrugged an explanation. What else?

"Okay, does that sound as vain to you as it did to me?" she asked quietly.

Anton shook his head and offered a smile. "No. I suspected you'd probably have a moment, but I thought you'd be okay after you'd seen it on."

So maybe they'd had a similar discussion once or twice. The day after she was brought home from the hospital, for example. A crazy amount of people had gathered at the Oceana house to welcome her back with a big dinner, and Viviana had been so overwhelmed that she hid in the master bedroom's bath. She'd still been covered in bandages, face marked up something awful, and her stress levels were out of control. It wasn't like she was trying to be rude, but Viviana didn't know how else to handle the sudden influx of people staring at her.

It had been much too much.

Anton, confused and worried, found her in her hiding spot. That was also the first time he all but forced her to look in a mirror after the accident. She'd been avoiding it like the plague. It hadn't been easy, but it served to prove a point she hadn't wanted to face.

Yes, she'd been hurt, her pretty skin was a little marked up, but hell, she was alive.

And *his*.

Subsequently, Anton went about showing her just how much as his hands lifted the knee-length black dress she wore, spread her legs wider, and fit himself tight behind to take her soft, sweet, and slow. Despite the still simmering pain from her injuries, she didn't feel a thing but him.

So fucking deep and good, his hands barricading hers on the bathroom counter as his blue eyes pierced into hers through the mirror's reflection. Viviana swore she could feel every inch of her sex holding his cock tighter, pulling him in farther. She couldn't even make sounds, just quiet breathy pants that fell from her parted lips against the side of his cheek.

Again, it had taken much too much, but in a whole new way.

Awestruck and spun.

Like it always had, sex seemed to fall somewhere in the lines of their communication.

They didn't connect fully, otherwise. Intimacy was their

link beyond words.

"Put it on," Anton murmured, drawing her out of her thoughts.

"But—"

"Don't. Put the dress on, Viviana. You can't go down there naked. I wouldn't get away with killing an entire room of men."

Instinctively, she flinched at the comment. Viviana still couldn't turn on a news channel for fear of seeing something about Sonny Carducci flashing over the screen. Anton might not have admitted it, but who else would have done it? Who else had the nerve? The question burned her tongue every time he got a little more quiet than normal. Viviana had to fill the silence just to keep from asking.

"Shit, baby … I'm sorry."

"Yeah, putting it on," she said, not wanting to dredge that up again.

Anton made his way to the bed, sitting on the edge as she fingered the ivory lace. Before she could pick the garment up, however, she found her wrist locked in the heat of his palm. With a gentle tug, her backside was firmly planted on his lap, legs dangling over the side of his thigh.

"*Ouch*, Anton."

"You sure you want to marry me?"

"A little late to say no," she quipped, pointing to her midsection.

As was his new favorite thing to do, his hand found her middle, lying flat with his fingers spread wide. The action always gave her butterflies, and this time was no exception. She liked it the very best when she woke to find his mouth kissing over her smooth flesh, sentimental tenderness reflecting in eyes that were so good at hiding what he usually felt.

Anton couldn't hide his enjoyment over her pregnancy at all.

"I suppose …"

The twitching of his shaft hardening against her ass

couldn't be ignored. Viviana squirmed under his hold, desire washing through her veins.

"We're going to be late."

Anton shrugged. "Suddenly don't care. I have no idea why."

"The dress …"

"Let me take these pants of yours off," he said, his tone turning husky as his fingers slipped under the cotton. When his hands came in contact with the lingerie she wore underneath, he hummed a lovely sound that had her core pulsing. "I don't know what these are, but they feel so fucking nice."

"Twice this morning," she reminded him, getting heated just at the memory. "Are you even going to have the energy left for tonight?"

"Are you questioning my more than proven stamina?"

The lift of his brow had her smirking before his fingers found a particularly sensitive spot on her thigh and began tickling. Viviana squealed, failing miserably to get out of his prison-like hold. Once she'd begged and pleaded enough, his evil hand left the confines of her pants to skim back up to her flat stomach.

Clearing her throat, she asked, "Did Sergei show up?"

Anton shook his head. "Not yet. I'm thinking he won't, which I prefer."

The wedding invitation had been offered to the Jersey Pakhan as a truce of sorts. Viviana knew Anton hadn't wanted to offer it at all, but it didn't look good on him to keep bad blood going. Repeated attempts for a sit-down had also been offered, which weren't refused, but they also weren't accepted.

Anton wanted and apology and so did Sergei. Viviana was afraid it might lead to something bad later if peace wasn't made soon.

"Don't worry about it," Anton added quietly. "What day is this, Vine?"

She furrowed her brow, confused. "December

twentieth?"

"Yeah," he agreed, laughing. "But, it's our day. I can see your worries in your eyes, so stop it."

Conceding with a sigh, she balefully stared at the dress again. "It should look perfect."

"It will. You're goddamn beautiful, huh? Like nobody else. There isn't a soul who gives any care about the marks on your skin, and who gives a shit if they do. You're mine, anyway, baby. So while everybody's looking at you, you're looking at me. And I'm looking back. That's what they see the most."

His hand on her back pushed her upward. On her feet, sweatpants were tugged down until they dropped to the floor. The silky camisole took the same path. With a smug grin, he helped her put the garter resting on top of the dress all the way up her thigh. It wasn't long before the ivory lace was in his grasp, too, falling down like a heavy sheet over her frame, hugging every inch.

The capped sleeves covered her shoulders, but her collarbones and neck were on display. Inlaid pearls had the lace bunched up just under her breasts. Lace spilled like rushing waves. His skillful fingers worked the few pearl buttons where they clasped together at the small of her back, and Viviana shivered when his hand skimmed all the way up her naked spine with a burning intent.

"Almost done," he said, all quiet and dark in her ear.

All of her hair had been pinned up into a simple, easy to manage up-do. The partial veil that hung off the mirror was plucked up in his hand and placed. Pins were carefully hidden so they wouldn't be seen. The ivory trim of the headpiece rested just above her nose, keeping her eyes shadowed by the partial veil.

Her painted red lips curved with a smile as his fingers skimmed along the line of her jaw. Makeup had been so meticulously applied, giving her eyes a darker appearance and her cheeks a rosy glow.

"Crazy beautiful. Where are the shoes?"

"Beside the bed," Viviana replied, not even wanting to say *no*, now.

A second later he was back, shoes placed at her feet. "I'll be right back. I have to get something before I forget."

Viviana nodded dumbly, going about resting her backside on the bed as she tugged on heels that would likely be the death of her before the night was out. By the time she managed to pull the deathtraps on, Anton was back with a silver case in hand. Immediately, she recognized it as the second case Richard had brought along with the engagement rings. The case that hadn't been opened.

"So, I have to go and get ready," Anton informed her. "Or someone—namely Sasha—is going to start screaming bloody murder."

Viviana laughed. She felt a whole hell of a lot better, now, anyway.

"Thank you for coming in here and calming me down."

"I love you, Viviana. Even when you're being ridiculous."

A kiss was placed on her cheek, her body lighting up all over again at the gesture.

"Tonight," he promised. "Or as soon as I can get you into the coat room."

"That's terrible."

"You fucking love it."

She wasn't even going to deny it.

When the case was placed on the bed, a key was slid into the lock. Anton held the top closed and sighed.

"This isn't from me. And while I know what it is, I don't know what else was included with it. I do know that Richard was given instructions to include something should you have found out about Nicoli."

"Okay," Viviana said, shrugging.

She'd already had a dozen and one gifts brought to her that morning. Some of them had special requests that she not open them until later in the evening, others were for her to open right then, and some were private for just her and

Anton. Viviana didn't think this would be any different.

His hand grabbed hers, holding it over the case to stop the top from popping open.

"Open it after I'm gone. That was his request."

One more kiss dropped down to the corner of her mouth before he winked and stood. When the door to the hotel room closed, Viviana removed her hand and chanced a glance down. Resting in grey velvet lay a matching necklace and earring set that had her heartbeat stuttering.

Similar in color and design to the engagement ring on her finger, glittering blue sapphires rested in crowns of white diamonds. The delicate white gold rope that held it all together would only be long enough to rest at the hollow of her throat. The cerulean-colored jewels and sparkling diamonds would fit her gown without taking anything away from it. Teardrop-style earrings rested just below a single folded-up piece of paper that had turned a yellowish tint from age.

With suddenly shaking hands, she plucked it up before she could second guess the choice and began to read scrawled words that were dated at the top over two decades before. Tears welled at the name written in black ink at the bottom.

It was the connection to a man she hadn't known she was looking for.

Viviana,

In my life, I've taken many things that weren't mine to own. A wife, a son, money, possessions, and lives. I did so without concern or care, and felt no guilt or remorse. I've bartered, stole, and coveted. I've cheated, hurt, and killed. There are no excuses worthy of the life I chose to live, but it was the one I made for myself nonetheless.

The only thing given to me that was finally mine to keep, I gave away: you.

I like to believe when decades have gone by, I won't feel quite as raw about it as I do now. Somehow, I doubt it.

Regret is a heavy weight to carry, and this is the first time I've worn it so wholly.

And forgive me for taking the one chance I had to someday have you back.

My grandfather called them old souls. A person with eyes so expressive just a blink appeared to be years traveled. People often wonder why I am so adept at finding the best matches in the worst situations, but it isn't difficult when the old souls are staring back, waiting for connection.

When they meet, it's hard not to take notice.

As I write this, Anton is but four years old. He's never spoken a word in English before today, and the first sentence out of his mouth when his mother woke him up was, "Where is Vine?" It was only yesterday evening that he met you, as did I. A tiny girl with the oldest eyes was the one little person he's spoken to outside of his mother, father, and me.

In the end, his old soul was just waiting to be brought back to yours.

I wish I could know if I made the right choice, sweet girl. In more ways than you know, I so wish for that. When you meet him at the end of the aisle today, I must have faith you will find the arrangement was made more of your own desires, than of others wills and mistakes.

And I hope he makes you live.

After all, this is just the beginning ...

Nicoli

*

Did you enjoy the first instalment of Anton and Vine's love story?

Read the second book in The Russian Guns series to continue the tale – *The Life* is live!

About the Author

Bethany-Kris is a Canadian author, lover of much, and mother to four young sons, three cats, and four dogs. A small town in Eastern Canada where she was born and raised is where she has always called home. With her boys under her feet, a snuggling cat, barking dogs, and a spouse calling over his shoulder, she is nearly always writing something ... when she can find the time.

Find Bethany-Kris at her:

www.bethanykris.com

Other Books

The Guzzi Legacy

Corrado
Alessio
Chris
Beni
Bene
Marcus

Renzo + Lucia

Privilege
Harbor
Contempt
Forever
Renzo + Lucia: The Complete Trilogy
Cusp

Andino + Haven

Duty
Vow
One Last Time
Andino + haven: The Complete Duet

John + Siena

Loyalty
Disgrace
John + Siena: The Complete Duet
John + Siena: Extended

Cross + Catherine

Always
Revere
Unruly
The Companion
Naz & Roz

Guzzi Duet

Unraveled, Book One
Entangled, Book Two
Cara & Gian: The Complete Duet

DeLuca Duet

Waste of Worth: Part One
Worth of Waste: Part Two

Standalone Titles

Fractured Ties: Boykov Bratva
Essence of Fear: Boykov Bratva
Pink
Pretty Lies
Dirty Pool
Effortless
Inflict
Cozen
Captivated
Dishonored

Donati Bloodlines

Thin Lies
Thin Lines
Thin Lives
Behind the Bloodlines
The Complete Trilogy

Filthy Marcellos

Antony
Lucian
Giovanni
Dante
Legacy
A Very Marcello Christmas
The Complete Collection

Seasons of Betrayal

Where the Sun Hides
Where the Snow Falls
Where the Wind Whispers
Seasons: The Complete Seasons of Betrayal Series

Gun Moll Trilogy

Gun Moll
Gangster Moll
Madame Moll

The Chicago War

Deathless & Divided
Reckless & Ruined
Scarless & Sacred
Breathless & Bloodstained
The Complete Series
Maldives & Mistletoe

The Russian Guns

The Arrangement
The Life
The Score
Demyan & Ana
Shattered
The Jersey Vignettes

FANTASY ROMANCE

The Hunted: A 9INE REALMS Novel

Find more on Bethany-Kris's website at
www.bethanykris.com.

www.ingramcontent.com/pod-product-compliance
Lightning Source LLC
Chambersburg PA
CBHW051331020726
47501CB00007B/2023